NORI
RUMI HARA

DRAWN & QUARTERLY

FOR MY
GRANDMOTHERS

drawnandquarterly.com
rumihara.com

978-1-77046-397-4
First edition: April 2020
Printed in China
10 9 8 7 6 5 4 3 2 1

Cataloguing data available from Library and Archives Canada

Published in the USA by Drawn & Quarterly, a client publisher of Farrar, Straus and Giroux
Published in Canada by Drawn & Quarterly, a client publisher of Raincoast Books
Published in the United Kingdom by Drawn & Quarterly, a client publisher of Publishers Group UK

THIS IS NORI.

NORI? IS THAT MY SWEATER?

THAT'S GRANDMA.

NORIKO IWASAKI
BORN AUGUST 8, 1982
LEO (AS YOU CAN SEE)
SHE LIVES IN A SMALL TOWN IN SUBURBAN OSAKA
WITH HER GRANDMA AND WORKING PARENTS.
THIS IS 1986...

1

NORI
AND THE
BATS
IN THE
HOUSE

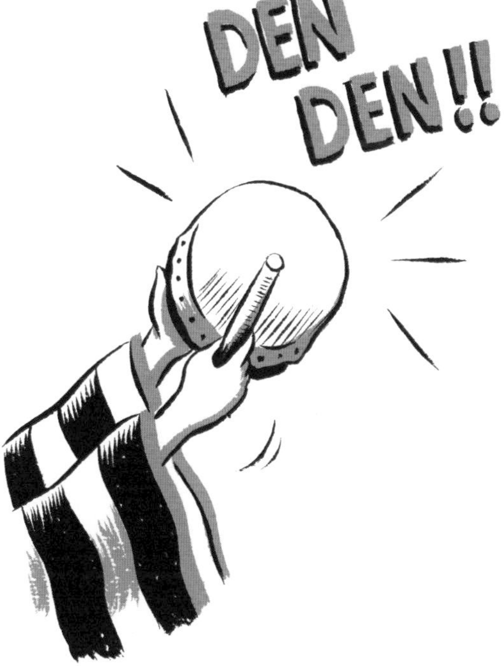
DEN
DEN!!

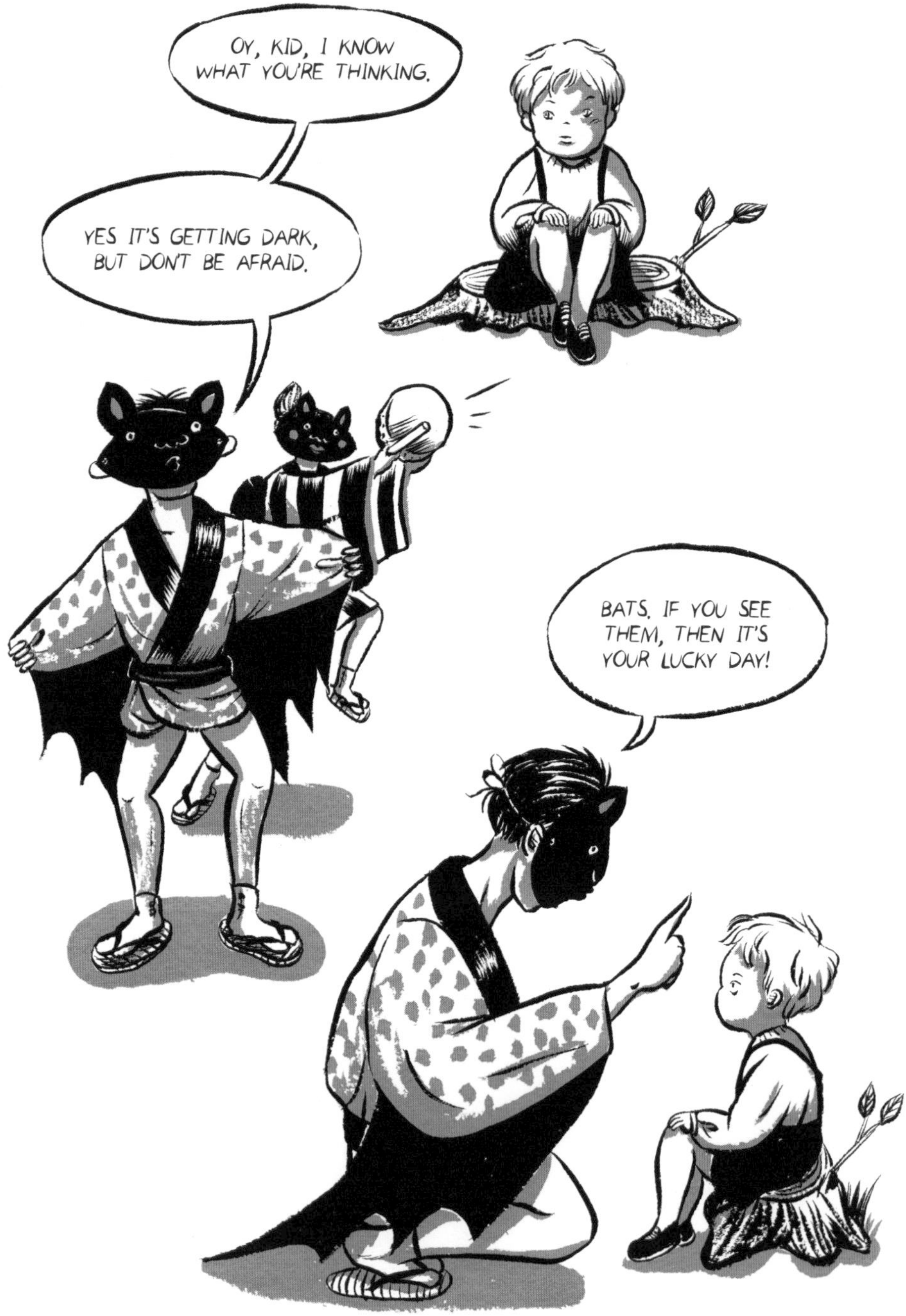
OY, KID, I KNOW WHAT YOU'RE THINKING.
YES IT'S GETTING DARK, BUT DON'T BE AFRAID.
BATS. IF YOU SEE THEM, THEN IT'S YOUR LUCKY DAY!

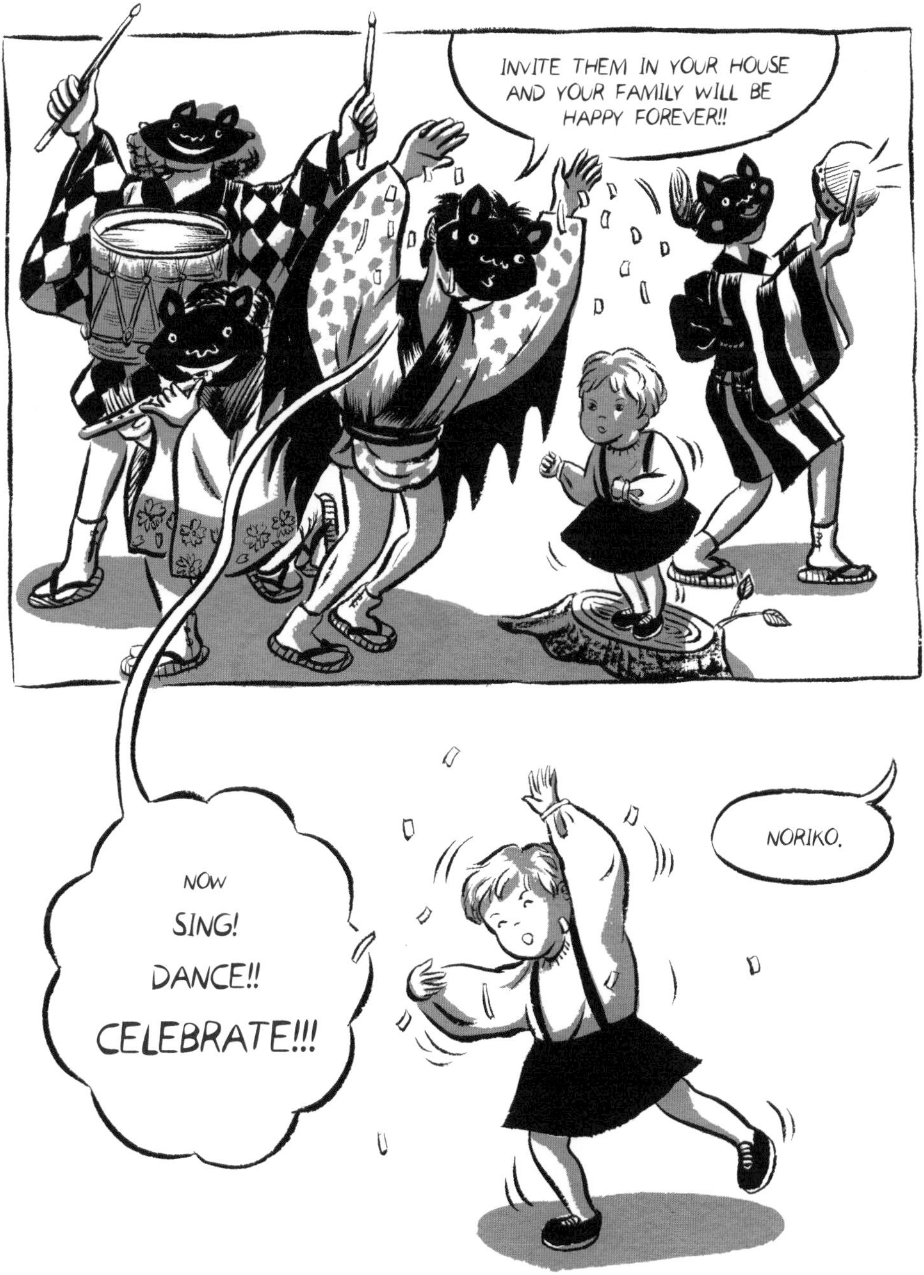
INVITE THEM IN YOUR HOUSE AND YOUR FAMILY WILL BE HAPPY FOREVER!!
NOW SING! DANCE!! CELEBRATE!!!
NORIKO.

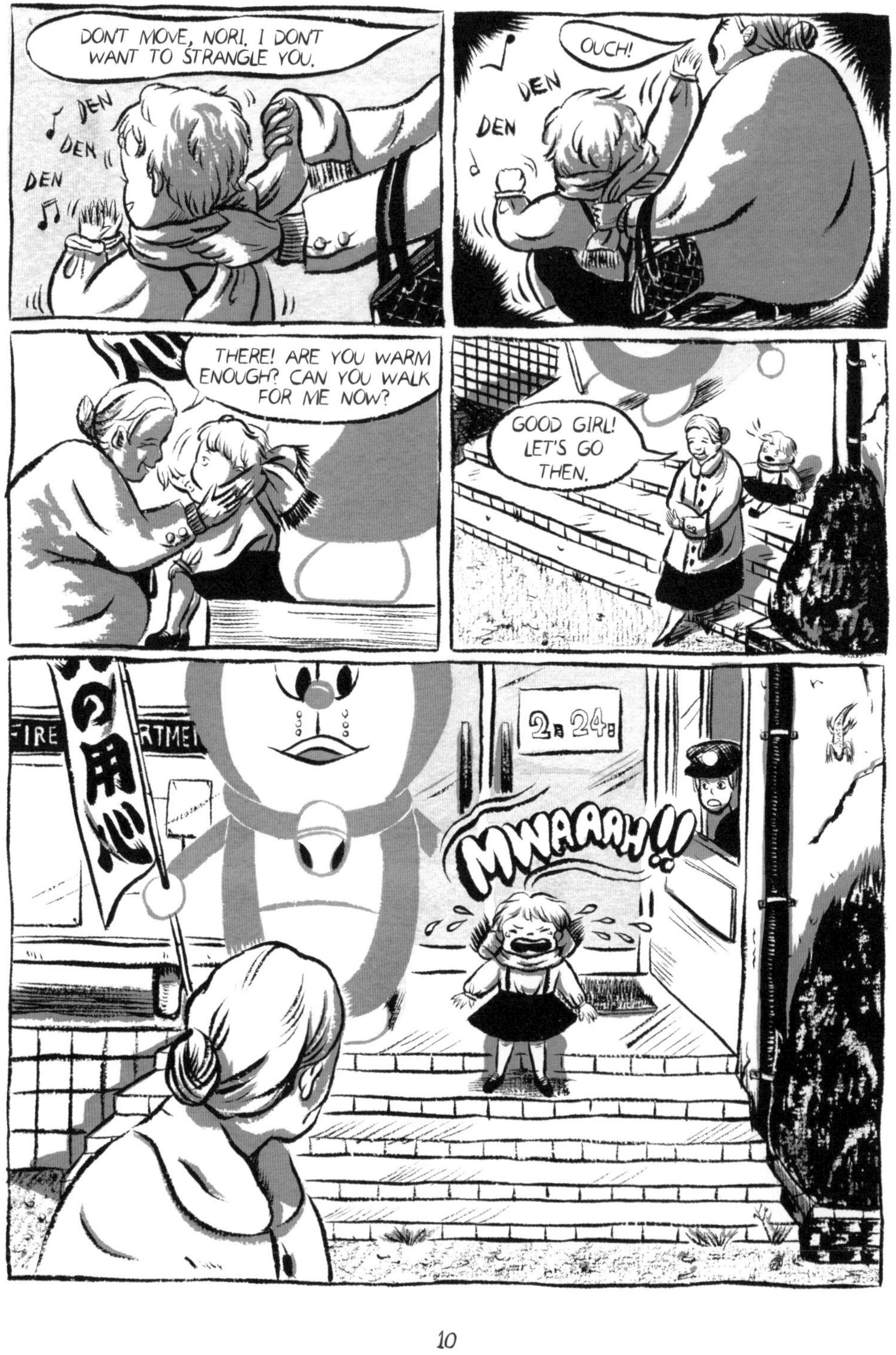
DON'T MOVE, NORI. I DON'T WANT TO STRANGLE YOU.
DEN
DEN
DEN
OUCH!
DEN
DEN
THERE! ARE YOU WARM ENOUGH? CAN YOU WALK FOR ME NOW?
GOOD GIRL! LET'S GO THEN.
FIRE
RTME
の用心
2月24日
MWAAAH!!

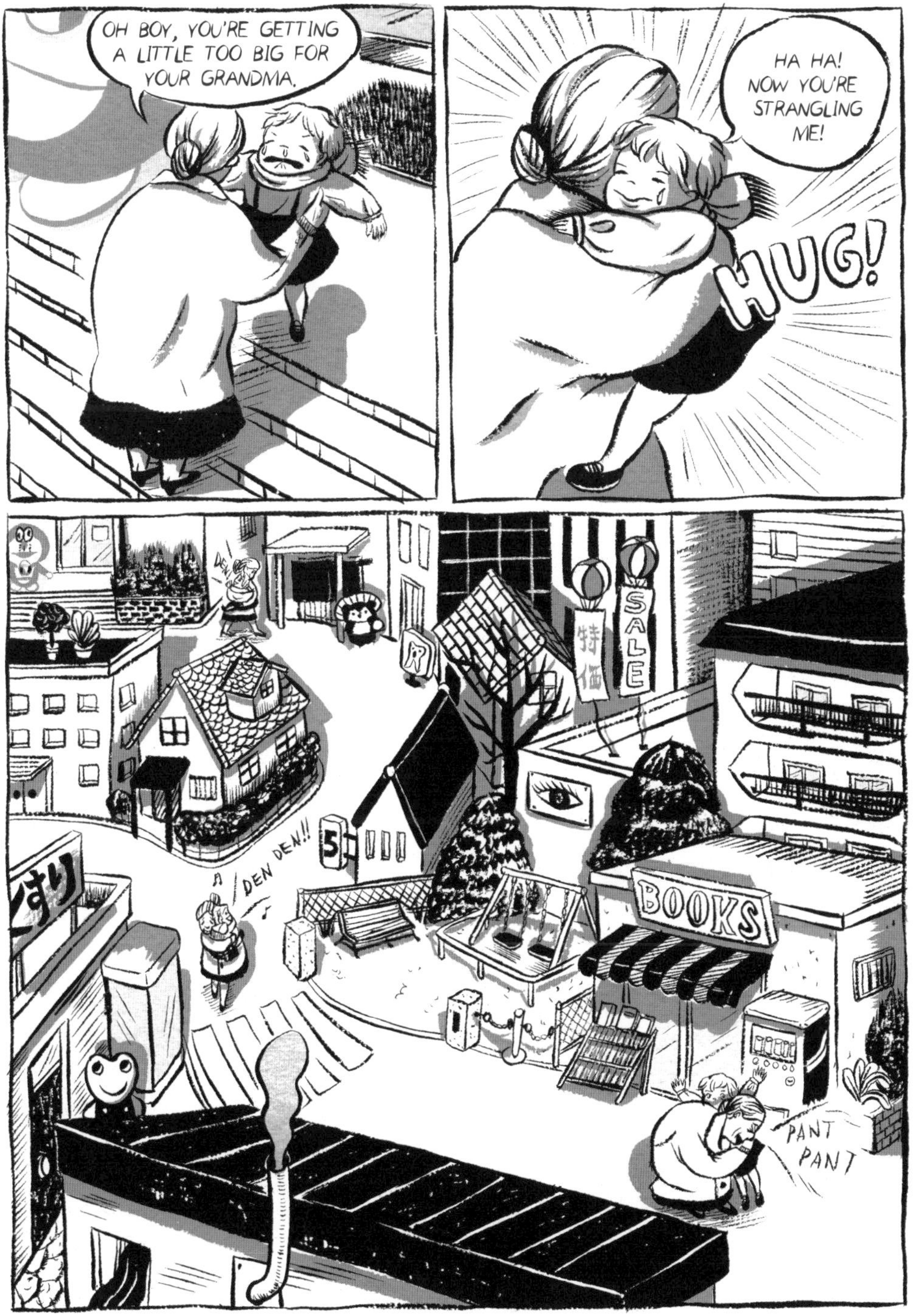
OH BOY, YOU'RE GETTING A LITTLE TOO BIG FOR YOUR GRANDMA.
HA HA! NOW YOU'RE STRANGLING ME!
HUG!
特価
SALE
DEN DEN!!
5
BOOKS
PANT PANT

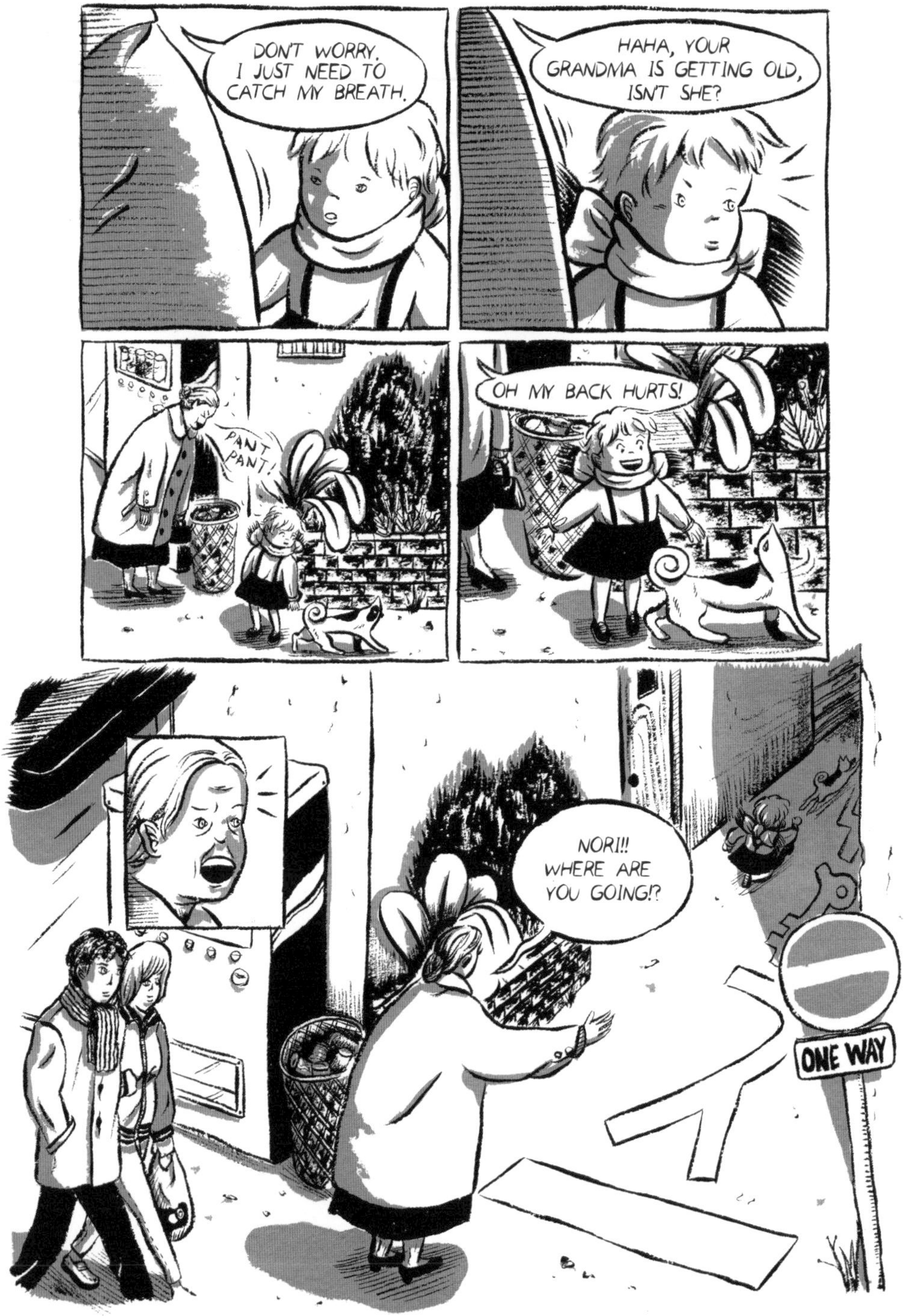
DON'T WORRY. I JUST NEED TO CATCH MY BREATH.
HAHA, YOUR GRANDMA IS GETTING OLD, ISN'T SHE?
PANT PANT!
OH MY BACK HURTS!
NORI!! WHERE ARE YOU GOING!?
ONE WAY

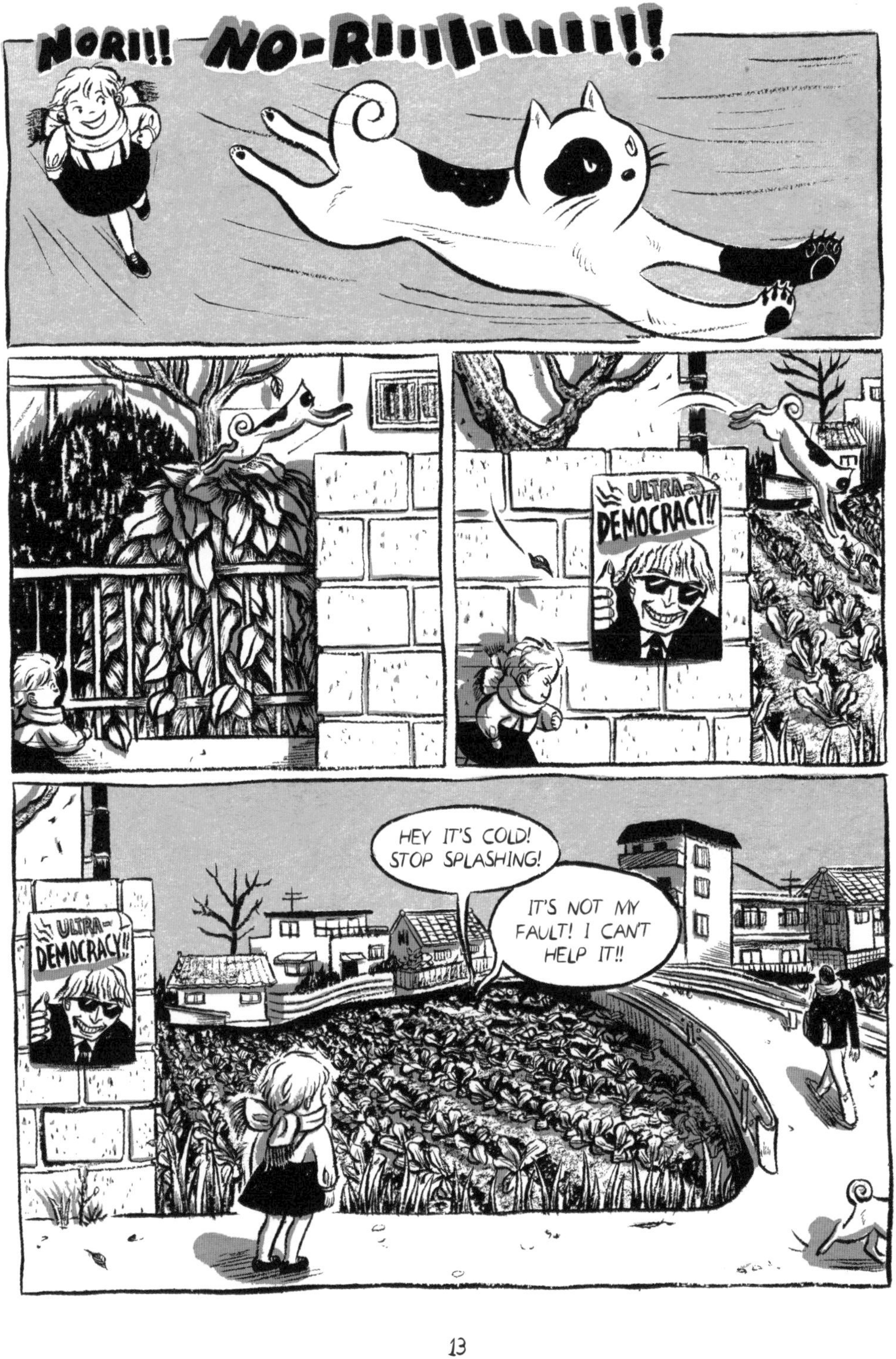
NORI!! NO-RIIIIIIIIIII!!
ULTRA-DEMOCRACY!!
ULTRA-DEMOCRACY!!
HEY IT'S COLD! STOP SPLASHING!
IT'S NOT MY FAULT! I CAN'T HELP IT!!

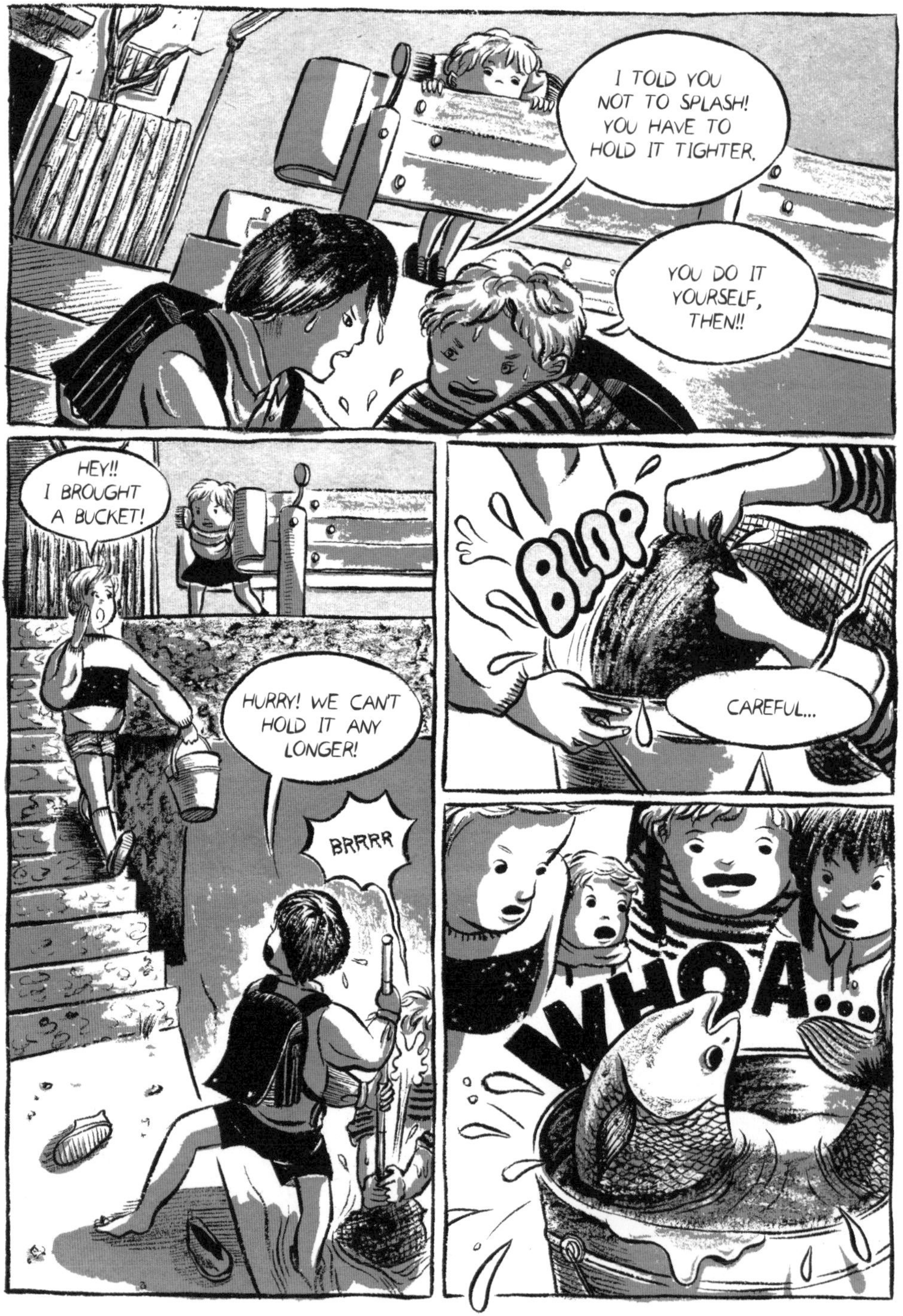
I TOLD YOU NOT TO SPLASH! YOU HAVE TO HOLD IT TIGHTER.
YOU DO IT YOURSELF, THEN!!
HEY!! I BROUGHT A BUCKET!
HURRY! WE CAN'T HOLD IT ANY LONGER!
BRRRR
BLOP
CAREFUL...
WHOA...

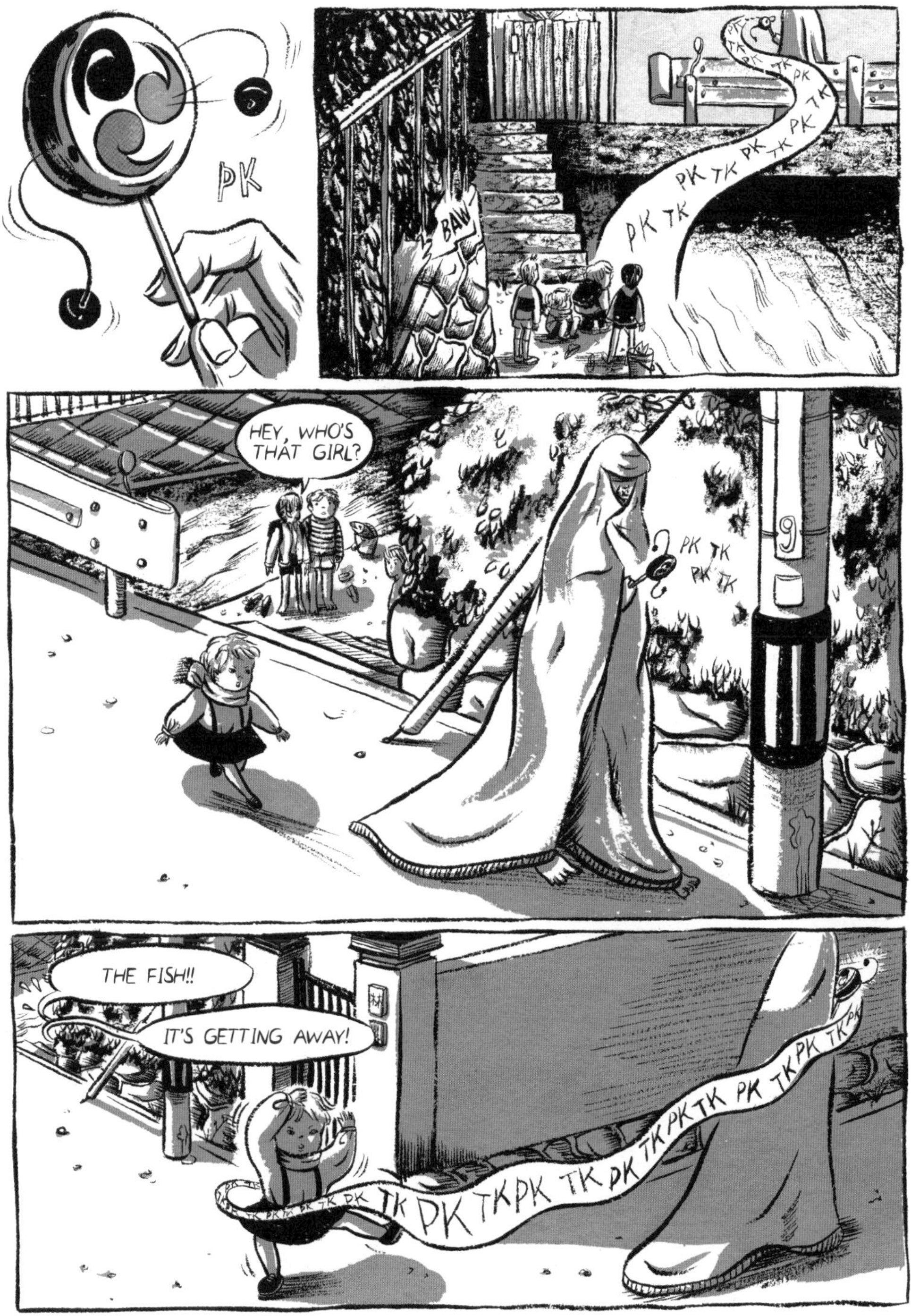
PK
BAW
PK TK PK TK PK TK PK TK PK TK
HEY, WHO'S THAT GIRL?
PK TK PK TK
THE FISH!!
IT'S GETTING AWAY!
TK PK TK PK TK PK TK PK TK PK TK PK TK PK

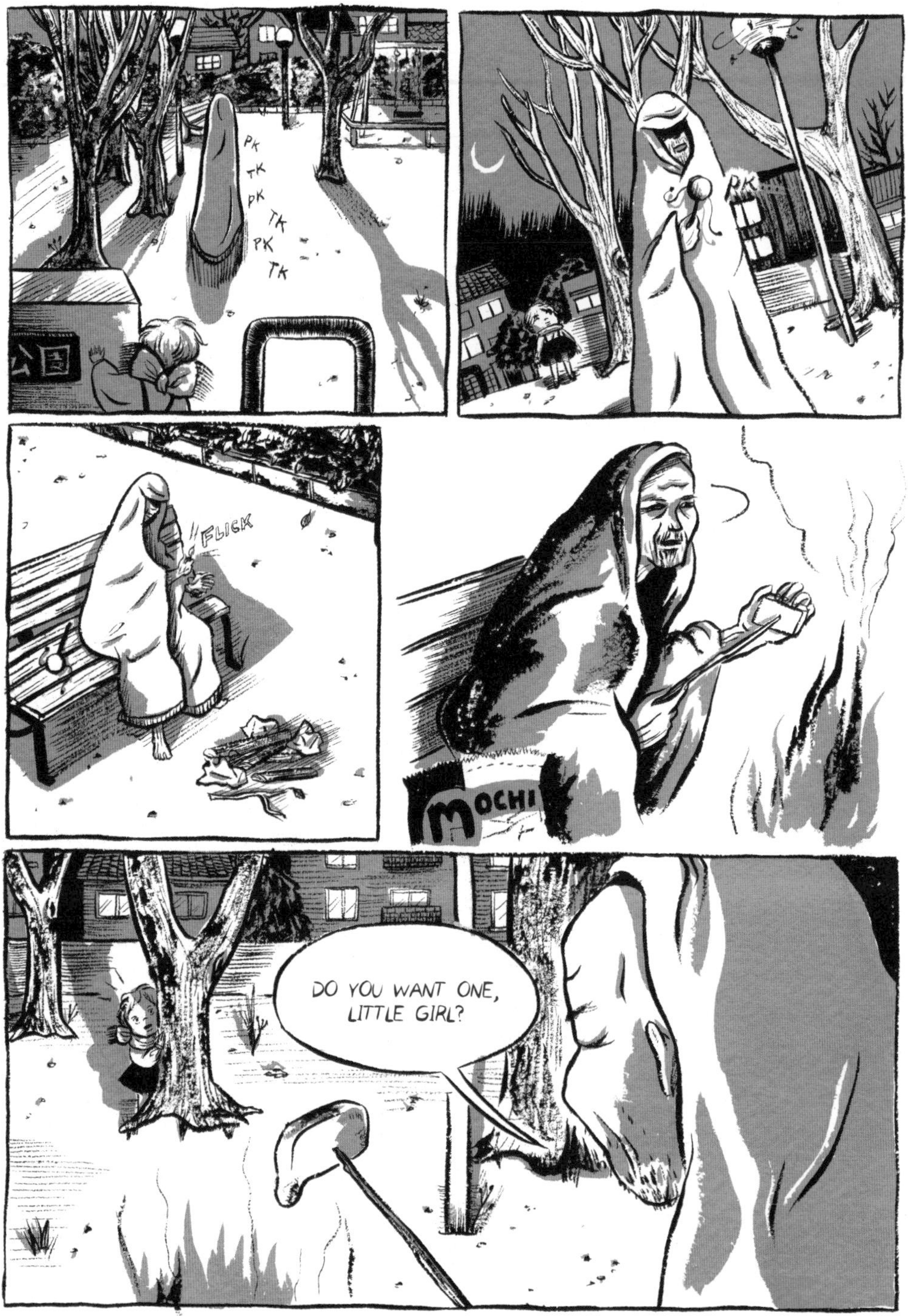
PK
TK
PK
TK
PK
TK
PK
FLICK
MOCHI
DO YOU WANT ONE, LITTLE GIRL?

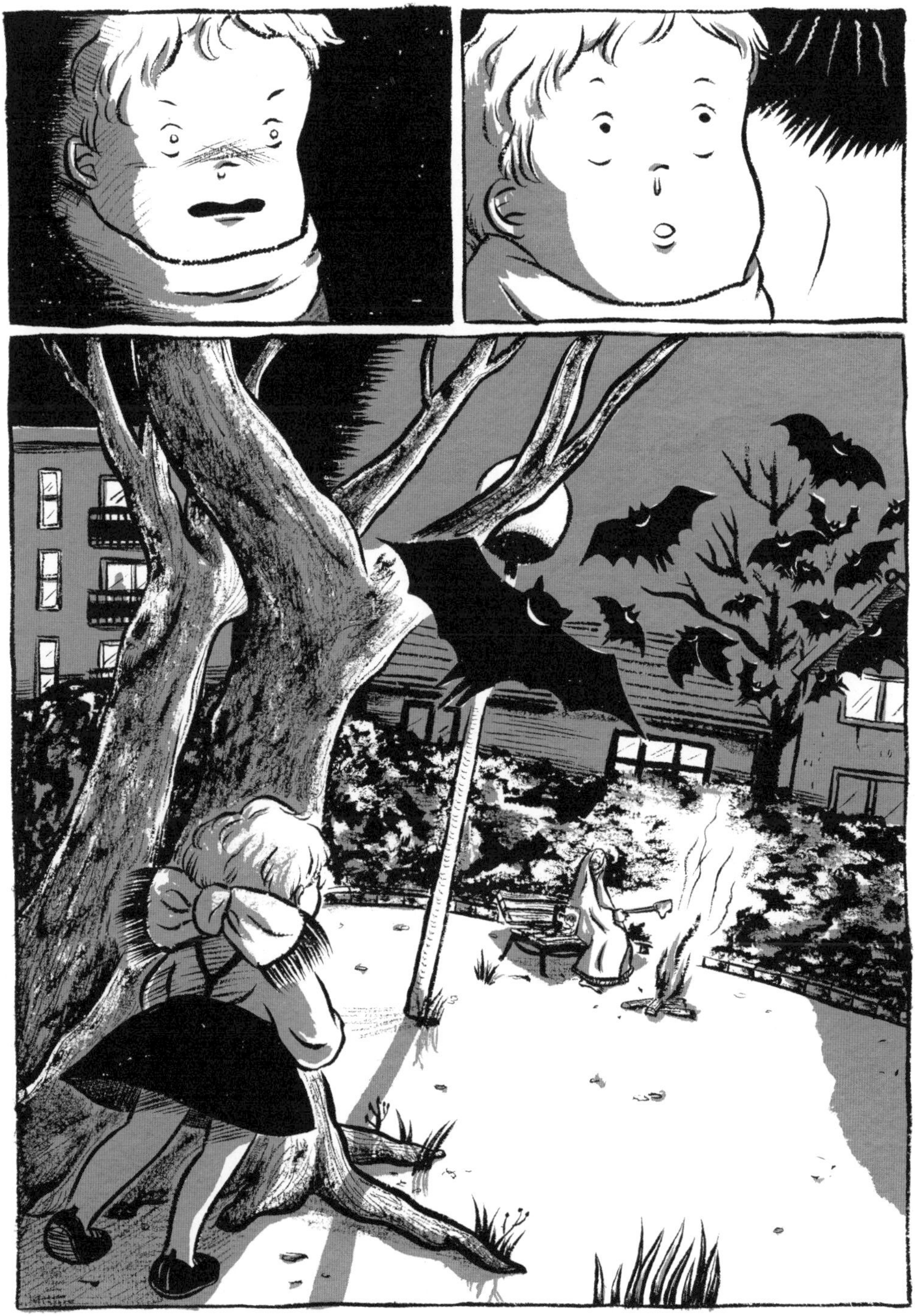

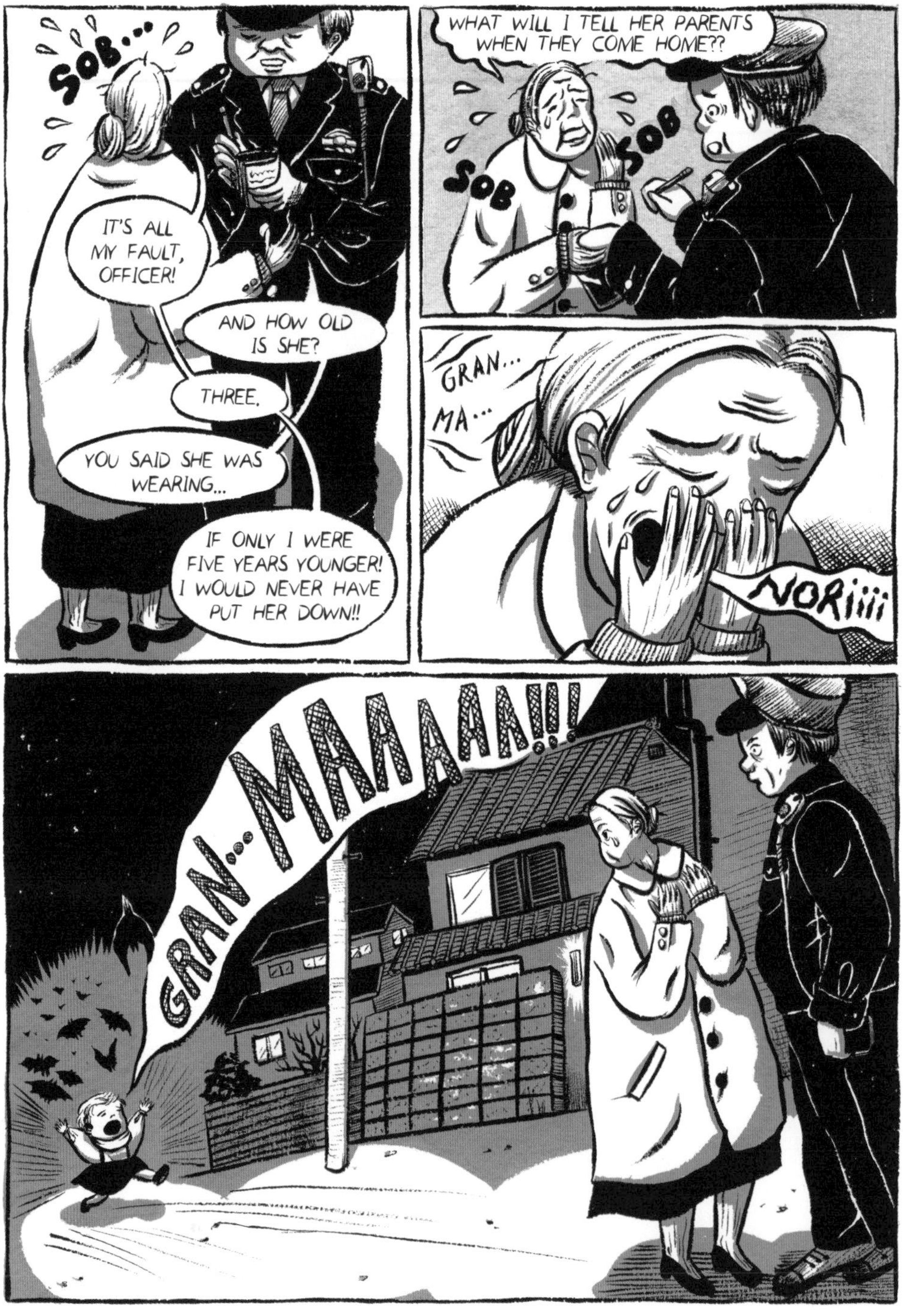
SOB...
IT'S ALL MY FAULT, OFFICER!
AND HOW OLD IS SHE?
THREE.
YOU SAID SHE WAS WEARING...
IF ONLY I WERE FIVE YEARS YOUNGER! I WOULD NEVER HAVE PUT HER DOWN!!
WHAT WILL I TELL HER PARENTS WHEN THEY COME HOME??
SOB
SOB
GRAN...
MA...
NORiiii
GRAN...MAAAAA!!!

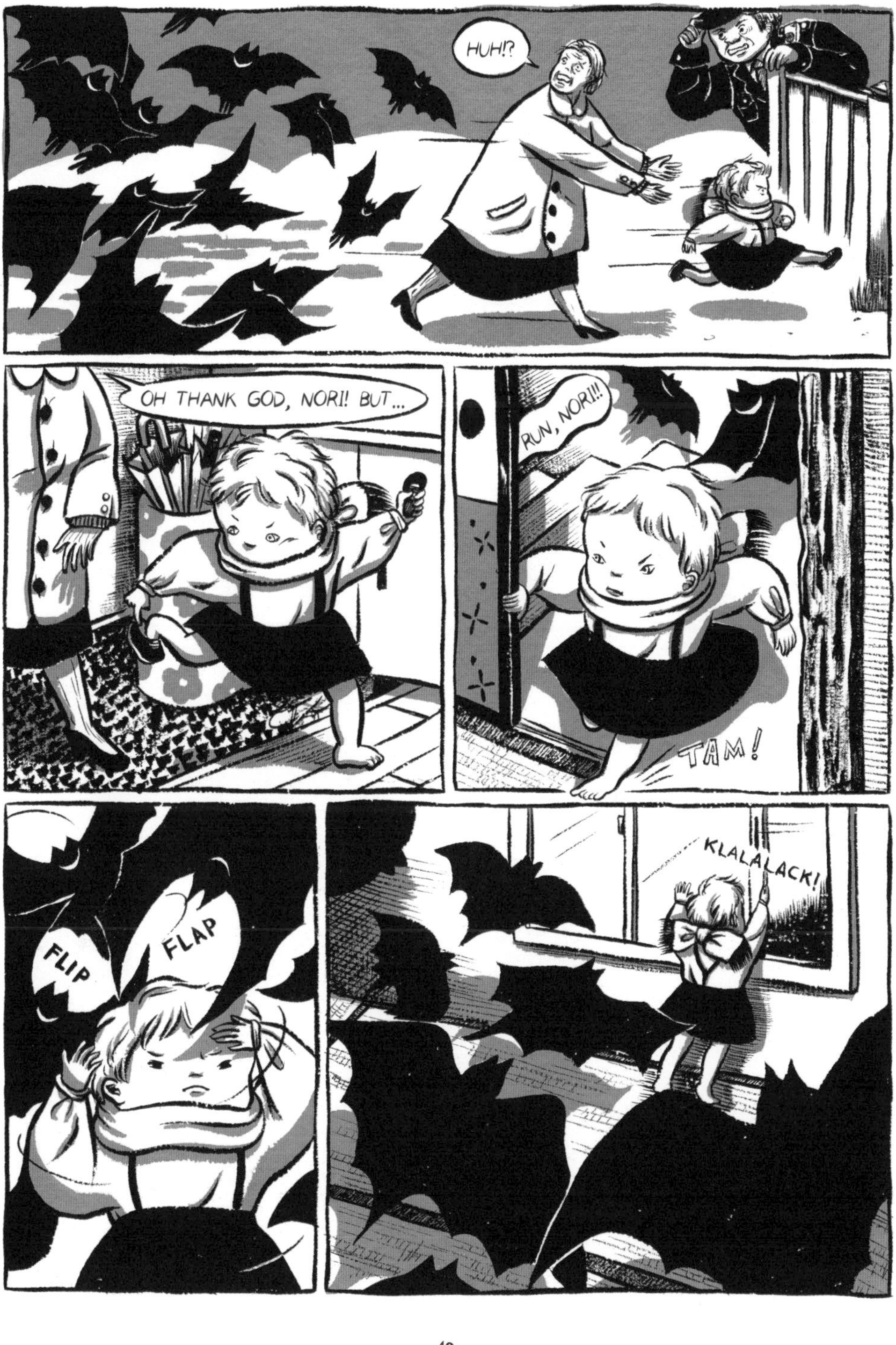
HUH!?
OH THANK GOD, NORI! BUT...
RUN, NORI!!!
TAM!
FLIP
FLAP
KLALALACK!

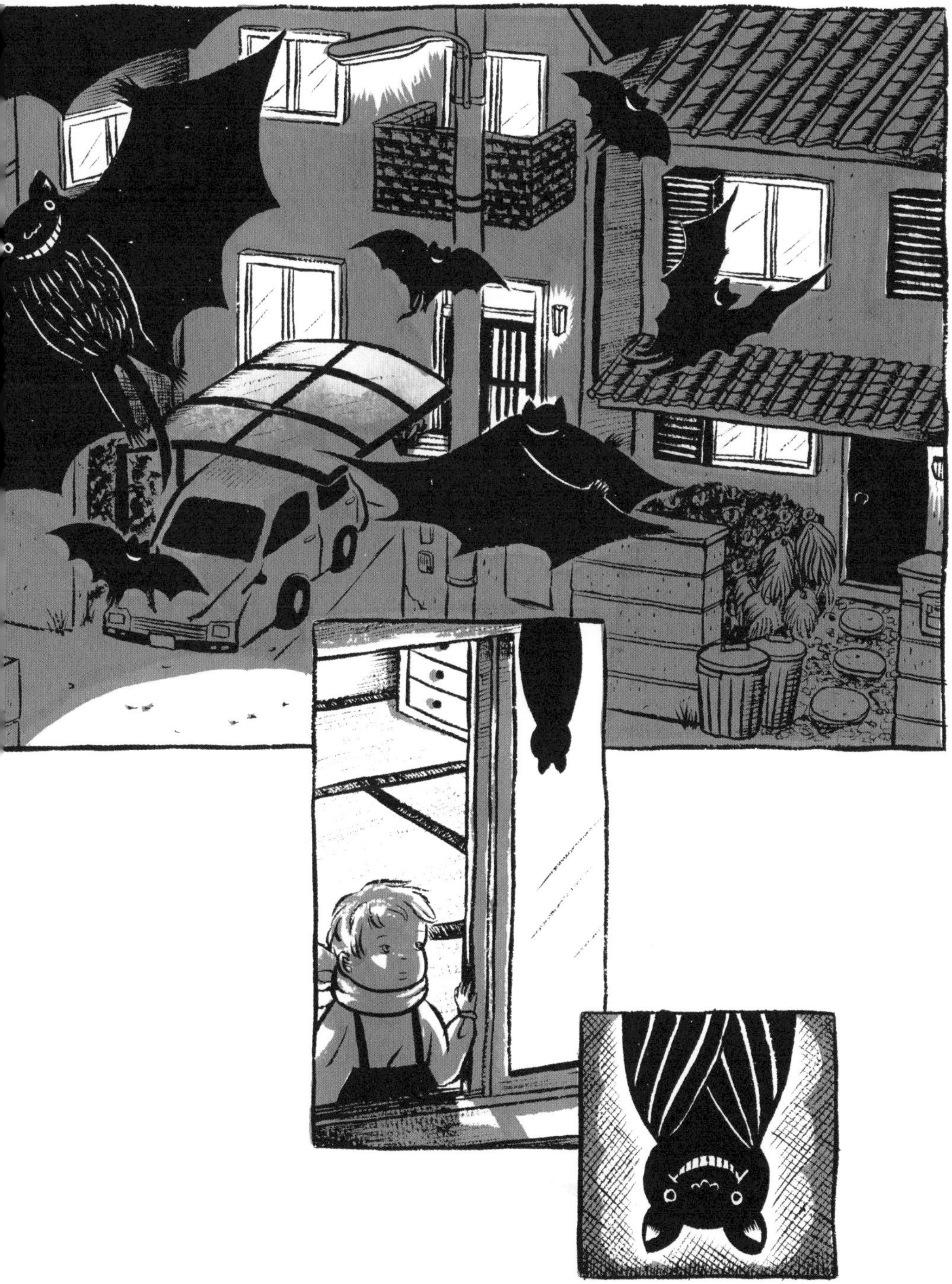

NORIKO.
DEN DEN!

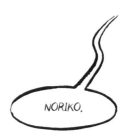

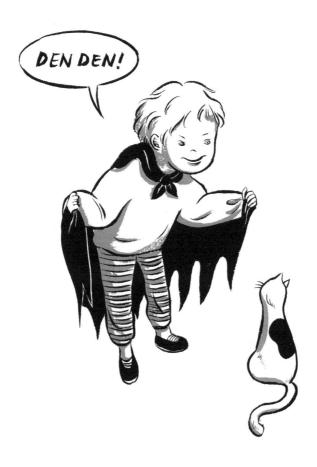

2

二

NORI

AND THE

RABBITS

OF THE

MOON

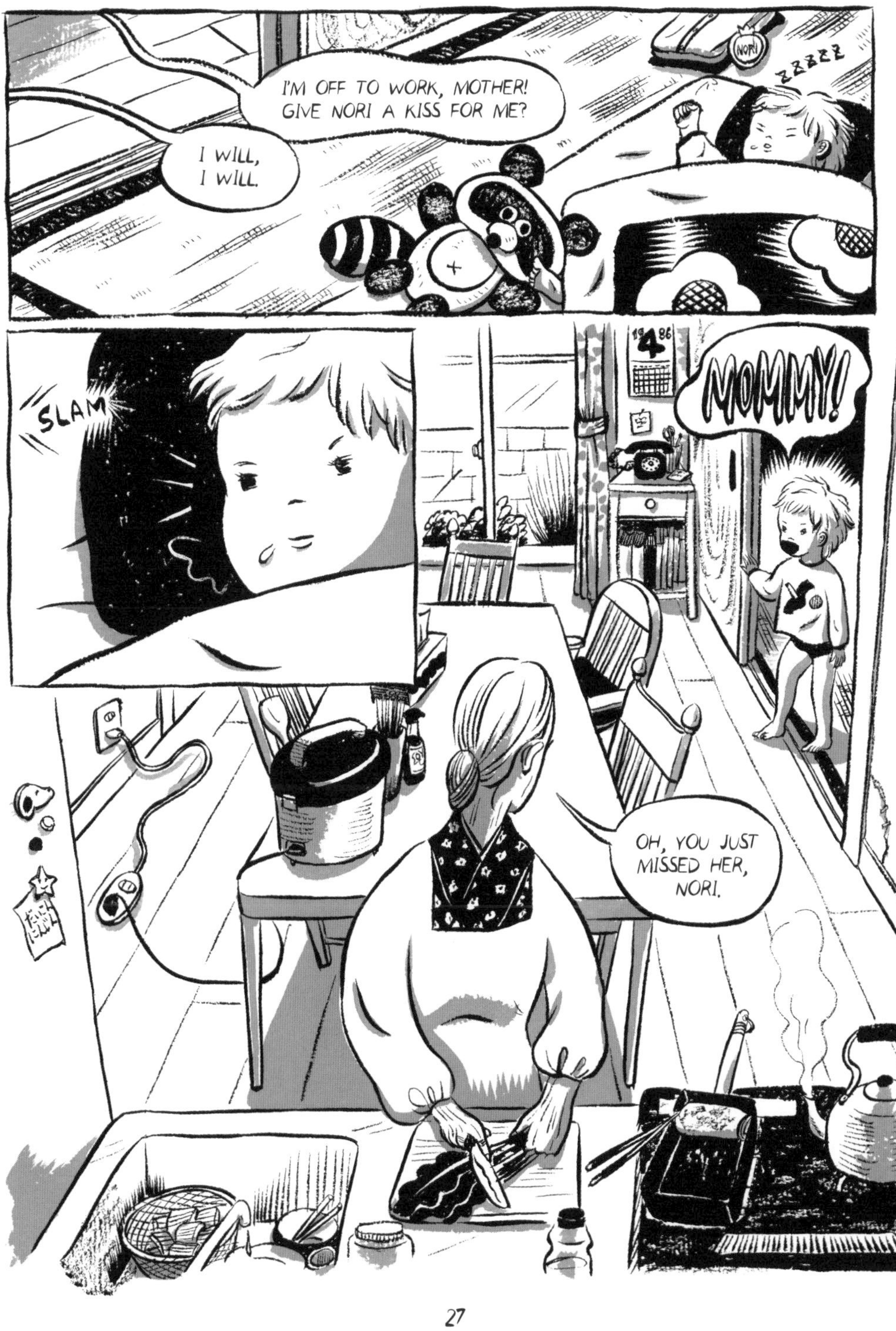
NORI
ZZZZZ
I'M OFF TO WORK, MOTHER! GIVE NORI A KISS FOR ME?
I WILL, I WILL.
SLAM
MOMMY!
OH, YOU JUST MISSED HER, NORI.

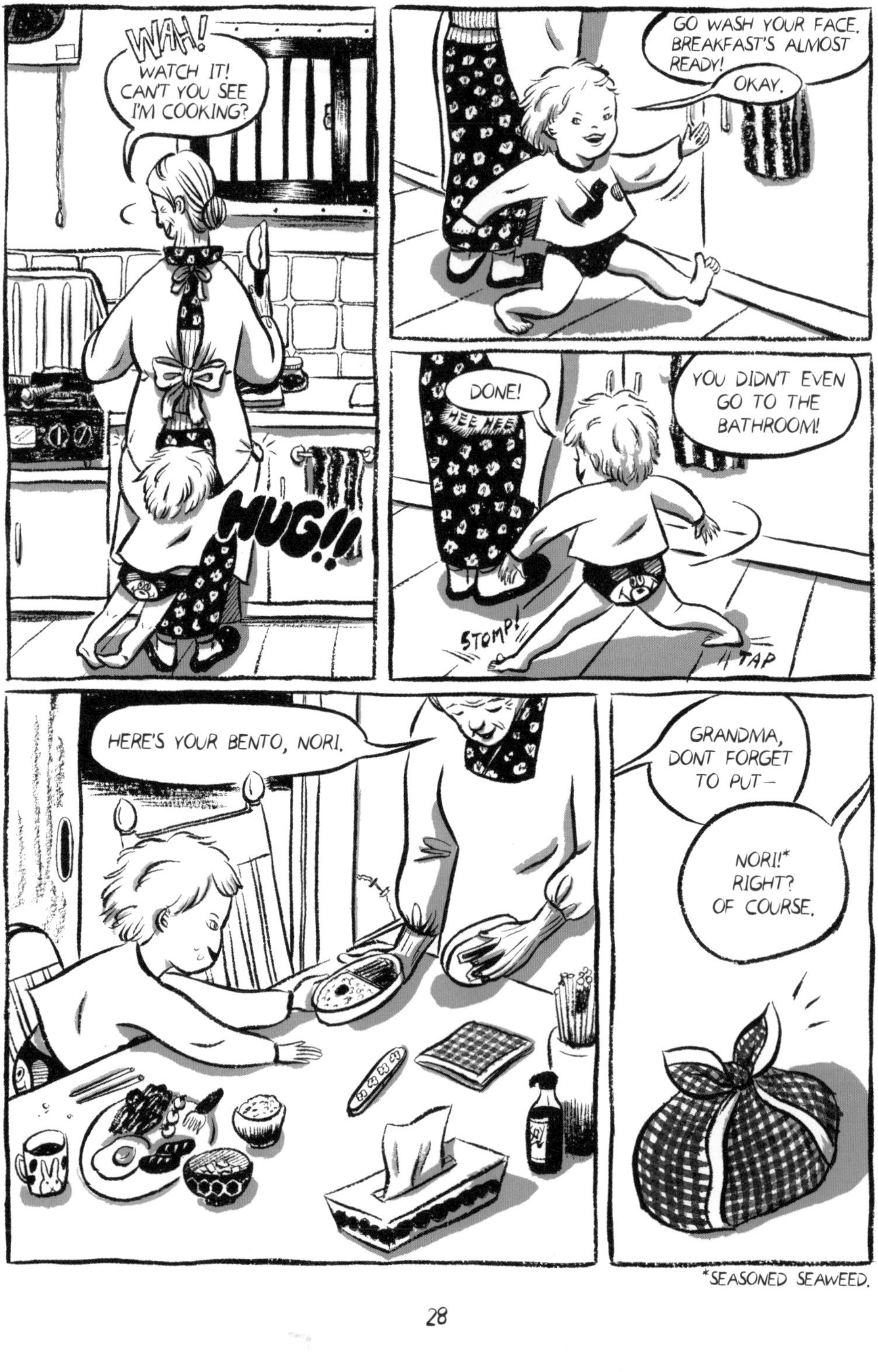
WAH!
WATCH IT! CAN'T YOU SEE I'M COOKING?
HUG!!
GO WASH YOUR FACE. BREAKFAST'S ALMOST READY!
OKAY.
DONE!
HEE HEE
YOU DIDN'T EVEN GO TO THE BATHROOM!
STOMP!
TAP
HERE'S YOUR BENTO, NORI.
GRANDMA, DONT FORGET TO PUT—
NORI!* RIGHT? OF COURSE.

*SEASONED SEAWEED.

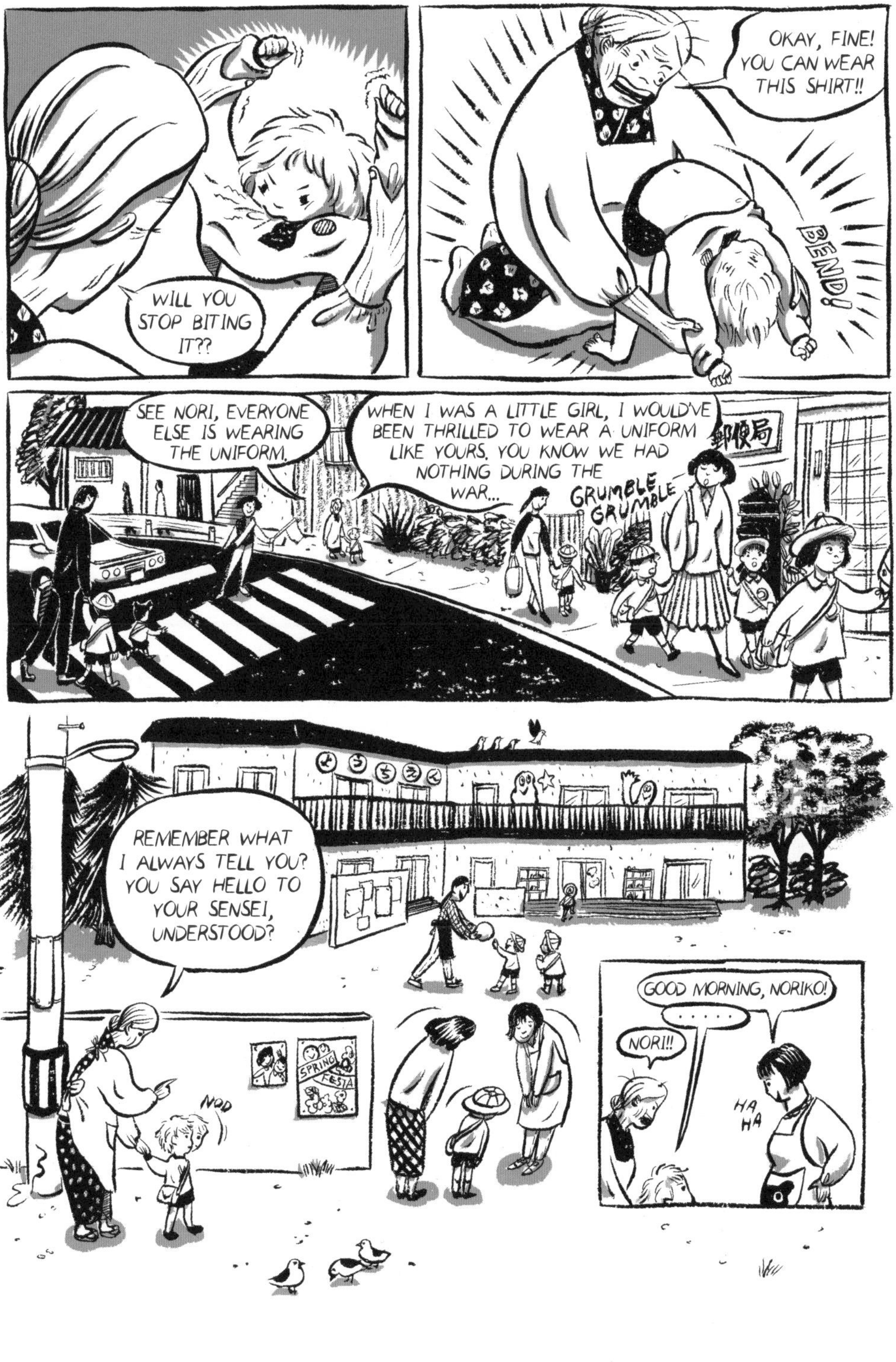

WILL YOU STOP BITING IT??
OKAY, FINE! YOU CAN WEAR THIS SHIRT!!
BEND!
SEE NORI, EVERYONE ELSE IS WEARING THE UNIFORM.
WHEN I WAS A LITTLE GIRL, I WOULD'VE BEEN THRILLED TO WEAR A UNIFORM LIKE YOURS. YOU KNOW WE HAD NOTHING DURING THE WAR...
GRUMBLE GRUMBLE
郵便局
ようちえん
REMEMBER WHAT I ALWAYS TELL YOU? YOU SAY HELLO TO YOUR SENSEI, UNDERSTOOD?
SPRING FESTA
NOD
GOOD MORNING, NORIKO!
. . . . .
NORI!!
HA HA

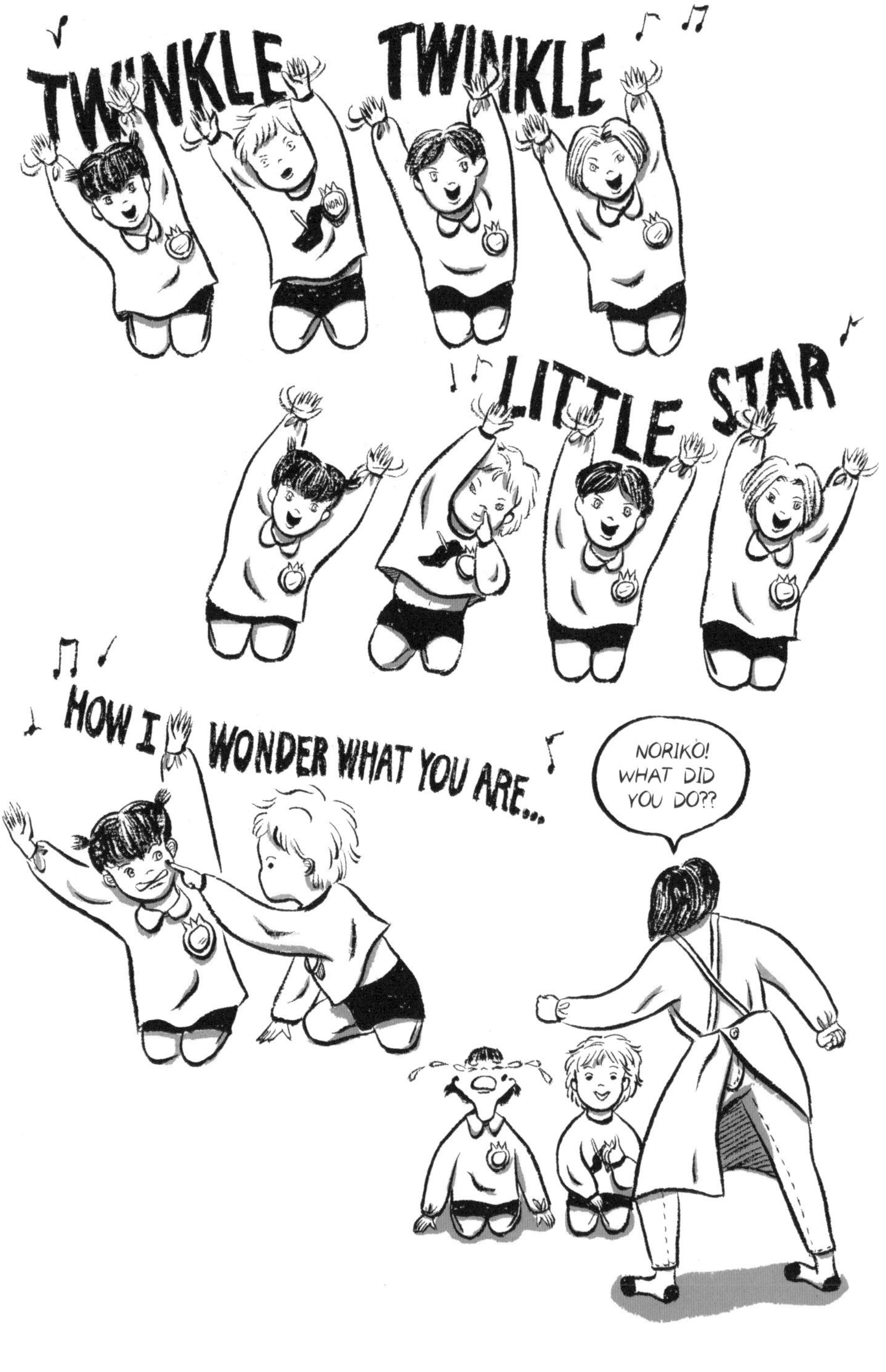
TWINKLE TWINKLE
NORI
LITTLE STAR
HOW I WONDER WHAT YOU ARE...
NORIKO! WHAT DID YOU DO??

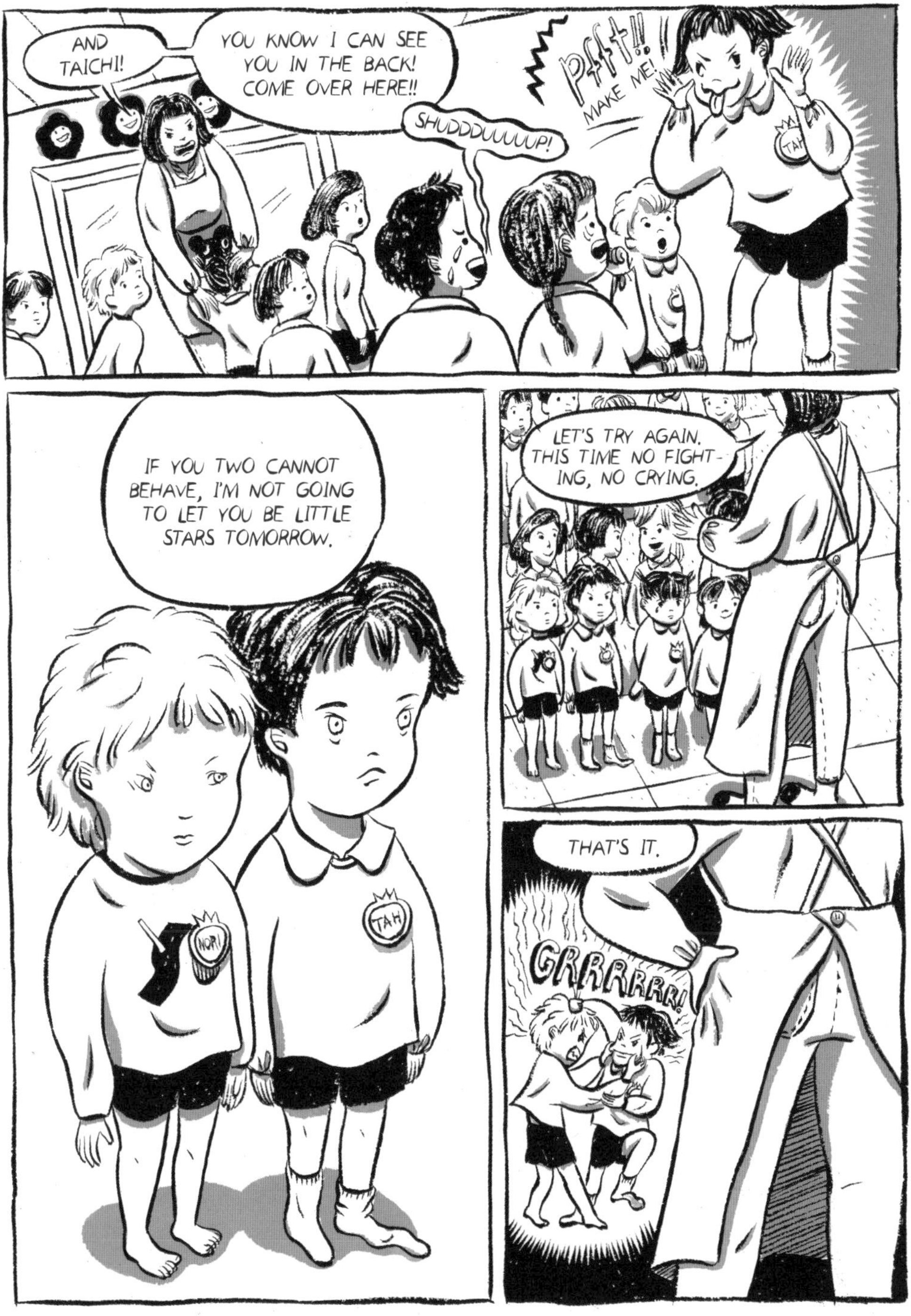
AND TAICHI!
YOU KNOW I CAN SEE YOU IN THE BACK! COME OVER HERE!!
SHUDDDUUUUUP!
pffft!!
MAKE ME!
TAH
IF YOU TWO CANNOT BEHAVE, I'M NOT GOING TO LET YOU BE LITTLE STARS TOMORROW.
NORI
TAH
LET'S TRY AGAIN. THIS TIME NO FIGHT-ING, NO CRYING.
THAT'S IT.
GRRRRRRR!

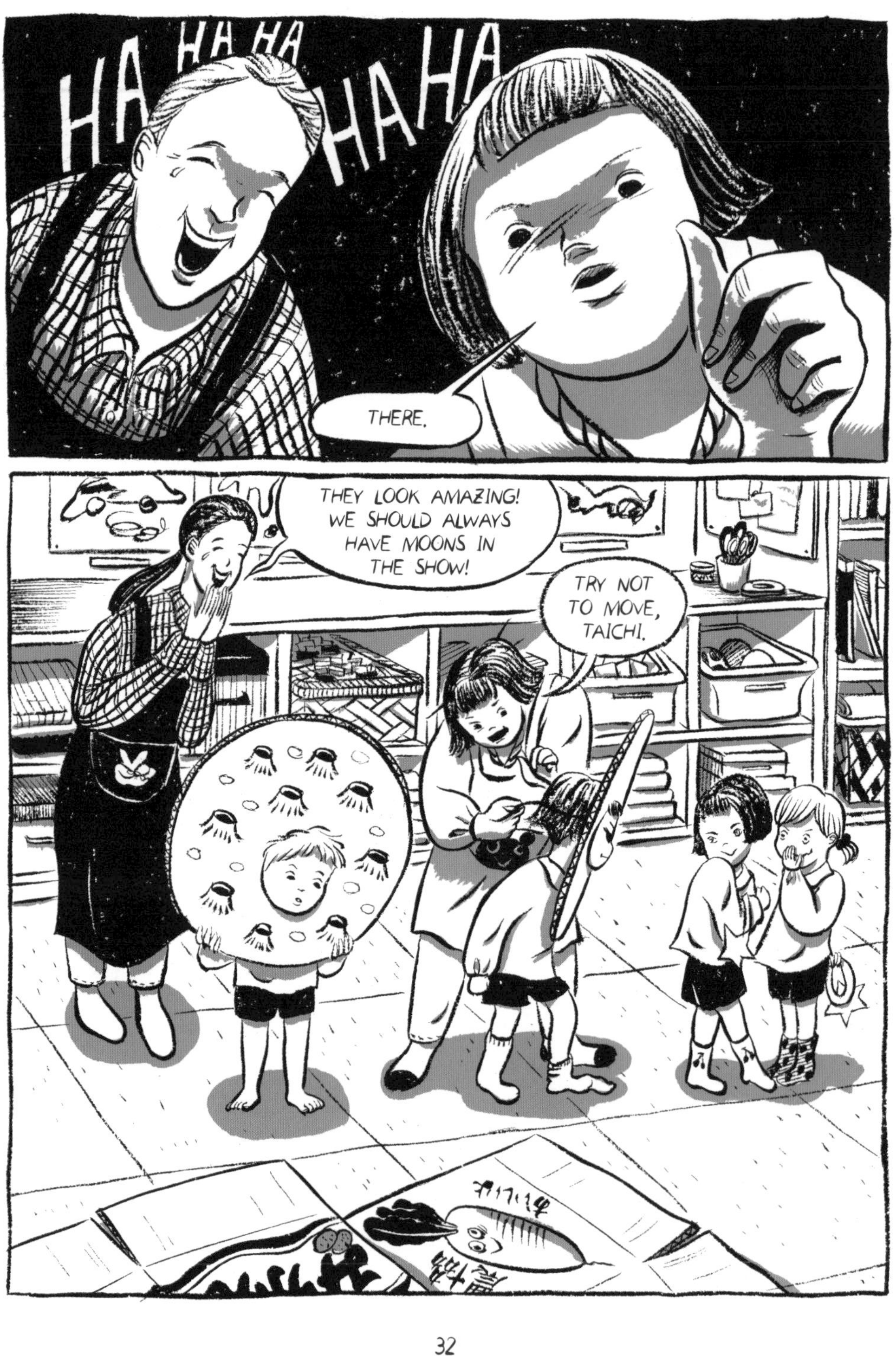
HA HA HA HAHA HA
THERE.
THEY LOOK AMAZING! WE SHOULD ALWAYS HAVE MOONS IN THE SHOW!
TRY NOT TO MOVE, TAICHI.

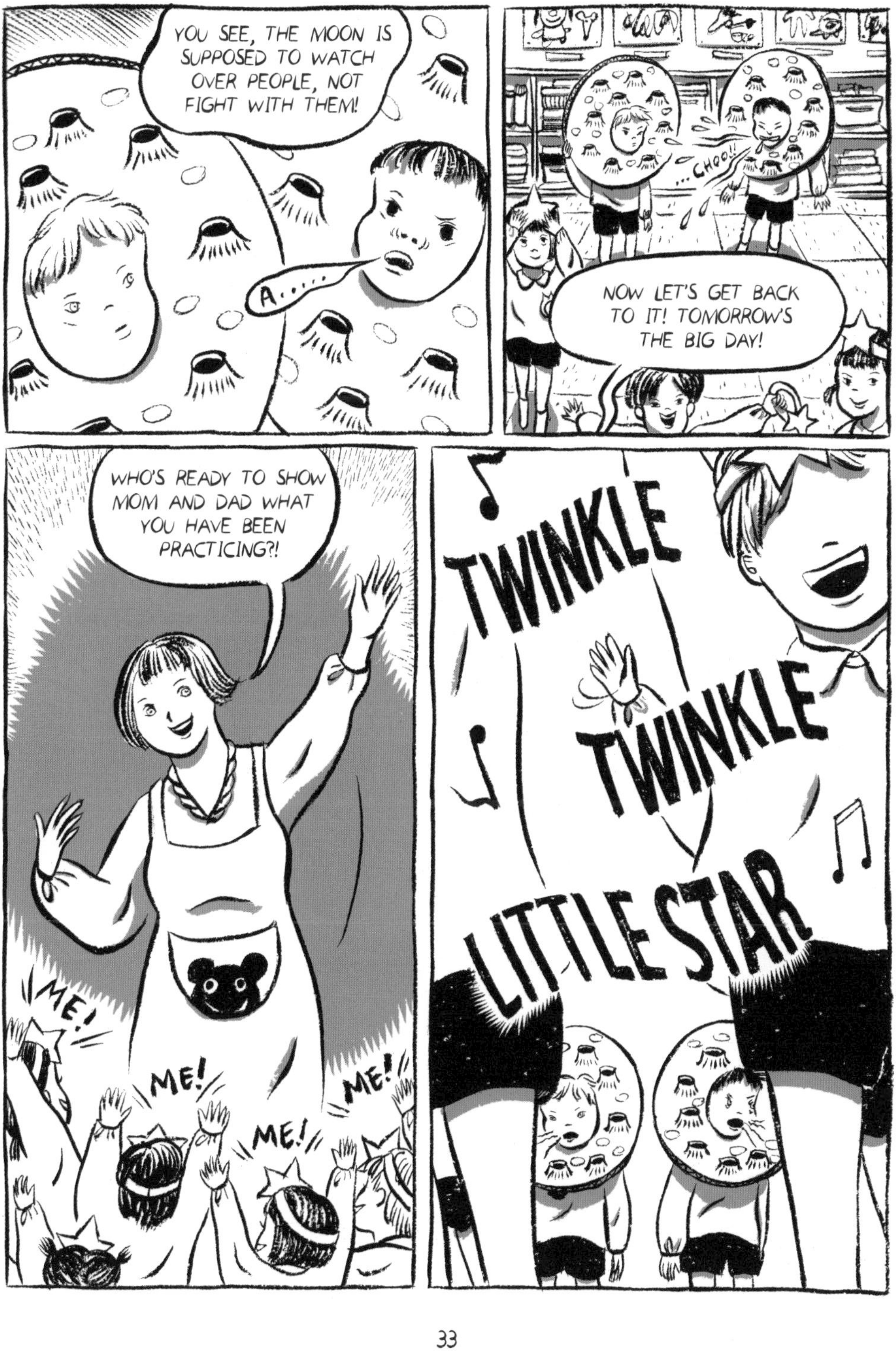
YOU SEE, THE MOON IS SUPPOSED TO WATCH OVER PEOPLE, NOT FIGHT WITH THEM!
A.....
...CHOO!!
NOW LET'S GET BACK TO IT! TOMORROW'S THE BIG DAY!
WHO'S READY TO SHOW MOM AND DAD WHAT YOU HAVE BEEN PRACTICING?!
ME!
ME!
ME!
ME!
TWINKLE
TWINKLE
LITTLE STAR

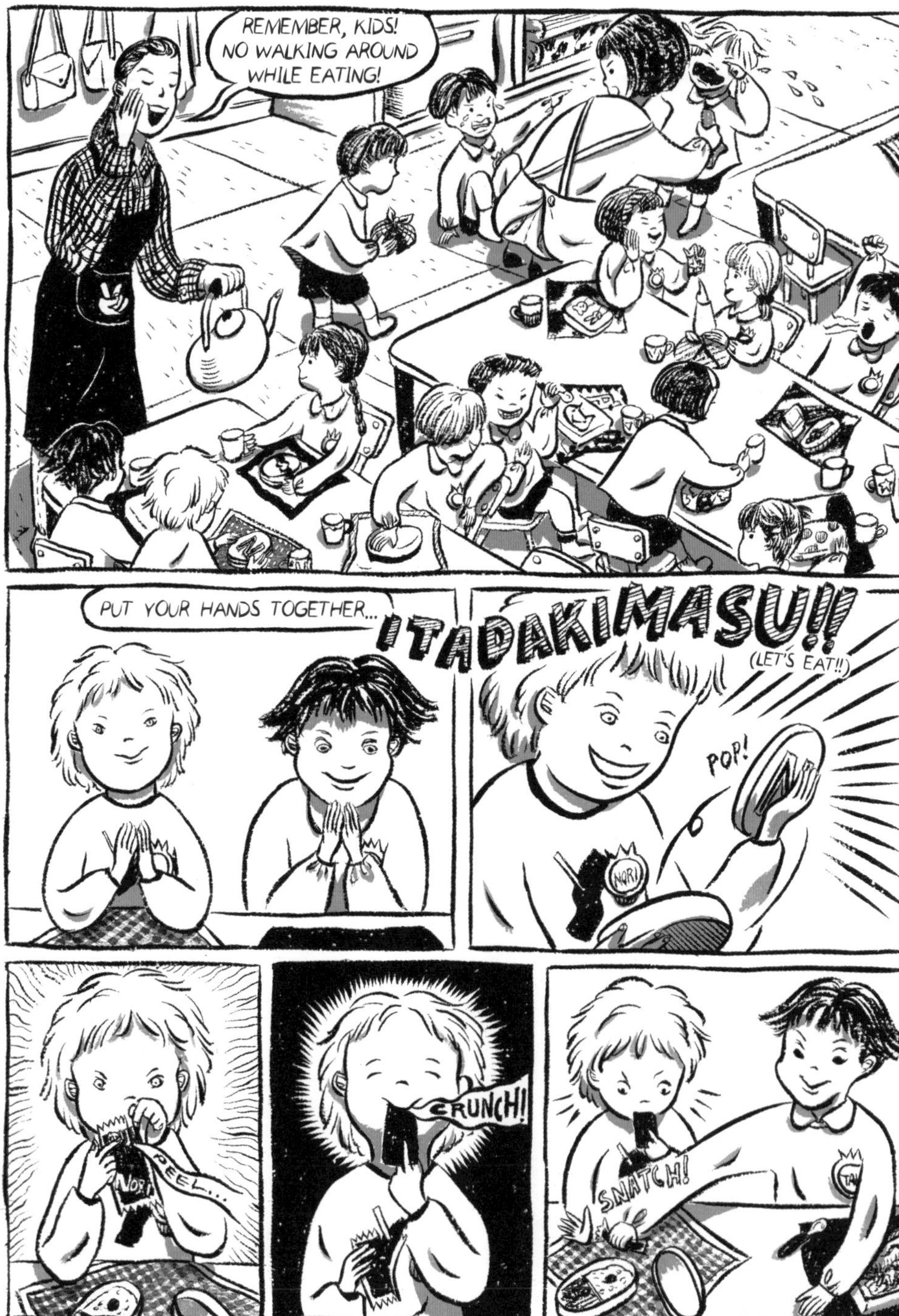

REMEMBER, KIDS! NO WALKING AROUND WHILE EATING!
PUT YOUR HANDS TOGETHER...
ITADAKIMASU!!
(LET'S EAT!!)
POP!
NORI
NORI
PEEL...
CRUNCH!
SNATCH!

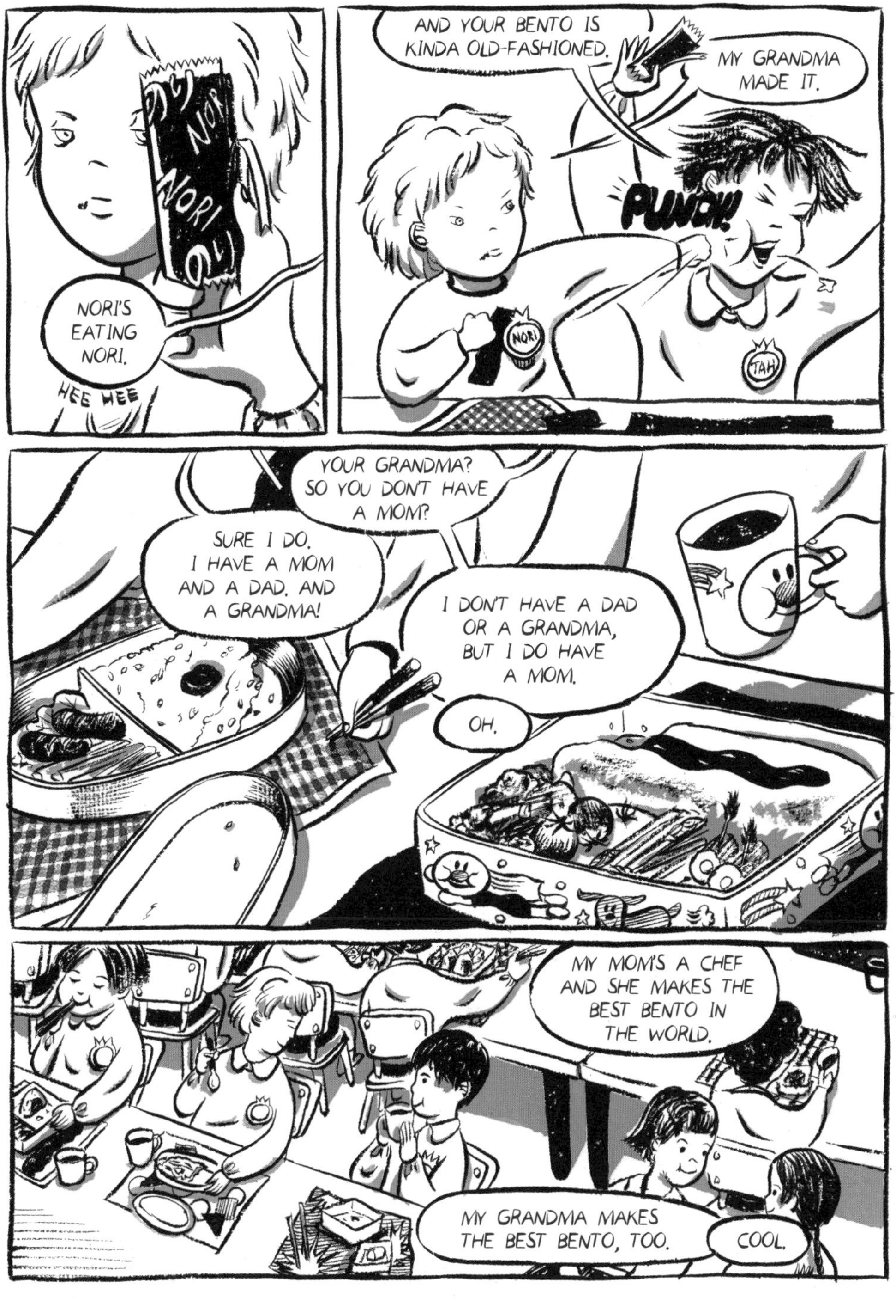
NORI
NORI
NORI'S EATING NORI.
HEE HEE
AND YOUR BENTO IS KINDA OLD-FASHIONED.
MY GRANDMA MADE IT.
PUNCH!
NORI
TAH
YOUR GRANDMA? SO YOU DON'T HAVE A MOM?
SURE I DO. I HAVE A MOM AND A DAD. AND A GRANDMA!
I DON'T HAVE A DAD OR A GRANDMA, BUT I DO HAVE A MOM.
OH.
MY MOM'S A CHEF AND SHE MAKES THE BEST BENTO IN THE WORLD.
MY GRANDMA MAKES THE BEST BENTO, TOO.
COOL.

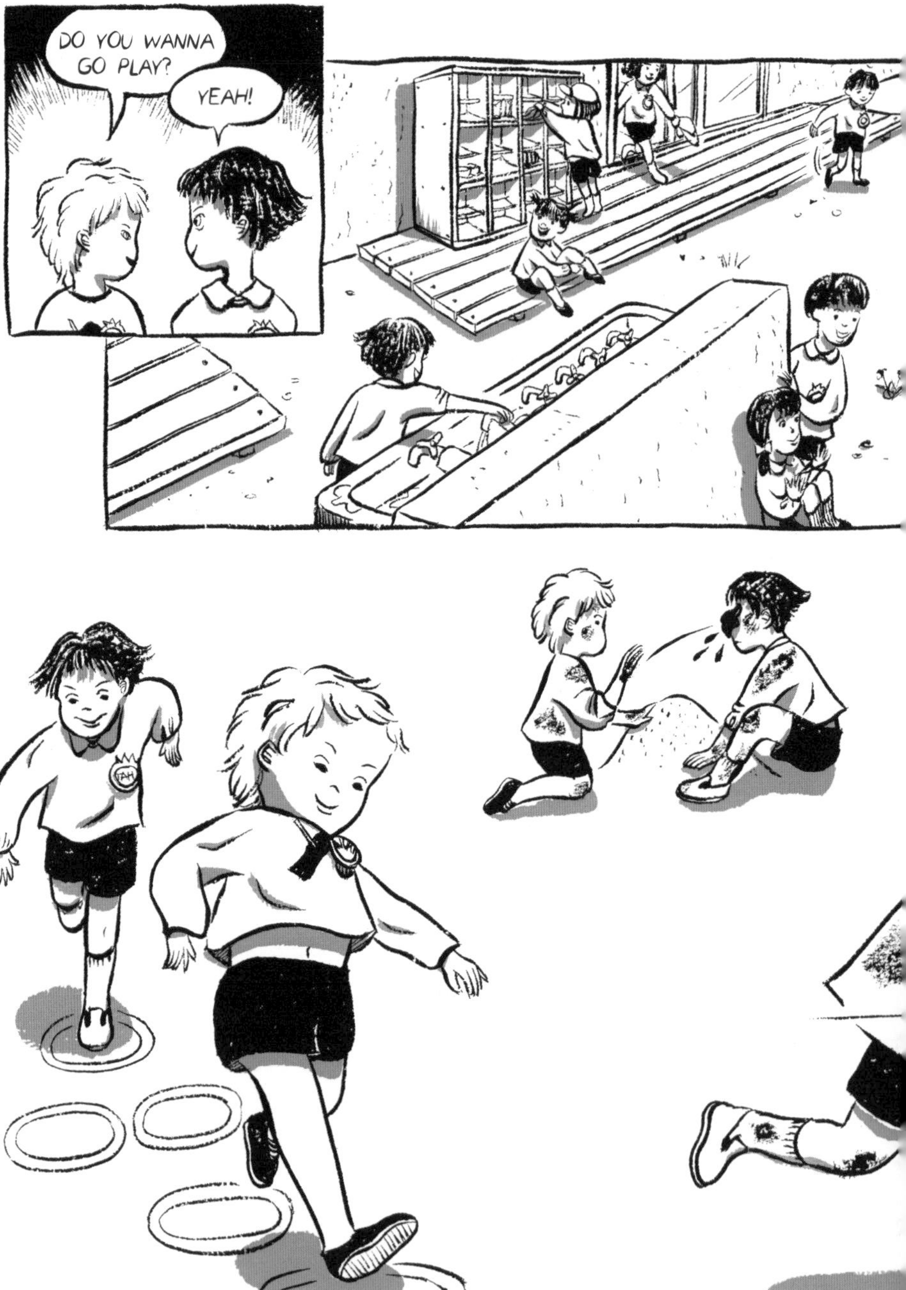

DO YOU WANNA GO PLAY?
YEAH!

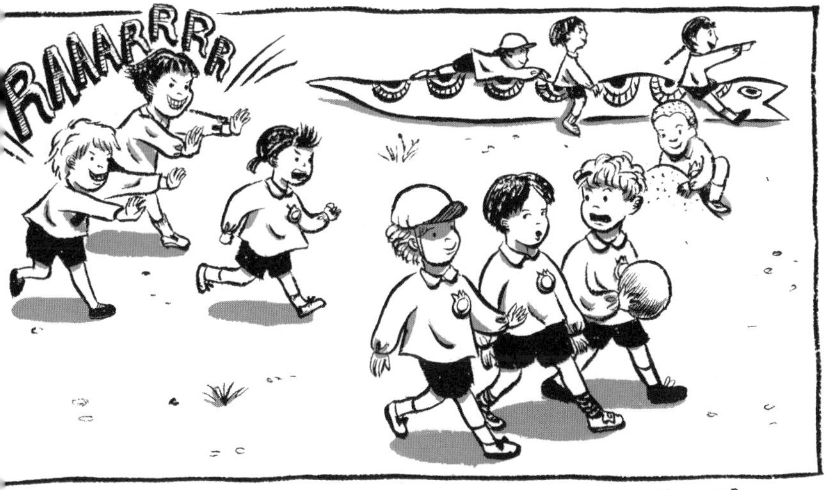
RAAARRRRR

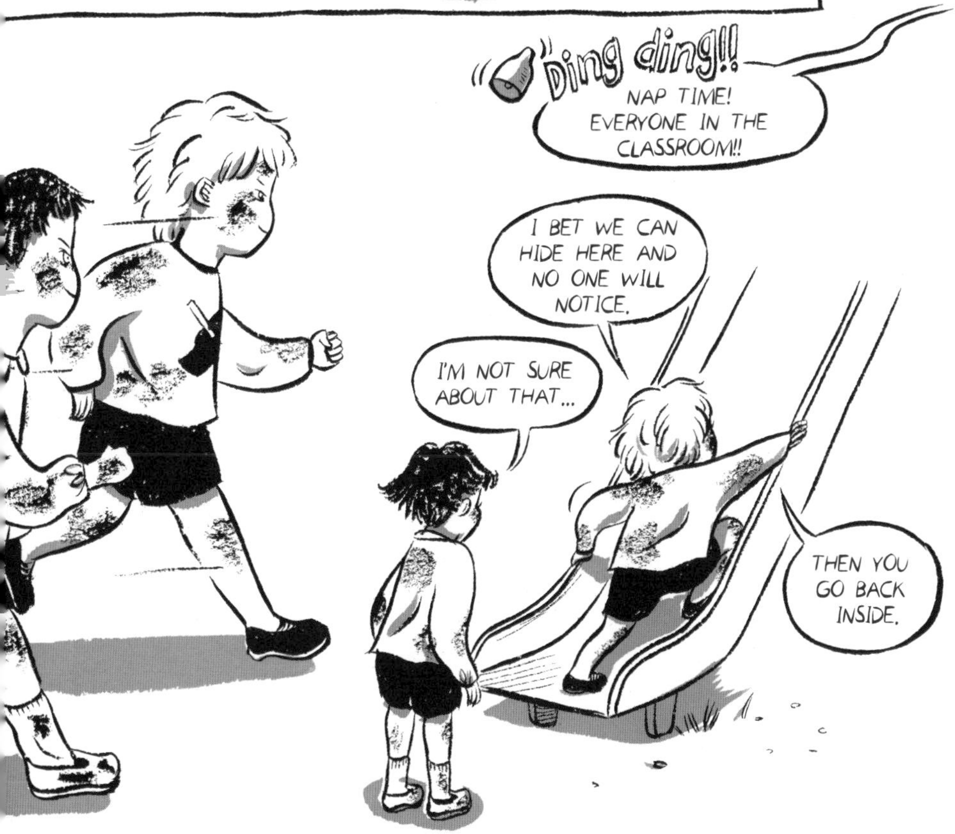
Ding ding!!
NAP TIME! EVERYONE IN THE CLASSROOM!!
I BET WE CAN HIDE HERE AND NO ONE WILL NOTICE.
I'M NOT SURE ABOUT THAT...
THEN YOU GO BACK INSIDE.

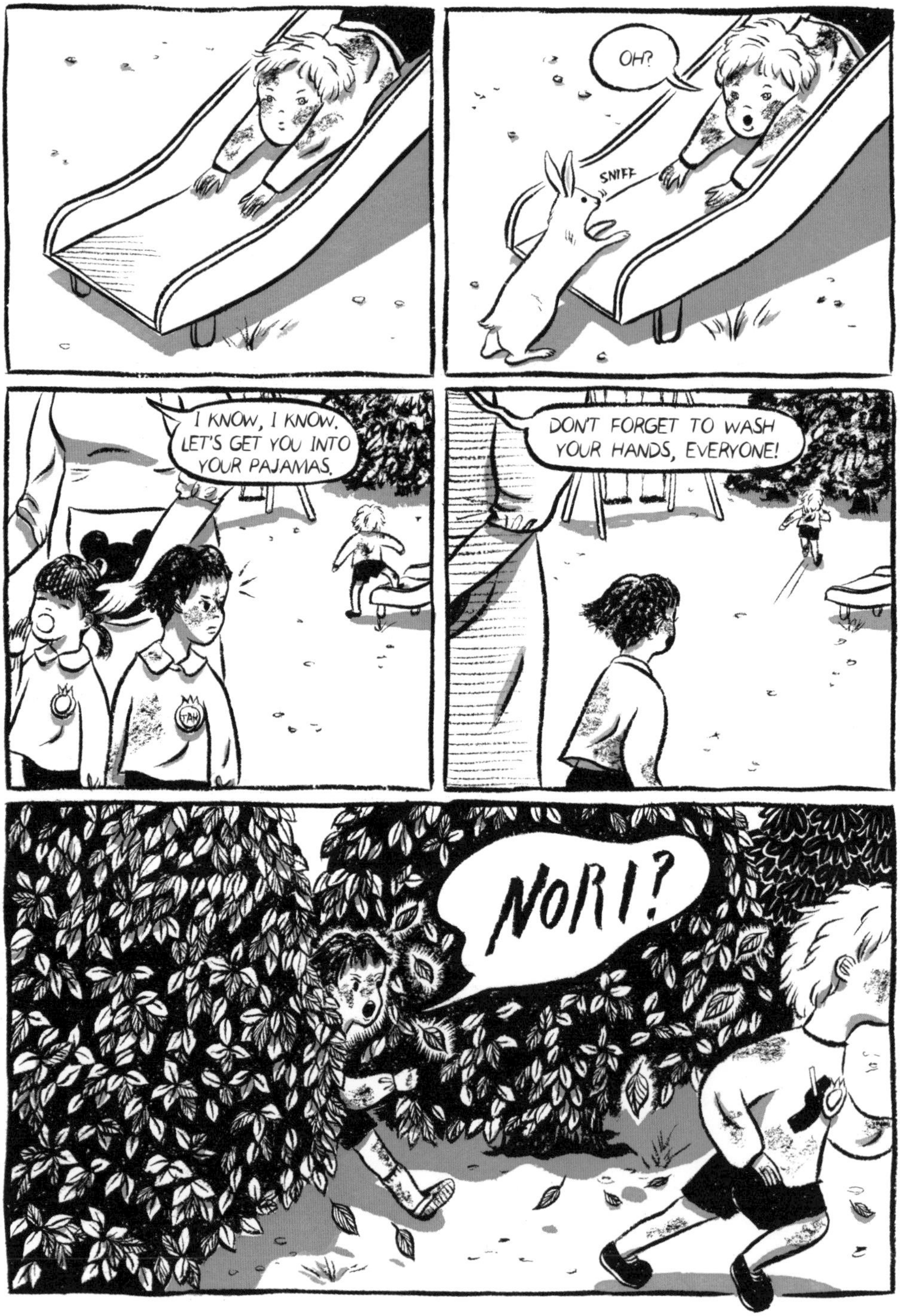
OH?
SNIFF
I KNOW, I KNOW. LET'S GET YOU INTO YOUR PAJAMAS.
DON'T FORGET TO WASH YOUR HANDS, EVERYONE!
NORI?

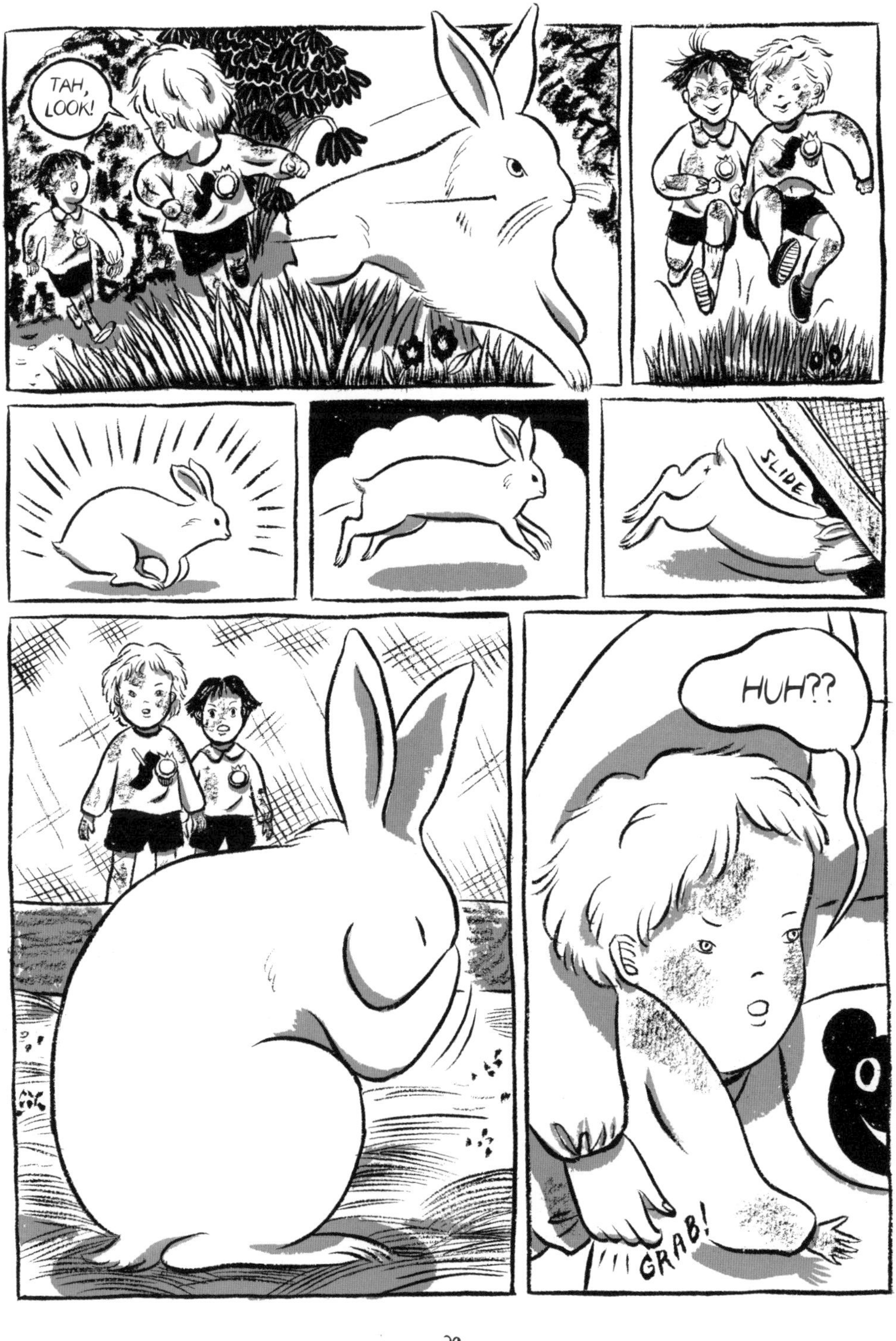
TAH, LOOK!
SLIDE
HUH??
GRAB!

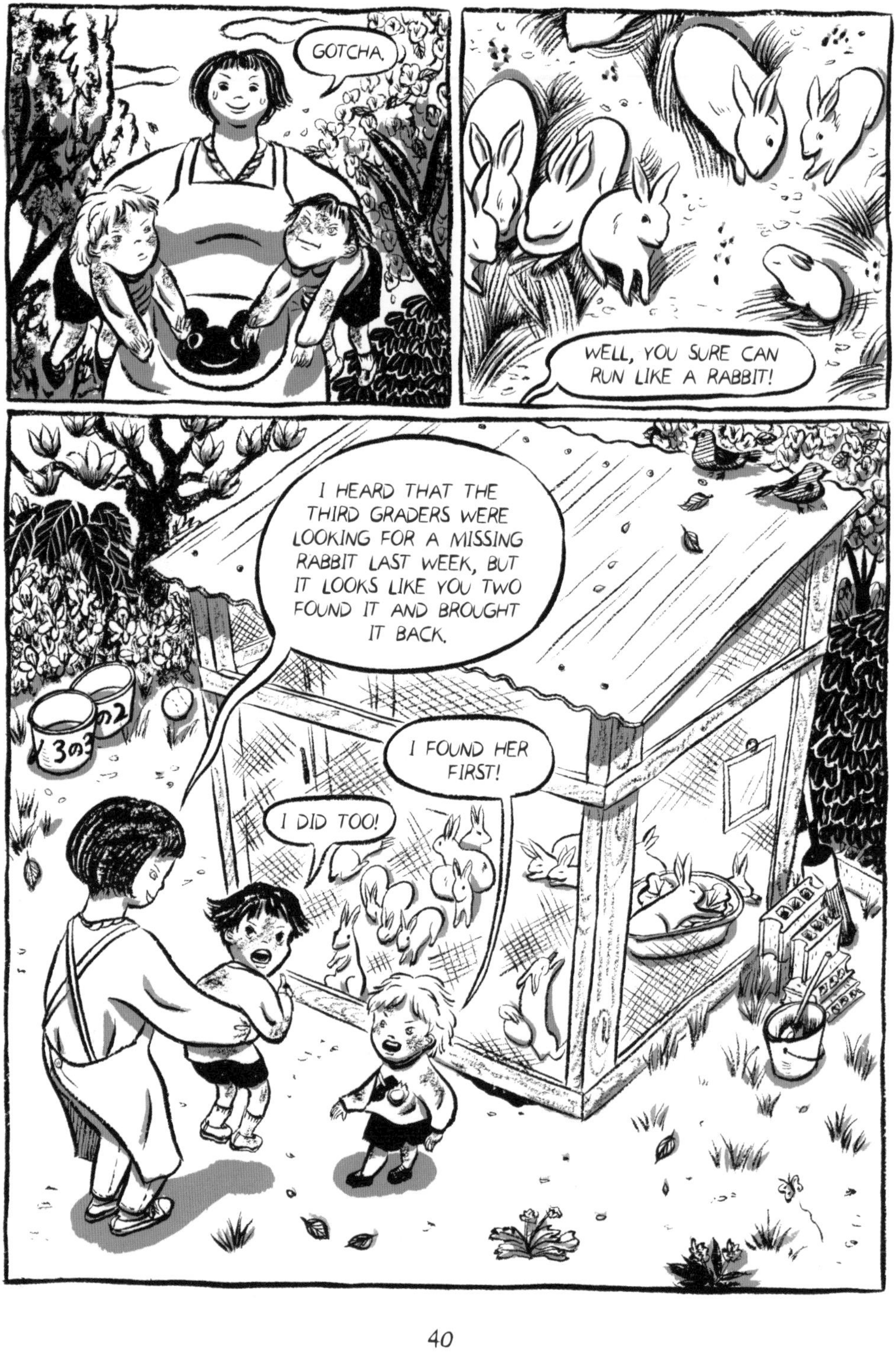
GOTCHA.
WELL, YOU SURE CAN RUN LIKE A RABBIT!
I HEARD THAT THE THIRD GRADERS WERE LOOKING FOR A MISSING RABBIT LAST WEEK, BUT IT LOOKS LIKE YOU TWO FOUND IT AND BROUGHT IT BACK.
I FOUND HER FIRST!
I DID TOO!

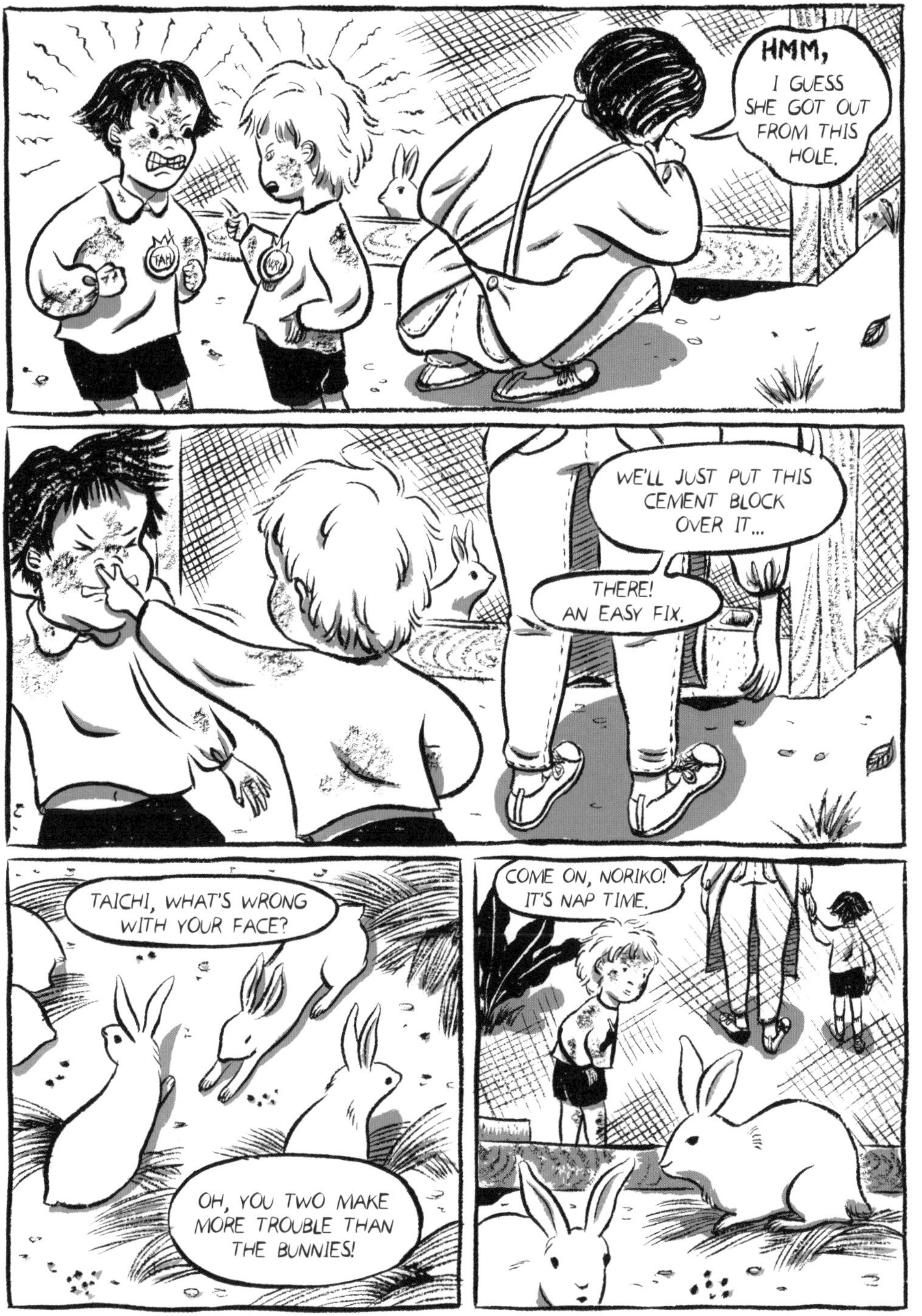
HMM, I GUESS SHE GOT OUT FROM THIS HOLE.
TAH
NRI
WE'LL JUST PUT THIS CEMENT BLOCK OVER IT...
THERE! AN EASY FIX.
TAICHI, WHAT'S WRONG WITH YOUR FACE?
OH, YOU TWO MAKE MORE TROUBLE THAN THE BUNNIES!
COME ON, NORIKO! IT'S NAP TIME.

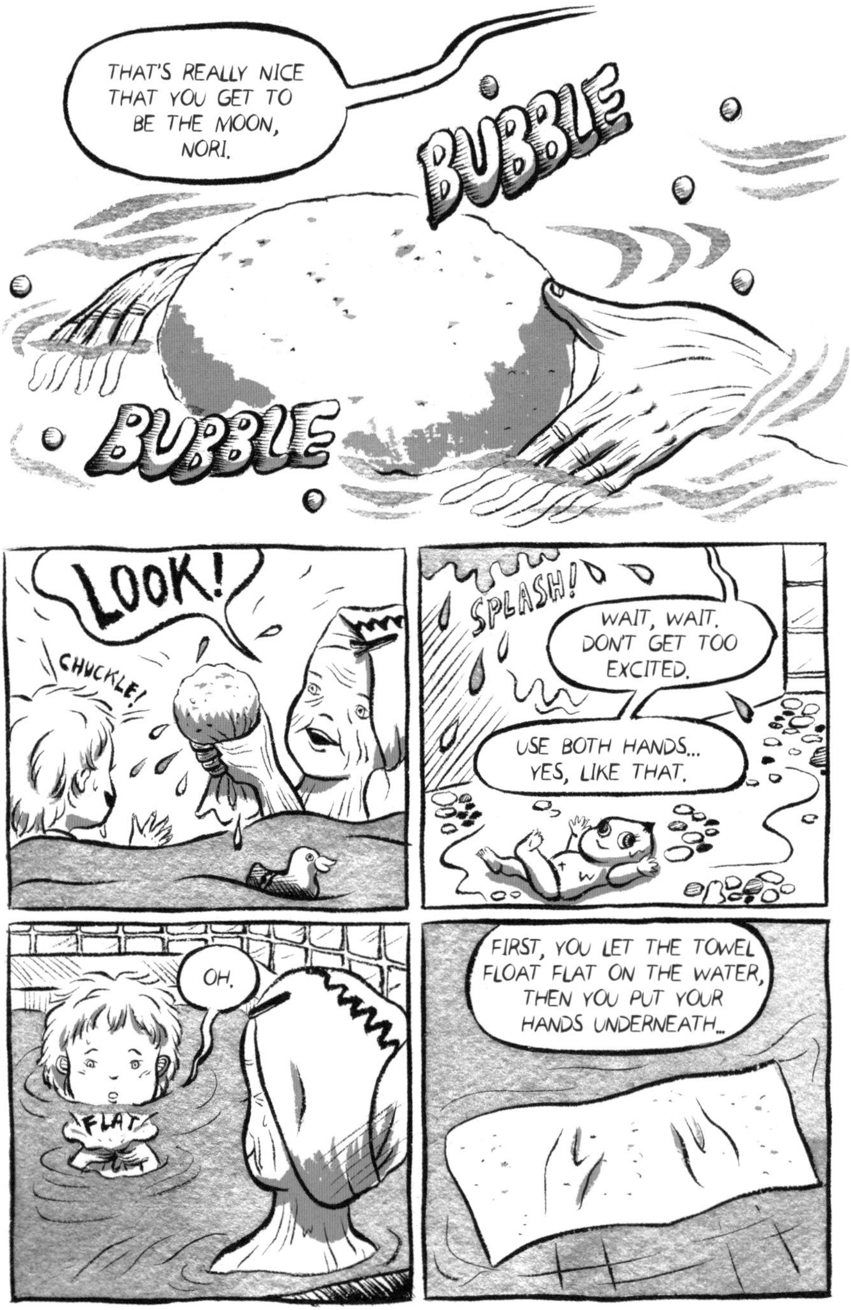
THAT'S REALLY NICE THAT YOU GET TO BE THE MOON, NORI.
BUBBLE
BUBBLE
LOOK!
CHUCKLE!
SPLASH!
WAIT, WAIT. DON'T GET TOO EXCITED.
USE BOTH HANDS... YES, LIKE THAT.
OH.
FLAT
FIRST, YOU LET THE TOWEL FLOAT FLAT ON THE WATER, THEN YOU PUT YOUR HANDS UNDERNEATH...

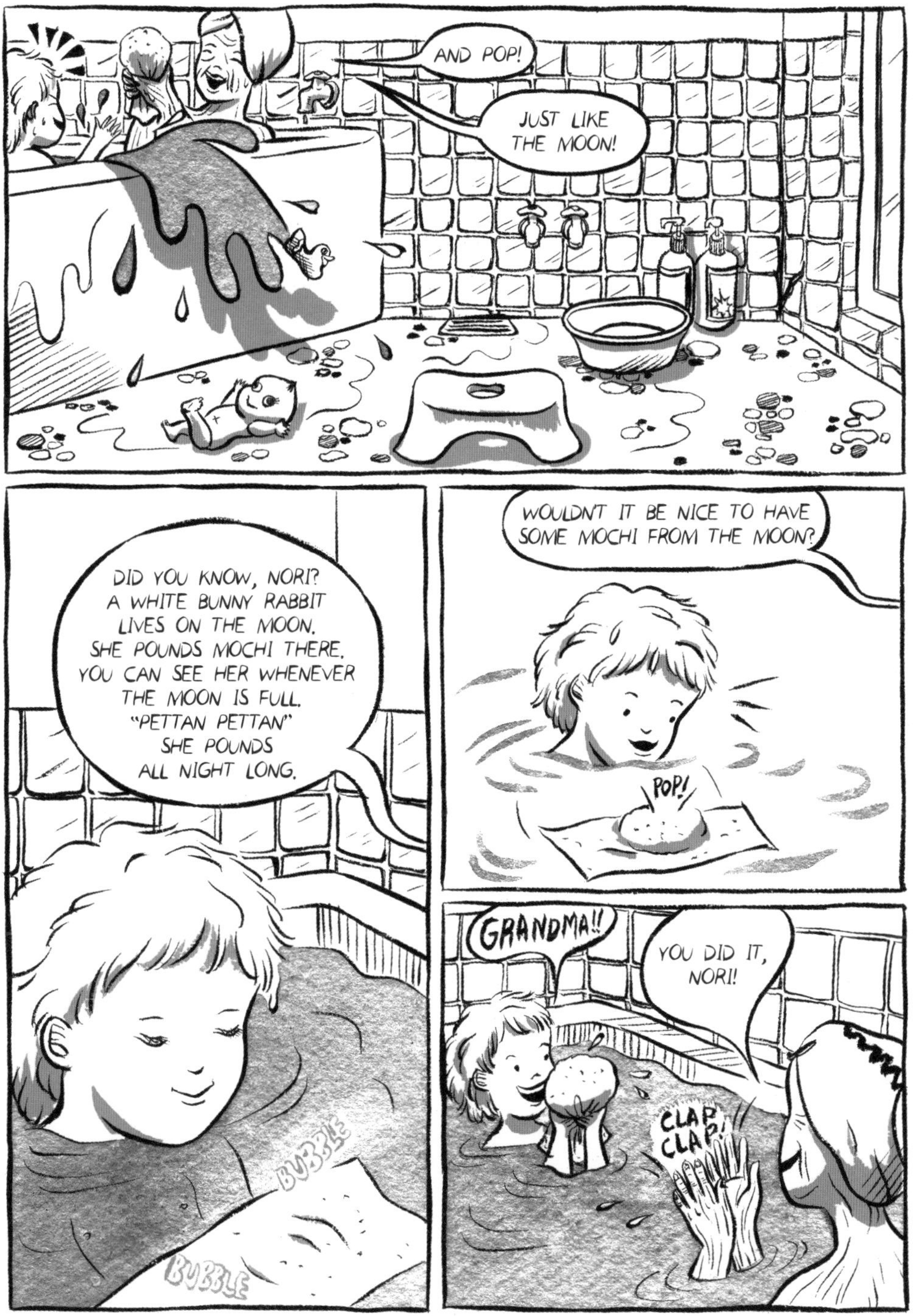
AND POP!
JUST LIKE THE MOON!
DID YOU KNOW, NORI? A WHITE BUNNY RABBIT LIVES ON THE MOON. SHE POUNDS MOCHI THERE. YOU CAN SEE HER WHENEVER THE MOON IS FULL. "PETTAN PETTAN" SHE POUNDS ALL NIGHT LONG.
BUBBLE
BUBBLE
WOULDN'T IT BE NICE TO HAVE SOME MOCHI FROM THE MOON?
POP!
GRANDMA!!
YOU DID IT, NORI!
CLAP, CLAP!

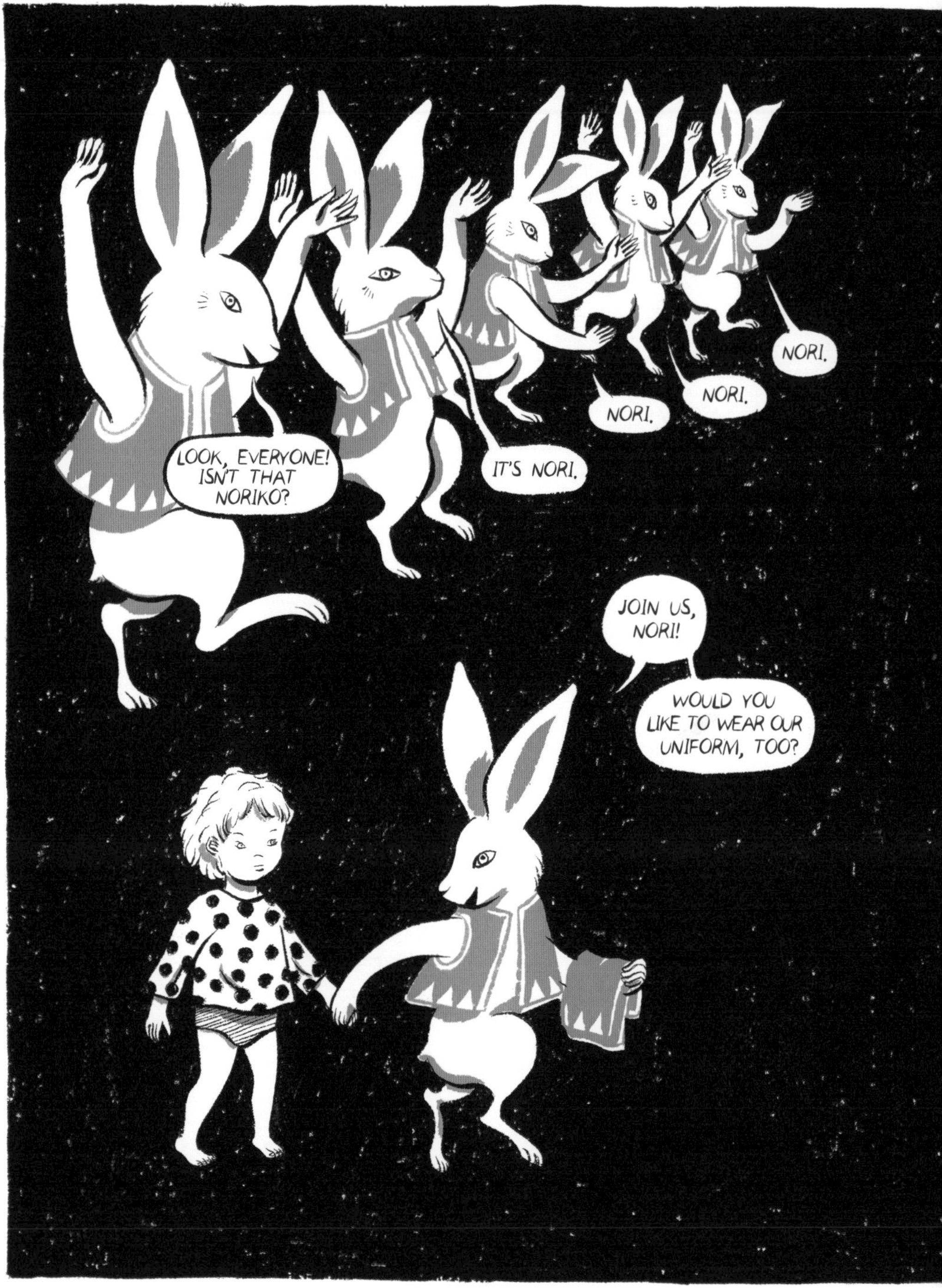
LOOK, EVERYONE! ISN'T THAT NORIKO?
IT'S NORI.
NORI.
NORI.
NORI.
JOIN US, NORI!
WOULD YOU LIKE TO WEAR OUR UNIFORM, TOO?

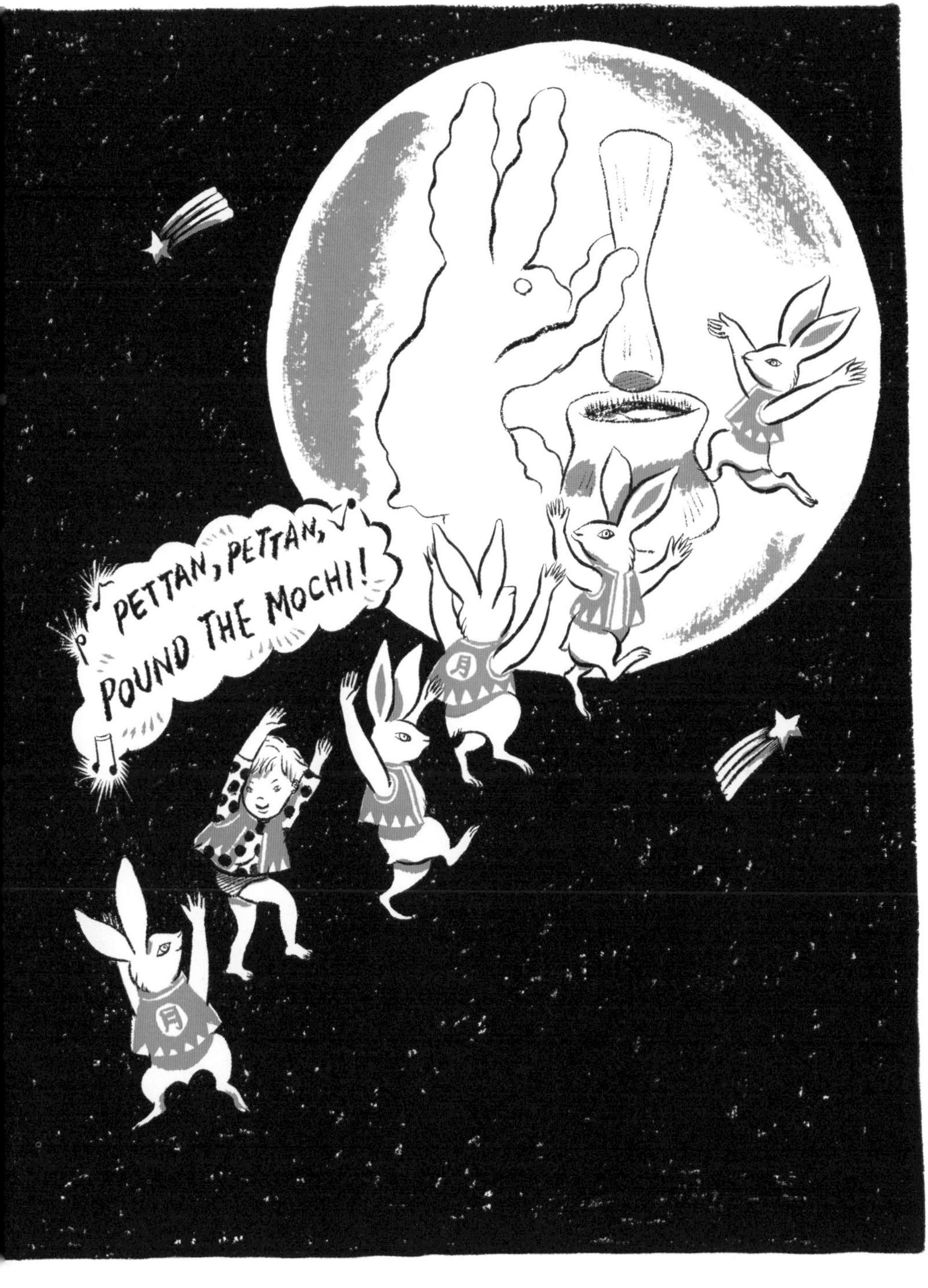
PETTAN, PETTAN, POUND THE MOCHI!

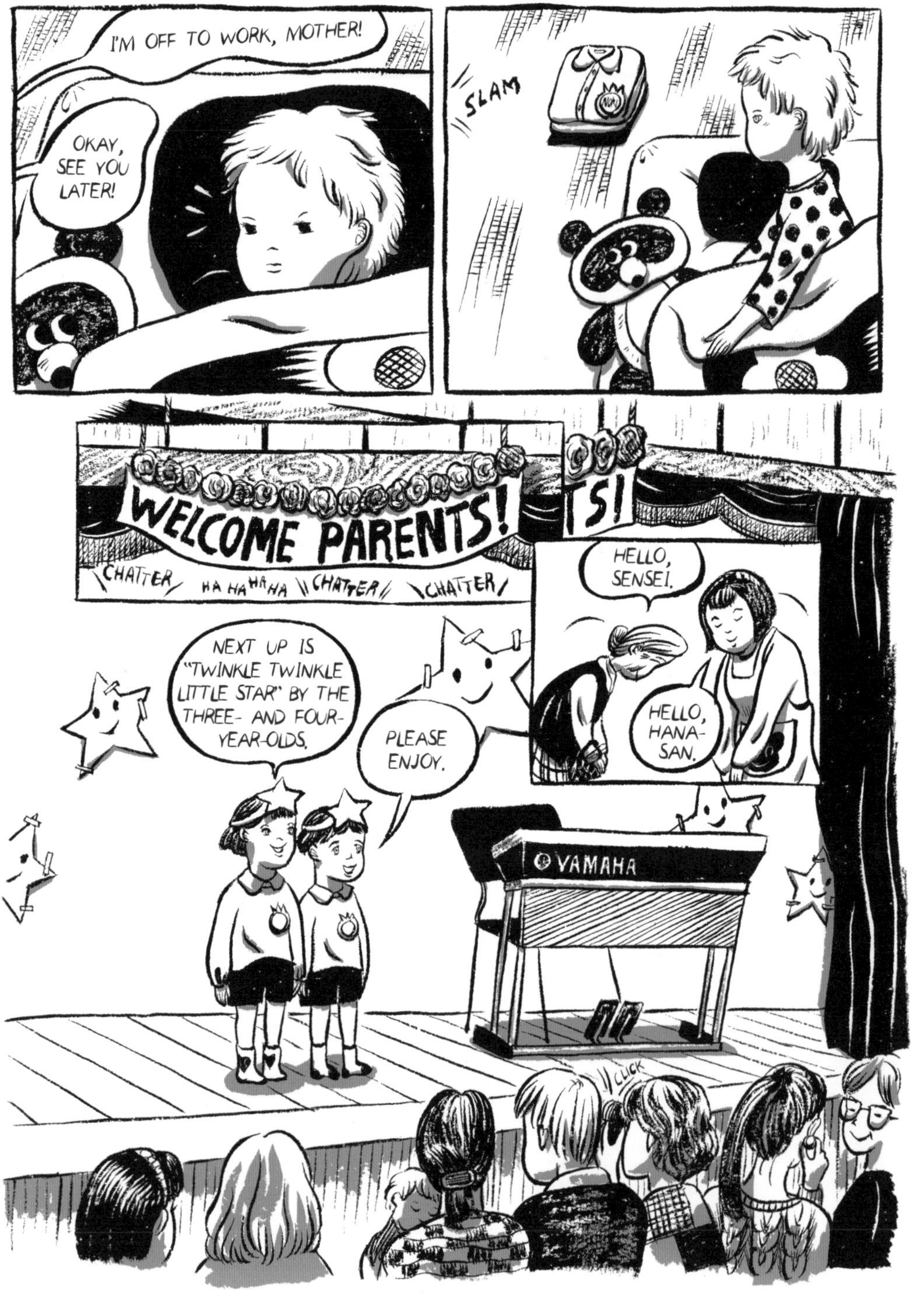
I'M OFF TO WORK, MOTHER!
OKAY, SEE YOU LATER!
SLAM
NUKI
WELCOME PARENTS!
TS!
CHATTER
HA HA HA HA
CHATTER
CHATTER
HELLO, SENSEI.
HELLO, HANA-SAN.
NEXT UP IS "TWINKLE TWINKLE LITTLE STAR" BY THE THREE- AND FOUR-YEAR-OLDS.
PLEASE ENJOY.
YAMAHA
CLICK

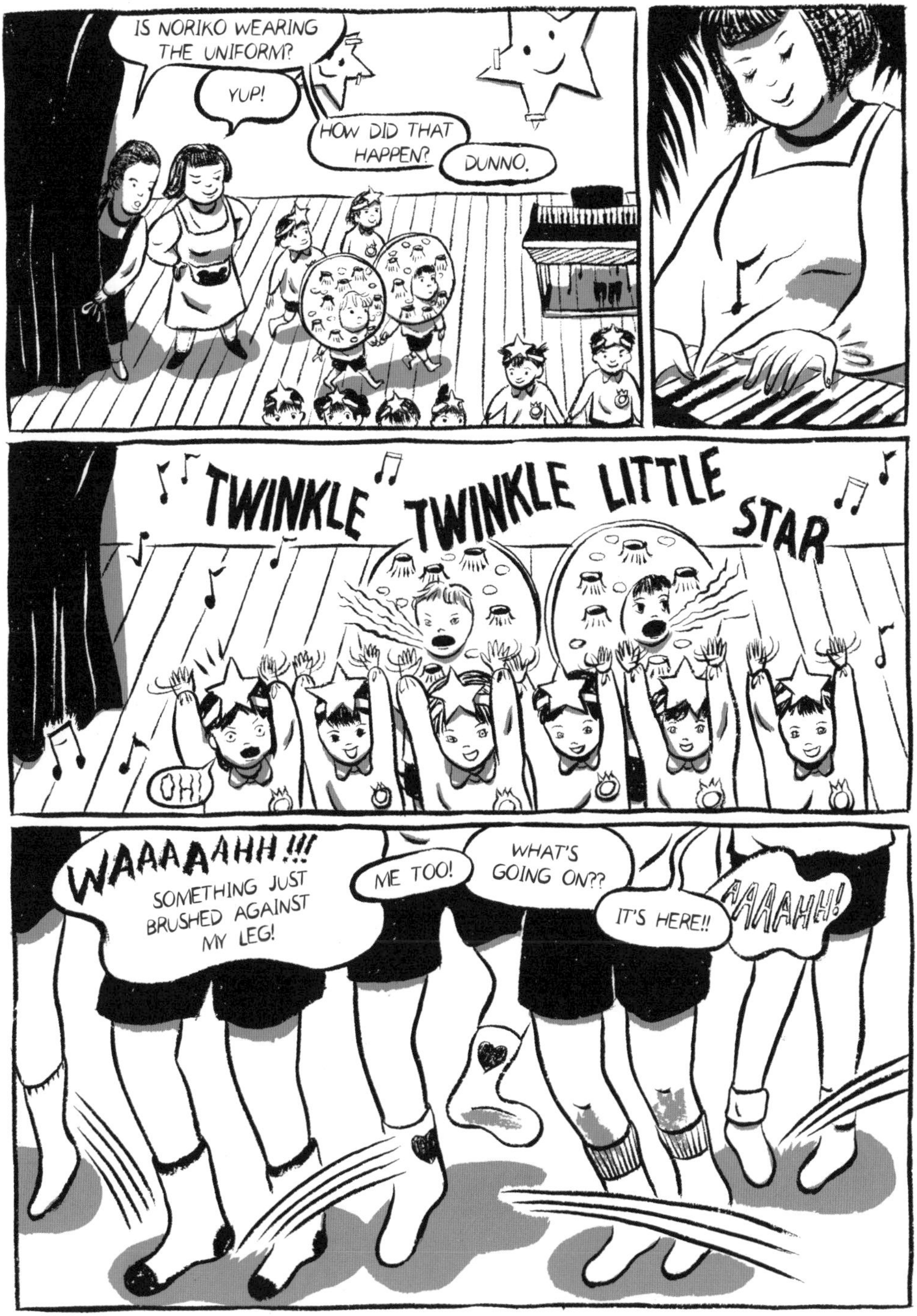
IS NORIKO WEARING THE UNIFORM?
YUP!
HOW DID THAT HAPPEN?
DUNNO.
TWINKLE TWINKLE LITTLE STAR
OH!
WAAAAAHH!!! SOMETHING JUST BRUSHED AGAINST MY LEG!
ME TOO!
WHAT'S GOING ON??
IT'S HERE!!
AAAAHH!

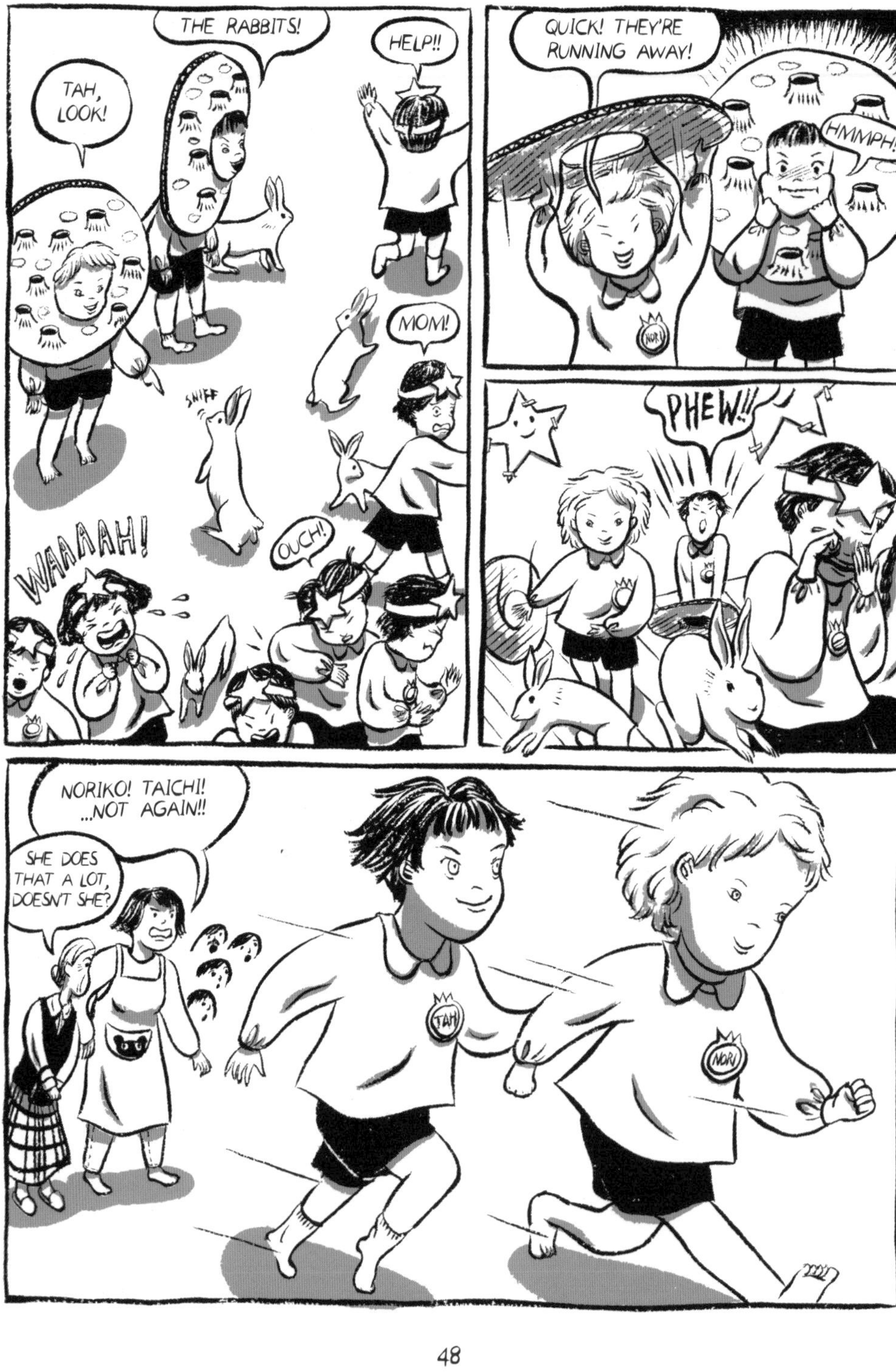
TAH, LOOK!
THE RABBITS!
HELP!!
SNIFF
MOM!
WAAAAH!
OUCH!
QUICK! THEY'RE RUNNING AWAY!
HMMPH!
NORI
PHEW!!
NORIKO! TAICHI! ...NOT AGAIN!!
SHE DOES THAT A LOT, DOESN'T SHE?
TAH
NORI

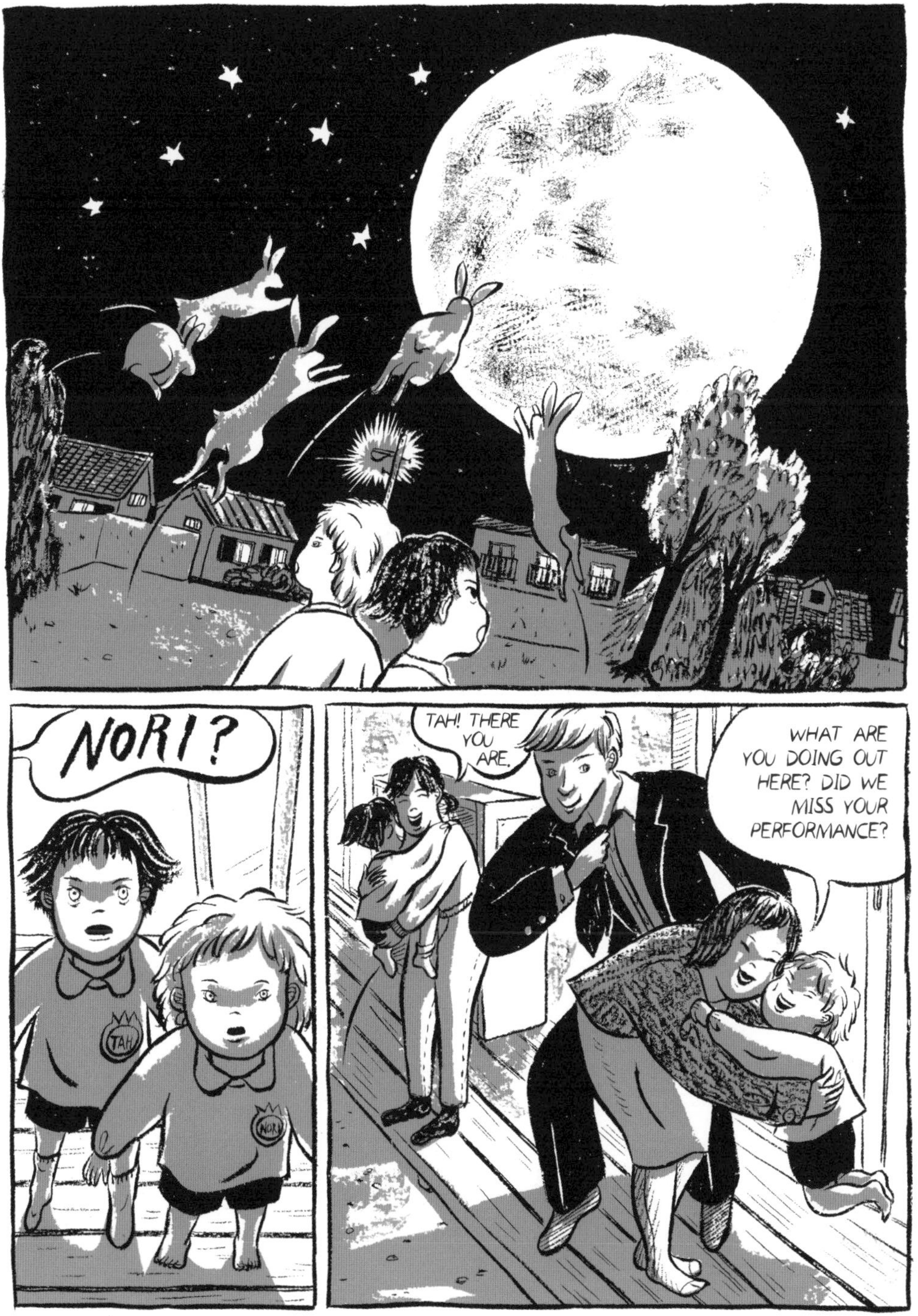
NORI?
TAH
NORI
TAH! THERE YOU ARE.
WHAT ARE YOU DOING OUT HERE? DID WE MISS YOUR PERFORMANCE?

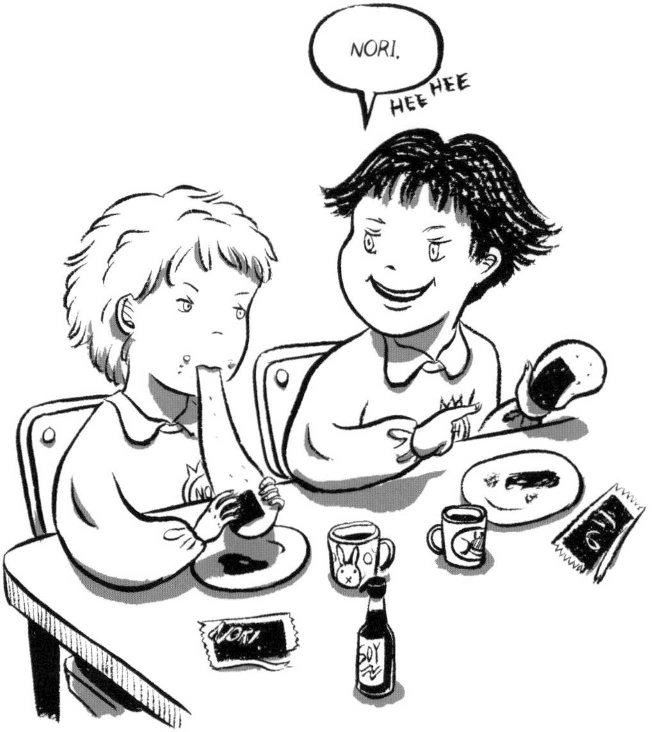
NORI.
HEE HEE
NORI
SOY

3

NORI

AND THE

CREATURES

OF A

DITCH

TAKE YOUR HANDS AND SQUEEZE THEM OPEN THEM PUT THEM TOGETHER...
CLAP CLAP

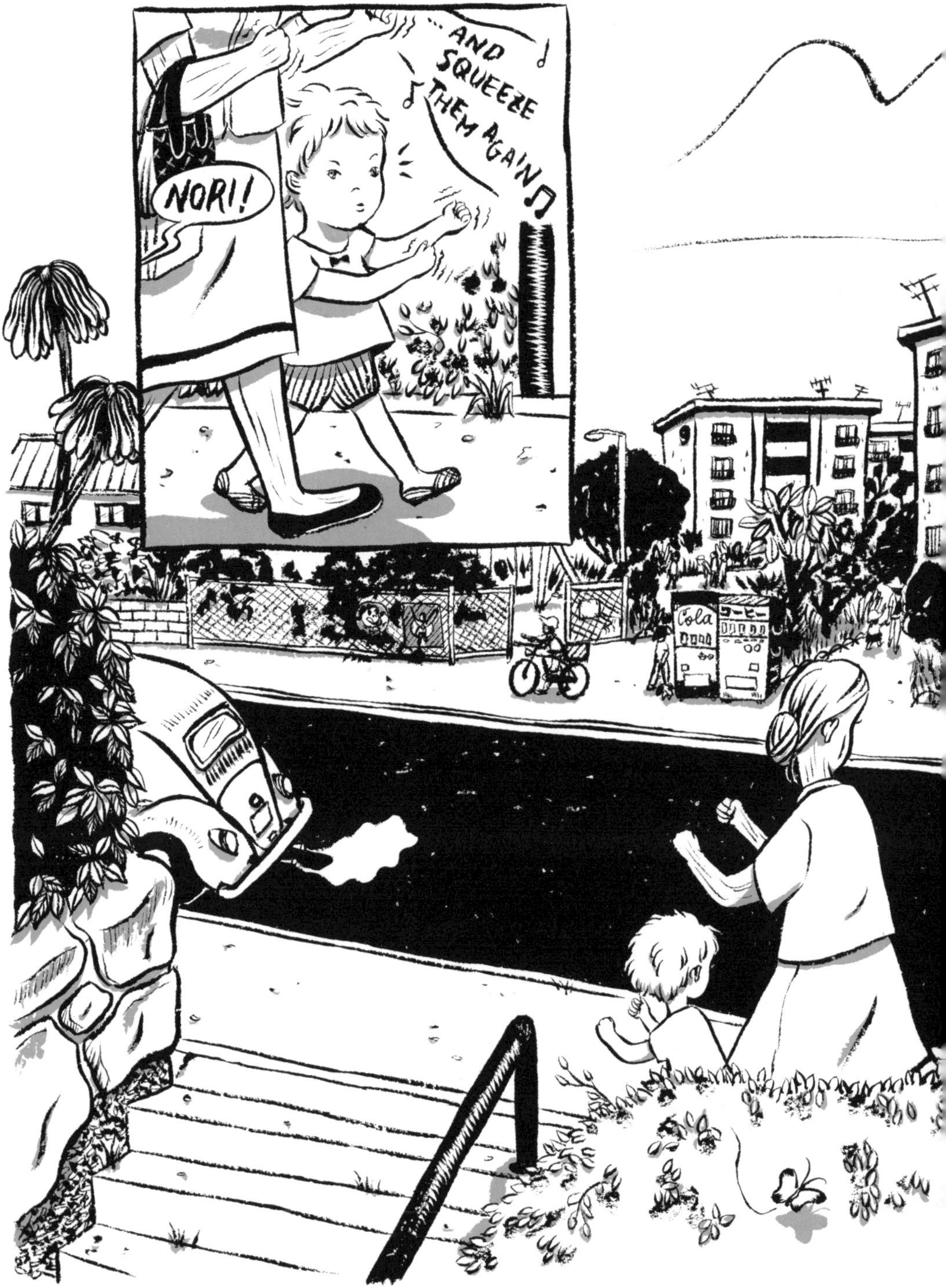
...AND SQUEEZE THEM AGAIN
NORI!
Cola
コーヒー

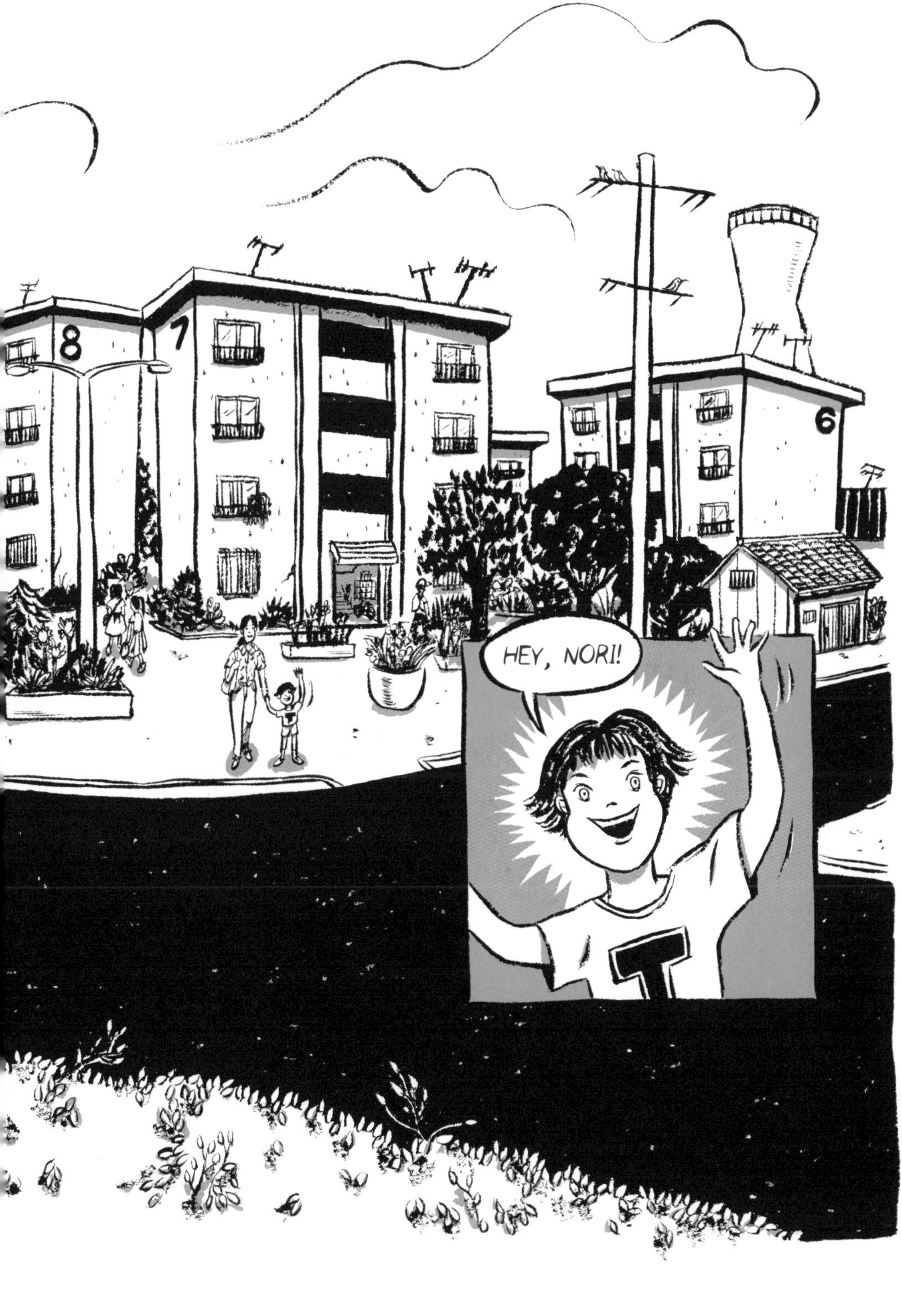
HEY, NORI!

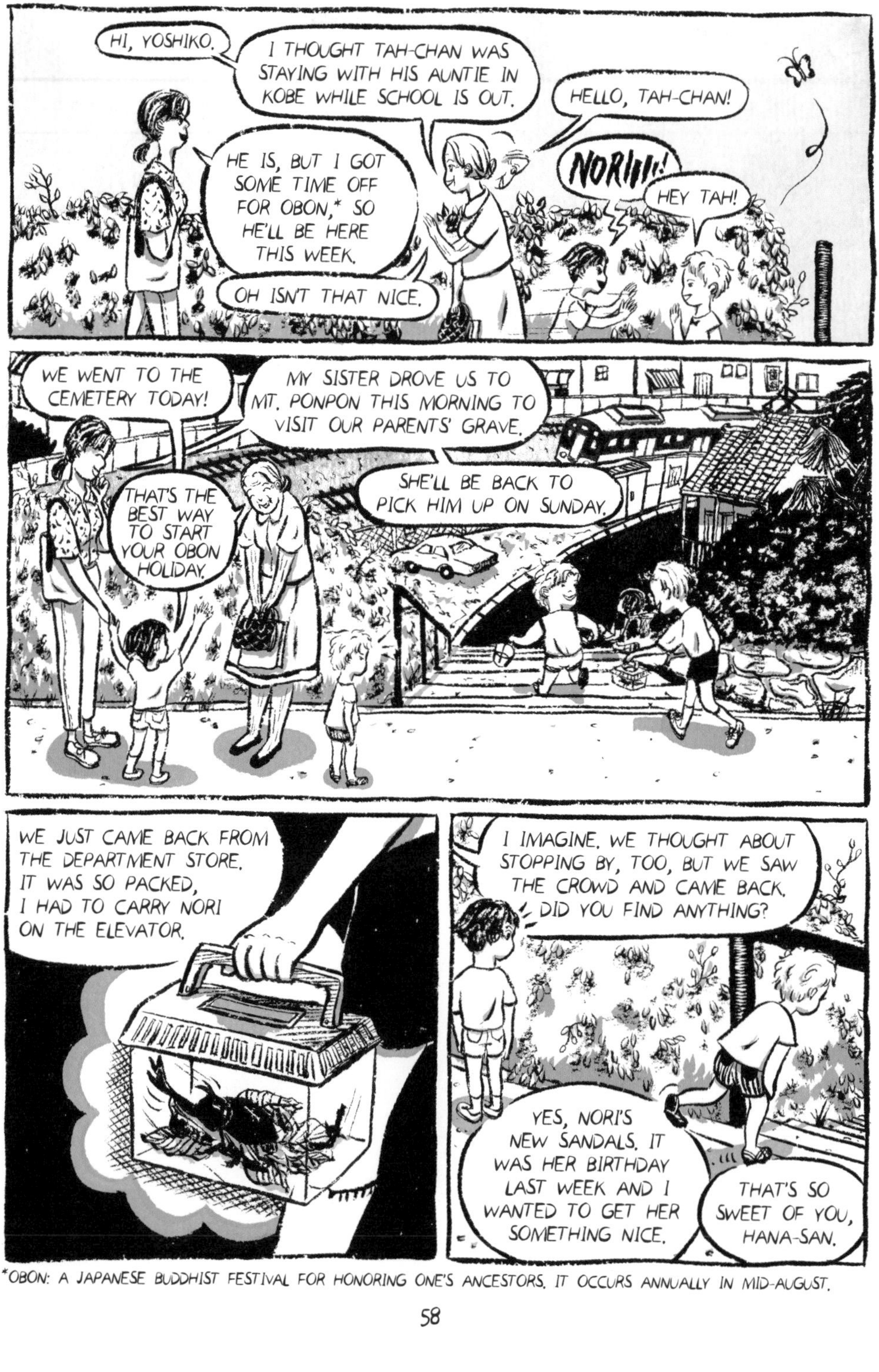
HI, YOSHIKO.
I THOUGHT TAH-CHAN WAS STAYING WITH HIS AUNTIE IN KOBE WHILE SCHOOL IS OUT.
HE IS, BUT I GOT SOME TIME OFF FOR OBON,* SO HE'LL BE HERE THIS WEEK.
OH ISN'T THAT NICE.
HELLO, TAH-CHAN!
NORI!!!
HEY TAH!
WE WENT TO THE CEMETERY TODAY!
MY SISTER DROVE US TO MT. PONPON THIS MORNING TO VISIT OUR PARENTS' GRAVE.
THAT'S THE BEST WAY TO START YOUR OBON HOLIDAY.
SHE'LL BE BACK TO PICK HIM UP ON SUNDAY.
WE JUST CAME BACK FROM THE DEPARTMENT STORE. IT WAS SO PACKED, I HAD TO CARRY NORI ON THE ELEVATOR.
I IMAGINE. WE THOUGHT ABOUT STOPPING BY, TOO, BUT WE SAW THE CROWD AND CAME BACK. DID YOU FIND ANYTHING?
YES, NORI'S NEW SANDALS. IT WAS HER BIRTHDAY LAST WEEK AND I WANTED TO GET HER SOMETHING NICE.
THAT'S SO SWEET OF YOU, HANA-SAN.

*OBON: A JAPANESE BUDDHIST FESTIVAL FOR HONORING ONE'S ANCESTORS. IT OCCURS ANNUALLY IN MID-AUGUST.

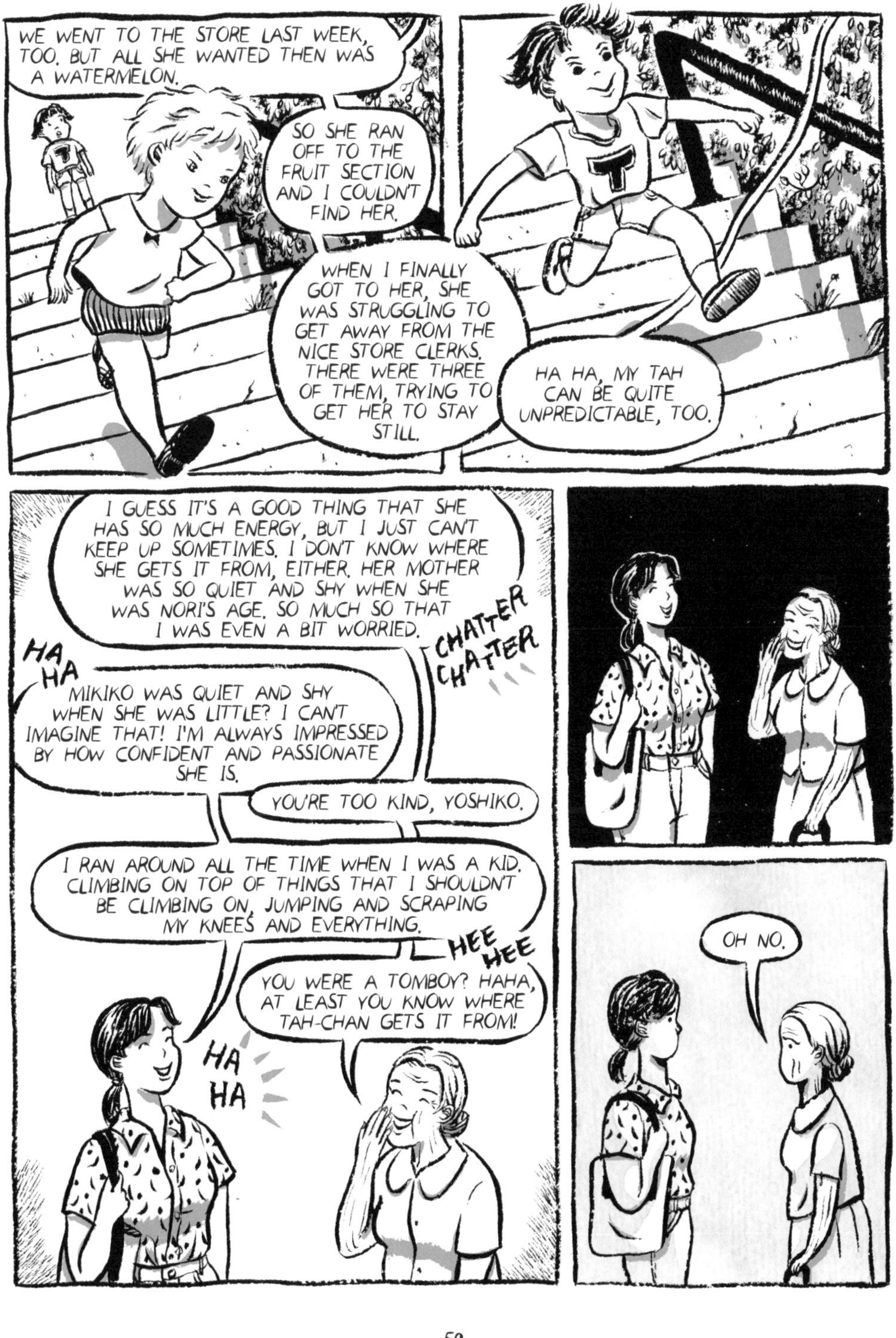
WE WENT TO THE STORE LAST WEEK, TOO. BUT ALL SHE WANTED THEN WAS A WATERMELON.
SO SHE RAN OFF TO THE FRUIT SECTION AND I COULDN'T FIND HER.
WHEN I FINALLY GOT TO HER, SHE WAS STRUGGLING TO GET AWAY FROM THE NICE STORE CLERKS. THERE WERE THREE OF THEM, TRYING TO GET HER TO STAY STILL.
HA HA, MY TAH CAN BE QUITE UNPREDICTABLE, TOO.
I GUESS IT'S A GOOD THING THAT SHE HAS SO MUCH ENERGY, BUT I JUST CAN'T KEEP UP SOMETIMES. I DON'T KNOW WHERE SHE GETS IT FROM, EITHER. HER MOTHER WAS SO QUIET AND SHY WHEN SHE WAS NORI'S AGE. SO MUCH SO THAT I WAS EVEN A BIT WORRIED.
CHATTER CHATTER
HA HA
MIKIKO WAS QUIET AND SHY WHEN SHE WAS LITTLE? I CAN'T IMAGINE THAT! I'M ALWAYS IMPRESSED BY HOW CONFIDENT AND PASSIONATE SHE IS.
YOU'RE TOO KIND, YOSHIKO.
I RAN AROUND ALL THE TIME WHEN I WAS A KID. CLIMBING ON TOP OF THINGS THAT I SHOULDN'T BE CLIMBING ON, JUMPING AND SCRAPING MY KNEES AND EVERYTHING.
HEE HEE
YOU WERE A TOMBOY? HAHA, AT LEAST YOU KNOW WHERE TAH-CHAN GETS IT FROM!
HA HA
OH NO.

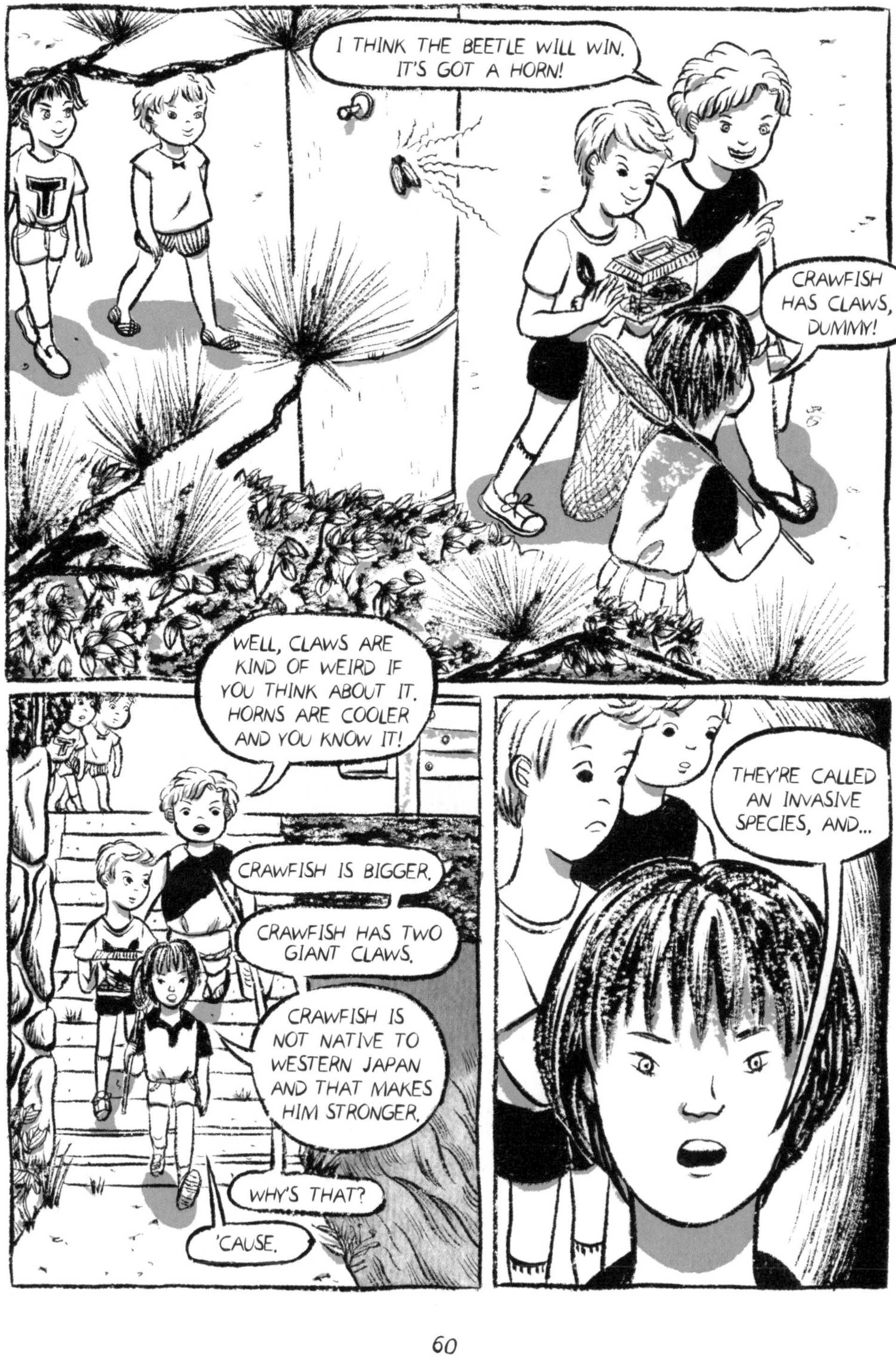
I THINK THE BEETLE WILL WIN. IT'S GOT A HORN!
CRAWFISH HAS CLAWS, DUMMY!
WELL, CLAWS ARE KIND OF WEIRD IF YOU THINK ABOUT IT. HORNS ARE COOLER AND YOU KNOW IT!
CRAWFISH IS BIGGER.
CRAWFISH HAS TWO GIANT CLAWS.
CRAWFISH IS NOT NATIVE TO WESTERN JAPAN AND THAT MAKES HIM STRONGER.
WHY'S THAT?
'CAUSE.
THEY'RE CALLED AN INVASIVE SPECIES, AND...

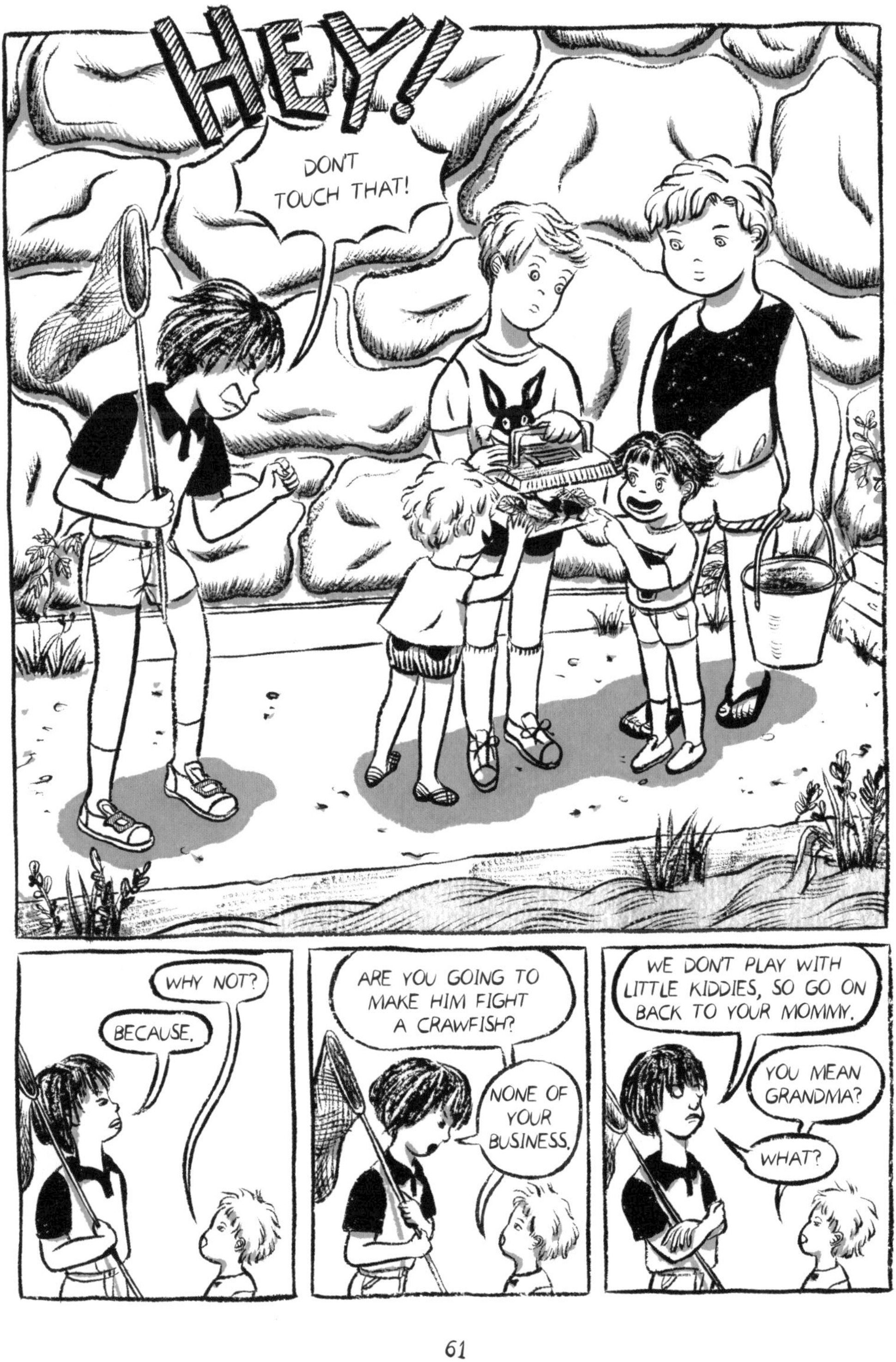
HEY!
DON'T TOUCH THAT!
WHY NOT?
BECAUSE.
ARE YOU GOING TO MAKE HIM FIGHT A CRAWFISH?
NONE OF YOUR BUSINESS.
WE DON'T PLAY WITH LITTLE KIDDIES, SO GO ON BACK TO YOUR MOMMY.
YOU MEAN GRANDMA?
WHAT?

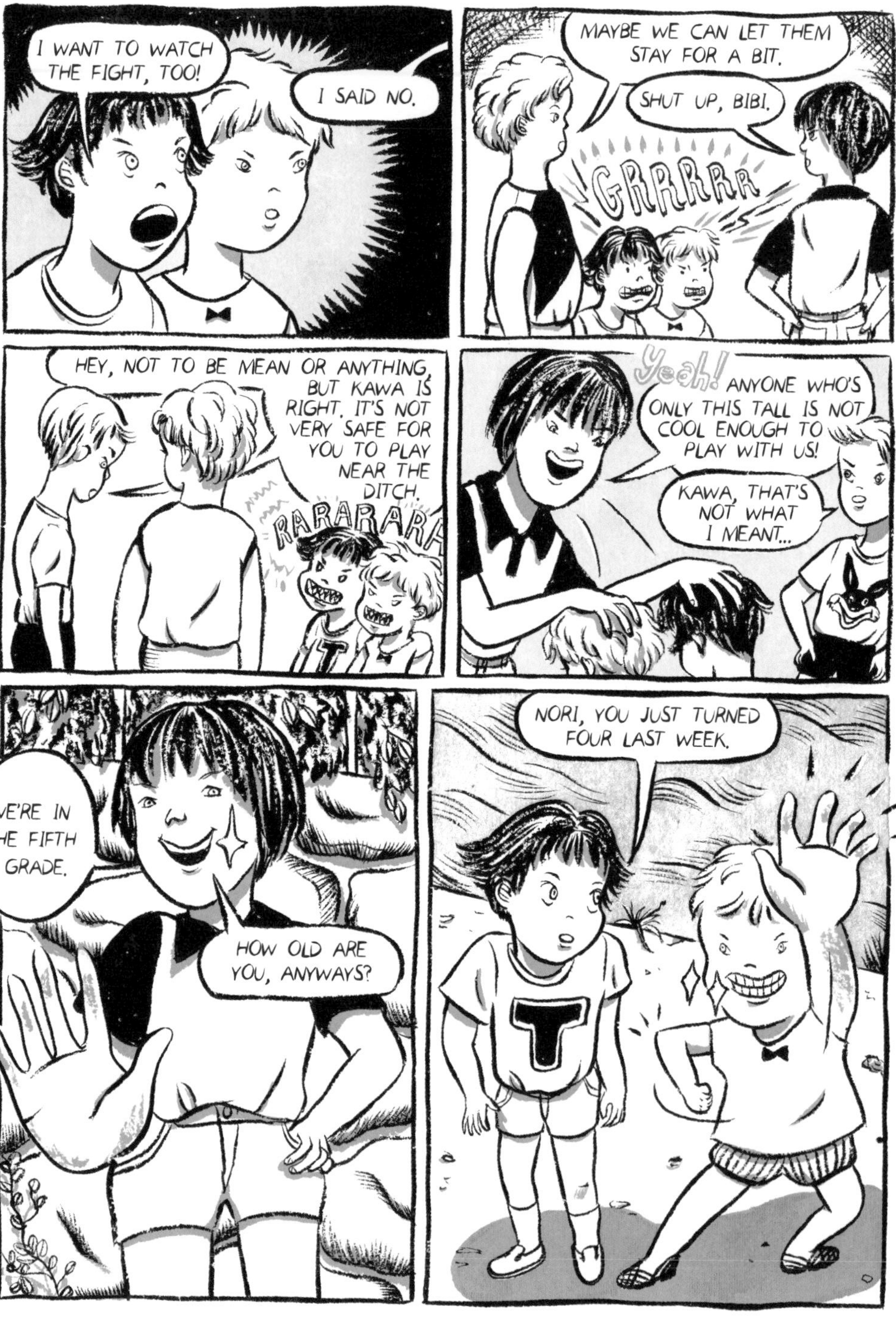
I WANT TO WATCH THE FIGHT, TOO!
I SAID NO.
MAYBE WE CAN LET THEM STAY FOR A BIT.
SHUT UP, BIBI.
GRRRRR
HEY, NOT TO BE MEAN OR ANYTHING, BUT KAWA IS RIGHT. IT'S NOT VERY SAFE FOR YOU TO PLAY NEAR THE DITCH.
RARARARA
Yeah!
ANYONE WHO'S ONLY THIS TALL IS NOT COOL ENOUGH TO PLAY WITH US!
KAWA, THAT'S NOT WHAT I MEANT...
WE'RE IN THE FIFTH GRADE.
HOW OLD ARE YOU, ANYWAYS?
NORI, YOU JUST TURNED FOUR LAST WEEK.

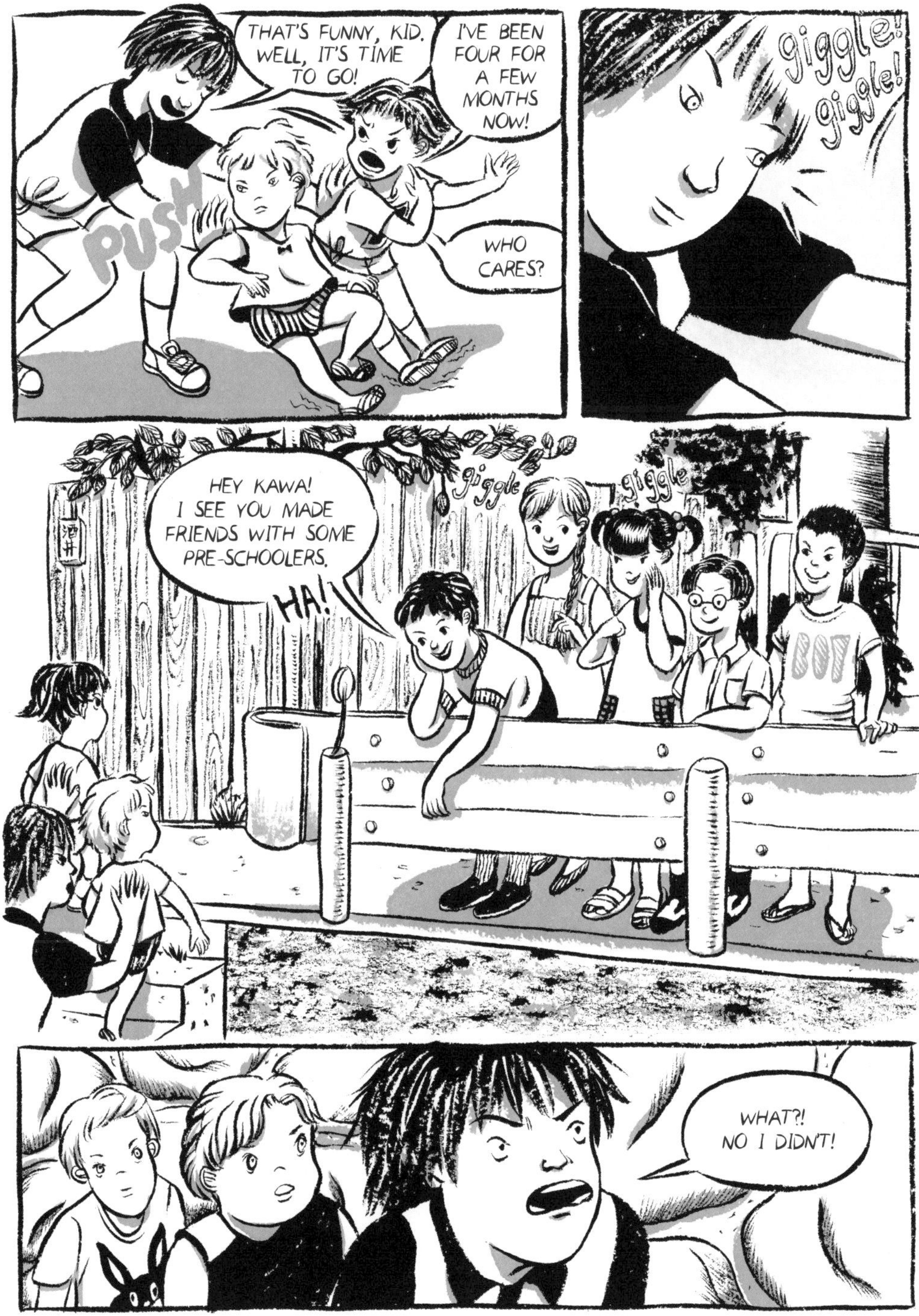
THAT'S FUNNY, KID. WELL, IT'S TIME TO GO!
I'VE BEEN FOUR FOR A FEW MONTHS NOW!
PUSH
WHO CARES?
giggle! giggle!
giggle
giggle
HEY KAWA! I SEE YOU MADE FRIENDS WITH SOME PRE-SCHOOLERS.
HA!
BOY
WHAT?! NO I DIDN'T!

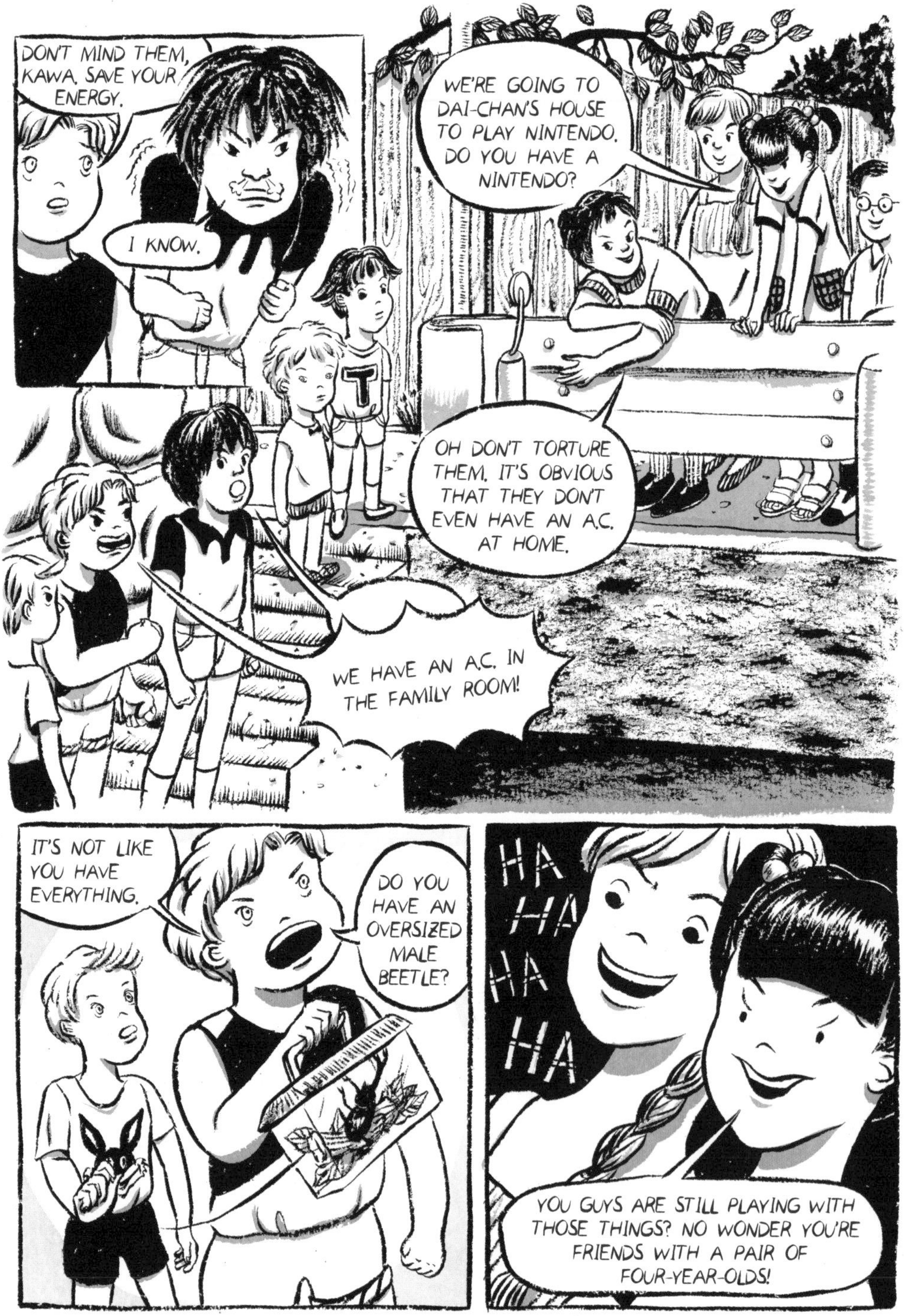

DON'T MIND THEM, KAWA. SAVE YOUR ENERGY.
I KNOW.
WE'RE GOING TO DAI-CHAN'S HOUSE TO PLAY NINTENDO. DO YOU HAVE A NINTENDO?
OH DON'T TORTURE THEM. IT'S OBVIOUS THAT THEY DON'T EVEN HAVE AN A.C. AT HOME.
WE HAVE AN A.C. IN THE FAMILY ROOM!
IT'S NOT LIKE YOU HAVE EVERYTHING.
DO YOU HAVE AN OVERSIZED MALE BEETLE?
HA HA HA HA
YOU GUYS ARE STILL PLAYING WITH THOSE THINGS? NO WONDER YOU'RE FRIENDS WITH A PAIR OF FOUR-YEAR-OLDS!

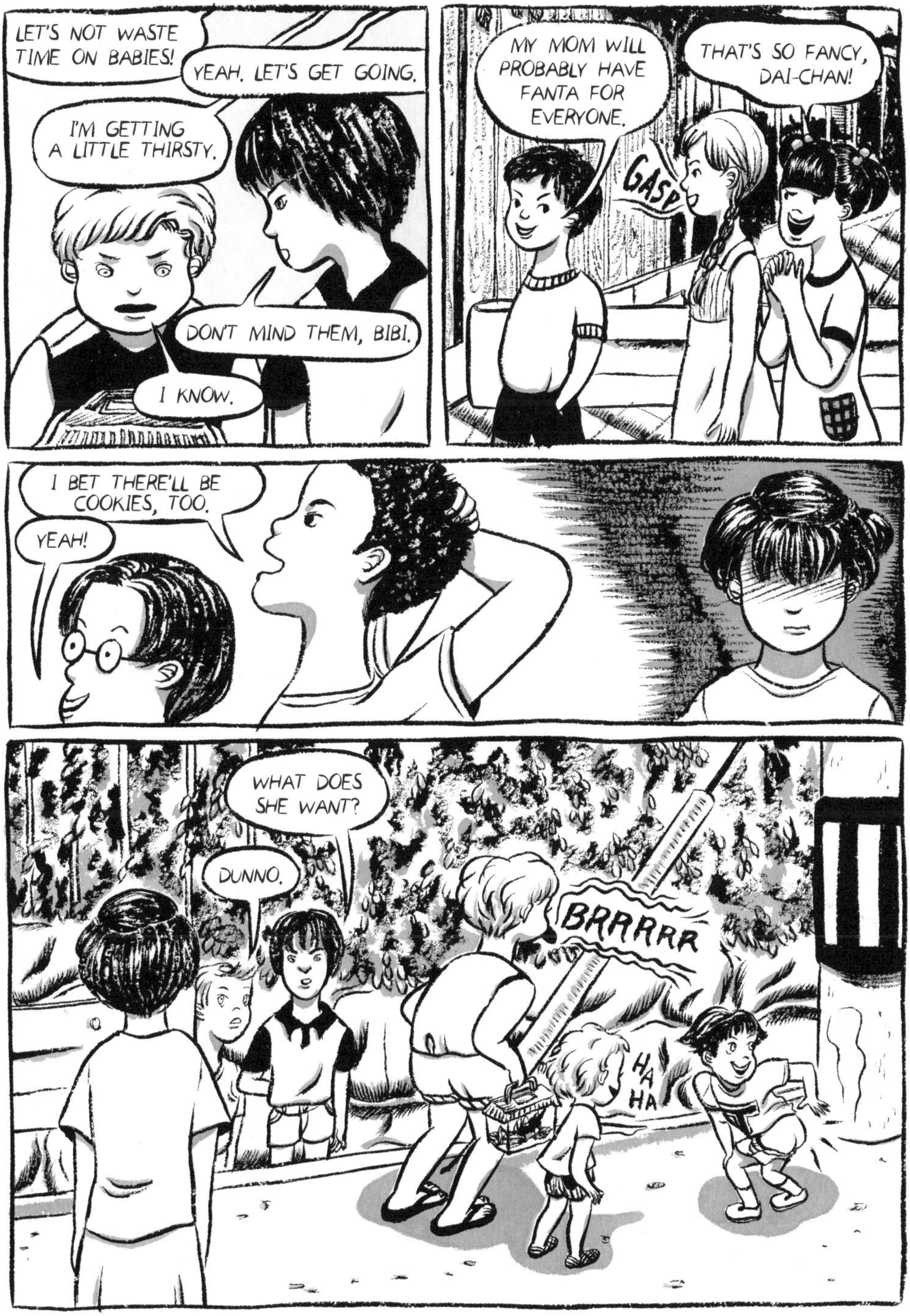
LET'S NOT WASTE TIME ON BABIES!
YEAH. LET'S GET GOING.
I'M GETTING A LITTLE THIRSTY.
DON'T MIND THEM, BIBI.
I KNOW.
MY MOM WILL PROBABLY HAVE FANTA FOR EVERYONE.
THAT'S SO FANCY, DAI-CHAN!
GASP
I BET THERE'LL BE COOKIES, TOO.
YEAH!
WHAT DOES SHE WANT?
DUNNO.
BRRRRR
HA HA

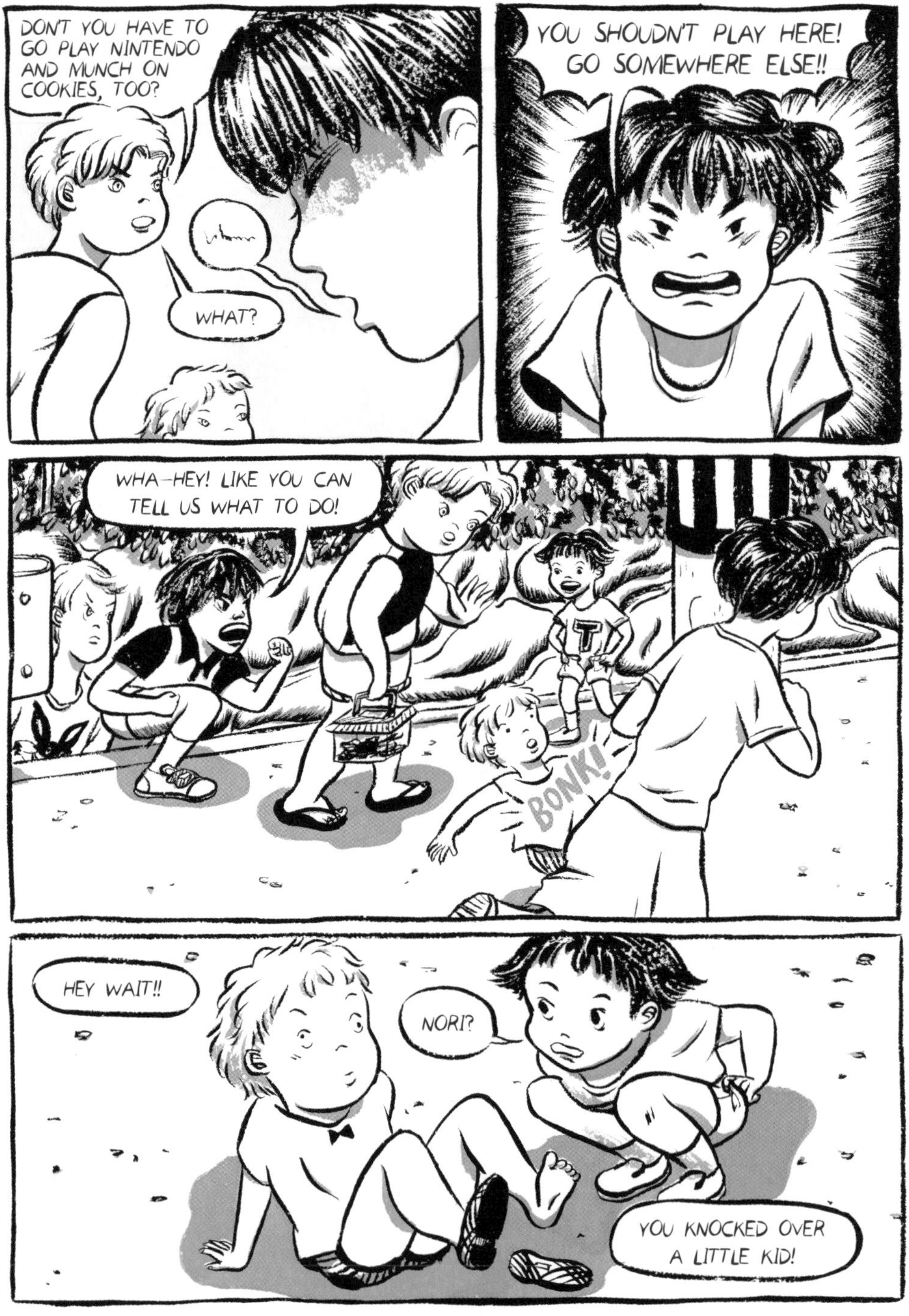
DON'T YOU HAVE TO GO PLAY NINTENDO AND MUNCH ON COOKIES, TOO?
WHAT?
YOU SHOUDN'T PLAY HERE! GO SOMEWHERE ELSE!!
WHA—HEY! LIKE YOU CAN TELL US WHAT TO DO!
T
BONK!
HEY WAIT!!
NORI?
YOU KNOCKED OVER A LITTLE KID!

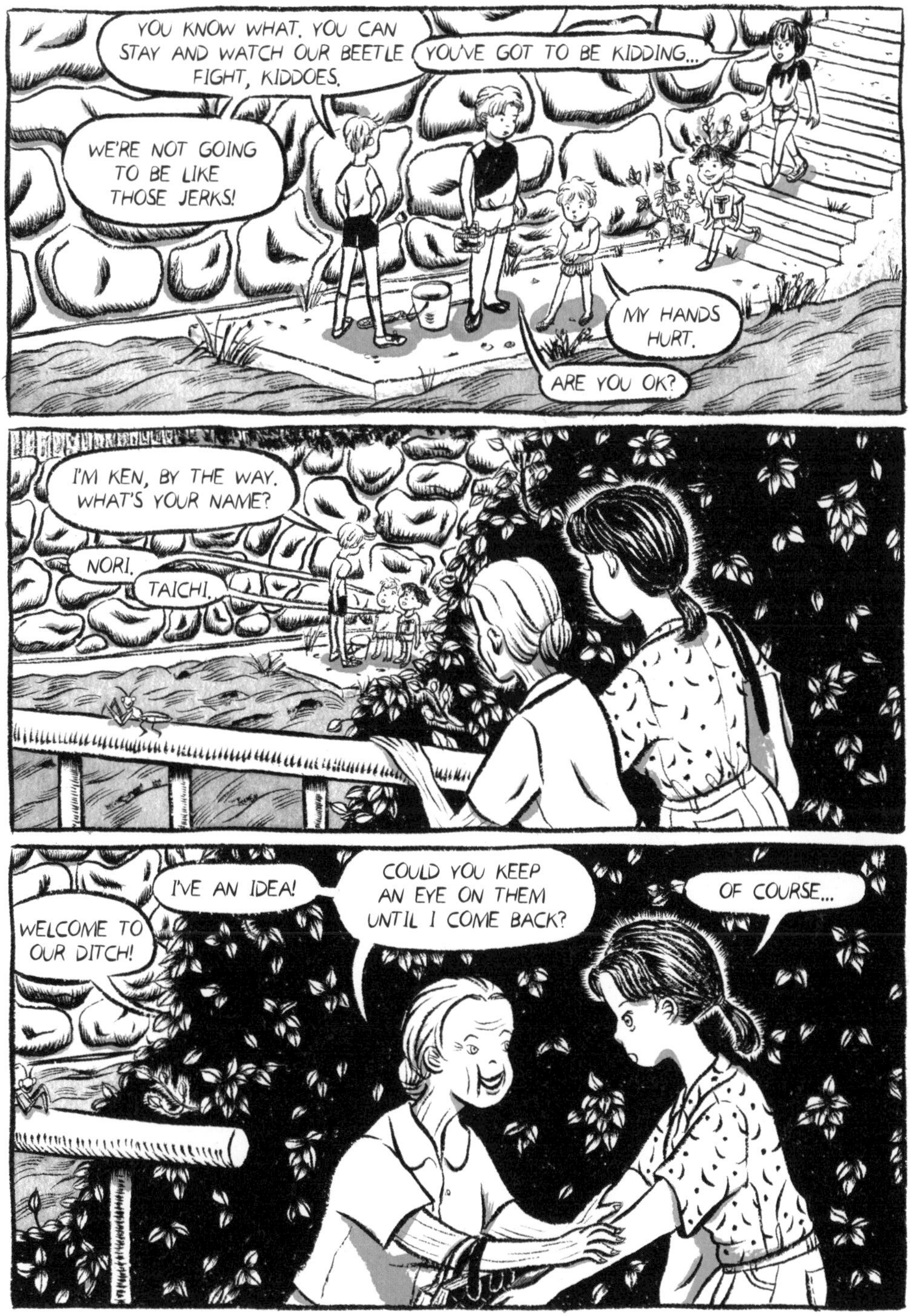
YOU KNOW WHAT. YOU CAN STAY AND WATCH OUR BEETLE FIGHT, KIDDOES.
YOU'VE GOT TO BE KIDDING...
WE'RE NOT GOING TO BE LIKE THOSE JERKS!
MY HANDS HURT.
ARE YOU OK?
I'M KEN, BY THE WAY. WHAT'S YOUR NAME?
NORI.
TAICHI.
WELCOME TO OUR DITCH!
I'VE AN IDEA!
COULD YOU KEEP AN EYE ON THEM UNTIL I COME BACK?
OF COURSE...

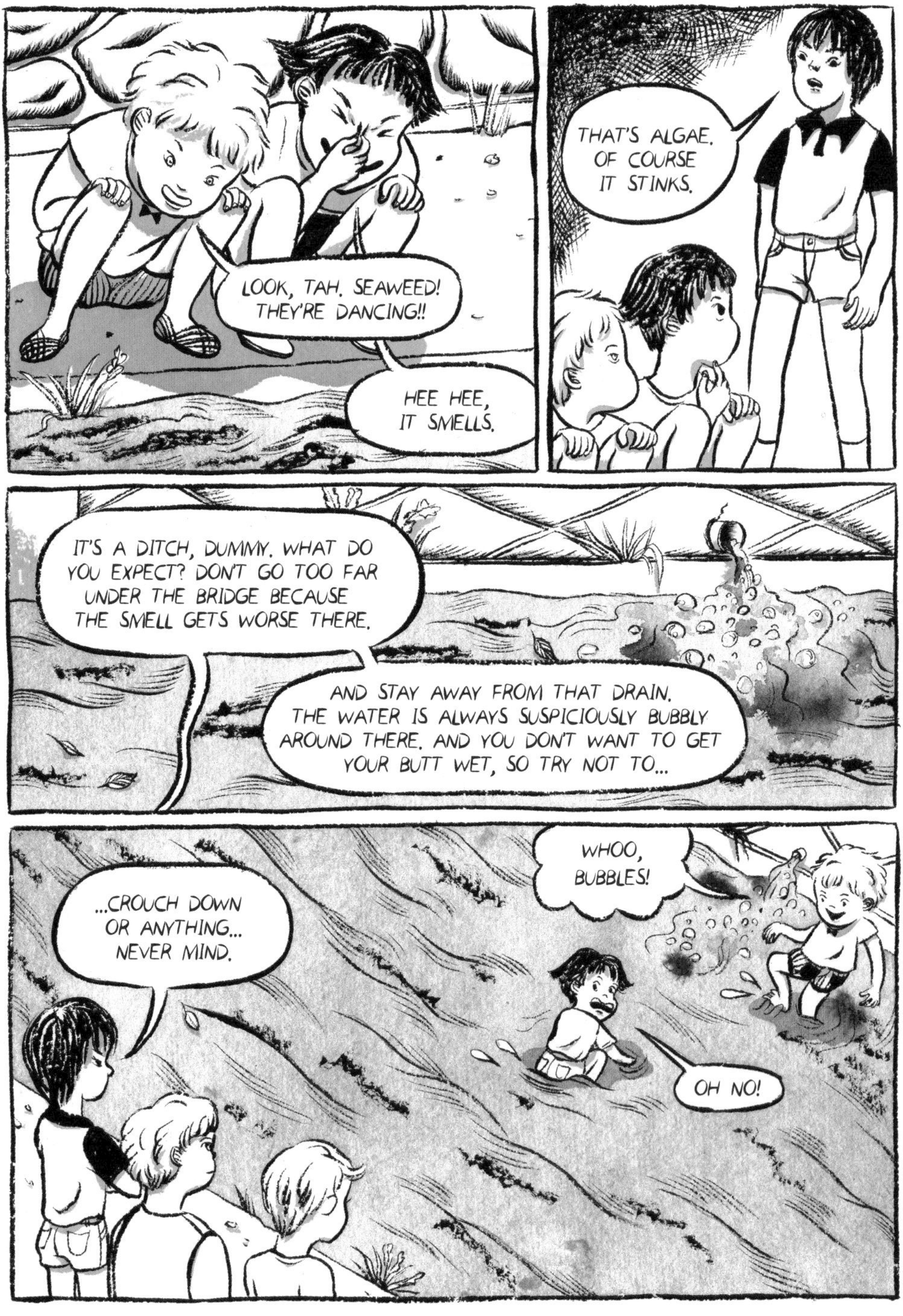
LOOK, TAH. SEAWEED! THEY'RE DANCING!!
HEE HEE, IT SMELLS.
THAT'S ALGAE. OF COURSE IT STINKS.
IT'S A DITCH, DUMMY. WHAT DO YOU EXPECT? DON'T GO TOO FAR UNDER THE BRIDGE BECAUSE THE SMELL GETS WORSE THERE.
AND STAY AWAY FROM THAT DRAIN. THE WATER IS ALWAYS SUSPICIOUSLY BUBBLY AROUND THERE. AND YOU DON'T WANT TO GET YOUR BUTT WET, SO TRY NOT TO...
...CROUCH DOWN OR ANYTHING... NEVER MIND.
WHOO, BUBBLES!
OH NO!

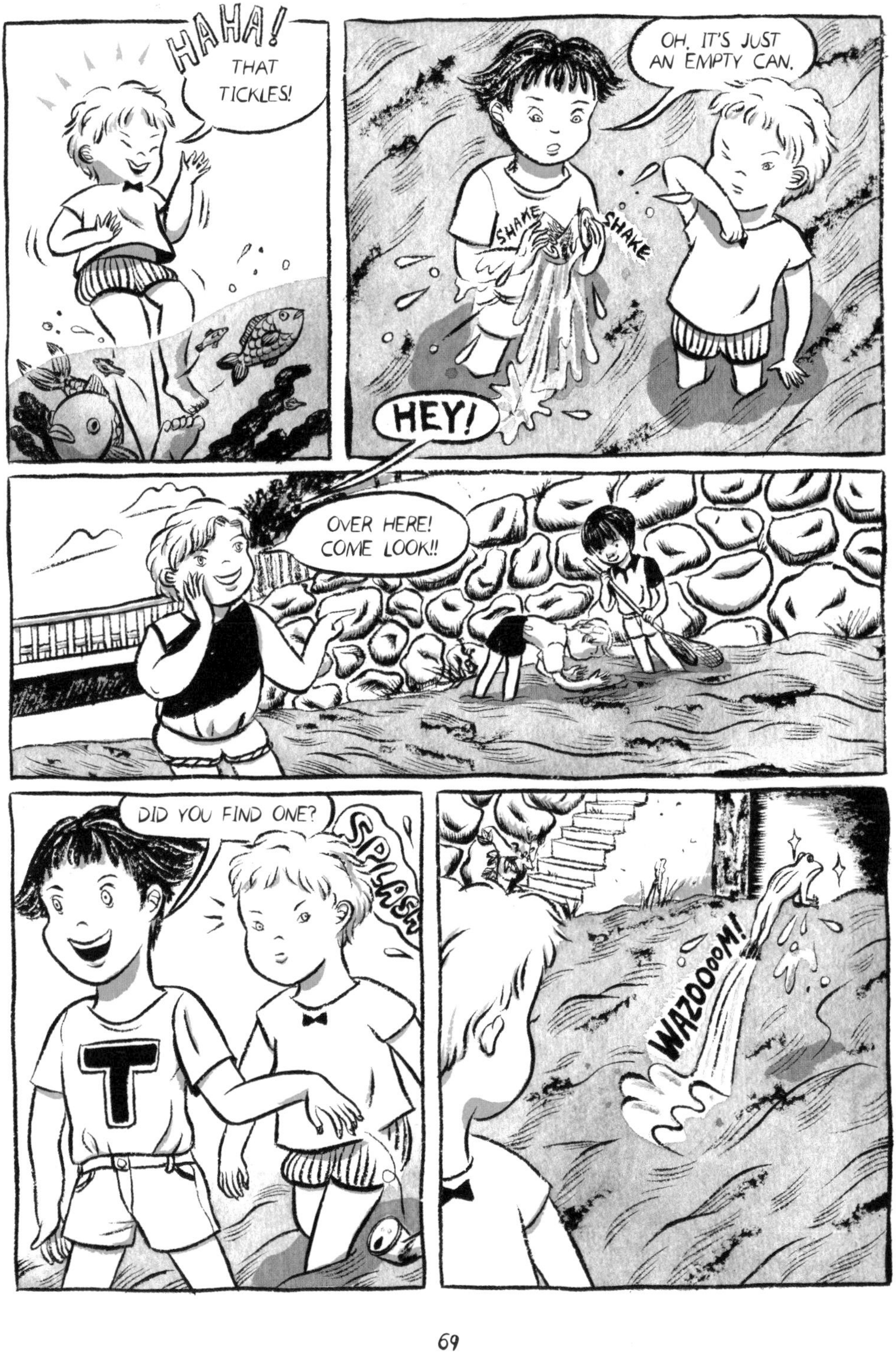
HAHA! THAT TICKLES!
OH, IT'S JUST AN EMPTY CAN.
SHAKE
SHAKE
HEY!
OVER HERE! COME LOOK!!
DID YOU FIND ONE?
SPLASH
WAZOOOOOM!

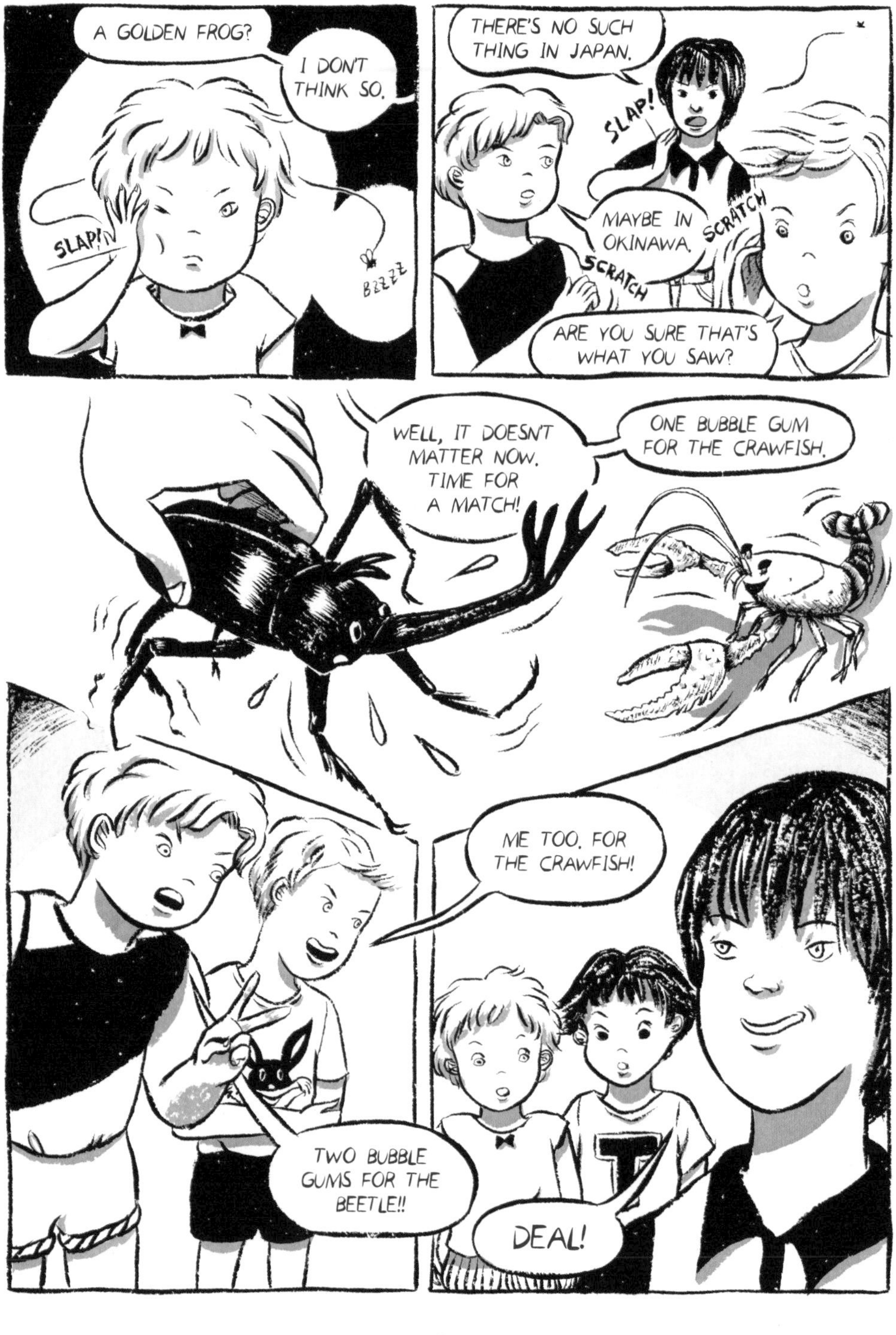
A GOLDEN FROG?
I DON'T THINK SO.
SLAP!
BZZZZ
THERE'S NO SUCH THING IN JAPAN.
SLAP!
MAYBE IN OKINAWA.
SCRATCH
SCRATCH
ARE YOU SURE THAT'S WHAT YOU SAW?
WELL, IT DOESN'T MATTER NOW. TIME FOR A MATCH!
ONE BUBBLE GUM FOR THE CRAWFISH.
ME TOO. FOR THE CRAWFISH!
TWO BUBBLE GUMS FOR THE BEETLE!!
DEAL!

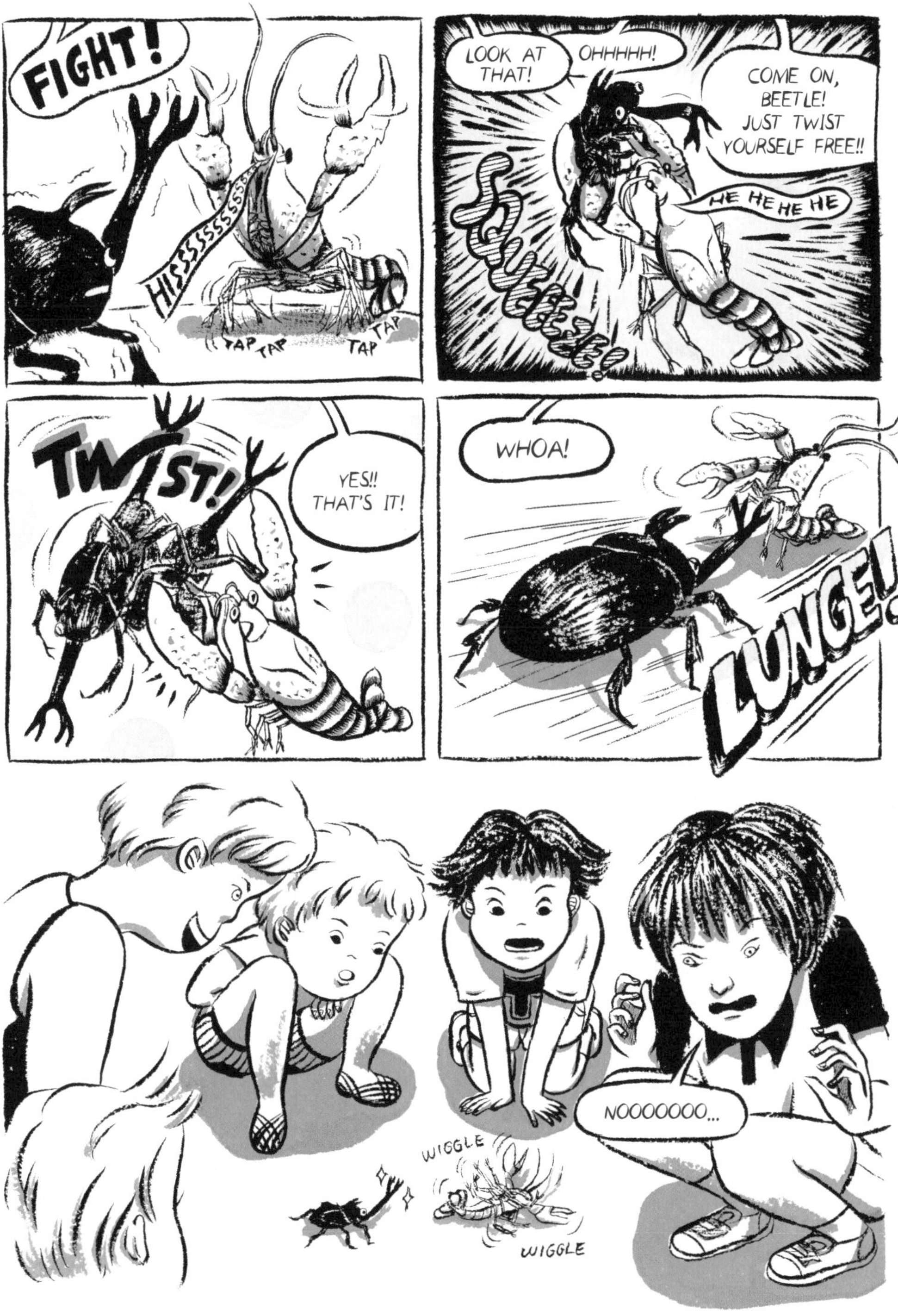
FIGHT!
HISSSSSSSSSSSS
TAP TAP TAP TAP
LOOK AT THAT!
OHHHHH!
COME ON, BEETLE! JUST TWIST YOURSELF FREE!!
HE HE HE HE
SQUEEZE!
TWIST!
YES!! THAT'S IT!
WHOA!
LUNGE!
NOOOOOOO...
WIGGLE
WIGGLE

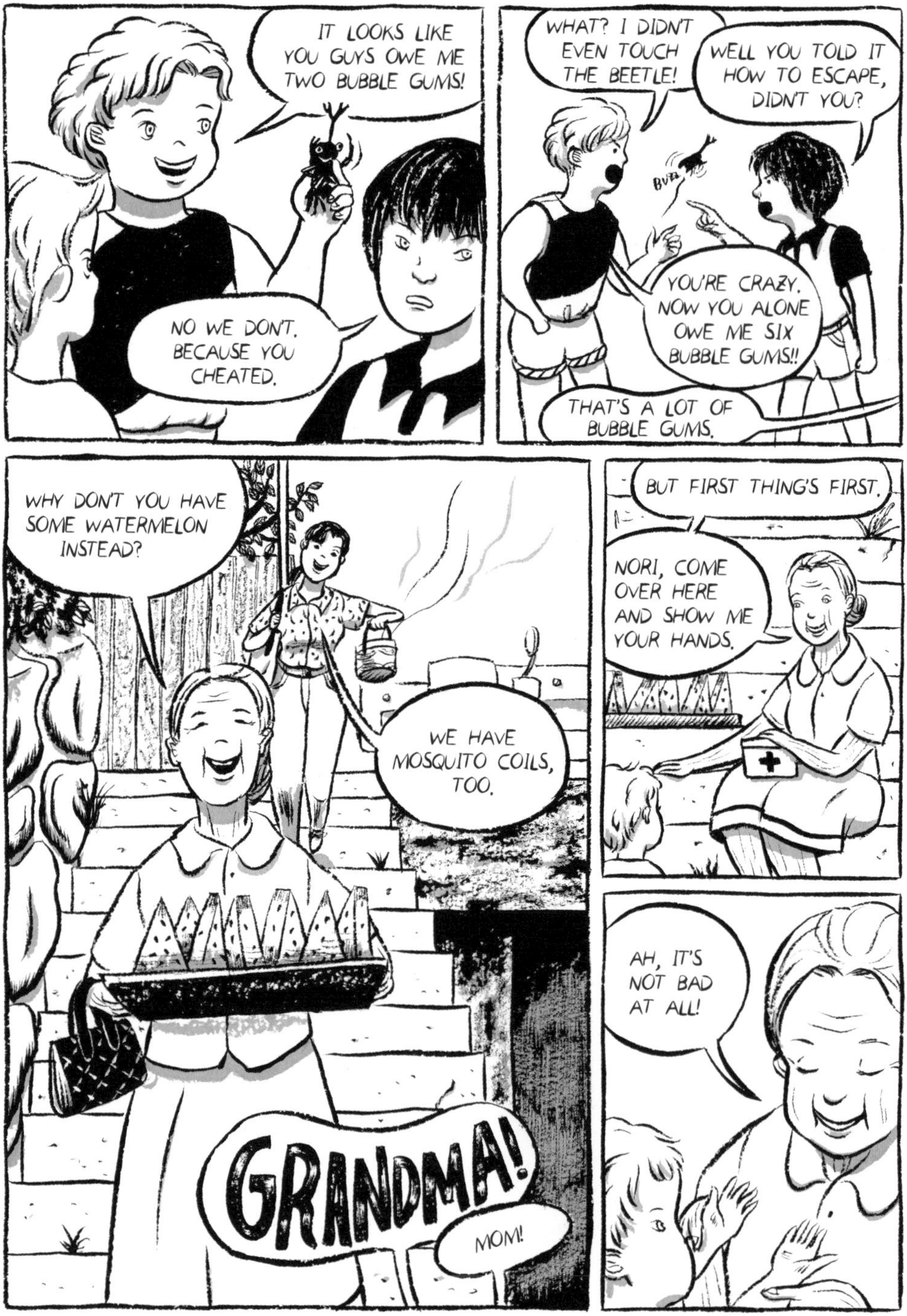
IT LOOKS LIKE YOU GUYS OWE ME TWO BUBBLE GUMS!
NO WE DON'T. BECAUSE YOU CHEATED.
WHAT? I DIDN'T EVEN TOUCH THE BEETLE!
WELL YOU TOLD IT HOW TO ESCAPE, DIDN'T YOU?
BUZZ
YOU'RE CRAZY. NOW YOU ALONE OWE ME SIX BUBBLE GUMS!!
THAT'S A LOT OF BUBBLE GUMS.
WHY DON'T YOU HAVE SOME WATERMELON INSTEAD?
WE HAVE MOSQUITO COILS, TOO.
GRANDMA!
MOM!
BUT FIRST THING'S FIRST.
NORI, COME OVER HERE AND SHOW ME YOUR HANDS.
AH, IT'S NOT BAD AT ALL!

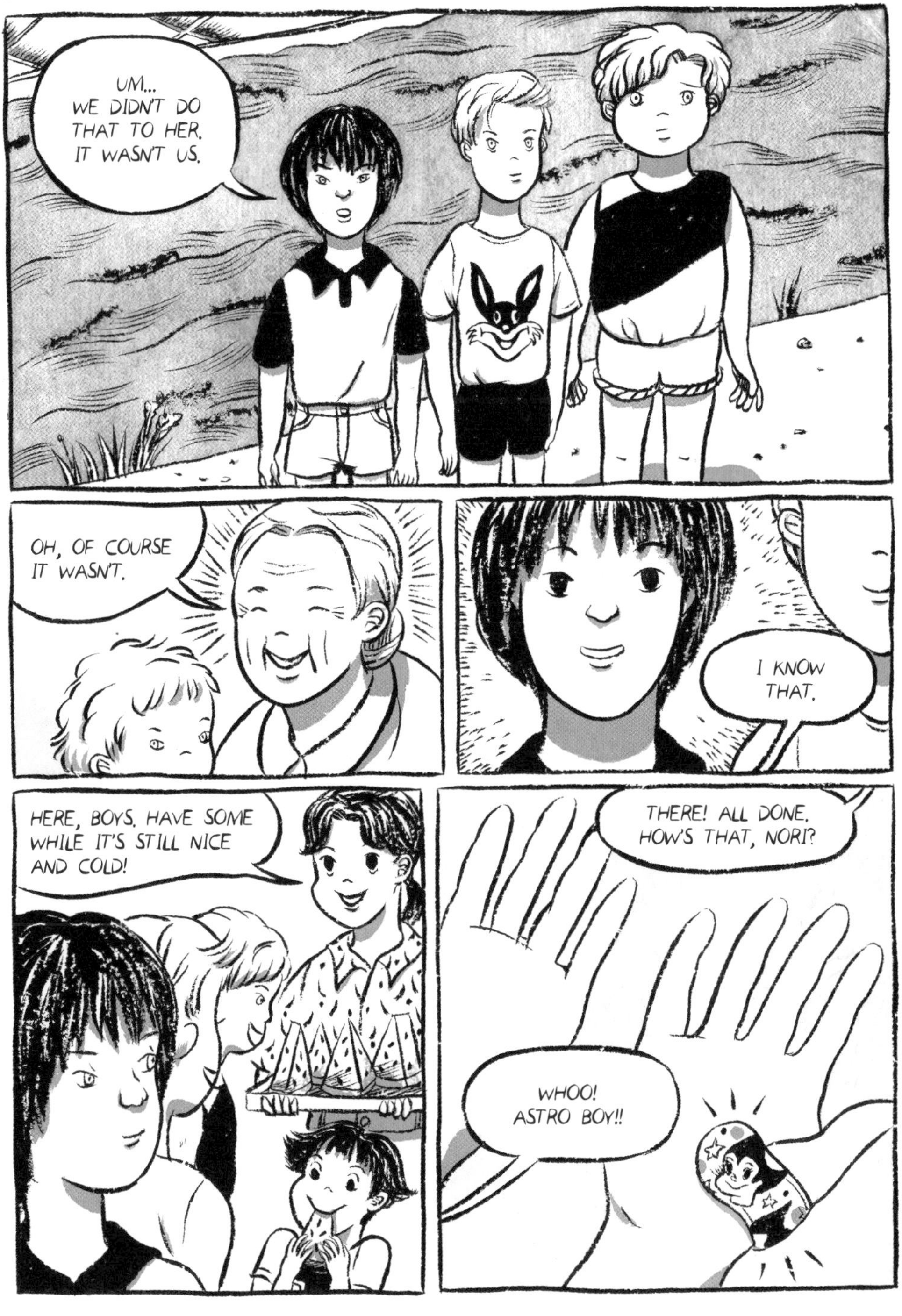
UM... WE DIDN'T DO THAT TO HER. IT WASN'T US.
OH, OF COURSE IT WASN'T.
I KNOW THAT.
HERE, BOYS. HAVE SOME WHILE IT'S STILL NICE AND COLD!
THERE! ALL DONE. HOW'S THAT, NORI?
WHOO! ASTRO BOY!!

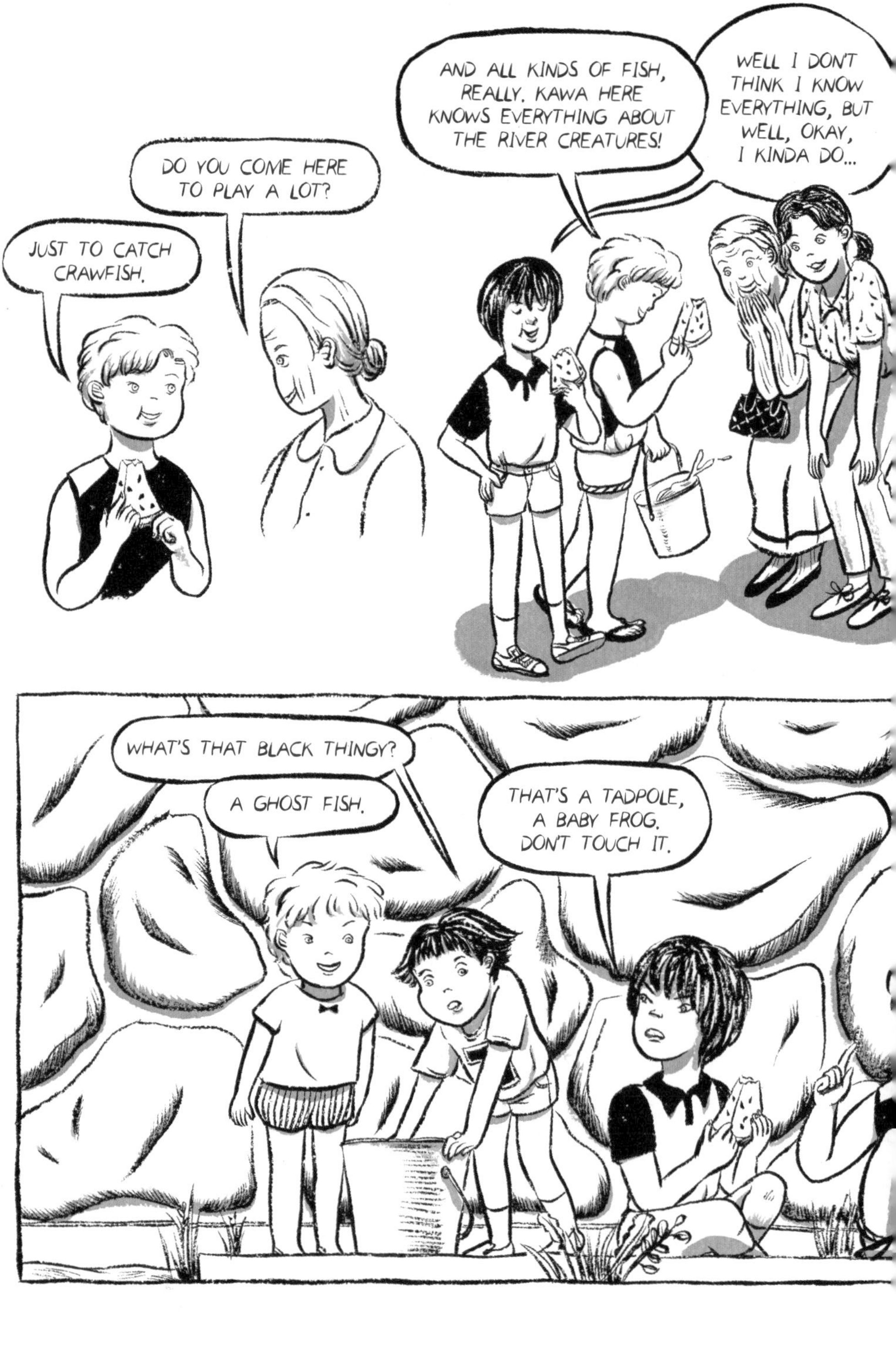

DO YOU COME HERE TO PLAY A LOT?
JUST TO CATCH CRAWFISH.
AND ALL KINDS OF FISH, REALLY. KAWA HERE KNOWS EVERYTHING ABOUT THE RIVER CREATURES!
WELL I DON'T THINK I KNOW EVERYTHING, BUT WELL, OKAY, I KINDA DO...
WHAT'S THAT BLACK THINGY?
A GHOST FISH.
THAT'S A TADPOLE, A BABY FROG. DON'T TOUCH IT.

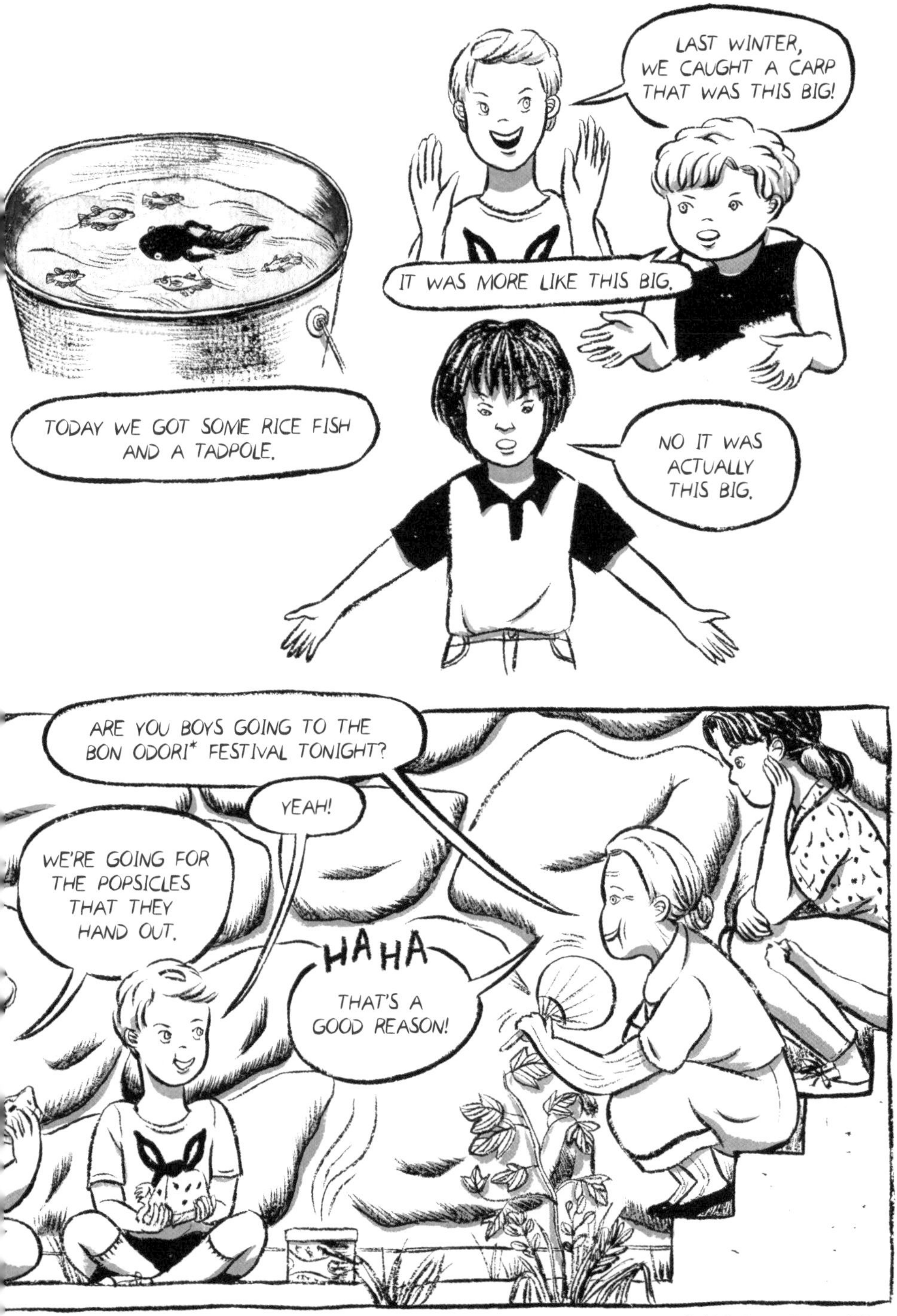

TODAY WE GOT SOME RICE FISH AND A TADPOLE.
LAST WINTER, WE CAUGHT A CARP THAT WAS THIS BIG!
IT WAS MORE LIKE THIS BIG.
NO IT WAS ACTUALLY THIS BIG.
ARE YOU BOYS GOING TO THE BON ODORI* FESTIVAL TONIGHT?
YEAH!
WE'RE GOING FOR THE POPSICLES THAT THEY HAND OUT.
HAHA
THAT'S A GOOD REASON!

*BON ODORI: BON DANCE, A DANCE DEDICATED TO THE SPIRITS OF ANCESTORS. IN A SMALL TOWN LIKE NORI'S, IT'S USUALLY A SMALL COMMUNITY EVENT WHERE NEIGHBORS GATHER AND DANCE TO FOLK SONGS AND POPULAR HITS. FOOD STALLS OPEN AT THE VENUE AND LOCAL ORGANIZATIONS USED TO HAND OUT CANDIES AND POPSICLES TO CHILDREN IN THE 1980s.

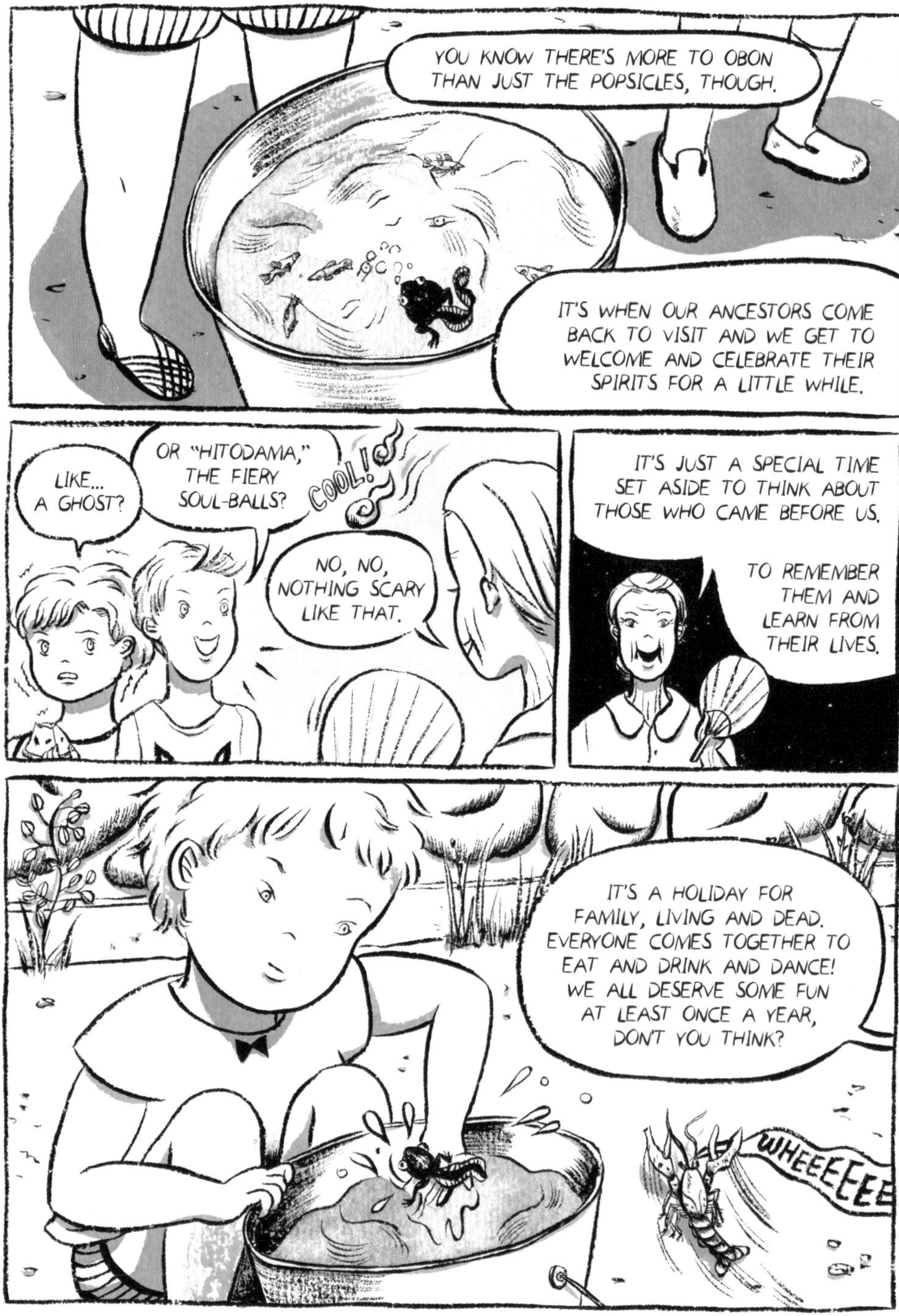
YOU KNOW THERE'S MORE TO OBON THAN JUST THE POPSICLES, THOUGH.
IT'S WHEN OUR ANCESTORS COME BACK TO VISIT AND WE GET TO WELCOME AND CELEBRATE THEIR SPIRITS FOR A LITTLE WHILE.
LIKE... A GHOST?
OR "HITODAMA," THE FIERY SOUL-BALLS?
COOL!
NO, NO, NOTHING SCARY LIKE THAT.
IT'S JUST A SPECIAL TIME SET ASIDE TO THINK ABOUT THOSE WHO CAME BEFORE US.
TO REMEMBER THEM AND LEARN FROM THEIR LIVES.
IT'S A HOLIDAY FOR FAMILY, LIVING AND DEAD. EVERYONE COMES TOGETHER TO EAT AND DRINK AND DANCE! WE ALL DESERVE SOME FUN AT LEAST ONCE A YEAR, DON'T YOU THINK?
WHEEEEEEE

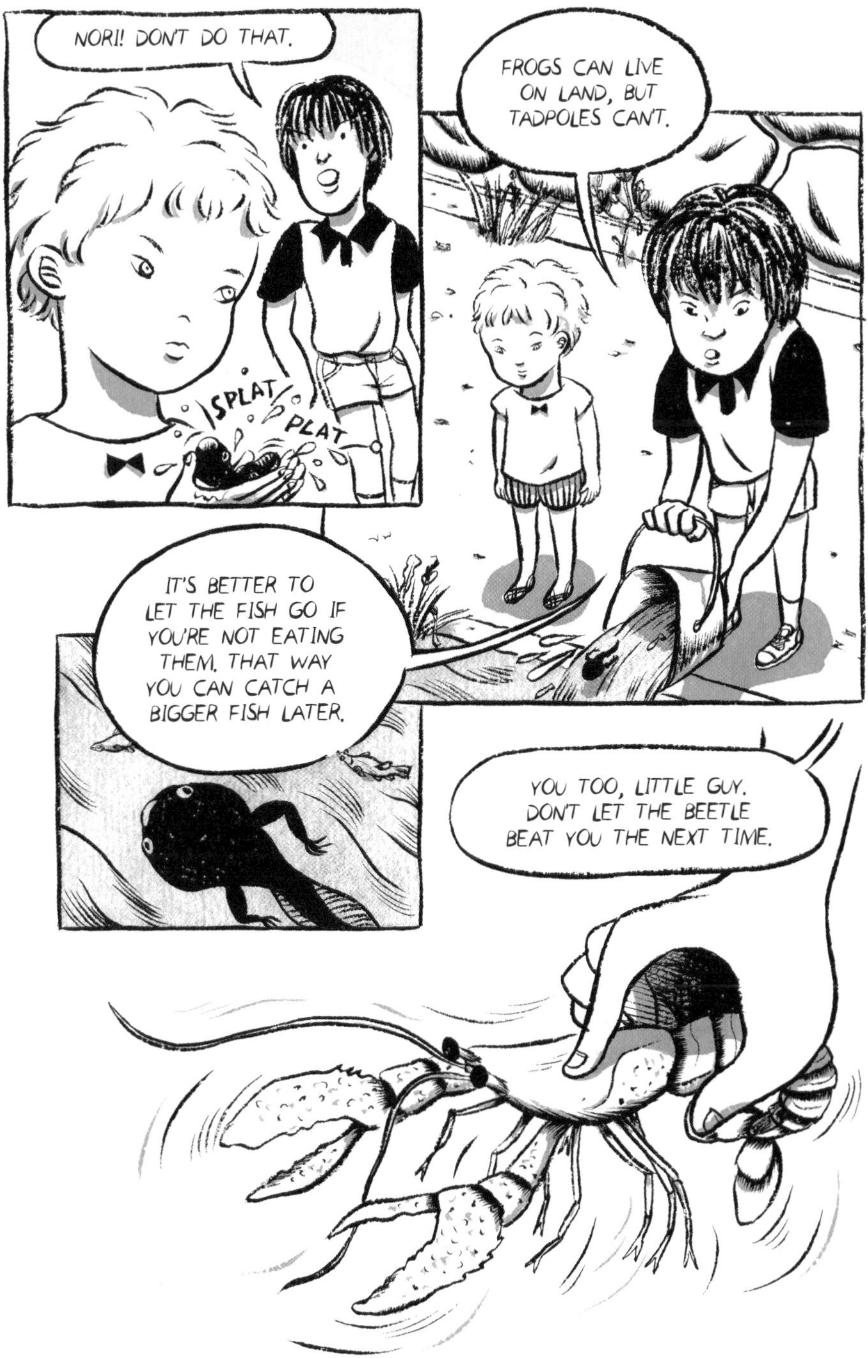
NORI! DON'T DO THAT.
SPLAT PLAT
FROGS CAN LIVE ON LAND, BUT TADPOLES CAN'T.
IT'S BETTER TO LET THE FISH GO IF YOU'RE NOT EATING THEM. THAT WAY YOU CAN CATCH A BIGGER FISH LATER.
YOU TOO, LITTLE GUY. DON'T LET THE BEETLE BEAT YOU THE NEXT TIME.

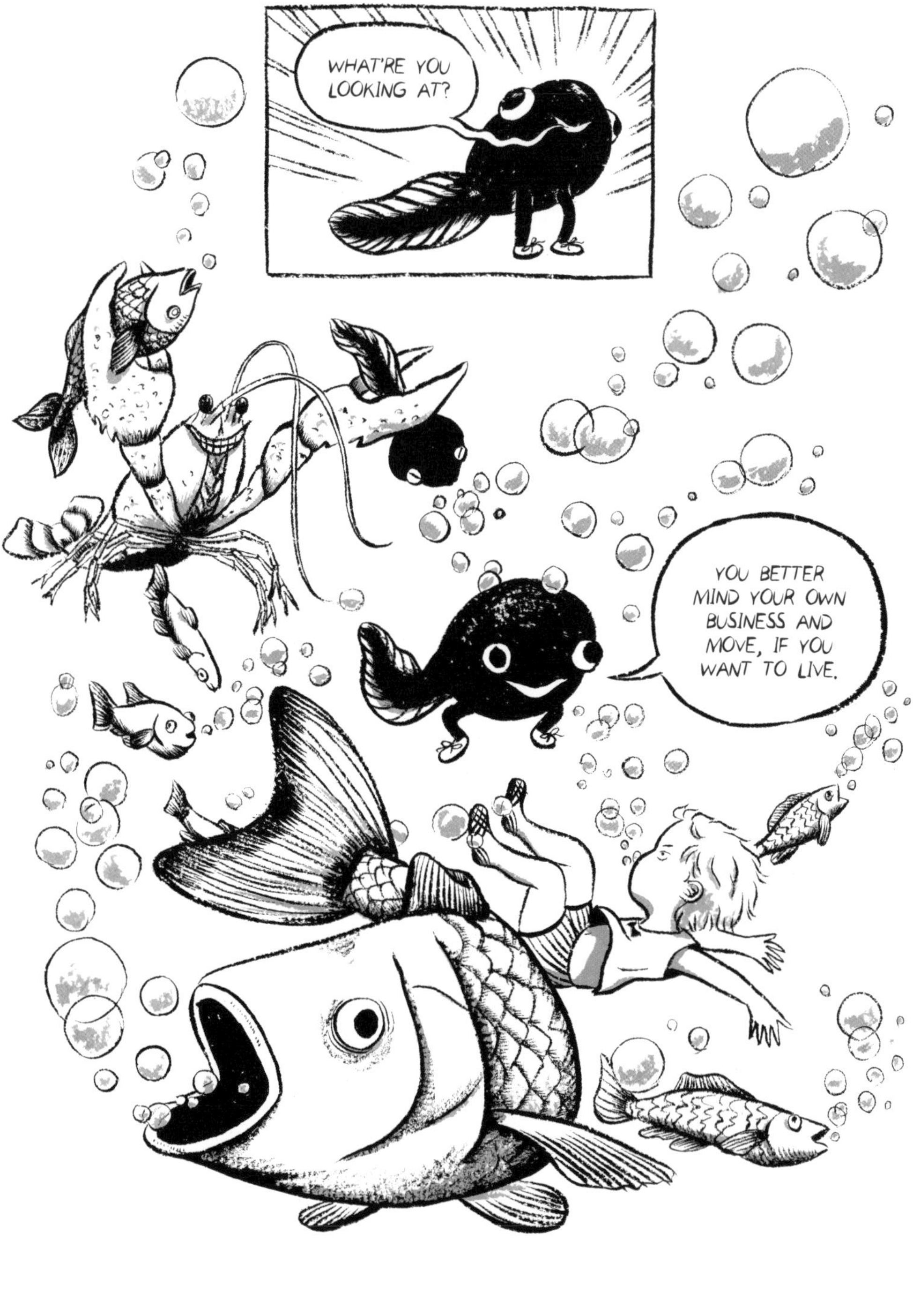
WHAT'RE YOU LOOKING AT?
YOU BETTER MIND YOUR OWN BUSINESS AND MOVE, IF YOU WANT TO LIVE.

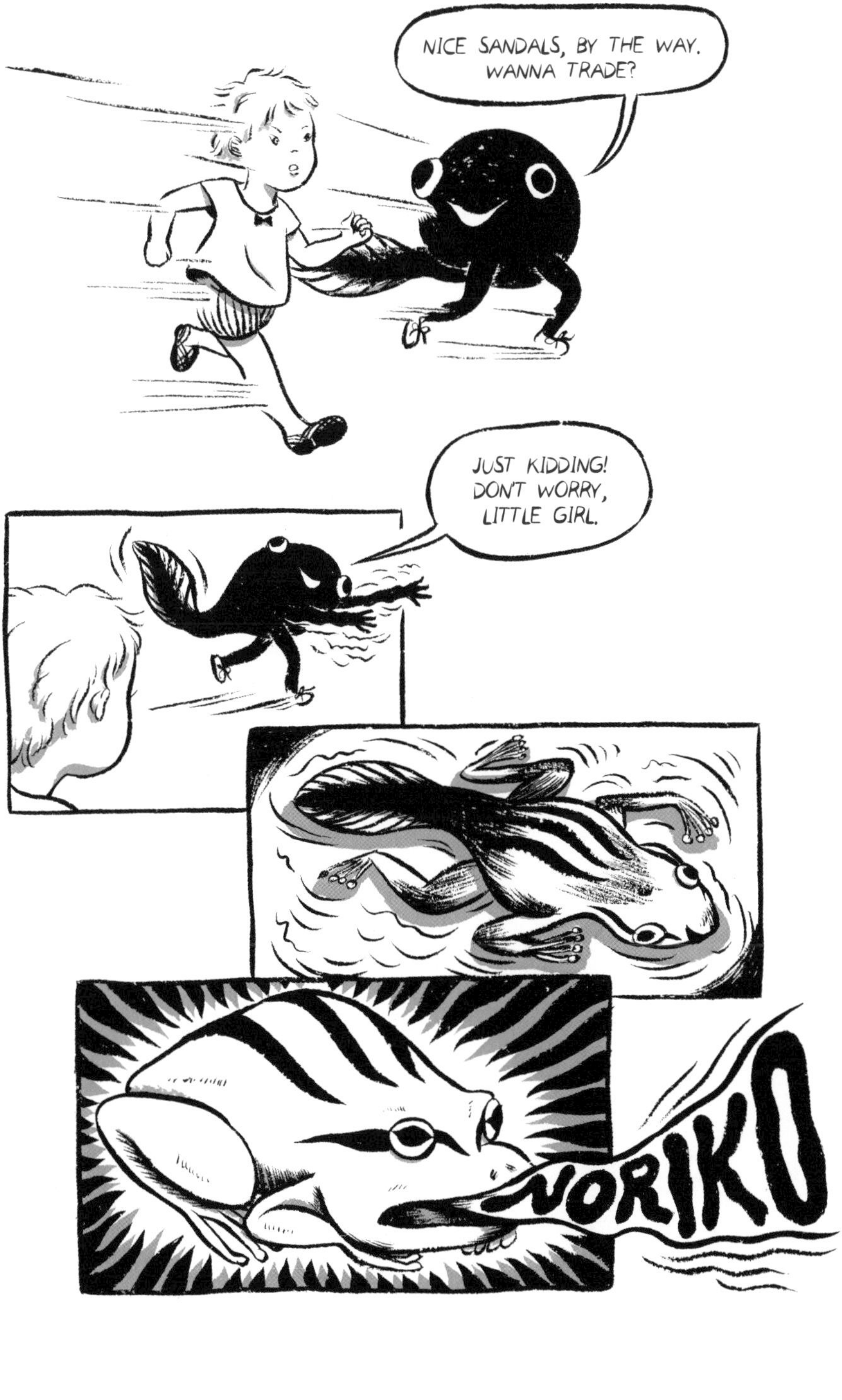
NICE SANDALS, BY THE WAY. WANNA TRADE?
JUST KIDDING! DON'T WORRY, LITTLE GIRL.
NORIKO

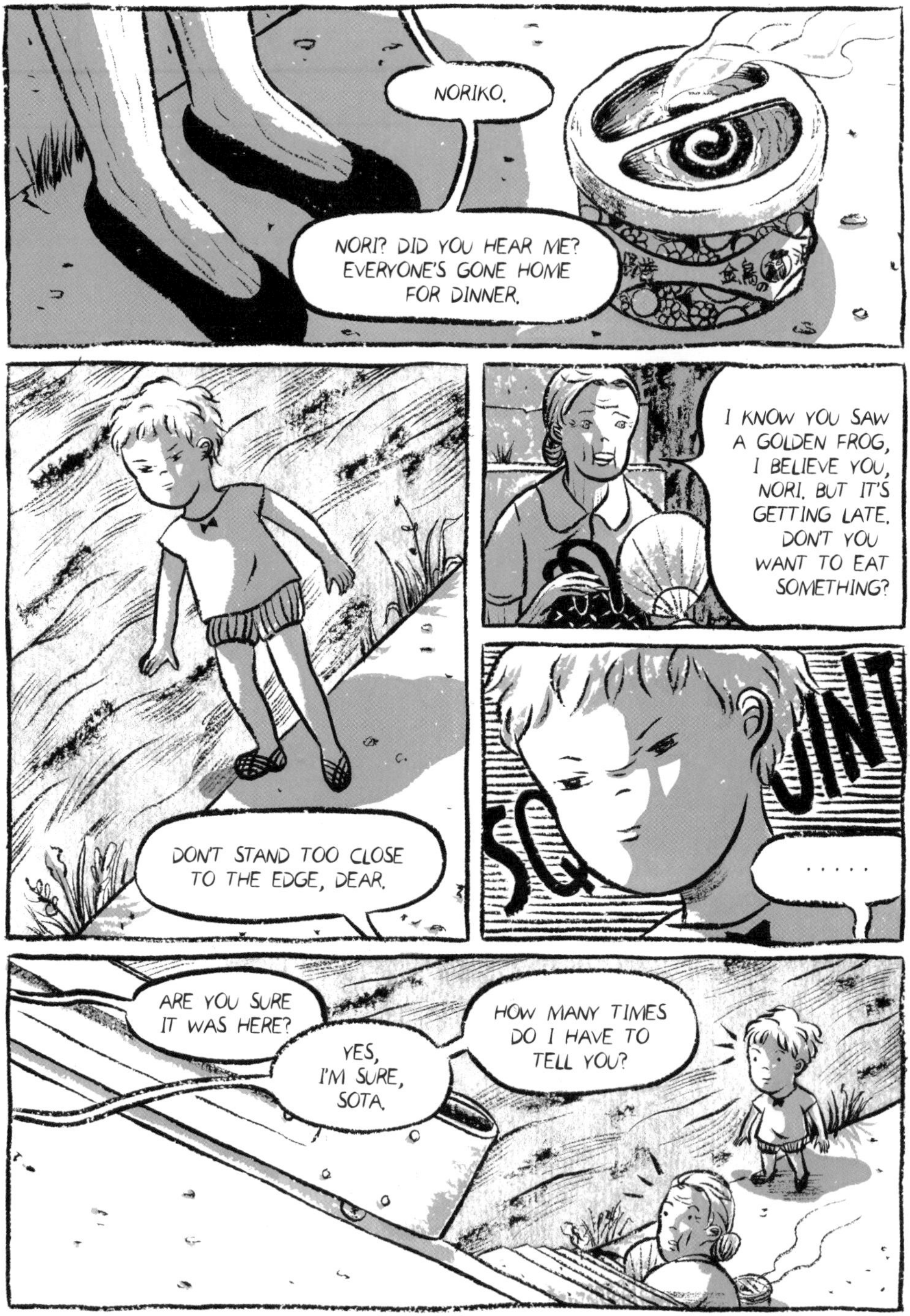
NORIKO.
NORI? DID YOU HEAR ME? EVERYONE'S GONE HOME FOR DINNER.
I KNOW YOU SAW A GOLDEN FROG, I BELIEVE YOU, NORI. BUT IT'S GETTING LATE. DON'T YOU WANT TO EAT SOMETHING?
DON'T STAND TOO CLOSE TO THE EDGE, DEAR.
SQUINT
. . . . .
ARE YOU SURE IT WAS HERE?
YES, I'M SURE, SOTA.
HOW MANY TIMES DO I HAVE TO TELL YOU?

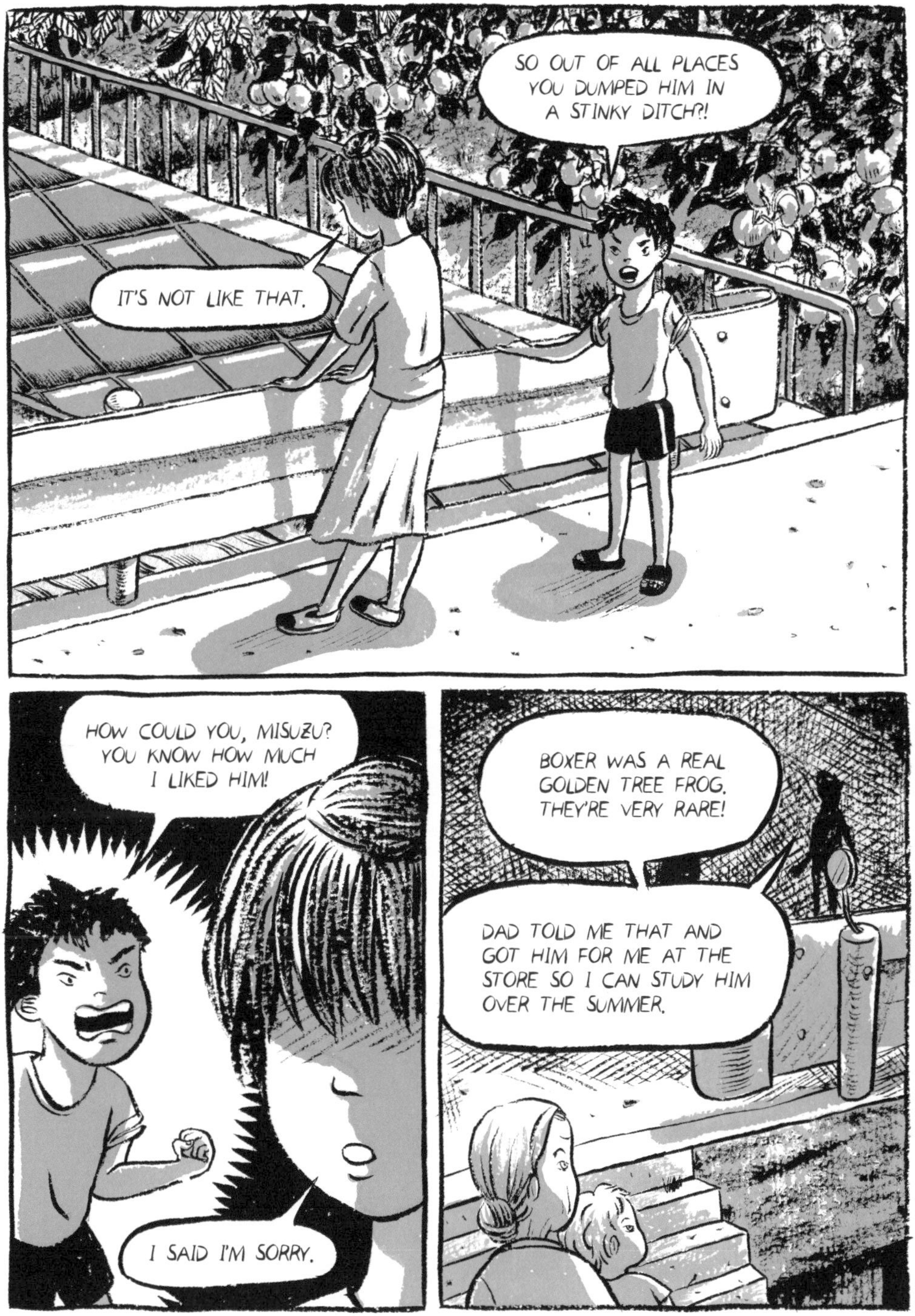
SO OUT OF ALL PLACES YOU DUMPED HIM IN A STINKY DITCH?!
IT'S NOT LIKE THAT.
HOW COULD YOU, MISUZU? YOU KNOW HOW MUCH I LIKED HIM!
I SAID I'M SORRY.
BOXER WAS A REAL GOLDEN TREE FROG. THEY'RE VERY RARE!
DAD TOLD ME THAT AND GOT HIM FOR ME AT THE STORE SO I CAN STUDY HIM OVER THE SUMMER.

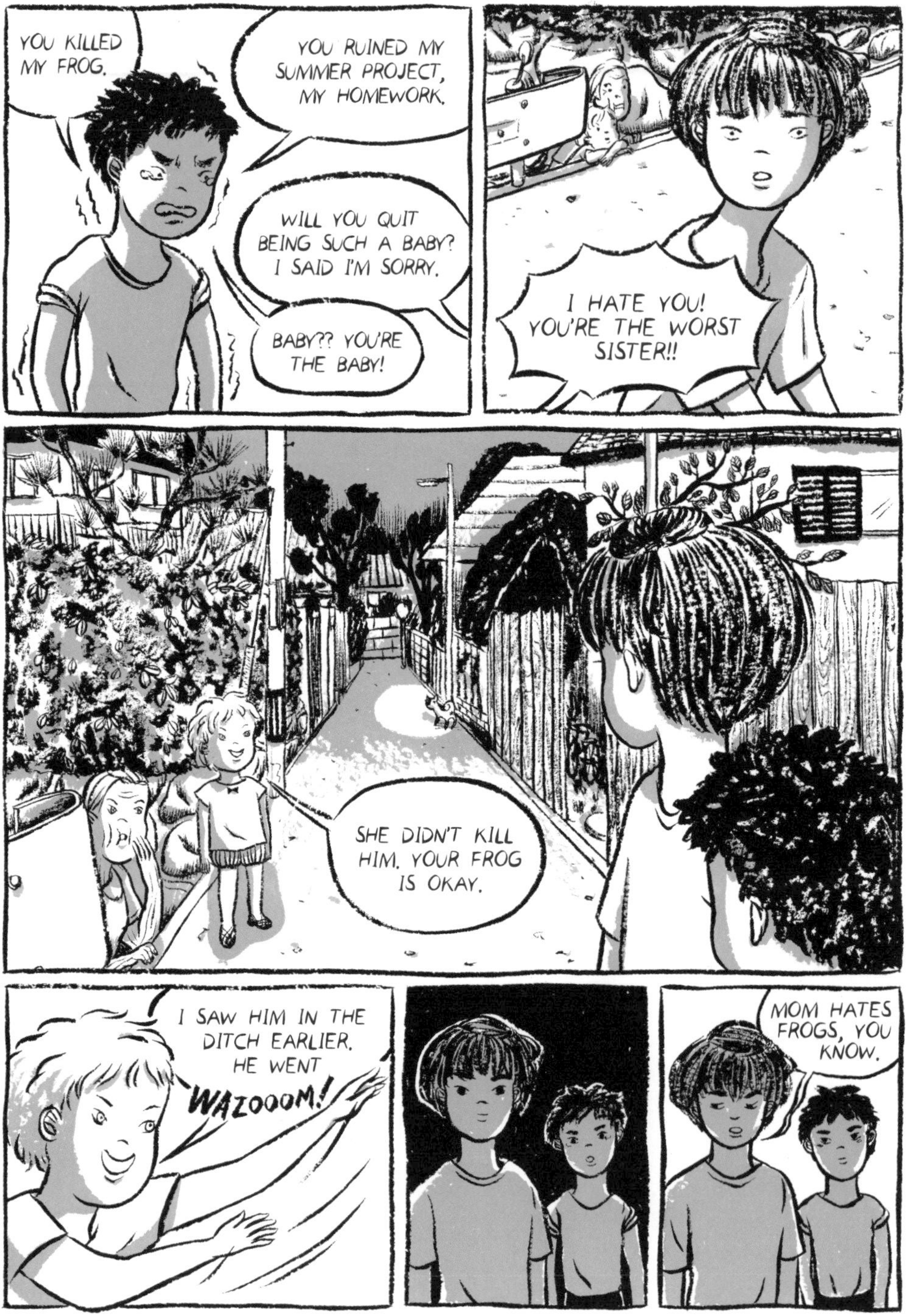

YOU KILLED MY FROG.
YOU RUINED MY SUMMER PROJECT, MY HOMEWORK.
WILL YOU QUIT BEING SUCH A BABY? I SAID I'M SORRY.
BABY?? YOU'RE THE BABY!
I HATE YOU! YOU'RE THE WORST SISTER!!
SHE DIDN'T KILL HIM. YOUR FROG IS OKAY.
I SAW HIM IN THE DITCH EARLIER. HE WENT
WAZOOOM!
MOM HATES FROGS, YOU KNOW.

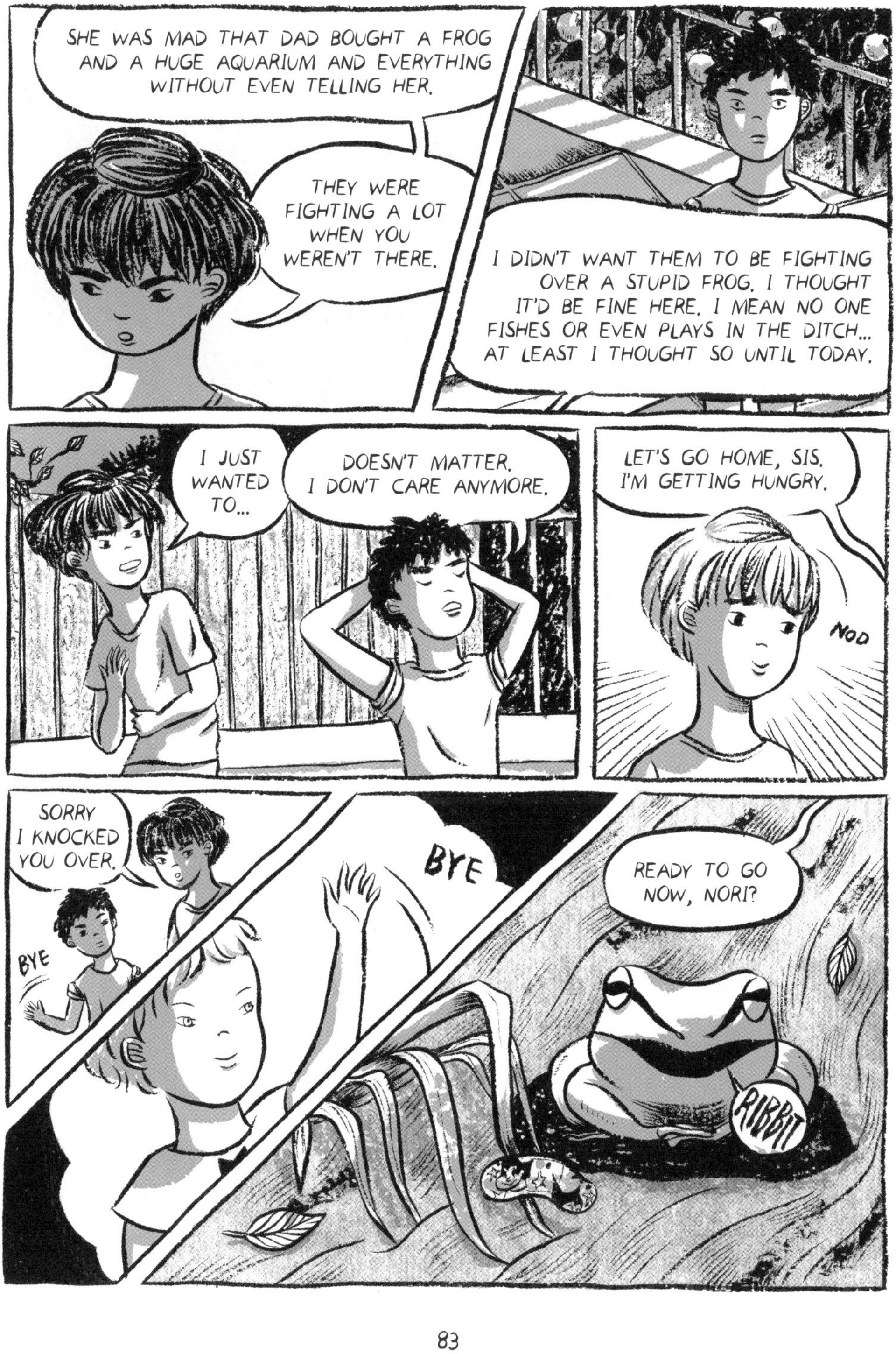

SHE WAS MAD THAT DAD BOUGHT A FROG AND A HUGE AQUARIUM AND EVERYTHING WITHOUT EVEN TELLING HER.
THEY WERE FIGHTING A LOT WHEN YOU WEREN'T THERE.
I DIDN'T WANT THEM TO BE FIGHTING OVER A STUPID FROG. I THOUGHT IT'D BE FINE HERE. I MEAN NO ONE FISHES OR EVEN PLAYS IN THE DITCH... AT LEAST I THOUGHT SO UNTIL TODAY.
I JUST WANTED TO...
DOESN'T MATTER. I DON'T CARE ANYMORE.
LET'S GO HOME, SIS. I'M GETTING HUNGRY.
NOD
SORRY I KNOCKED YOU OVER.
BYE
BYE
READY TO GO NOW, NORI?
RIBBIT

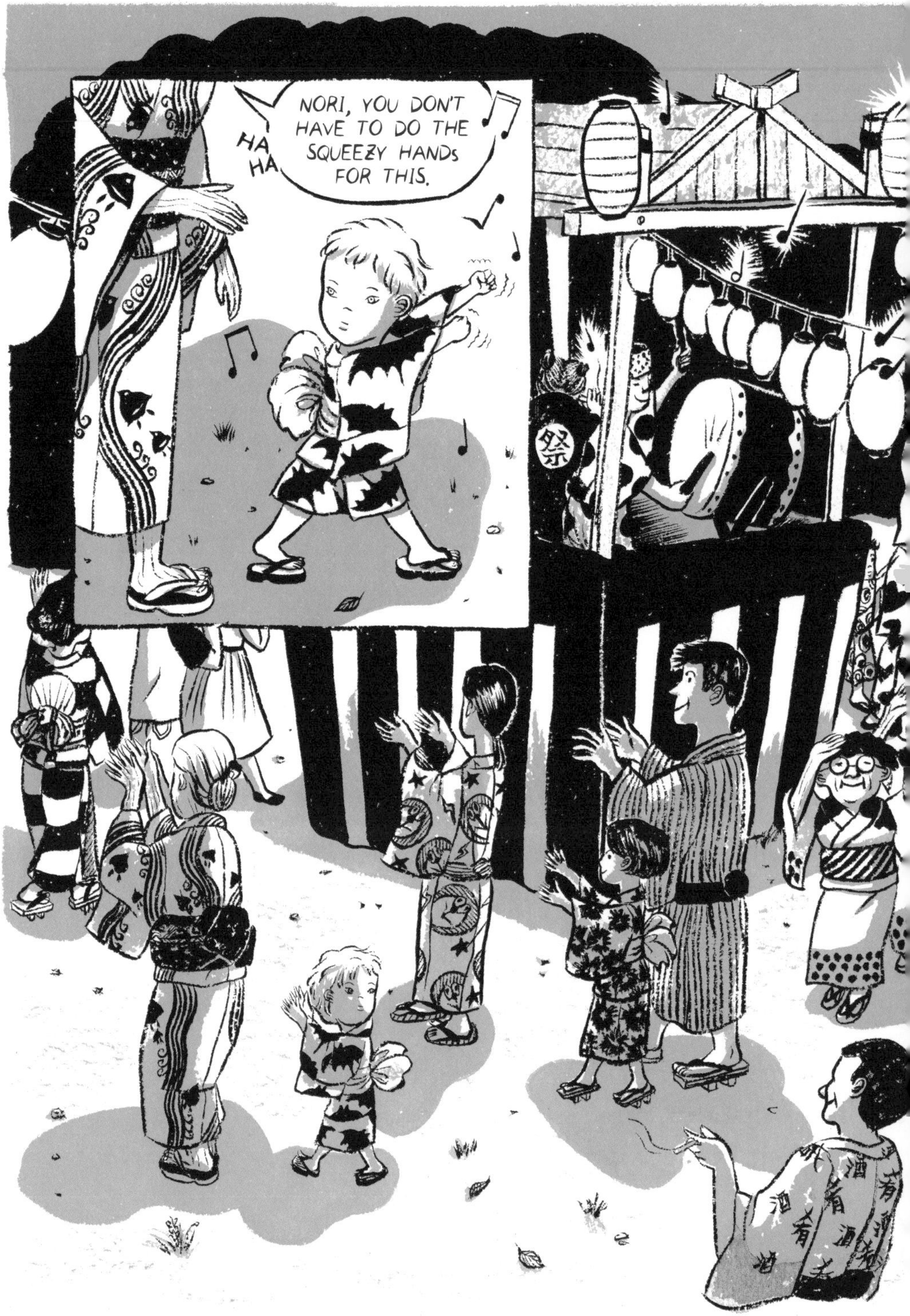
HA HA
NORI, YOU DON'T HAVE TO DO THE SQUEEZY HANDS FOR THIS.
祭

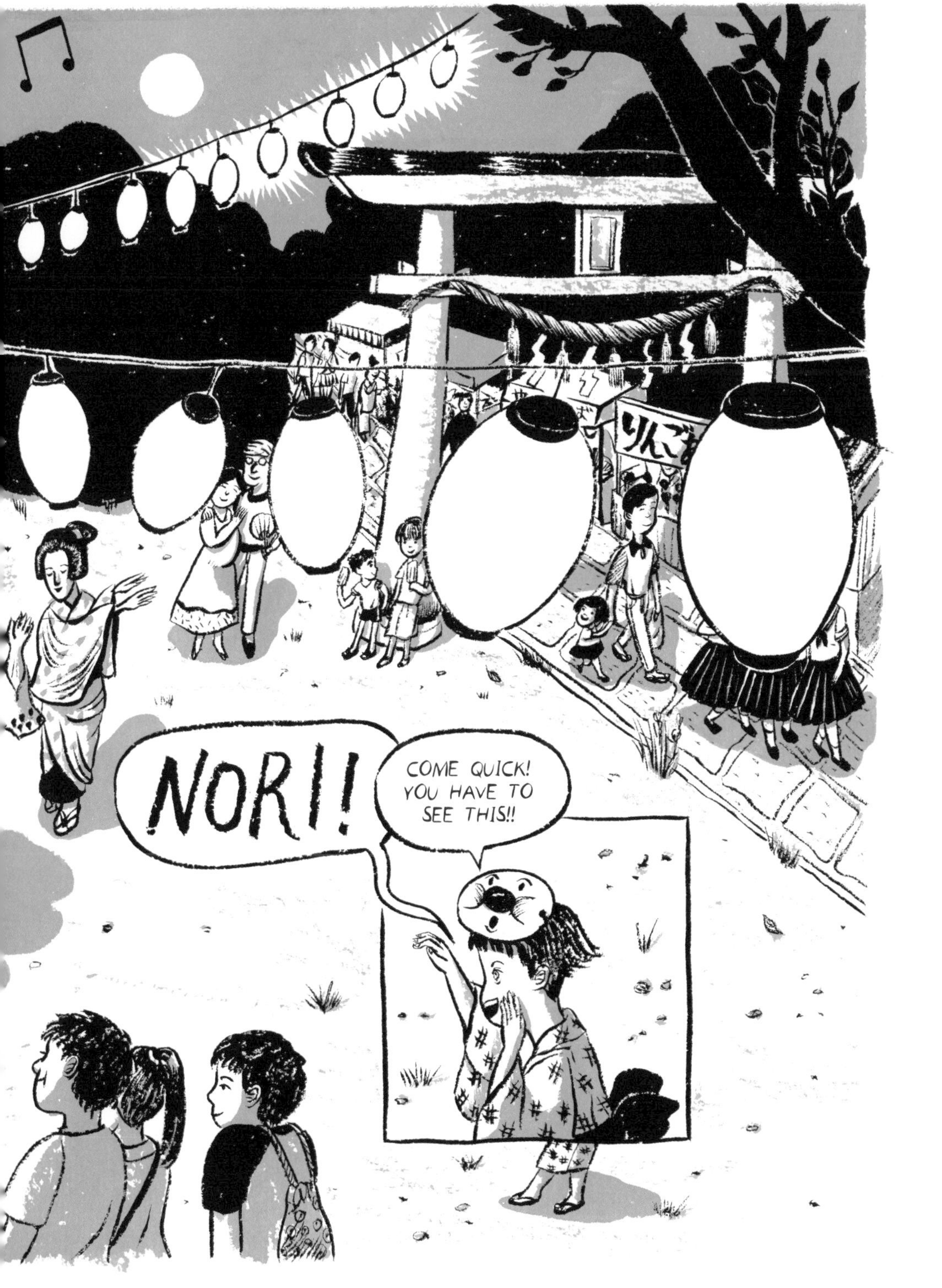
りんご
NORI!
COME QUICK! YOU HAVE TO SEE THIS!!

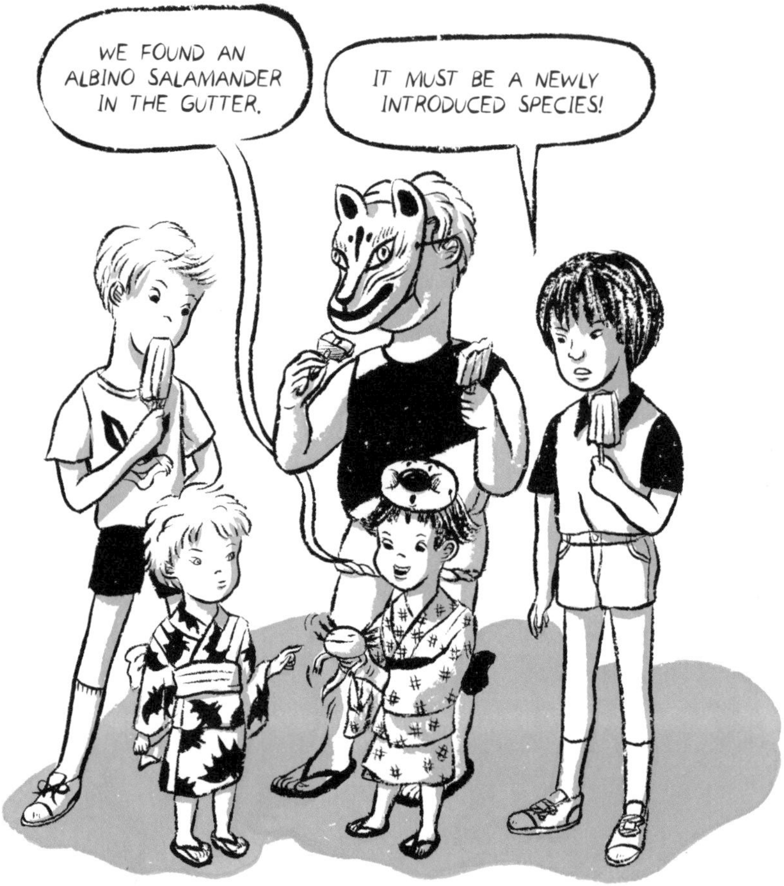
WE FOUND AN ALBINO SALAMANDER IN THE GUTTER.
IT MUST BE A NEWLY INTRODUCED SPECIES!

4

四

NORI
IN . THE
Tropics

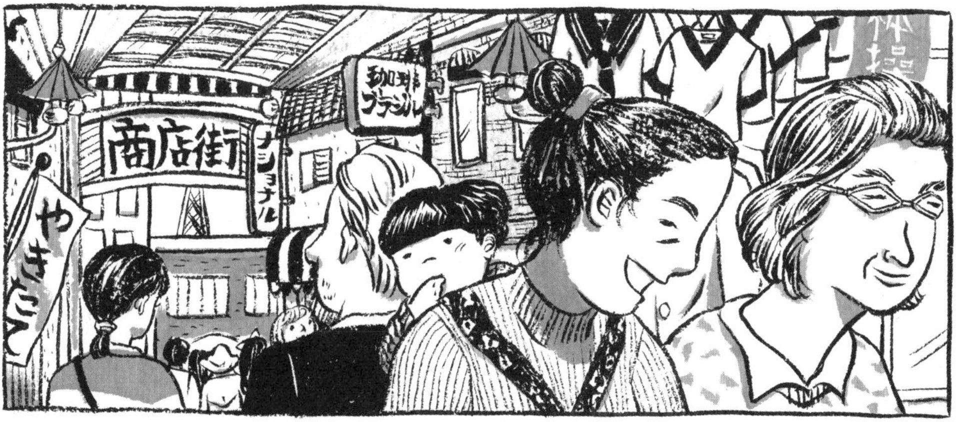
商店街
ナショナル

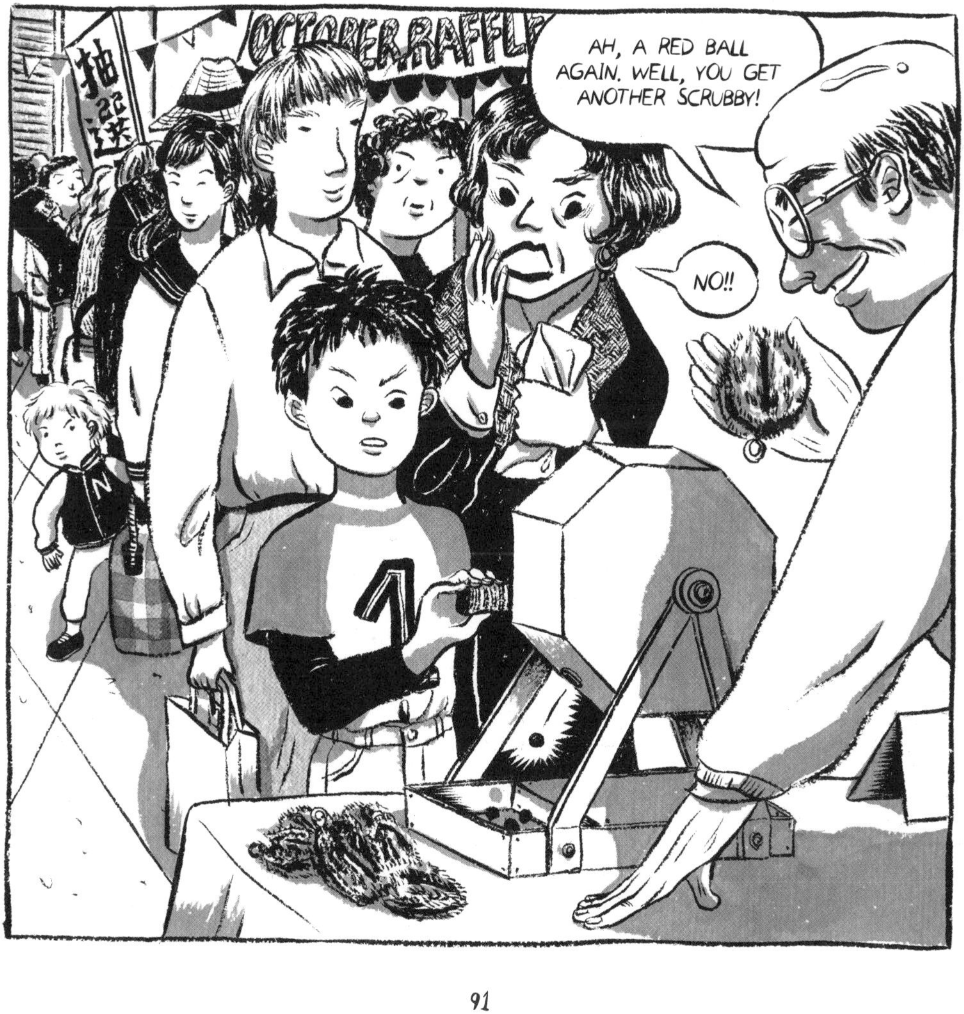
AH, A RED BALL AGAIN. WELL, YOU GET ANOTHER SCRUBBY!
NO!!

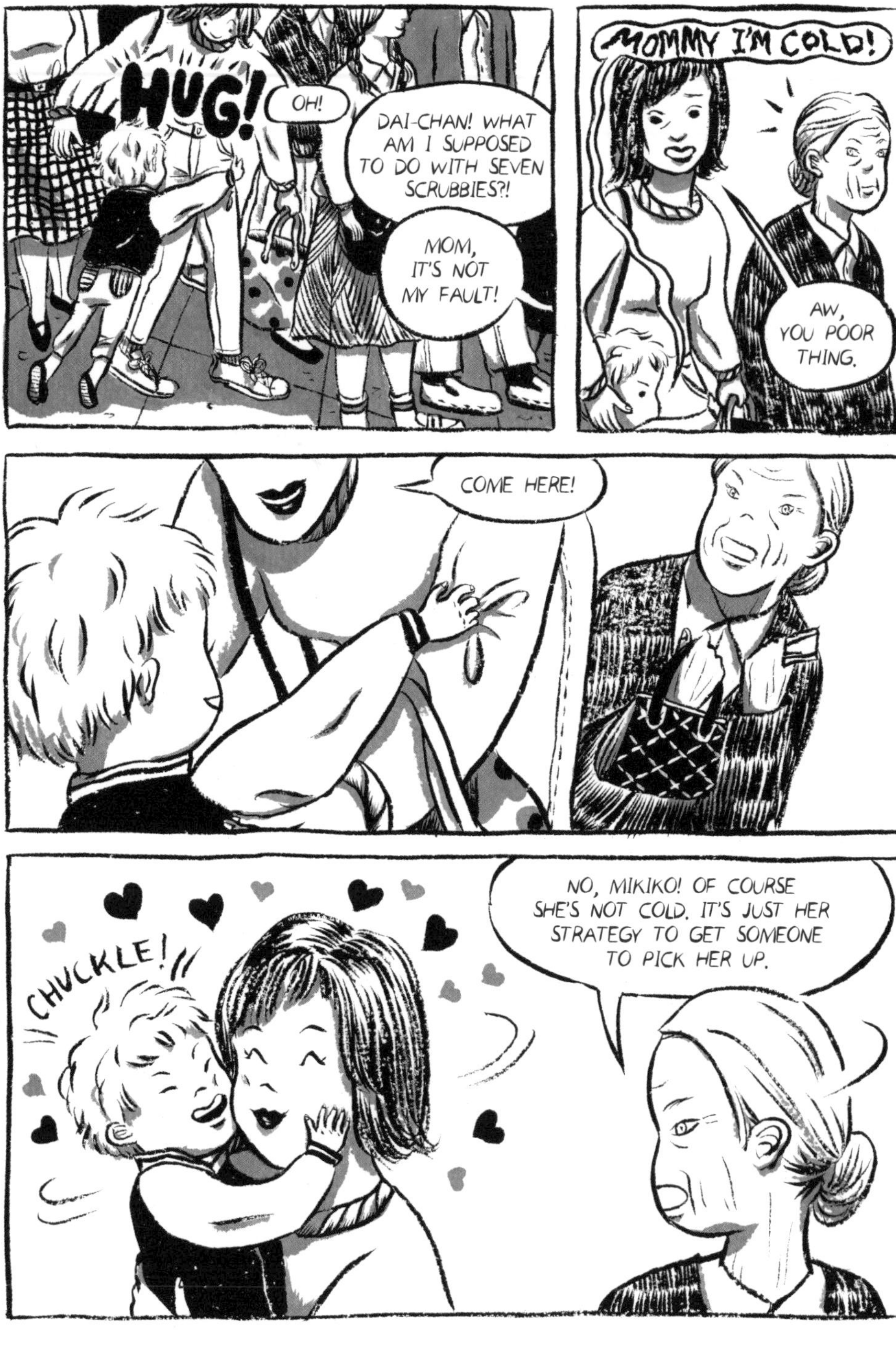
HUG!
OH!
DAI-CHAN! WHAT AM I SUPPOSED TO DO WITH SEVEN SCRUBBIES?!
MOM, IT'S NOT MY FAULT!
MOMMY I'M COLD!
AW, YOU POOR THING.
COME HERE!
CHUCKLE!
NO, MIKIKO! OF COURSE SHE'S NOT COLD. IT'S JUST HER STRATEGY TO GET SOMEONE TO PICK HER UP.

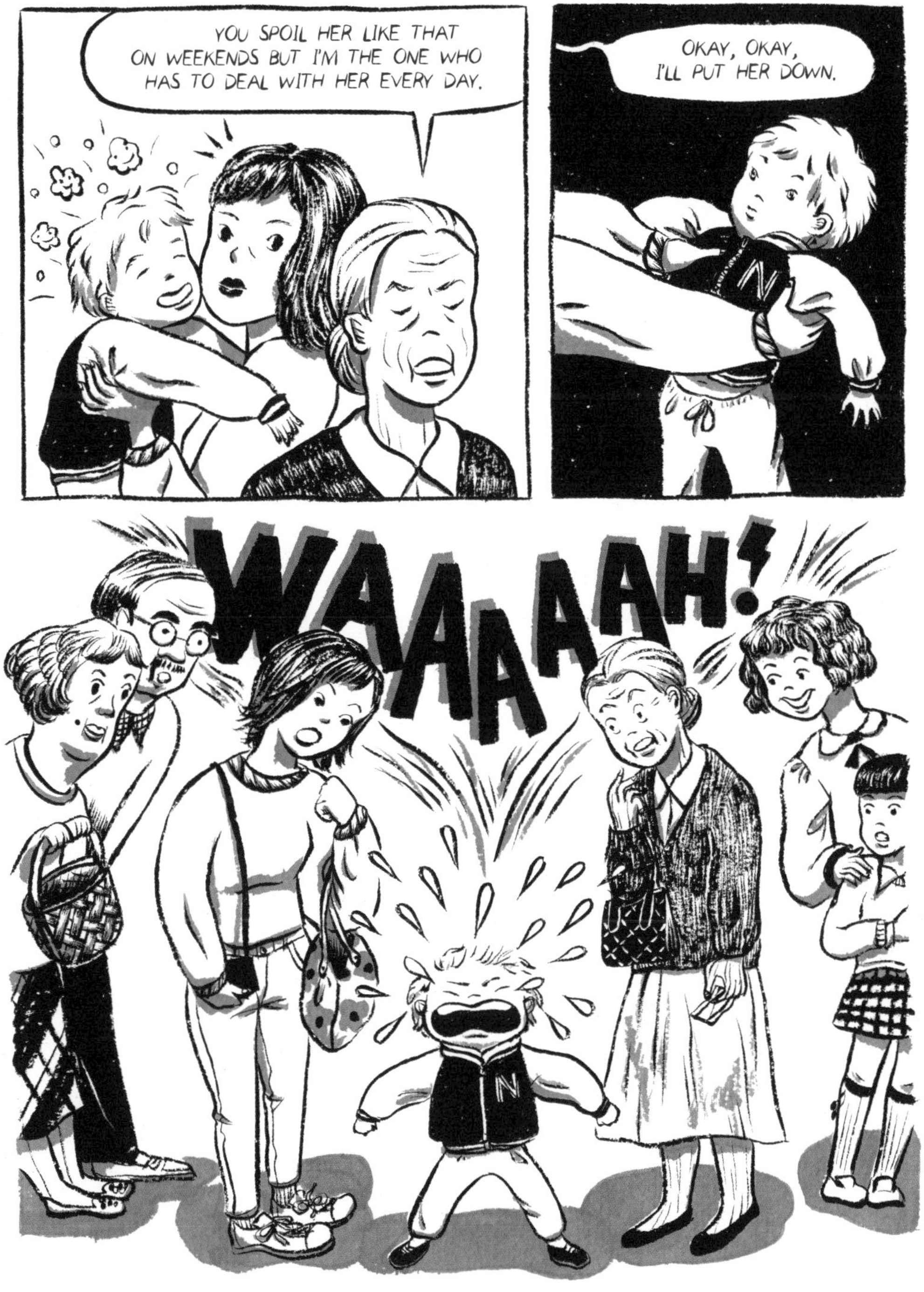
YOU SPOIL HER LIKE THAT ON WEEKENDS BUT I'M THE ONE WHO HAS TO DEAL WITH HER EVERY DAY.
OKAY, OKAY, I'LL PUT HER DOWN.
WAAAAAH!

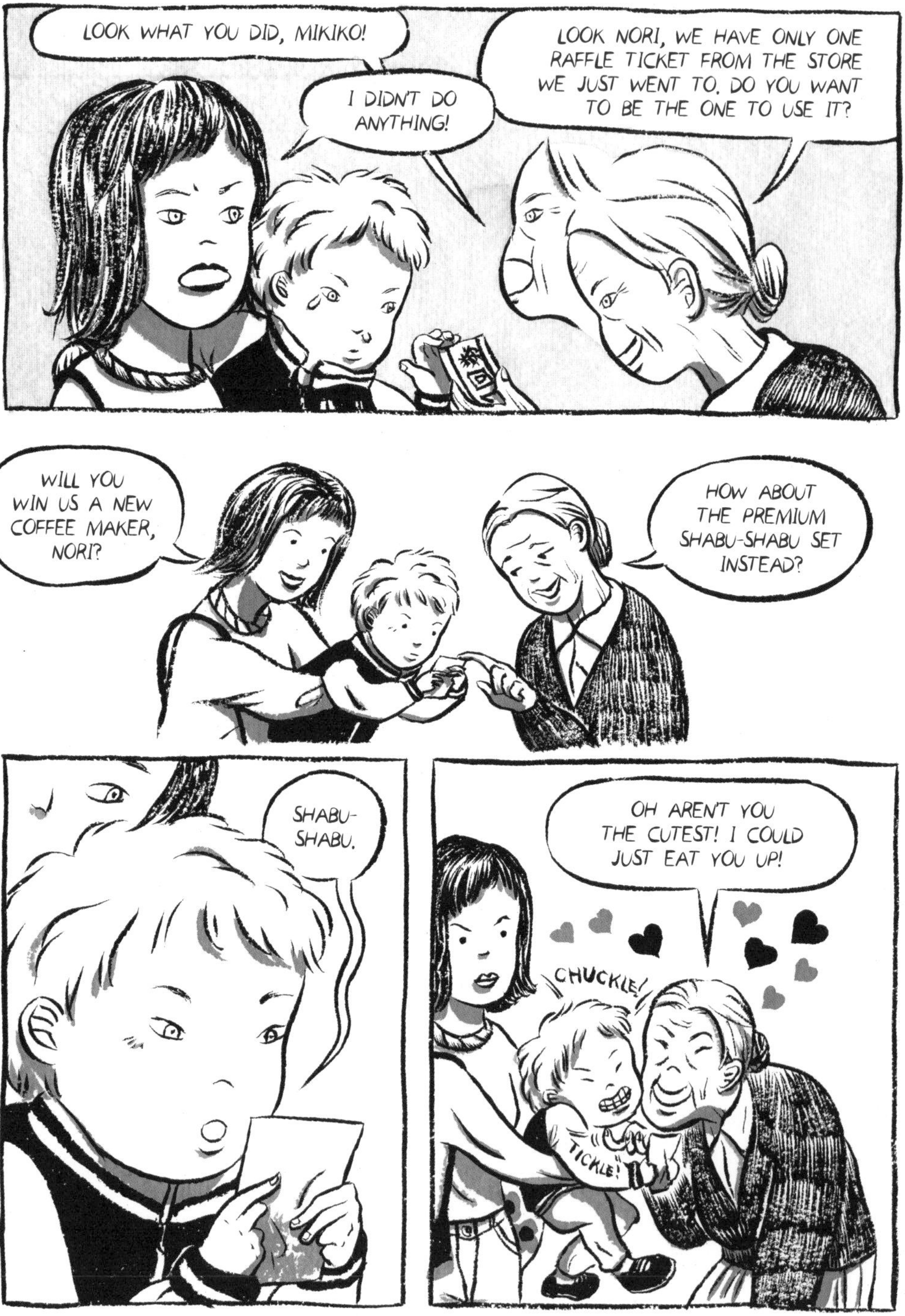
LOOK WHAT YOU DID, MIKIKO!
I DIDN'T DO ANYTHING!
LOOK NORI, WE HAVE ONLY ONE RAFFLE TICKET FROM THE STORE WE JUST WENT TO. DO YOU WANT TO BE THE ONE TO USE IT?
WILL YOU WIN US A NEW COFFEE MAKER, NORI?
HOW ABOUT THE PREMIUM SHABU-SHABU SET INSTEAD?
SHABU-SHABU.
OH AREN'T YOU THE CUTEST! I COULD JUST EAT YOU UP!
CHUCKLE!
TICKLE!

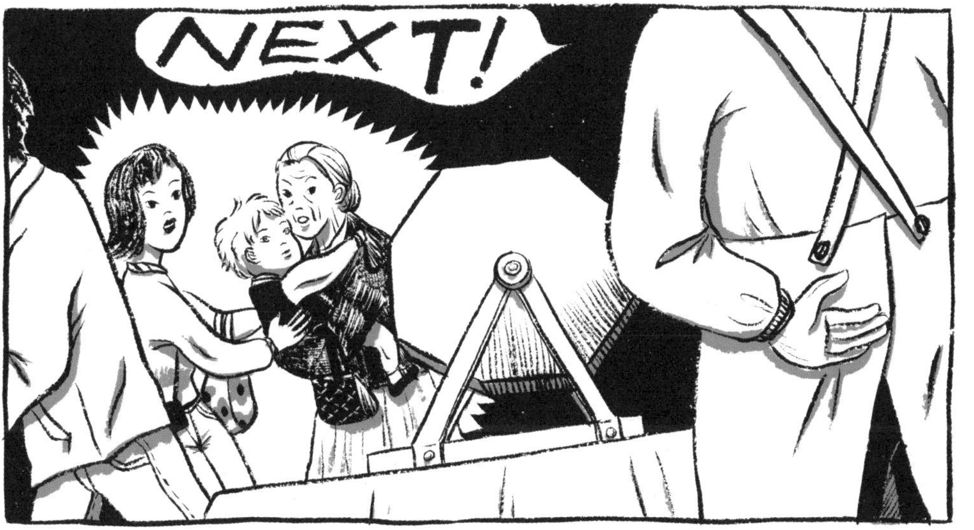
NEXT!

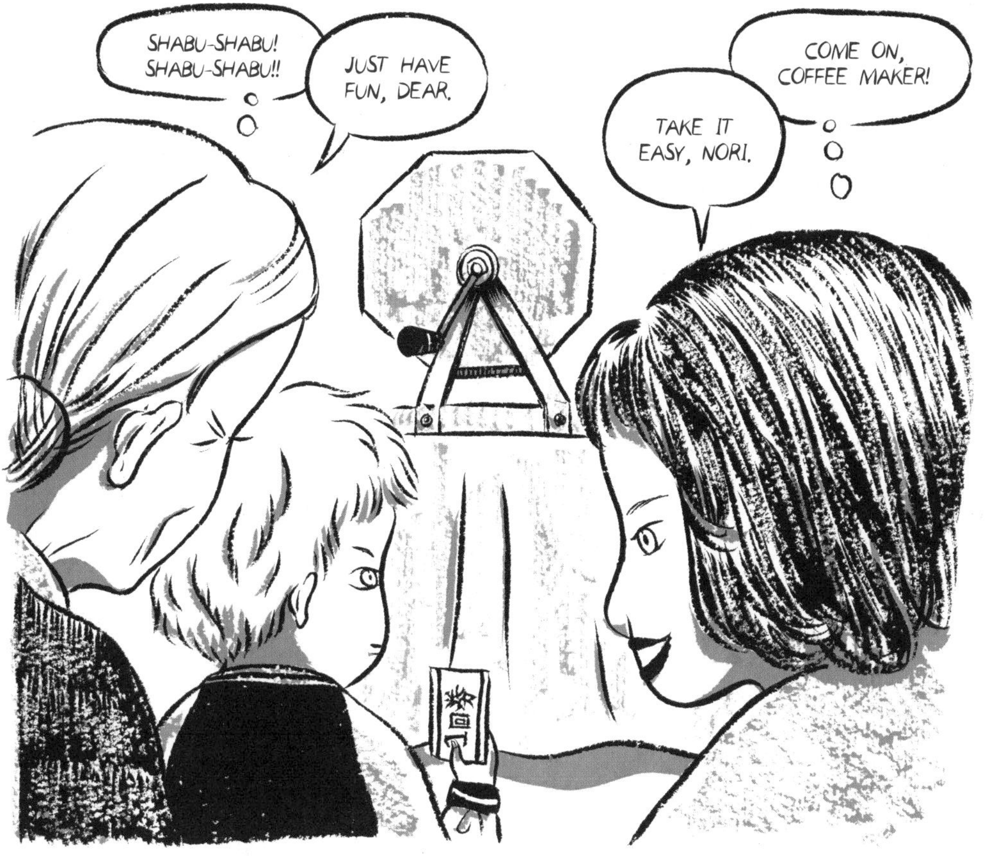
SHABU-SHABU! SHABU-SHABU!!
JUST HAVE FUN, DEAR.
COME ON, COFFEE MAKER!
TAKE IT EASY, NORI.

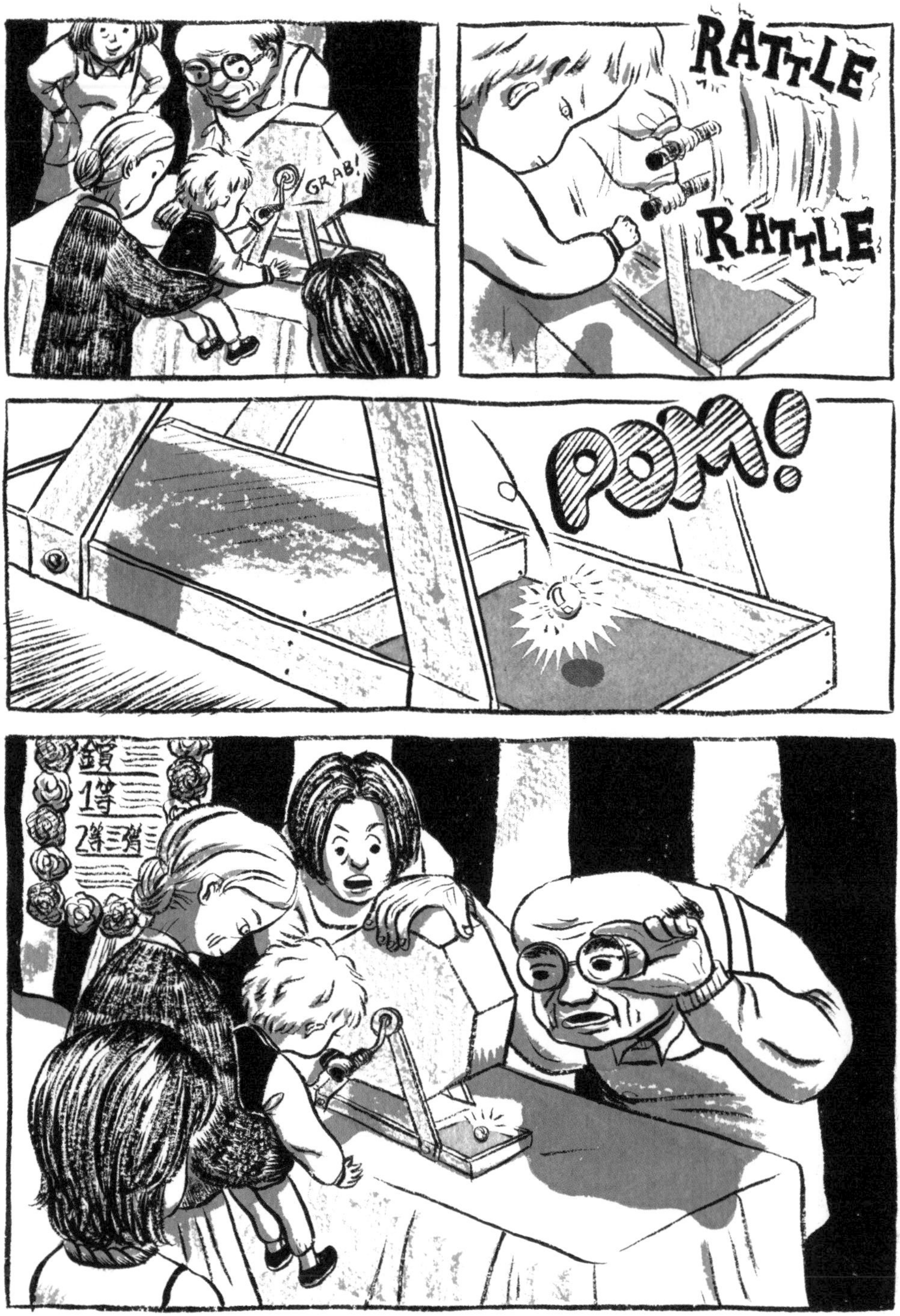
GRAB!
RATTLE
RATTLE
POM!
1等

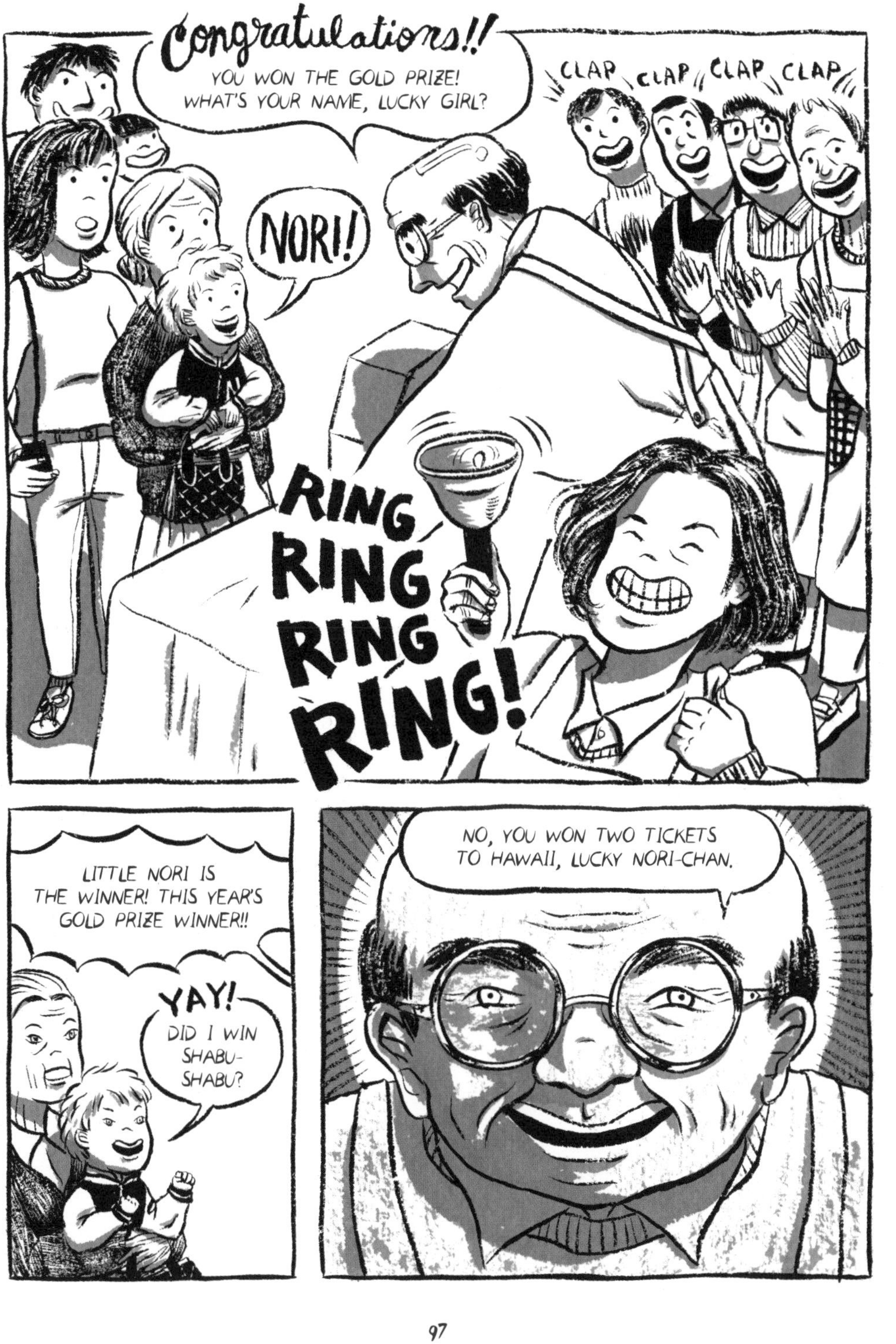
Congratulations!!
YOU WON THE GOLD PRIZE! WHAT'S YOUR NAME, LUCKY GIRL?
CLAP CLAP CLAP CLAP
NORI!
RING RING RING RING!
LITTLE NORI IS THE WINNER! THIS YEAR'S GOLD PRIZE WINNER!!
YAY! DID I WIN SHABU-SHABU?
NO, YOU WON TWO TICKETS TO HAWAII, LUCKY NORI-CHAN.

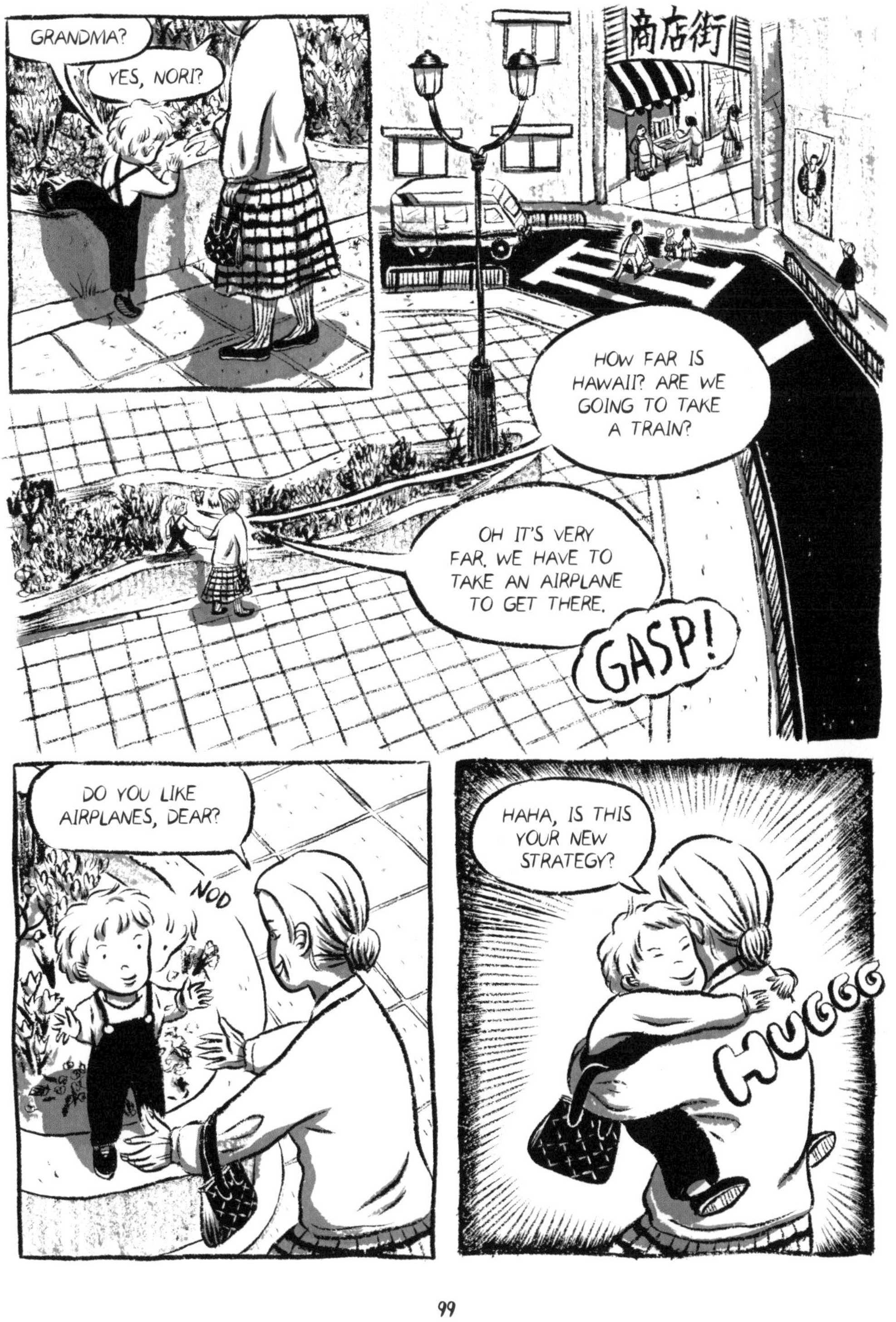

GRANDMA?
YES, NORI?
商店街
HOW FAR IS HAWAII? ARE WE GOING TO TAKE A TRAIN?
OH IT'S VERY FAR. WE HAVE TO TAKE AN AIRPLANE TO GET THERE.
GASP!
DO YOU LIKE AIRPLANES, DEAR?
NOD
HAHA, IS THIS YOUR NEW STRATEGY?
HUGGG

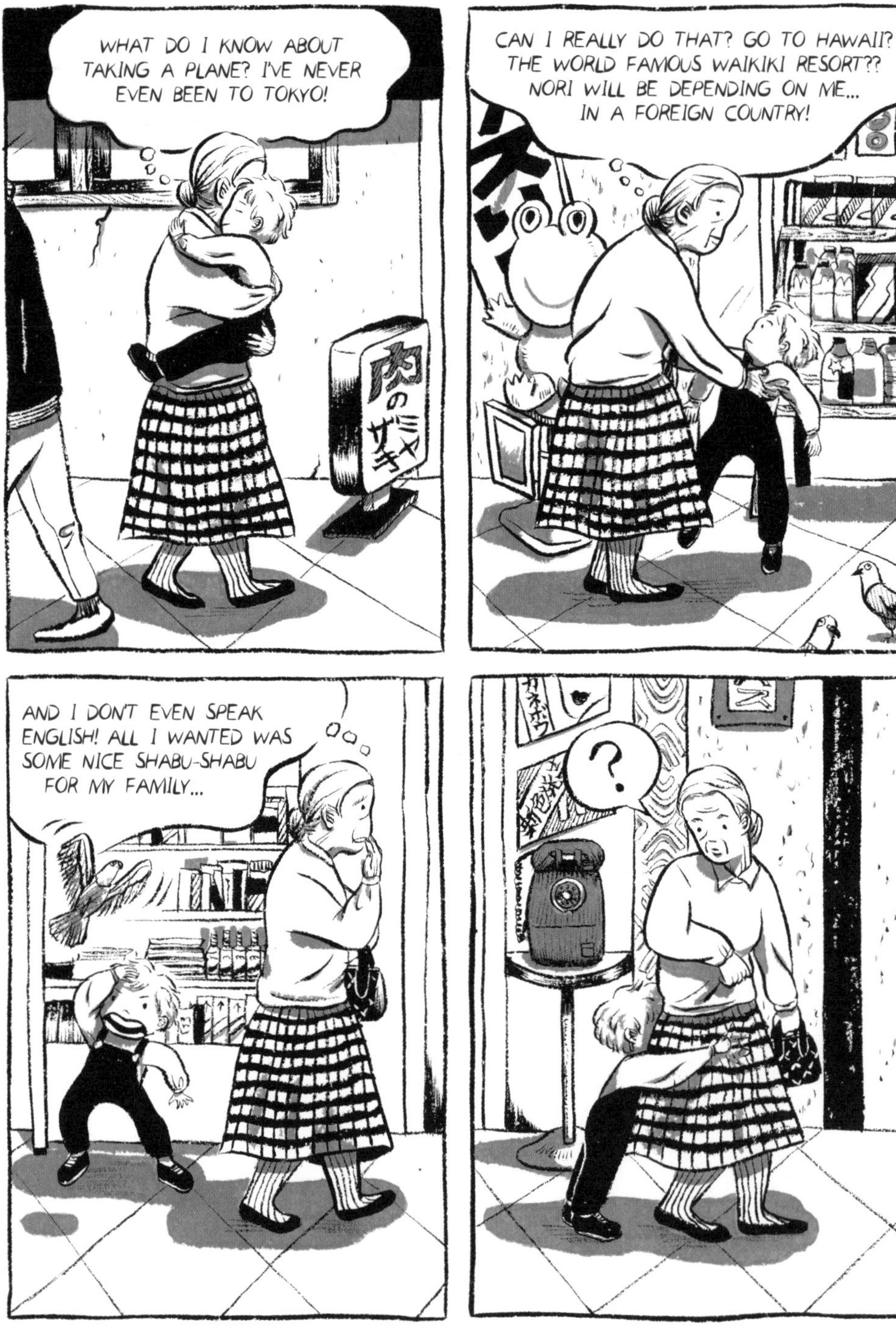
WHAT DO I KNOW ABOUT TAKING A PLANE? I'VE NEVER EVEN BEEN TO TOKYO!
肉のミヤザキ
CAN I REALLY DO THAT? GO TO HAWAII? THE WORLD FAMOUS WAIKIKI RESORT?? NORI WILL BE DEPENDING ON ME... IN A FOREIGN COUNTRY!
AND I DON'T EVEN SPEAK ENGLISH! ALL I WANTED WAS SOME NICE SHABU-SHABU FOR MY FAMILY...
?

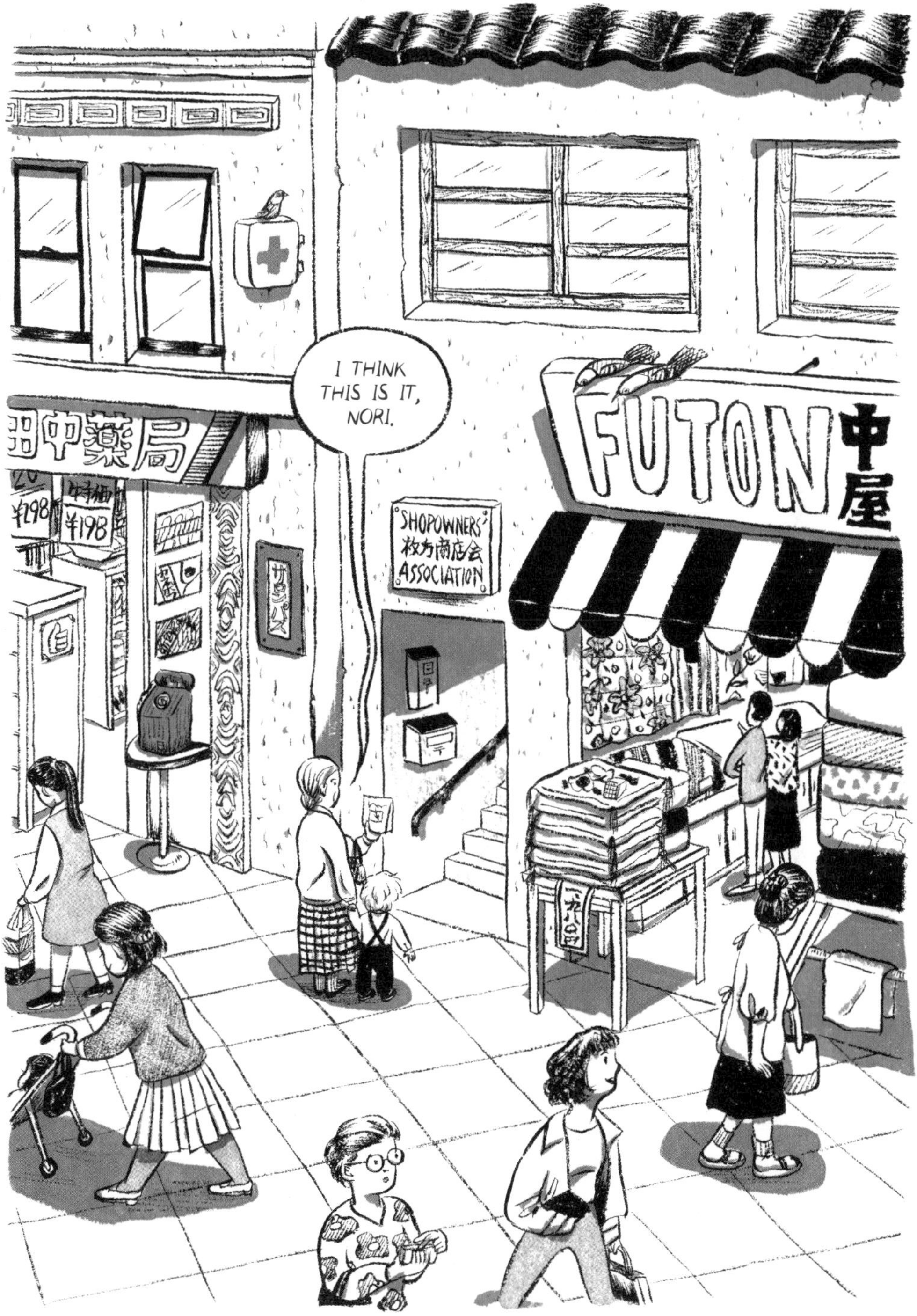

I THINK THIS IS IT, NORI.
中薬局
¥198
FUTON 中屋
SHOPOWNERS' 枚方商店会 ASSOCIATION

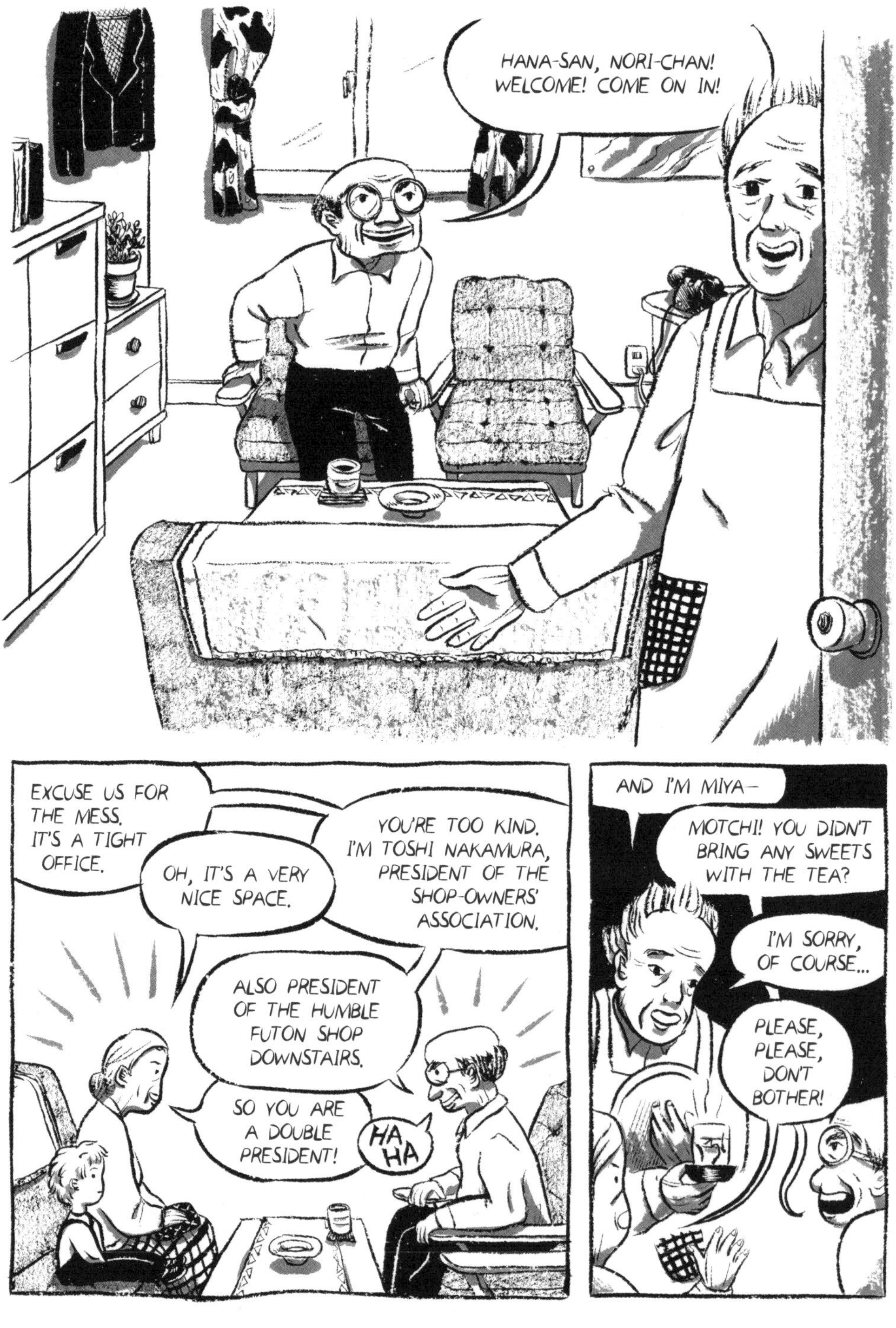
HANA-SAN, NORI-CHAN! WELCOME! COME ON IN!
EXCUSE US FOR THE MESS. IT'S A TIGHT OFFICE.
OH, IT'S A VERY NICE SPACE.
YOU'RE TOO KIND. I'M TOSHI NAKAMURA, PRESIDENT OF THE SHOP-OWNERS' ASSOCIATION.
ALSO PRESIDENT OF THE HUMBLE FUTON SHOP DOWNSTAIRS.
SO YOU ARE A DOUBLE PRESIDENT!
HA HA
AND I'M MIYA—
MOTCHI! YOU DIDN'T BRING ANY SWEETS WITH THE TEA?
I'M SORRY, OF COURSE...
PLEASE, PLEASE, DON'T BOTHER!

SIT UP STRAIGHT, NORI.

CONGRATULATIONS AGAIN FOR WINNING THE GOLD PRIZE!

I HEAR YOU ONLY HAD ONE TICKET, TOO. IMPRESSIVE!

POF!

NORI!

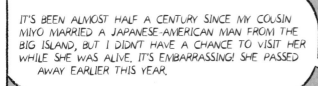

IT'S BEEN ALMOST HALF A CENTURY SINCE MY COUSIN MIYO MARRIED A JAPANESE-AMERICAN MAN FROM THE BIG ISLAND, BUT I DIDN'T HAVE A CHANCE TO VISIT HER WHILE SHE WAS ALIVE. IT'S EMBARRASSING! SHE PASSED AWAY EARLIER THIS YEAR.

I'M SO SORRY TO HEAR THAT.

SHE WAS BEAUTIFUL AND KIND. I USED TO HAVE A HUGE CRUSH ON HER AS A BOY!

OH!

SOME ORANGE JUICE FOR YOU, NORI-CHAN?

MOCHI!

IT'S ACTUALLY MOT-CHI, SHORT FOR MIYAMOTO.

MOCHI?

MOT-CHI!

SHE WAS ABOUT TEN YEARS OLDER THAN ME, AND I WAS HER FAVORITE LITTLE COUSIN. SHE USED TO SEND ME PICTURES OF HILO SEVERAL TIMES A YEAR. BEAUTIFUL PLACE! YOU AND NORI-CHAN WILL LOVE IT THERE!

HOW NICE. BUT MR...

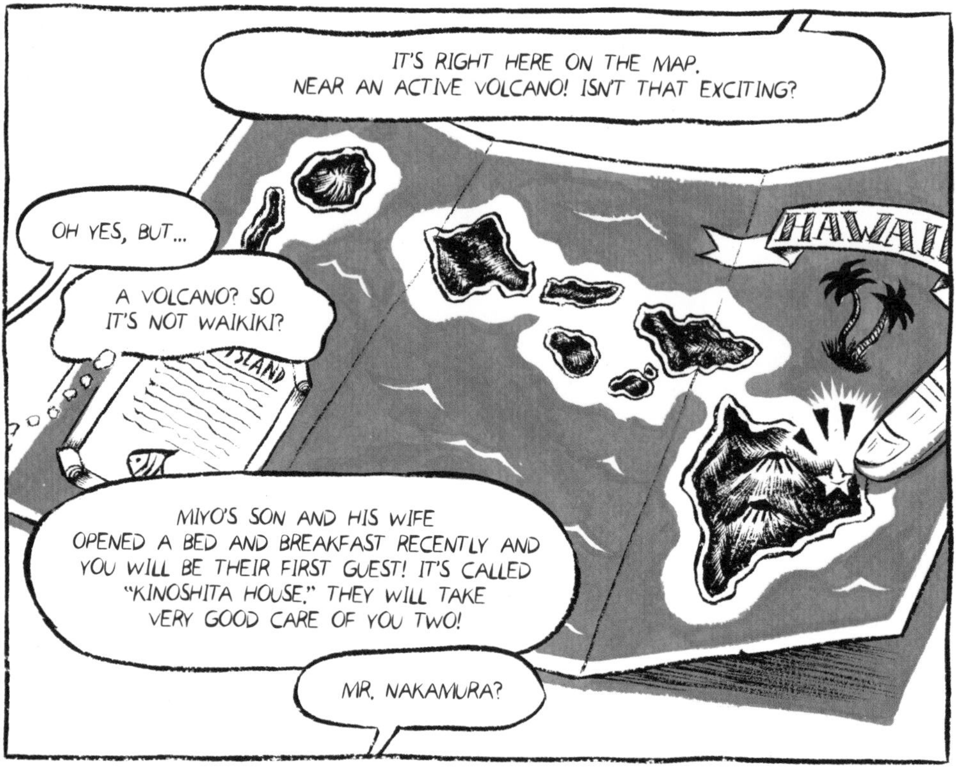
IT'S RIGHT HERE ON THE MAP. NEAR AN ACTIVE VOLCANO! ISN'T THAT EXCITING?
OH YES, BUT...
A VOLCANO? SO IT'S NOT WAIKIKI?
HAWAII
MIYO'S SON AND HIS WIFE OPENED A BED AND BREAKFAST RECENTLY AND YOU WILL BE THEIR FIRST GUEST! IT'S CALLED "KINOSHITA HOUSE." THEY WILL TAKE VERY GOOD CARE OF YOU TWO!
MR. NAKAMURA?

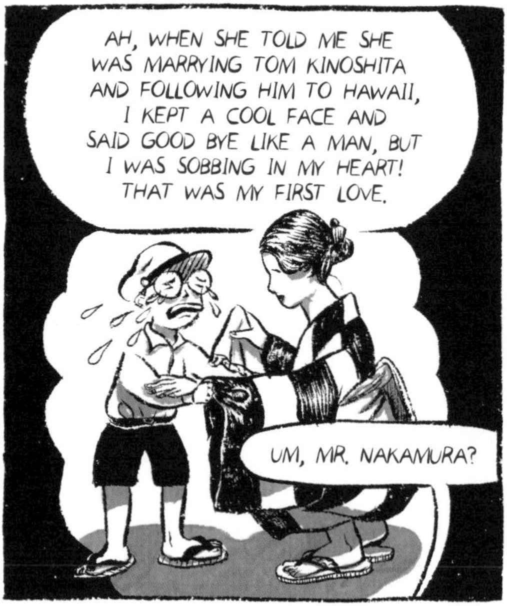
AH, WHEN SHE TOLD ME SHE WAS MARRYING TOM KINOSHITA AND FOLLOWING HIM TO HAWAII, I KEPT A COOL FACE AND SAID GOOD BYE LIKE A MAN, BUT I WAS SOBBING IN MY HEART! THAT WAS MY FIRST LOVE.
UM, MR. NAKAMURA?

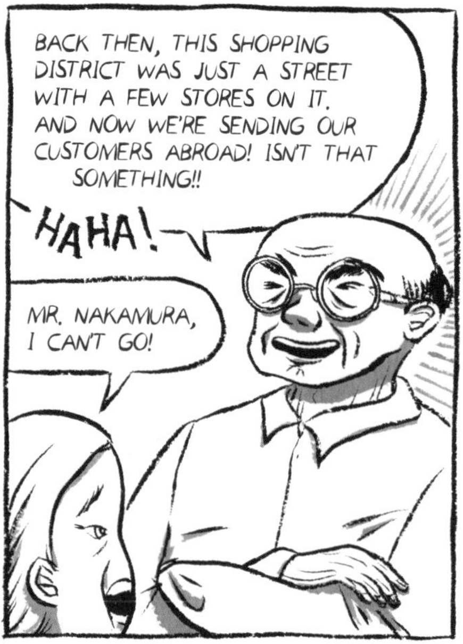
BACK THEN, THIS SHOPPING DISTRICT WAS JUST A STREET WITH A FEW STORES ON IT. AND NOW WE'RE SENDING OUR CUSTOMERS ABROAD! ISN'T THAT SOMETHING!!
HAHA!
MR. NAKAMURA, I CAN'T GO!

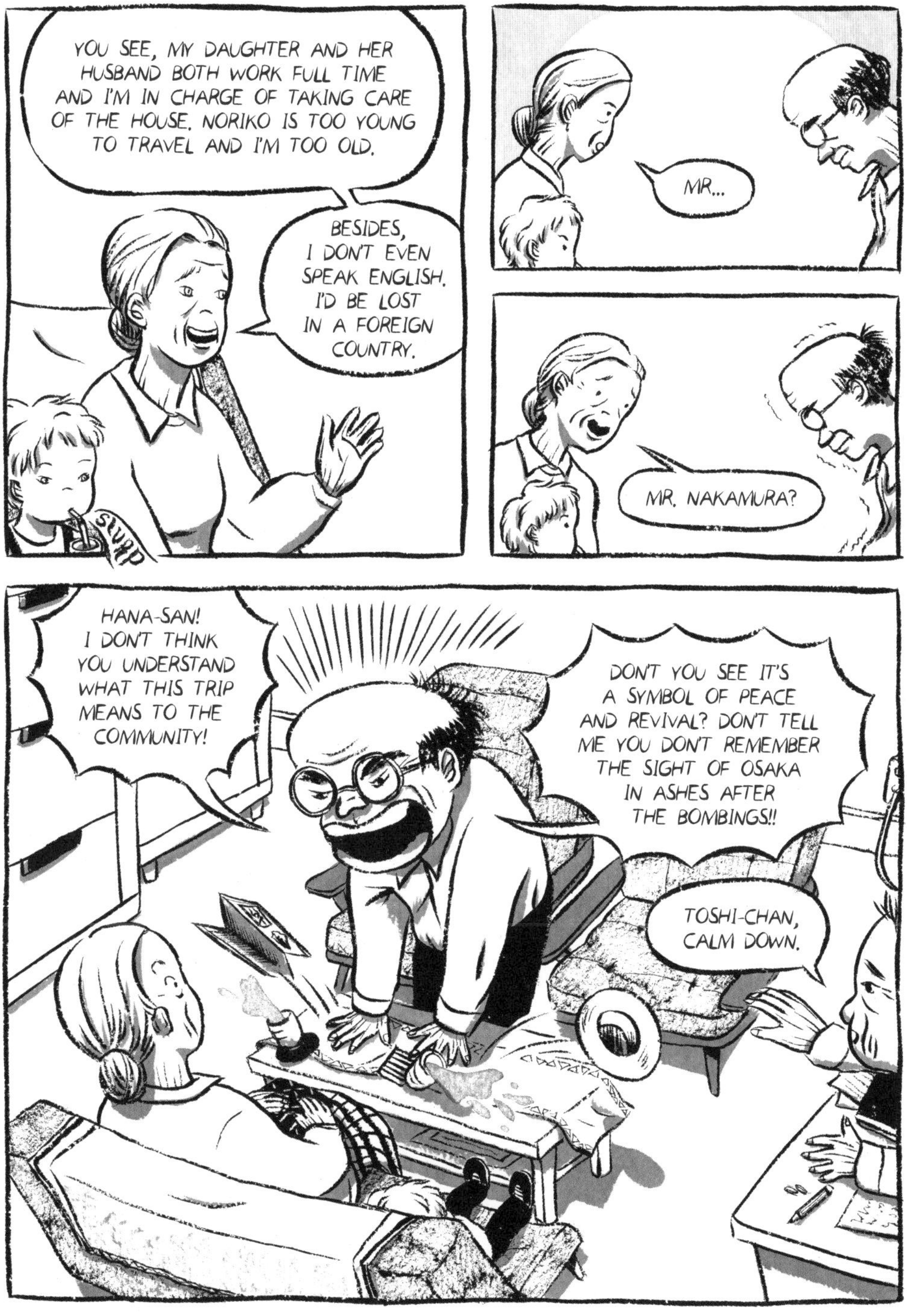
YOU SEE, MY DAUGHTER AND HER HUSBAND BOTH WORK FULL TIME AND I'M IN CHARGE OF TAKING CARE OF THE HOUSE. NORIKO IS TOO YOUNG TO TRAVEL AND I'M TOO OLD.
BESIDES, I DON'T EVEN SPEAK ENGLISH. I'D BE LOST IN A FOREIGN COUNTRY.
SLURP
MR...
MR. NAKAMURA?
HANA-SAN! I DON'T THINK YOU UNDERSTAND WHAT THIS TRIP MEANS TO THE COMMUNITY!
DON'T YOU SEE IT'S A SYMBOL OF PEACE AND REVIVAL? DON'T TELL ME YOU DON'T REMEMBER THE SIGHT OF OSAKA IN ASHES AFTER THE BOMBINGS!!
TOSHI-CHAN, CALM DOWN.

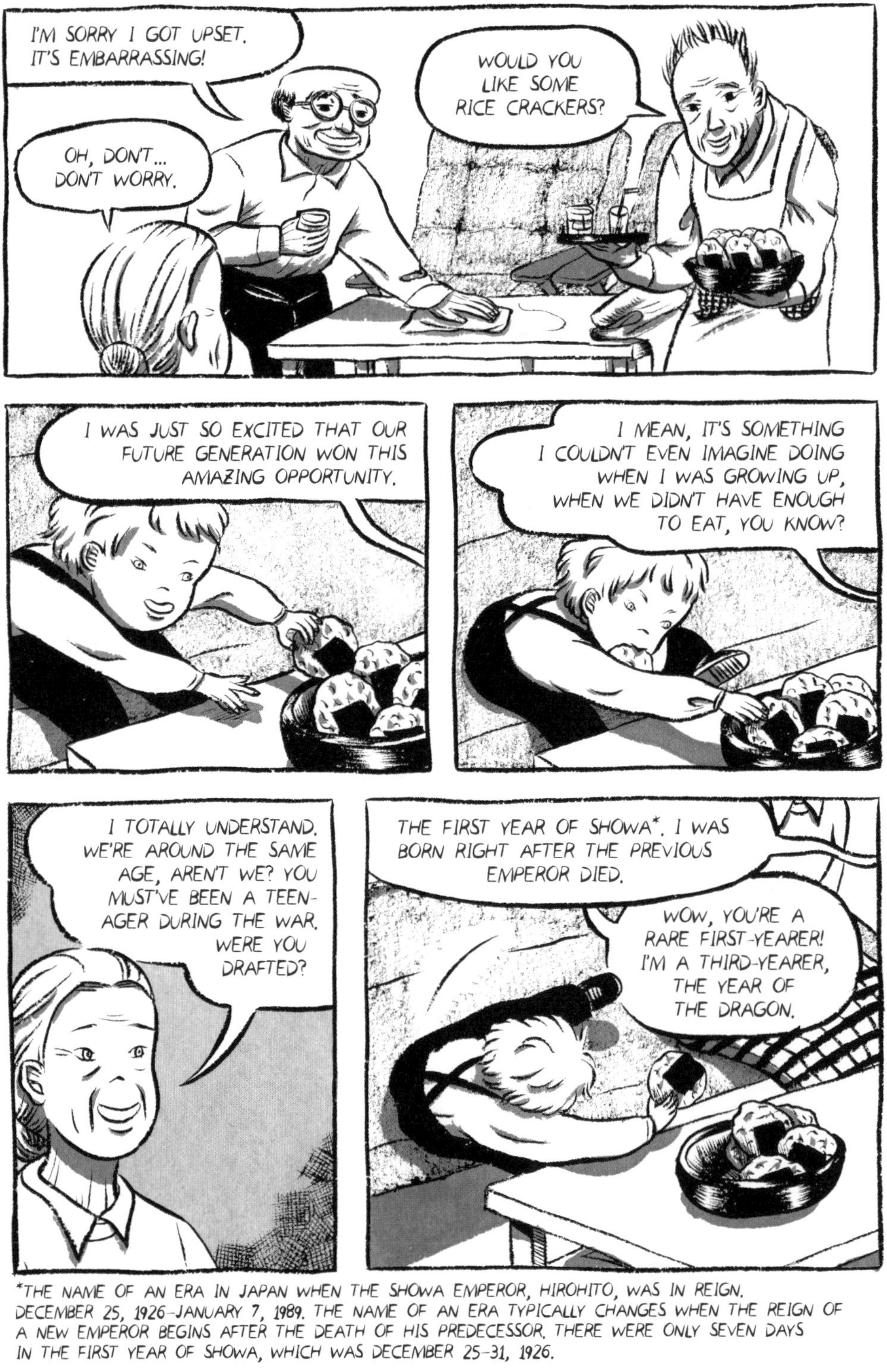
I'M SORRY I GOT UPSET. IT'S EMBARRASSING!
OH, DON'T... DON'T WORRY.
WOULD YOU LIKE SOME RICE CRACKERS?
I WAS JUST SO EXCITED THAT OUR FUTURE GENERATION WON THIS AMAZING OPPORTUNITY.
I MEAN, IT'S SOMETHING I COULDN'T EVEN IMAGINE DOING WHEN I WAS GROWING UP, WHEN WE DIDN'T HAVE ENOUGH TO EAT, YOU KNOW?
I TOTALLY UNDERSTAND. WE'RE AROUND THE SAME AGE, AREN'T WE? YOU MUST'VE BEEN A TEEN-AGER DURING THE WAR. WERE YOU DRAFTED?
THE FIRST YEAR OF SHOWA*. I WAS BORN RIGHT AFTER THE PREVIOUS EMPEROR DIED.
WOW, YOU'RE A RARE FIRST-YEARER! I'M A THIRD-YEARER, THE YEAR OF THE DRAGON.

*THE NAME OF AN ERA IN JAPAN WHEN THE SHOWA EMPEROR, HIROHITO, WAS IN REIGN. DECEMBER 25, 1926–JANUARY 7, 1989. THE NAME OF AN ERA TYPICALLY CHANGES WHEN THE REIGN OF A NEW EMPEROR BEGINS AFTER THE DEATH OF HIS PREDECESSOR. THERE WERE ONLY SEVEN DAYS IN THE FIRST YEAR OF SHOWA, WHICH WAS DECEMBER 25–31, 1926.

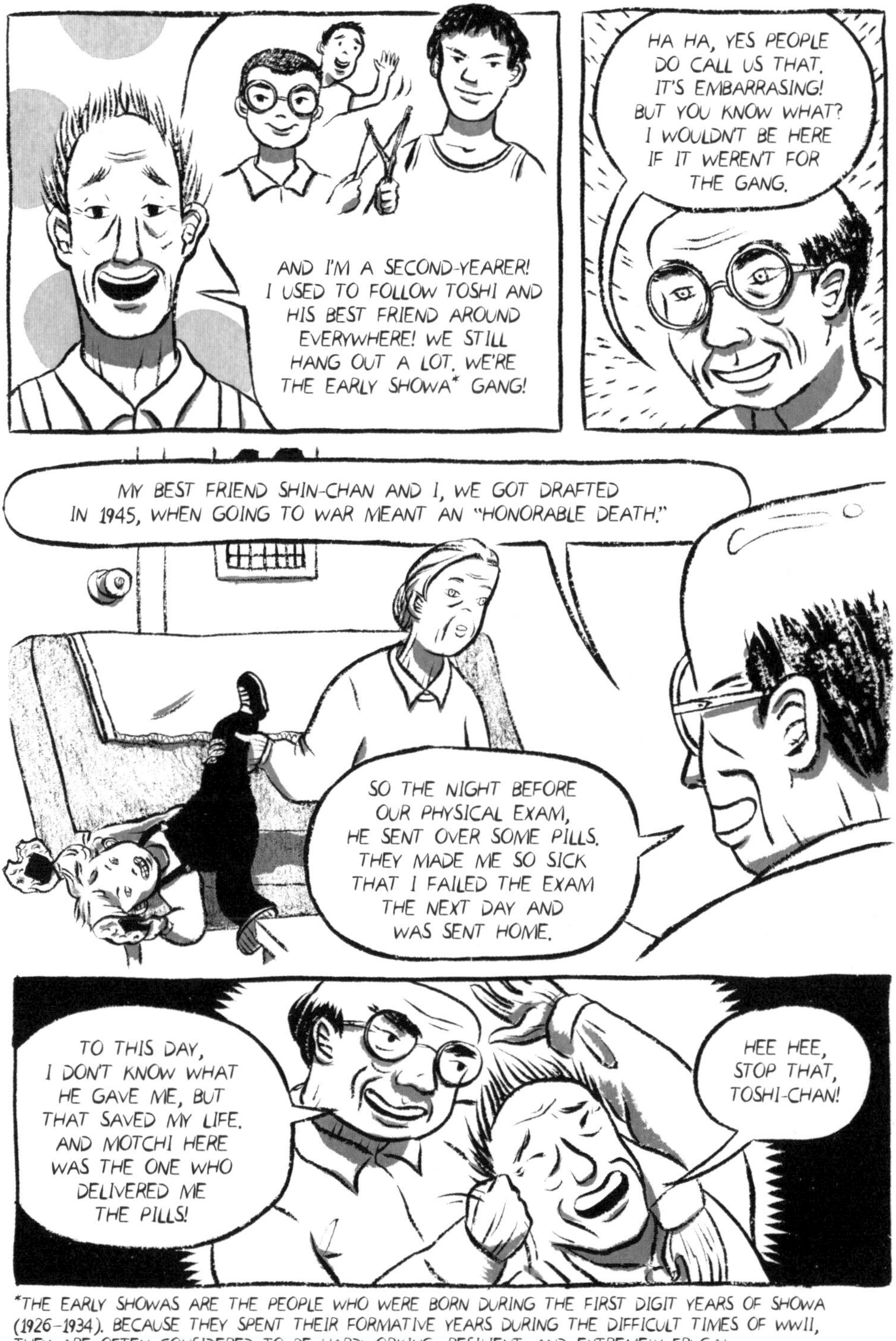
AND I'M A SECOND-YEARER! I USED TO FOLLOW TOSHI AND HIS BEST FRIEND AROUND EVERYWHERE! WE STILL HANG OUT A LOT. WE'RE THE EARLY SHOWA* GANG!
HA HA, YES PEOPLE DO CALL US THAT. IT'S EMBARRASING! BUT YOU KNOW WHAT? I WOULDN'T BE HERE IF IT WEREN'T FOR THE GANG.
MY BEST FRIEND SHIN-CHAN AND I, WE GOT DRAFTED IN 1945, WHEN GOING TO WAR MEANT AN "HONORABLE DEATH."
SO THE NIGHT BEFORE OUR PHYSICAL EXAM, HE SENT OVER SOME PILLS. THEY MADE ME SO SICK THAT I FAILED THE EXAM THE NEXT DAY AND WAS SENT HOME.
TO THIS DAY, I DON'T KNOW WHAT HE GAVE ME, BUT THAT SAVED MY LIFE. AND MOTCHI HERE WAS THE ONE WHO DELIVERED ME THE PILLS!
HEE HEE, STOP THAT, TOSHI-CHAN!

*THE EARLY SHOWAS ARE THE PEOPLE WHO WERE BORN DURING THE FIRST DIGIT YEARS OF SHOWA (1926–1934). BECAUSE THEY SPENT THEIR FORMATIVE YEARS DURING THE DIFFICULT TIMES OF WWII, THEY ARE OFTEN CONSIDERED TO BE HARDWORKING, RESILIENT, AND EXTREMELY FRUGAL.

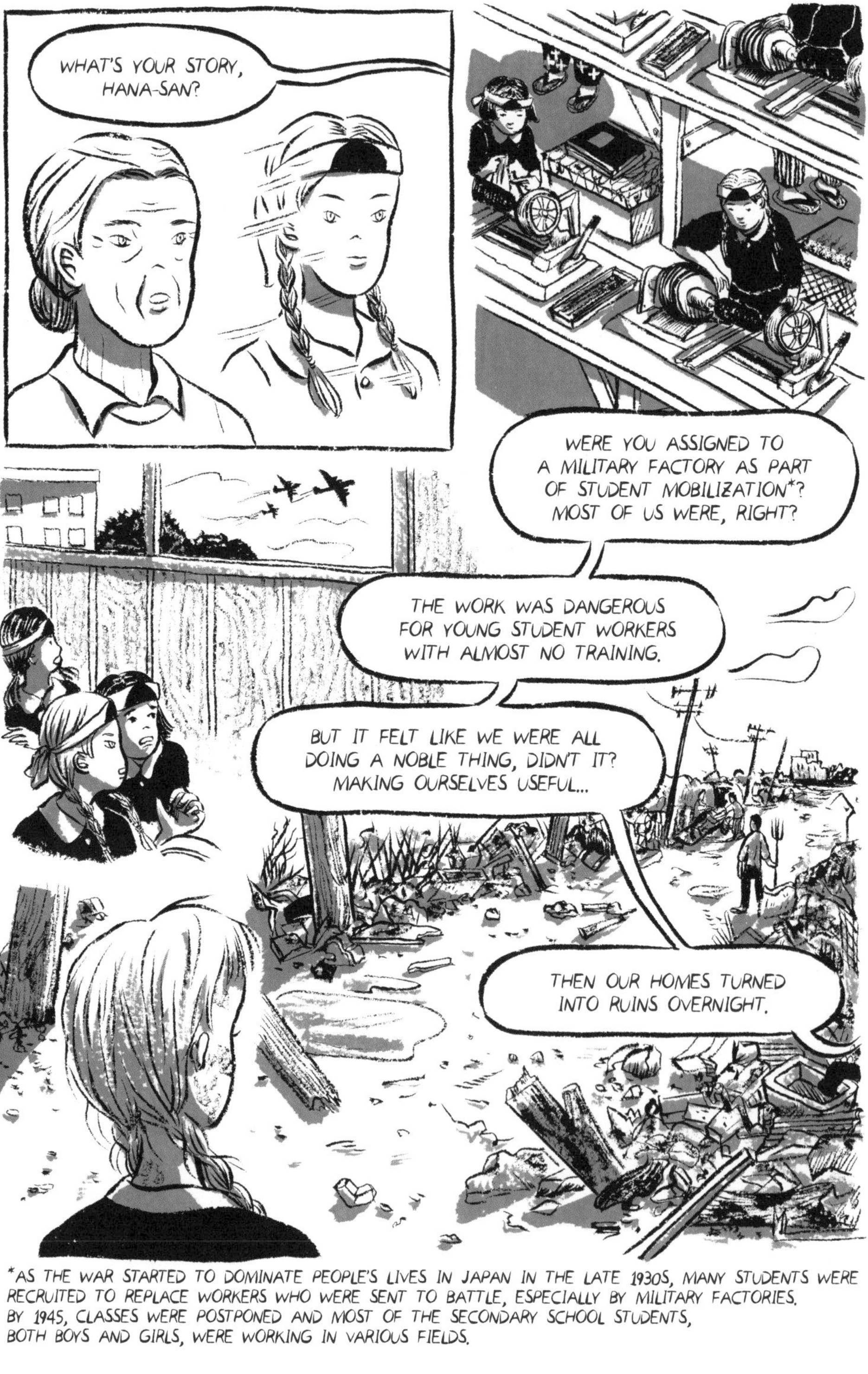
WHAT'S YOUR STORY, HANA-SAN?
WERE YOU ASSIGNED TO A MILITARY FACTORY AS PART OF STUDENT MOBILIZATION*? MOST OF US WERE, RIGHT?
THE WORK WAS DANGEROUS FOR YOUNG STUDENT WORKERS WITH ALMOST NO TRAINING.
BUT IT FELT LIKE WE WERE ALL DOING A NOBLE THING, DIDN'T IT? MAKING OURSELVES USEFUL...
THEN OUR HOMES TURNED INTO RUINS OVERNIGHT.

*AS THE WAR STARTED TO DOMINATE PEOPLE'S LIVES IN JAPAN IN THE LATE 1930S, MANY STUDENTS WERE RECRUITED TO REPLACE WORKERS WHO WERE SENT TO BATTLE, ESPECIALLY BY MILITARY FACTORIES. BY 1945, CLASSES WERE POSTPONED AND MOST OF THE SECONDARY SCHOOL STUDENTS, BOTH BOYS AND GIRLS, WERE WORKING IN VARIOUS FIELDS.

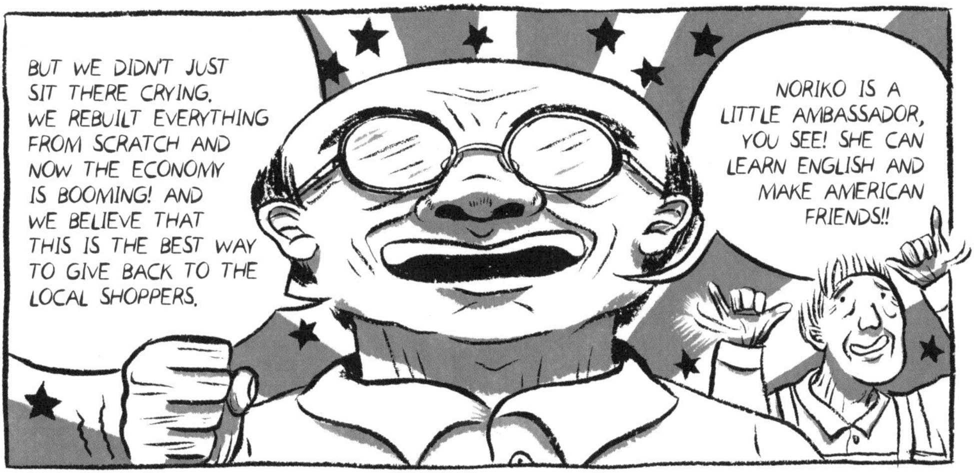
BUT WE DIDN'T JUST SIT THERE CRYING. WE REBUILT EVERYTHING FROM SCRATCH AND NOW THE ECONOMY IS BOOMING! AND WE BELIEVE THAT THIS IS THE BEST WAY TO GIVE BACK TO THE LOCAL SHOPPERS.
NORIKO IS A LITTLE AMBASSADOR, YOU SEE! SHE CAN LEARN ENGLISH AND MAKE AMERICAN FRIENDS!!

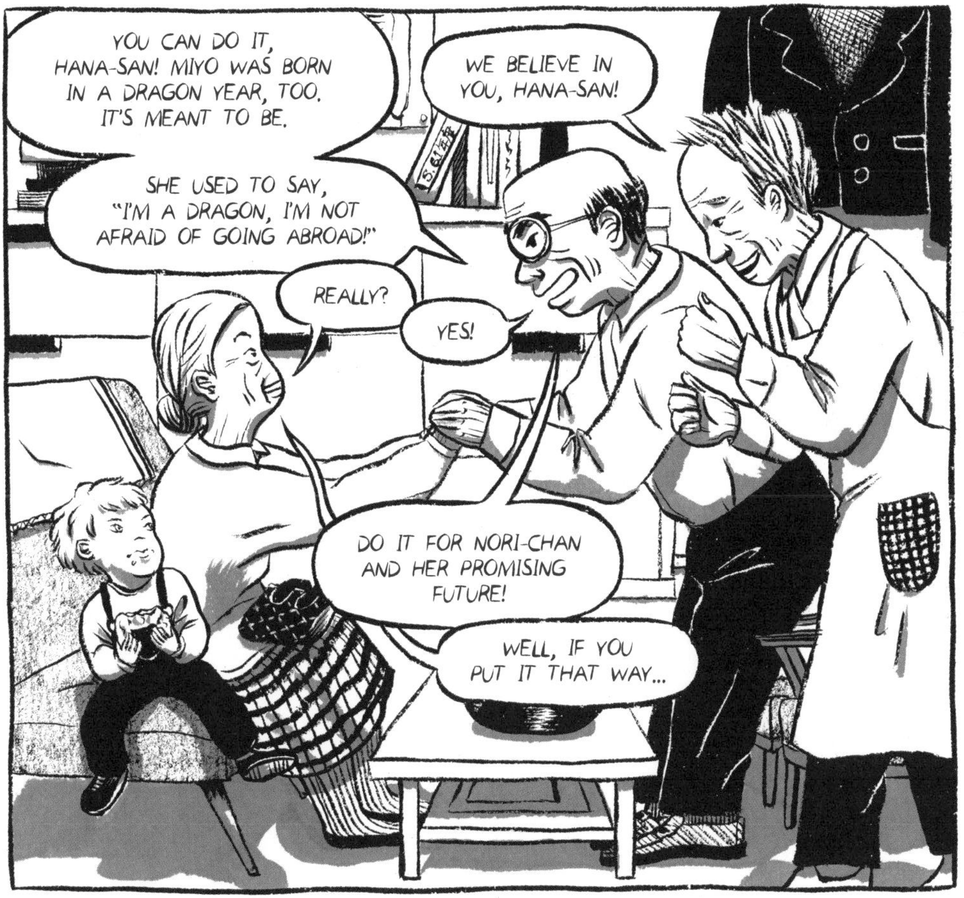
YOU CAN DO IT, HANA-SAN! MIYO WAS BORN IN A DRAGON YEAR, TOO. IT'S MEANT TO BE.
WE BELIEVE IN YOU, HANA-SAN!
SHE USED TO SAY, "I'M A DRAGON, I'M NOT AFRAID OF GOING ABROAD!"
REALLY?
YES!
DO IT FOR NORI-CHAN AND HER PROMISING FUTURE!
WELL, IF YOU PUT IT THAT WAY...

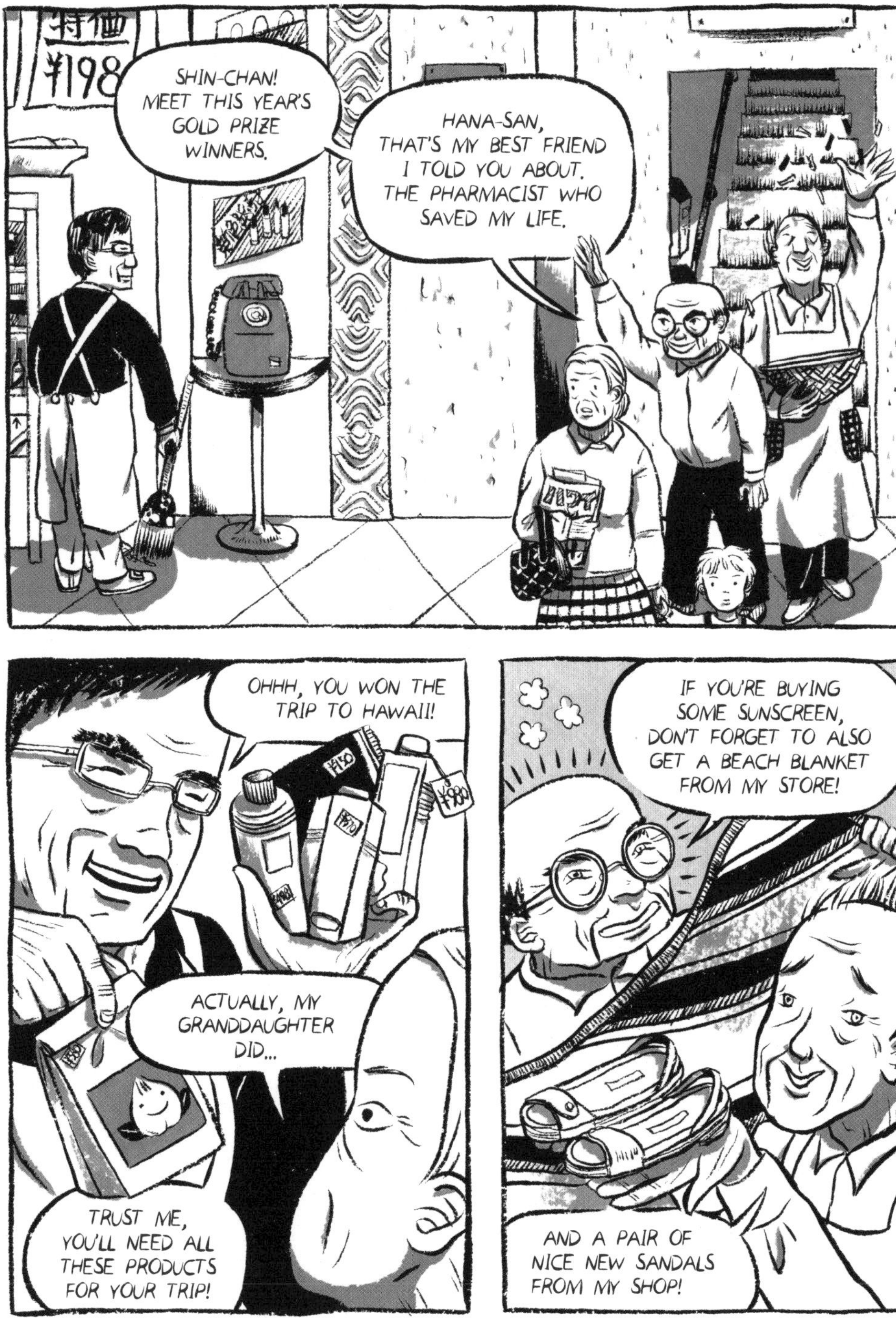
特価
¥198
SHIN-CHAN! MEET THIS YEAR'S GOLD PRIZE WINNERS.
HANA-SAN, THAT'S MY BEST FRIEND I TOLD YOU ABOUT. THE PHARMACIST WHO SAVED MY LIFE.
OHHH, YOU WON THE TRIP TO HAWAII!
ACTUALLY, MY GRANDDAUGHTER DID...
TRUST ME, YOU'LL NEED ALL THESE PRODUCTS FOR YOUR TRIP!
IF YOU'RE BUYING SOME SUNSCREEN, DON'T FORGET TO ALSO GET A BEACH BLANKET FROM MY STORE!
AND A PAIR OF NICE NEW SANDALS FROM MY SHOP!

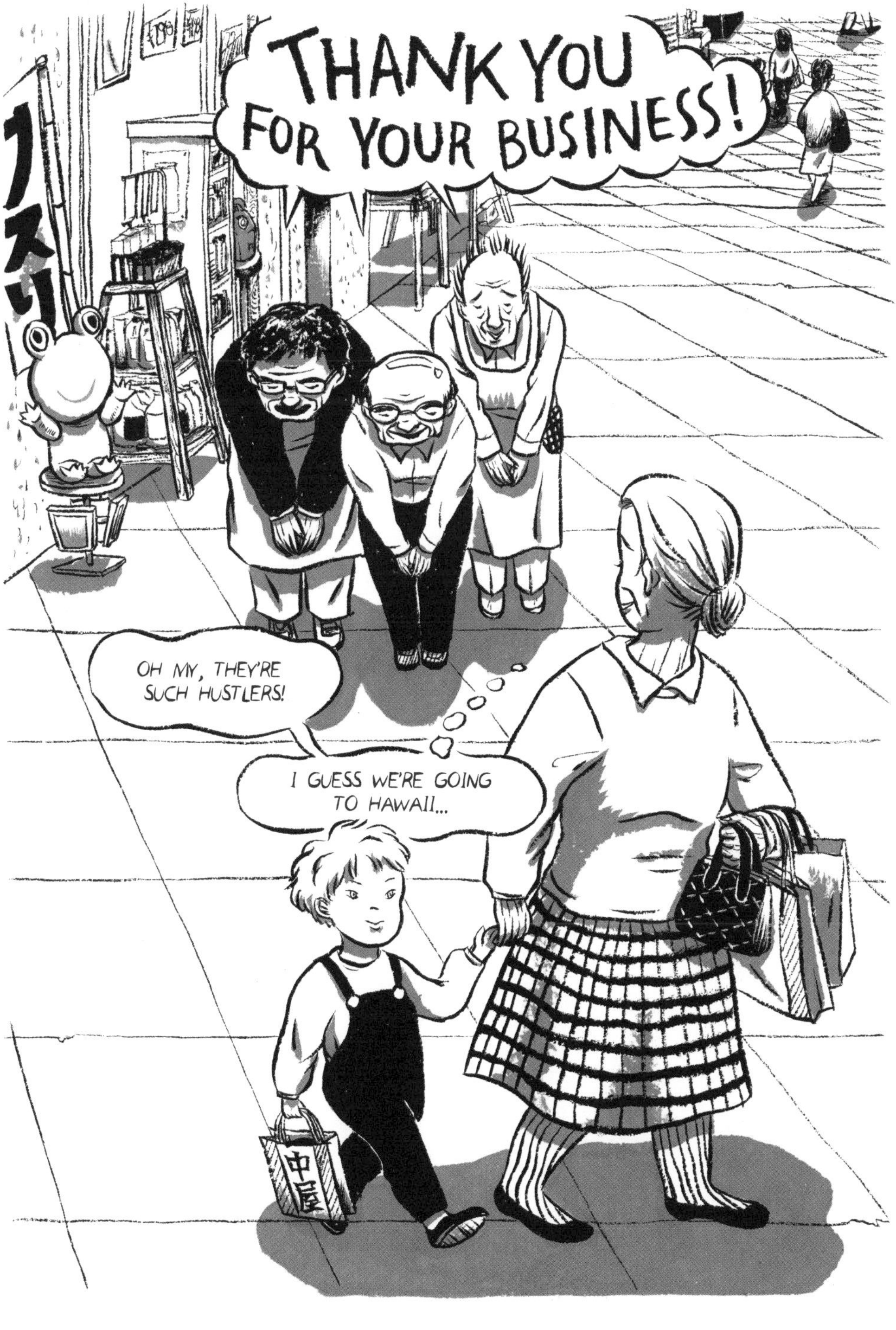
クスリ
THANK YOU FOR YOUR BUSINESS!
OH MY, THEY'RE SUCH HUSTLERS!
I GUESS WE'RE GOING TO HAWAII...
中屋

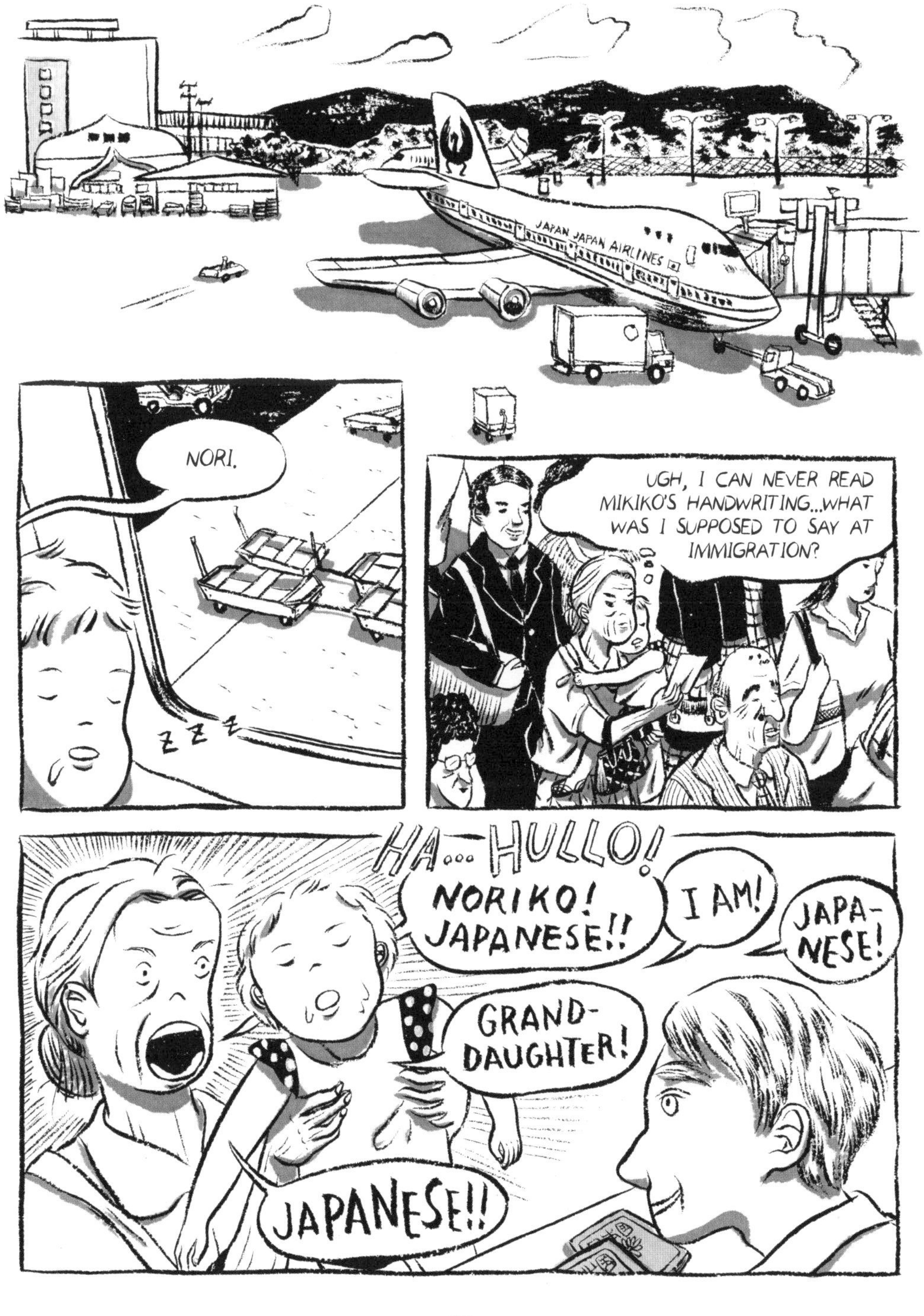
JAPAN JAPAN AIRLINES
NORI.
Z Z Z
UGH, I CAN NEVER READ MIKIKO'S HANDWRITING...WHAT WAS I SUPPOSED TO SAY AT IMMIGRATION?
HA... HULLO!
NORIKO! JAPANESE!!
I AM!
JAPA-NESE!
GRAND-DAUGHTER!
JAPANESE!!

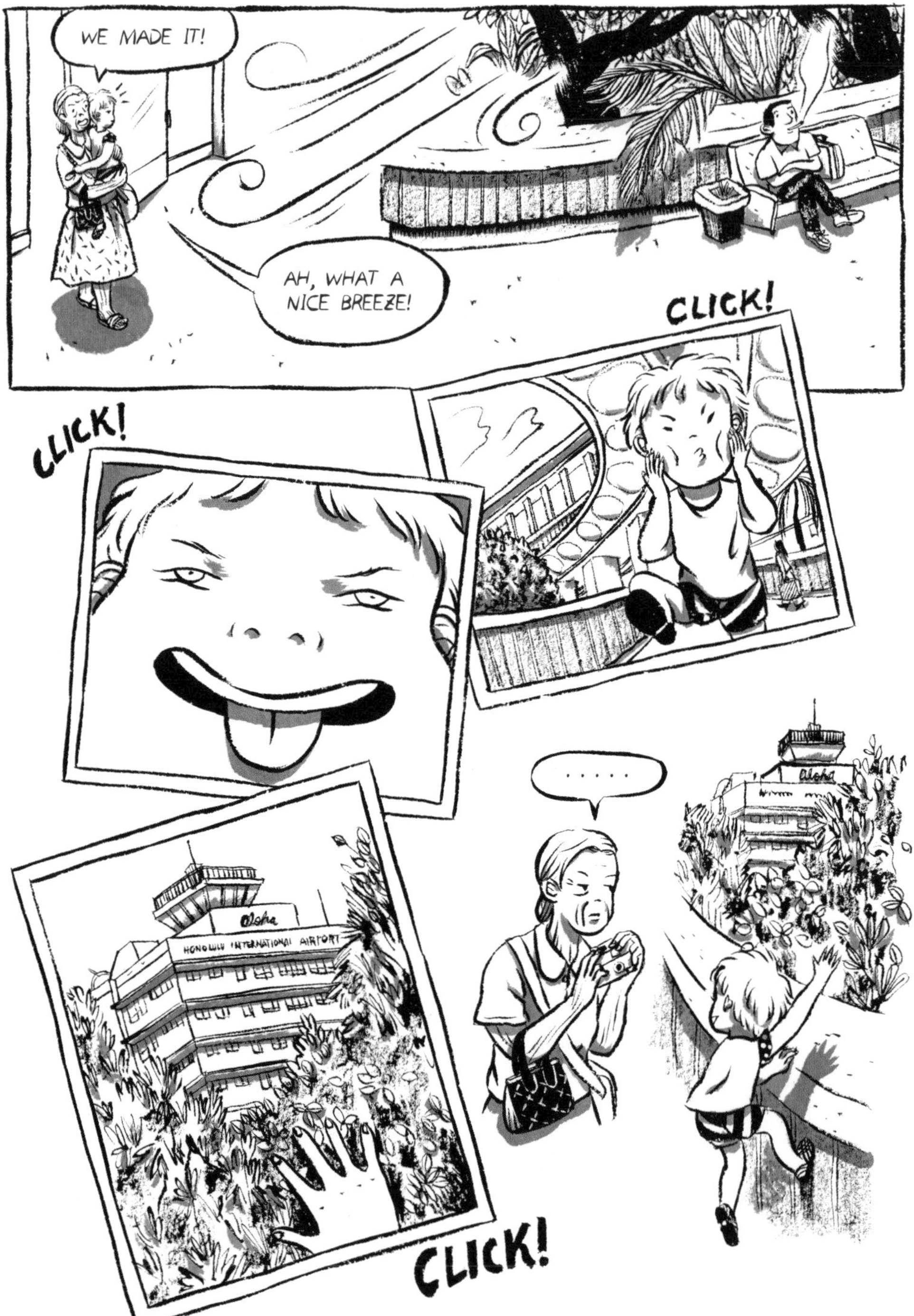
WE MADE IT!
AH, WHAT A NICE BREEZE!
CLICK!
CLICK!
. . . . .
Aloha
HONOLULU INTERNATIONAL AIRPORT
CLICK!

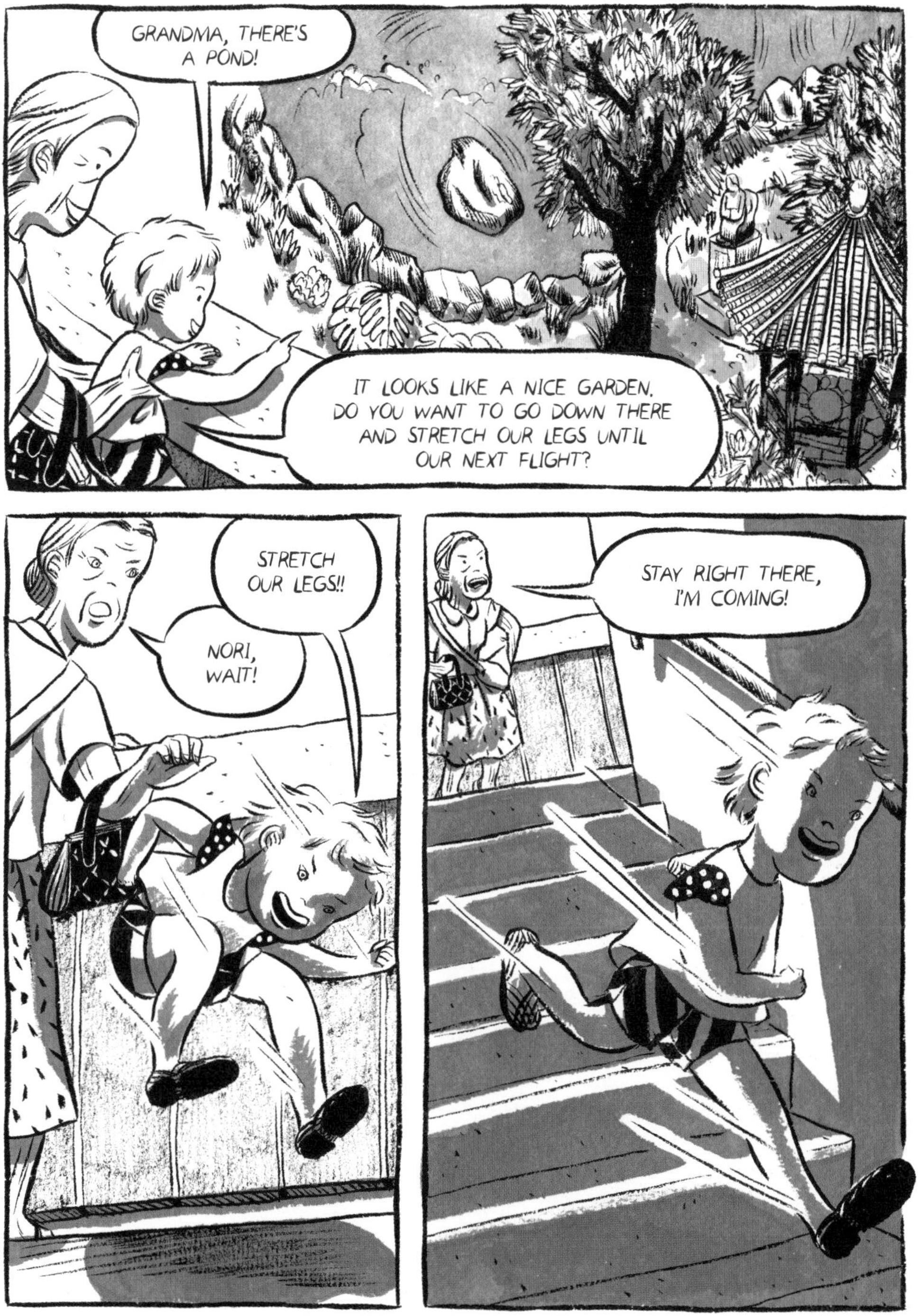
GRANDMA, THERE'S A POND!
IT LOOKS LIKE A NICE GARDEN. DO YOU WANT TO GO DOWN THERE AND STRETCH OUR LEGS UNTIL OUR NEXT FLIGHT?
STRETCH OUR LEGS!!
NORI, WAIT!
STAY RIGHT THERE, I'M COMING!

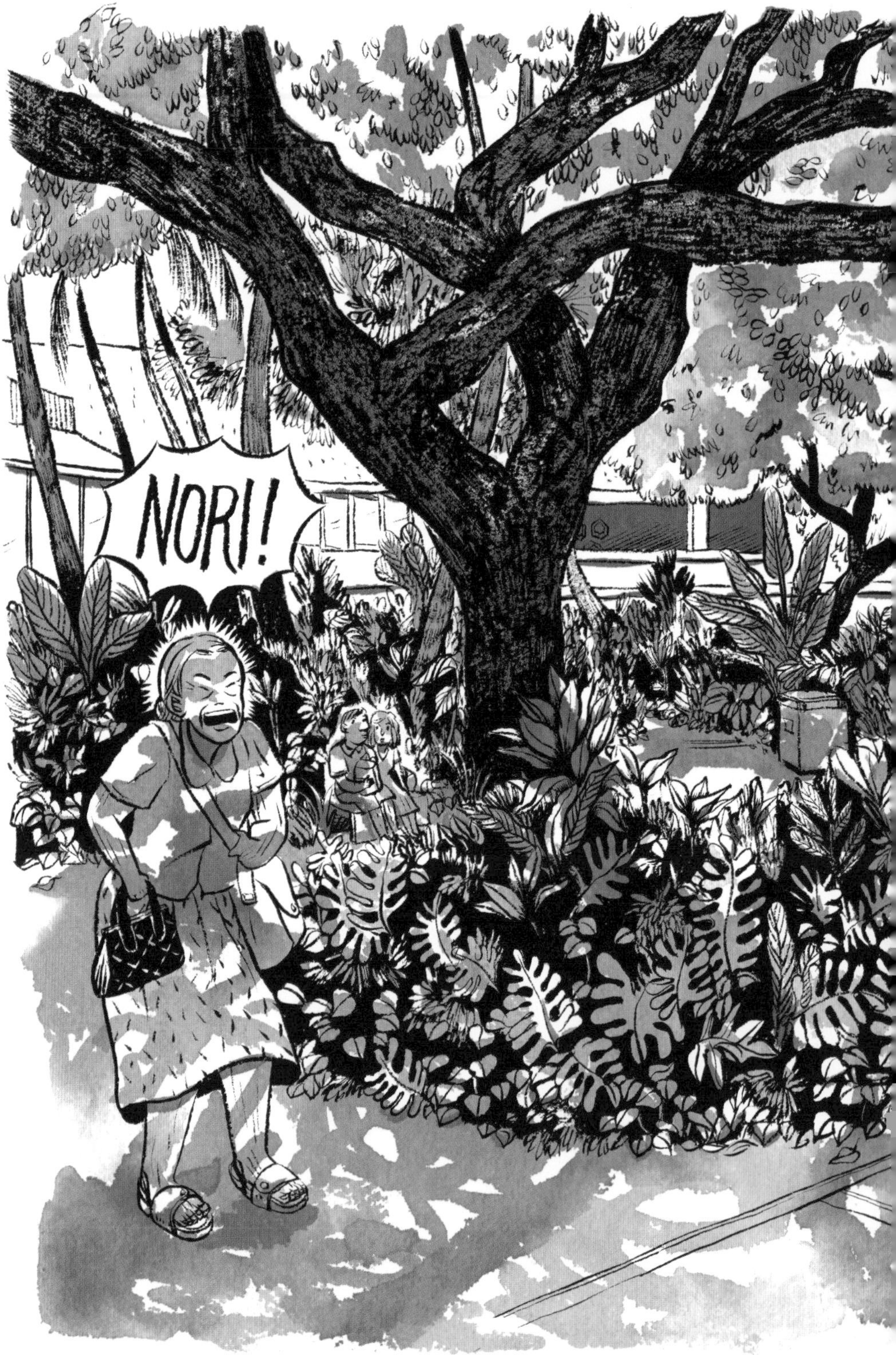
NORI!

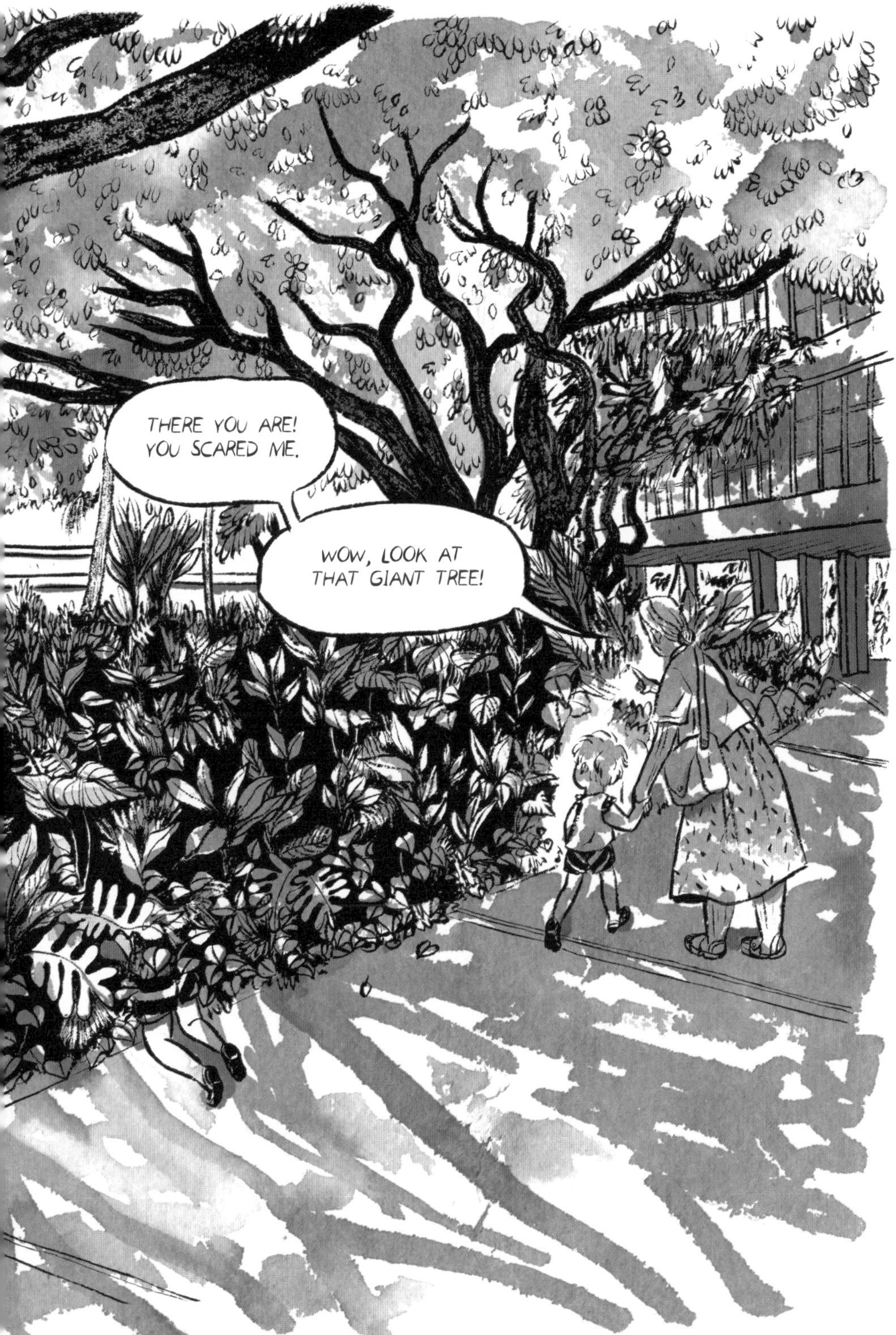
THERE YOU ARE! YOU SCARED ME.
WOW, LOOK AT THAT GIANT TREE!

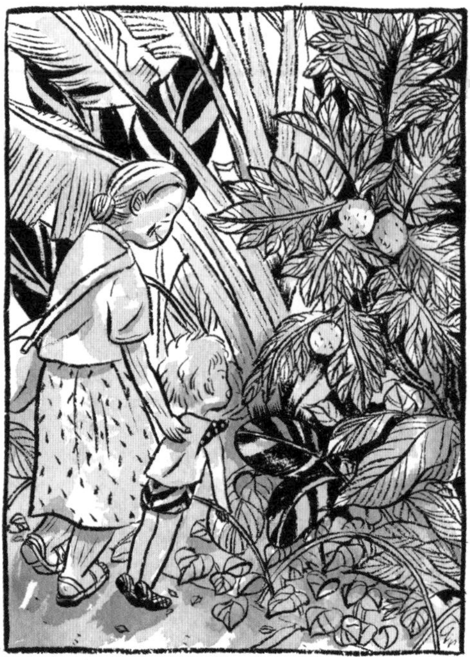

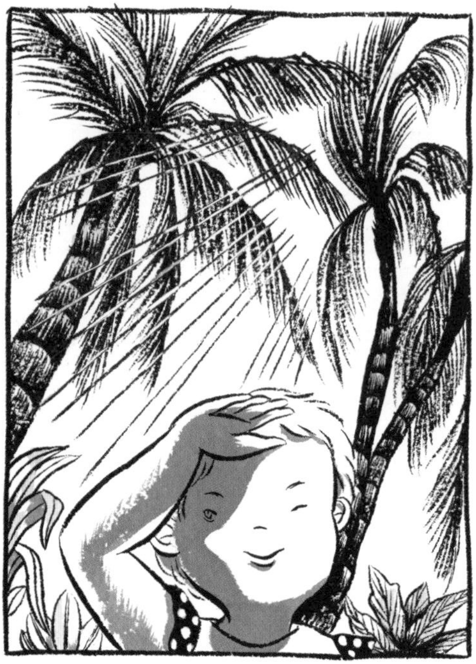

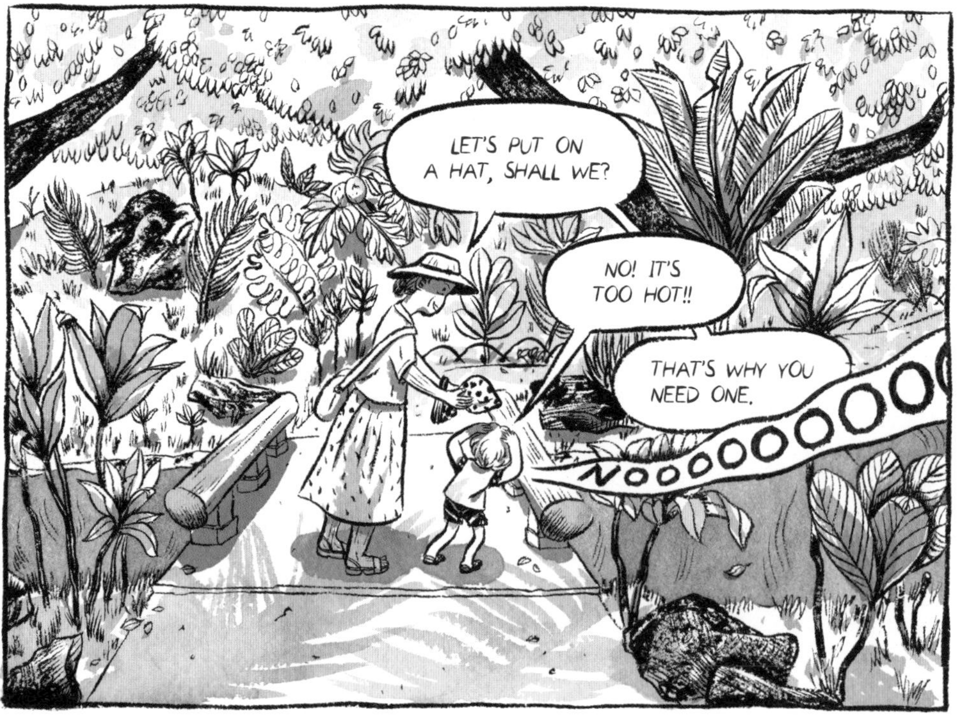
LET'S PUT ON A HAT, SHALL WE?
NO! IT'S TOO HOT!!
THAT'S WHY YOU NEED ONE.
NOOOOOOOOOOOOO

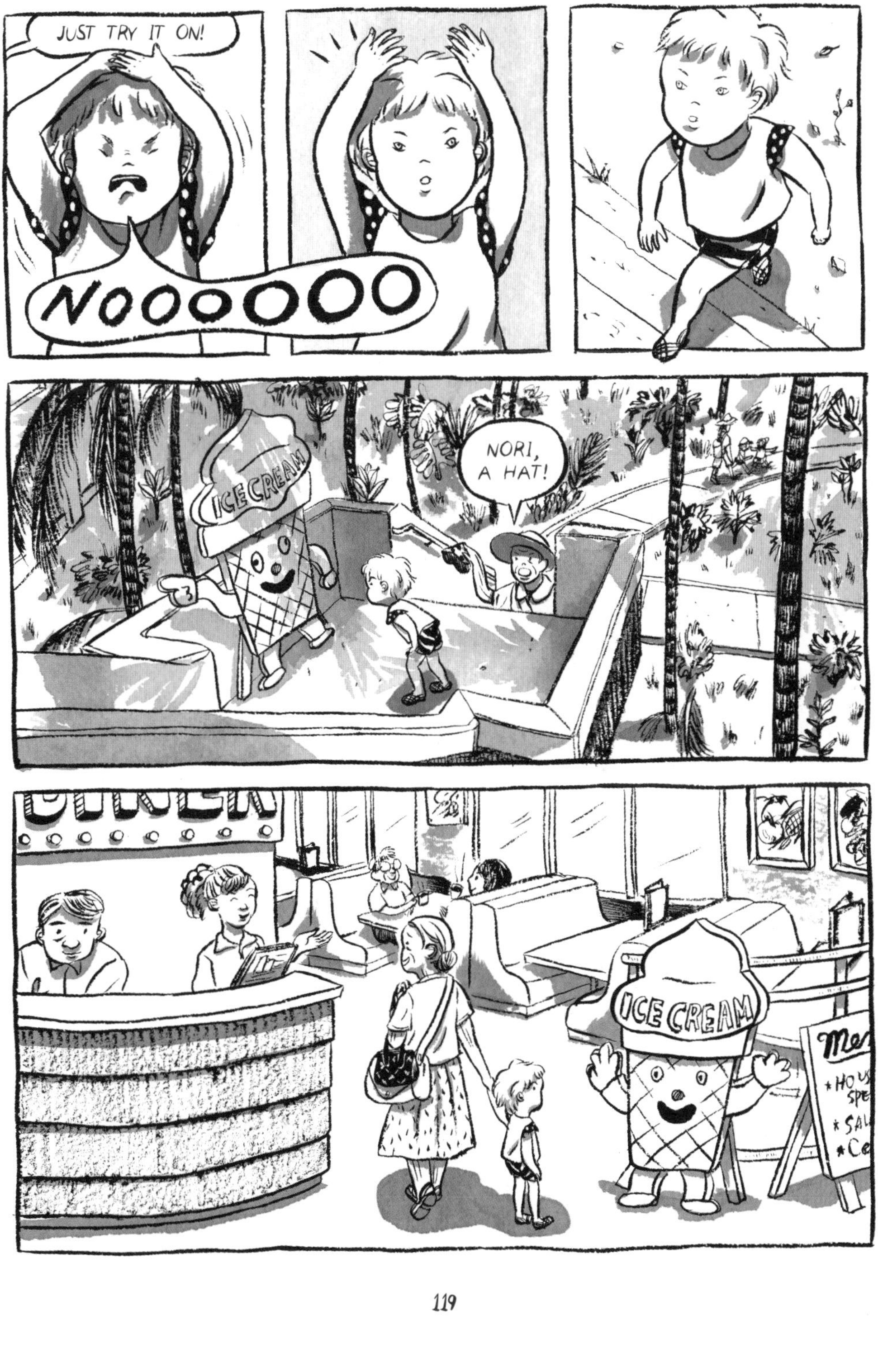
JUST TRY IT ON!
NOOOOOO
ICECREAM
NORI, A HAT!
ICE CREAM

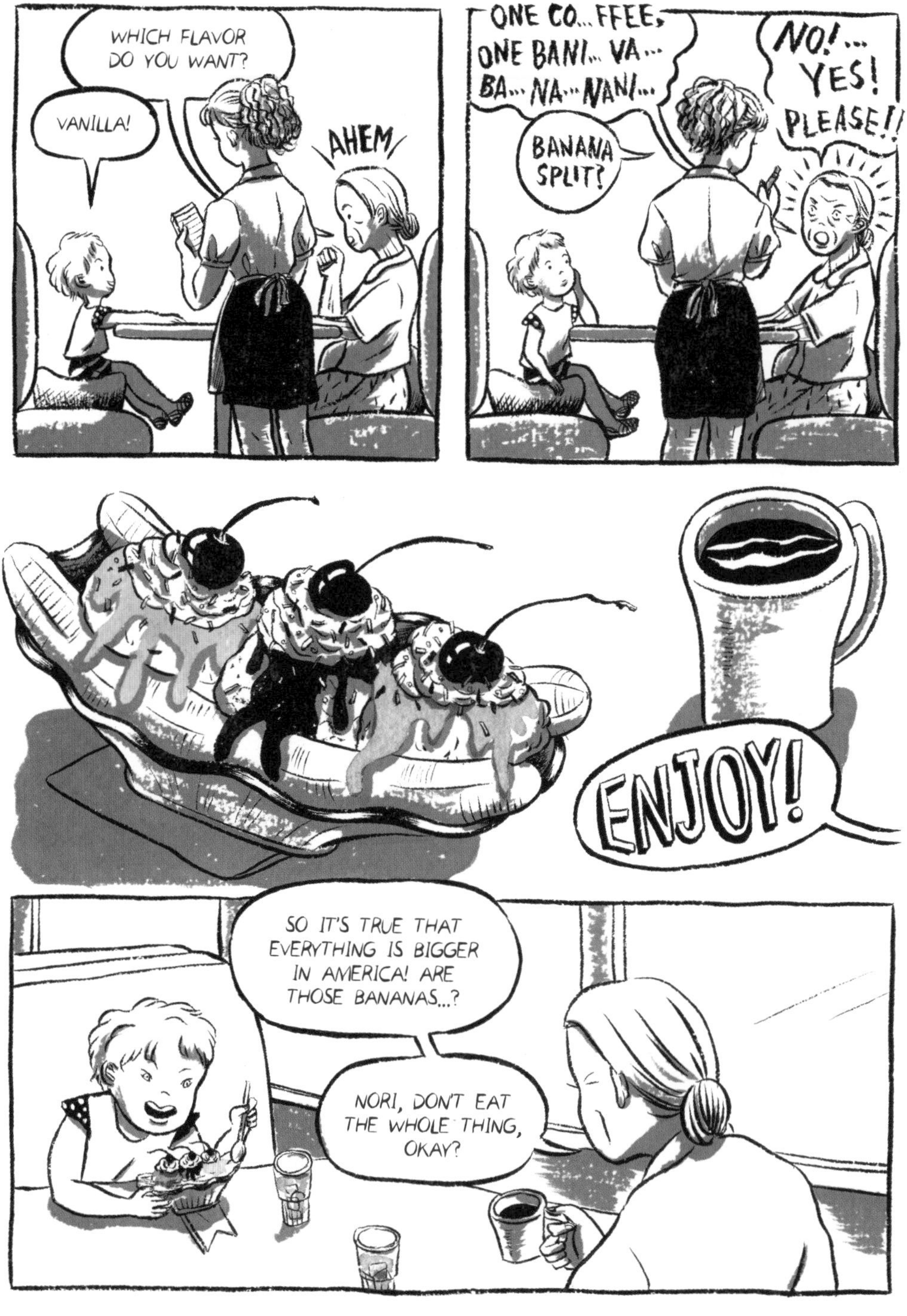
WHICH FLAVOR DO YOU WANT?
VANILLA!
AHEM
ONE CO... FFEE, ONE BANI... VA... BA... NA... NANI...
BANANA SPLIT?
NO! ... YES! PLEASE!!
ENJOY!
SO IT'S TRUE THAT EVERYTHING IS BIGGER IN AMERICA! ARE THOSE BANANAS...?
NORI, DON'T EAT THE WHOLE THING, OKAY?

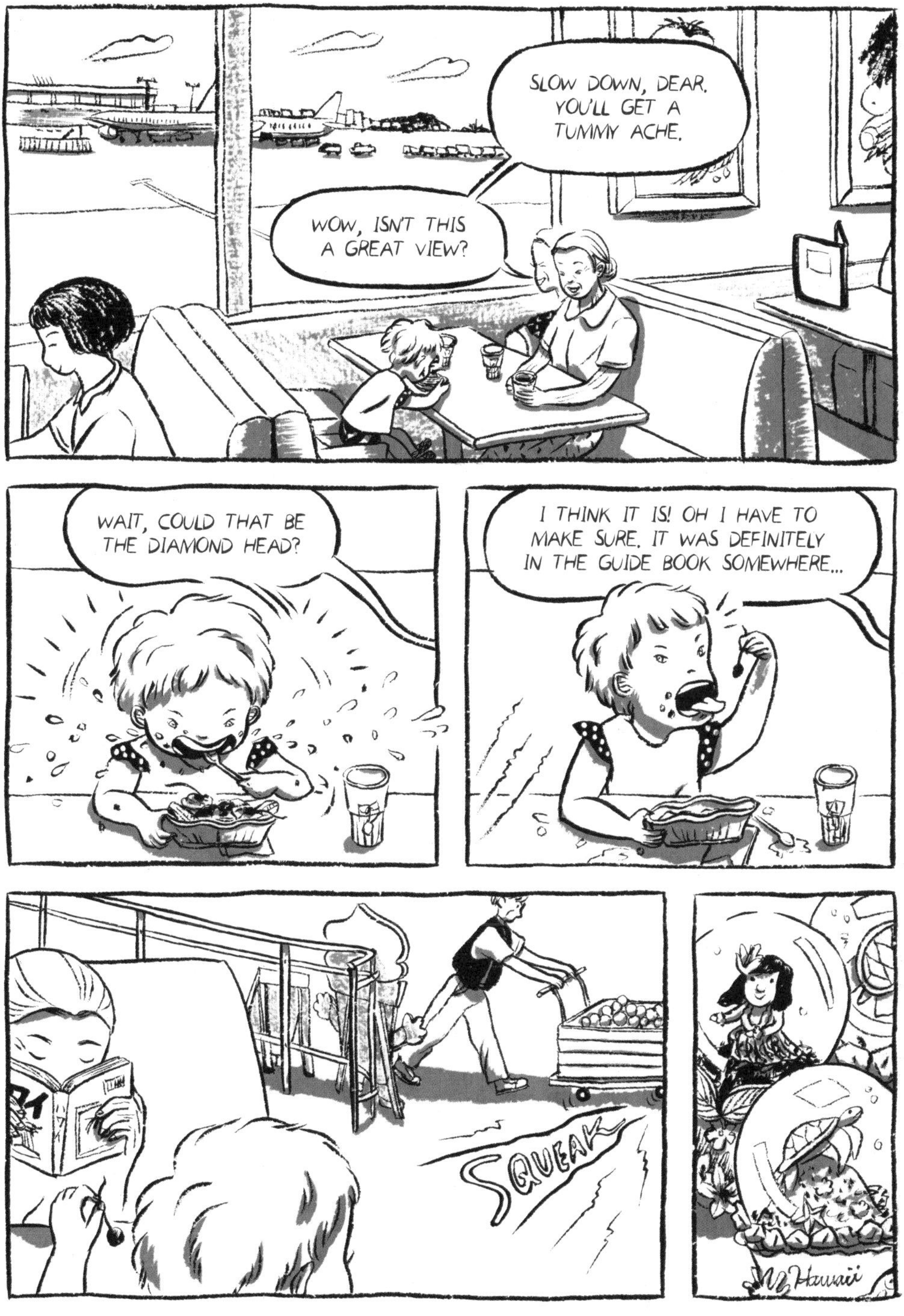
WOW, ISN'T THIS A GREAT VIEW?
SLOW DOWN, DEAR. YOU'LL GET A TUMMY ACHE.
WAIT, COULD THAT BE THE DIAMOND HEAD?
I THINK IT IS! OH I HAVE TO MAKE SURE. IT WAS DEFINITELY IN THE GUIDE BOOK SOMEWHERE...
SQUEAK
Hawaii

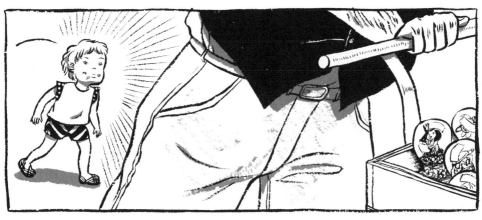

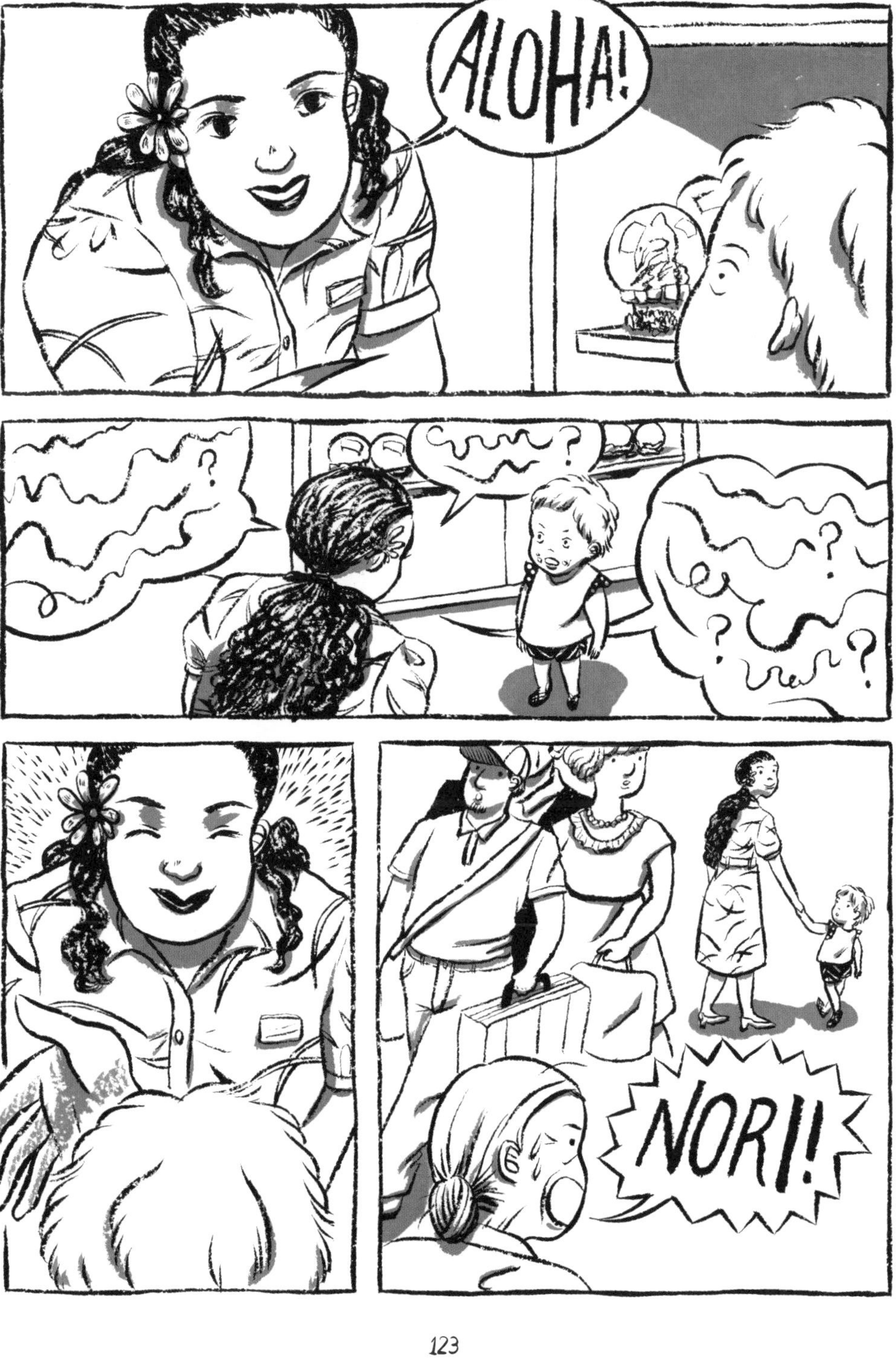
ALOHA!
NORI!

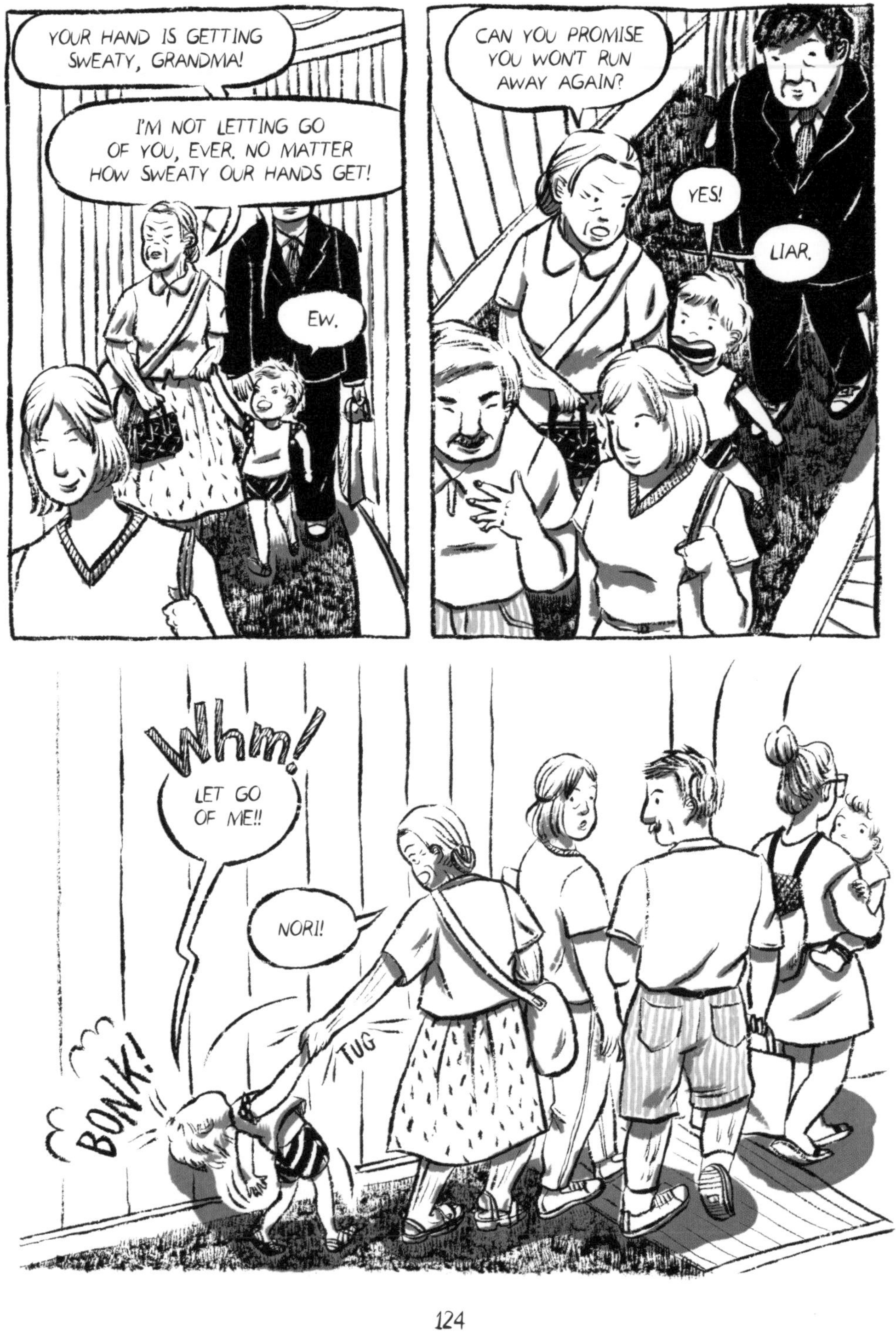
YOUR HAND IS GETTING SWEATY, GRANDMA!
I'M NOT LETTING GO OF YOU, EVER. NO MATTER HOW SWEATY OUR HANDS GET!
EW.
CAN YOU PROMISE YOU WON'T RUN AWAY AGAIN?
YES!
LIAR.
Whm!
LET GO OF ME!!
NORI!
TUG
BONK!

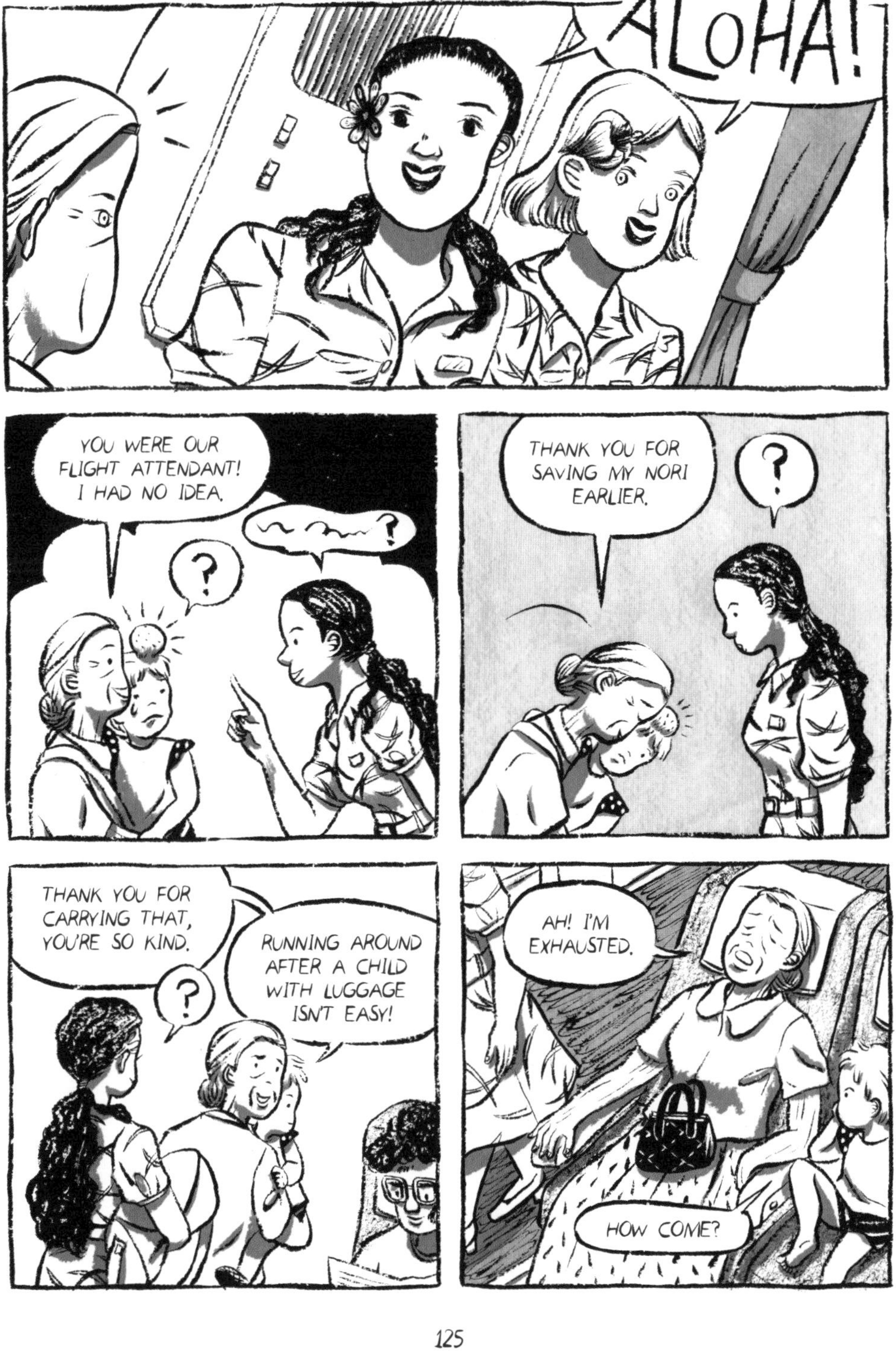
ALOHA!
YOU WERE OUR FLIGHT ATTENDANT! I HAD NO IDEA.
?
?
THANK YOU FOR SAVING MY NORI EARLIER.
?
THANK YOU FOR CARRYING THAT, YOU'RE SO KIND.
?
RUNNING AROUND AFTER A CHILD WITH LUGGAGE ISN'T EASY!
AH! I'M EXHAUSTED.
HOW COME?

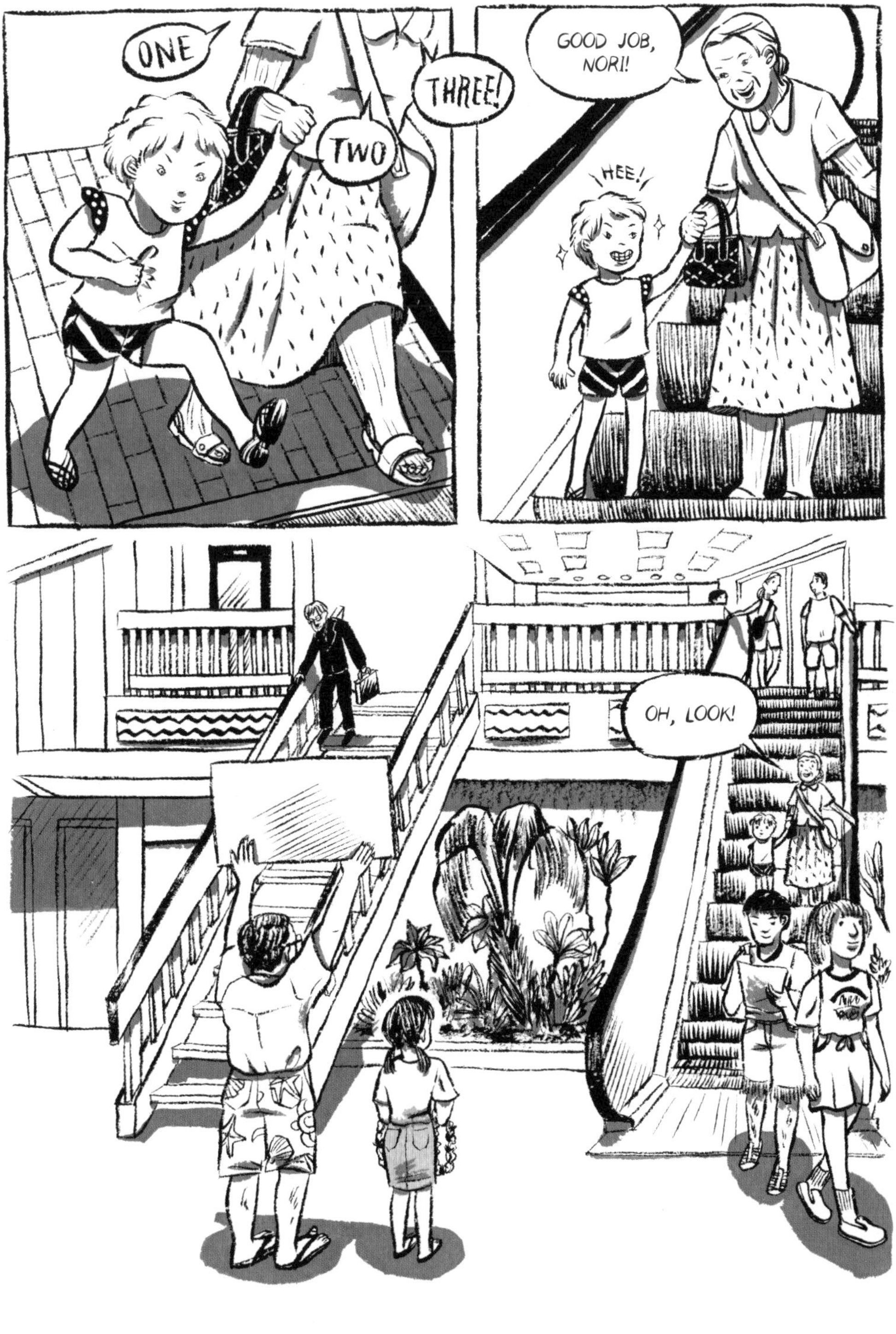
ONE
TWO
THREE!
GOOD JOB, NORI!
HEE!
OH, LOOK!

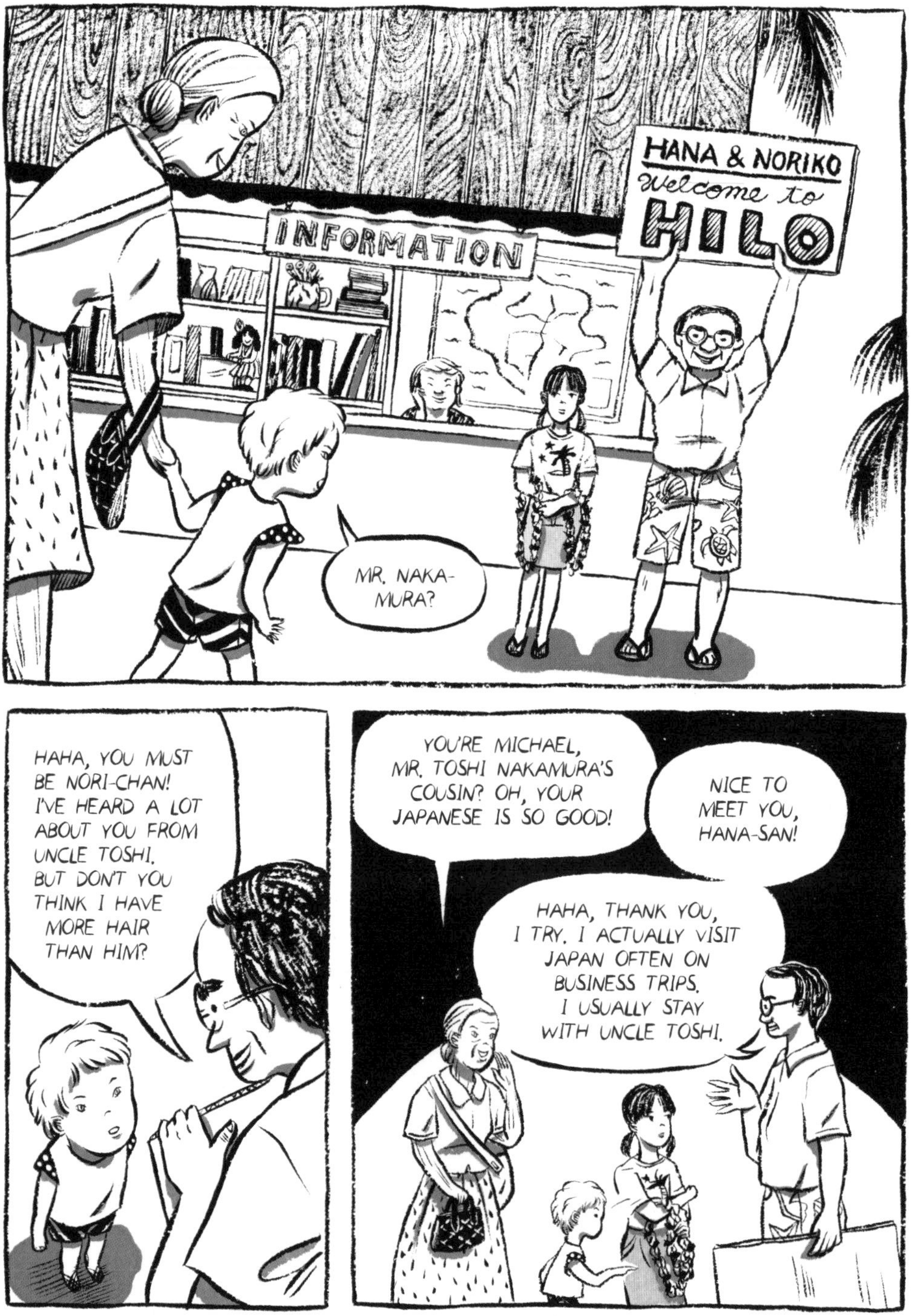
HANA & NORIKO
Welcome to
HILO
INFORMATION
MR. NAKA-MURA?
HAHA, YOU MUST BE NORI-CHAN! I'VE HEARD A LOT ABOUT YOU FROM UNCLE TOSHI. BUT DON'T YOU THINK I HAVE MORE HAIR THAN HIM?
YOU'RE MICHAEL, MR. TOSHI NAKAMURA'S COUSIN? OH, YOUR JAPANESE IS SO GOOD!
NICE TO MEET YOU, HANA-SAN!
HAHA, THANK YOU, I TRY. I ACTUALLY VISIT JAPAN OFTEN ON BUSINESS TRIPS. I USUALLY STAY WITH UNCLE TOSHI.

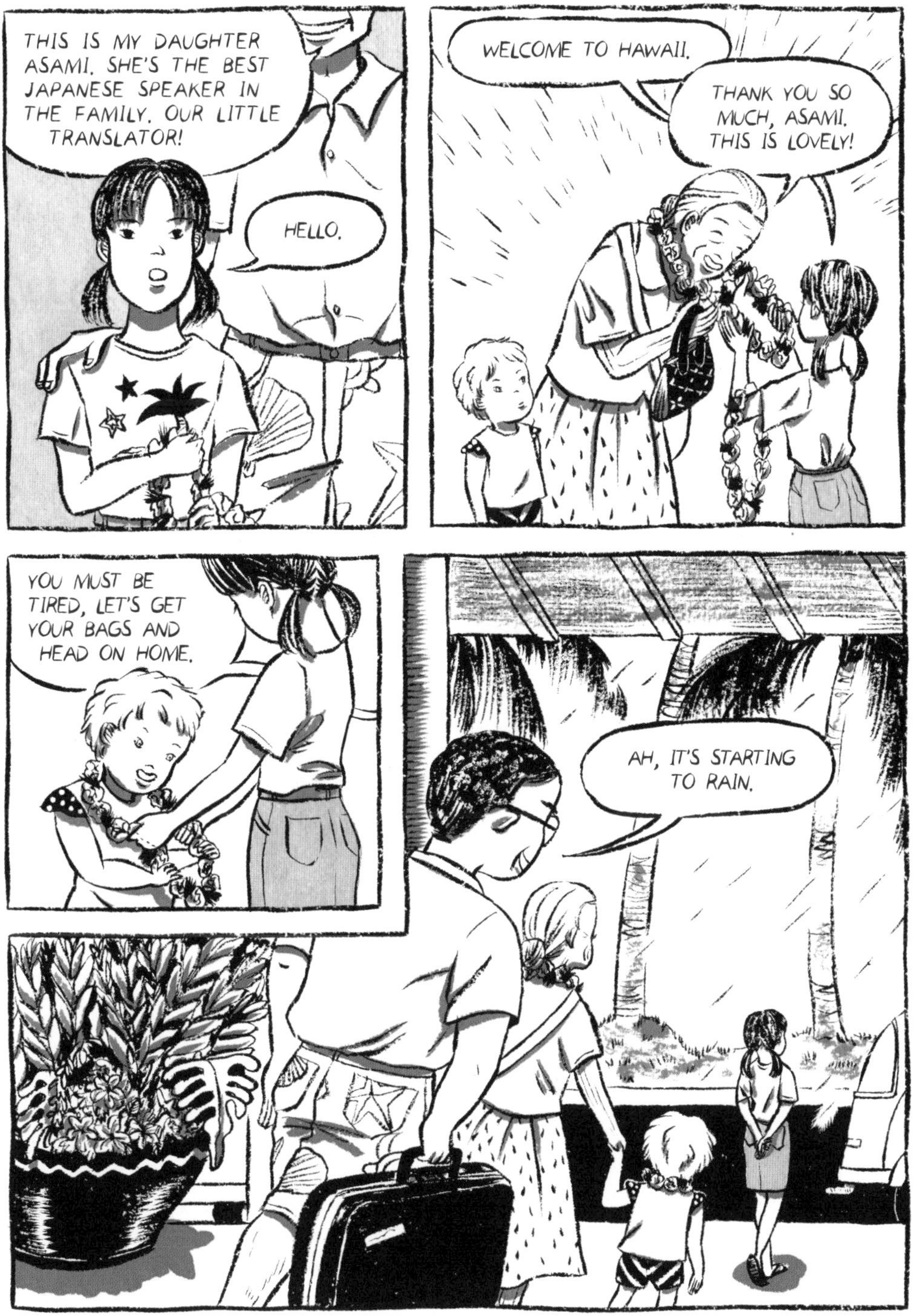
THIS IS MY DAUGHTER ASAMI. SHE'S THE BEST JAPANESE SPEAKER IN THE FAMILY. OUR LITTLE TRANSLATOR!
HELLO.
WELCOME TO HAWAII.
THANK YOU SO MUCH, ASAMI. THIS IS LOVELY!
YOU MUST BE TIRED, LET'S GET YOUR BAGS AND HEAD ON HOME.
AH, IT'S STARTING TO RAIN.

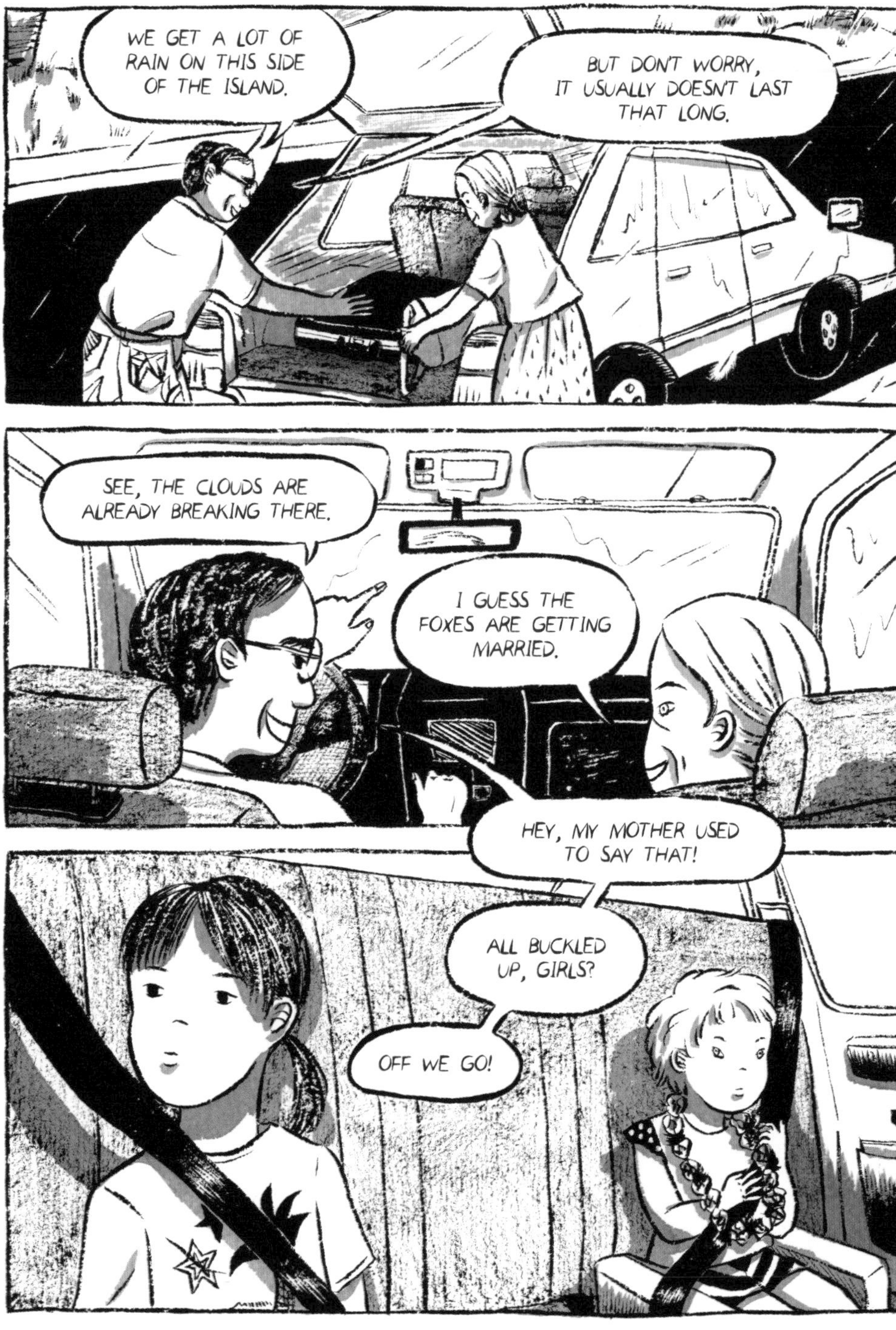
WE GET A LOT OF RAIN ON THIS SIDE OF THE ISLAND.
BUT DON'T WORRY, IT USUALLY DOESN'T LAST THAT LONG.
SEE, THE CLOUDS ARE ALREADY BREAKING THERE.
I GUESS THE FOXES ARE GETTING MARRIED.
HEY, MY MOTHER USED TO SAY THAT!
ALL BUCKLED UP, GIRLS?
OFF WE GO!

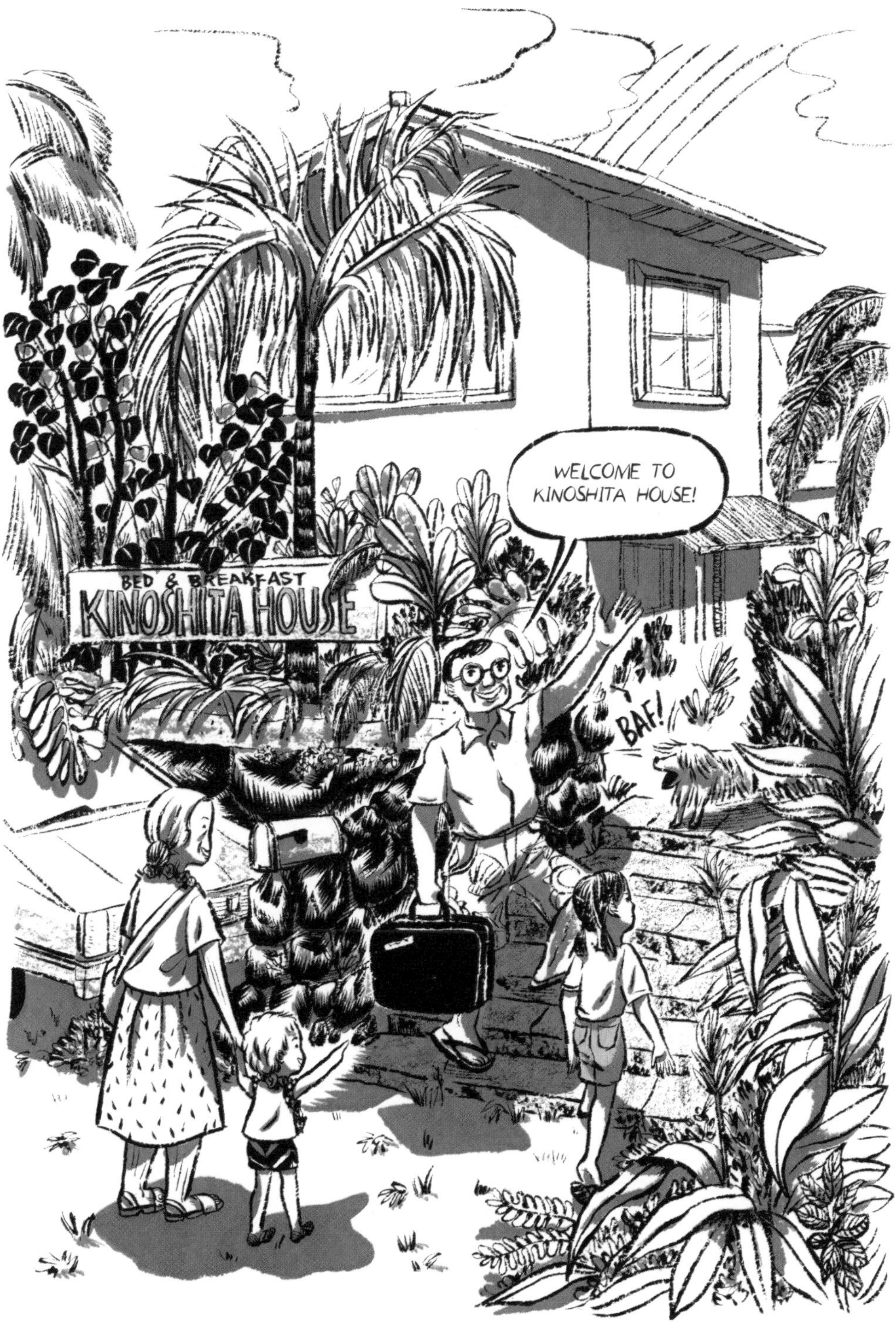
BED & BREAKFAST
KINOSHITA HOUSE
WELCOME TO KINOSHITA HOUSE!
BAF!

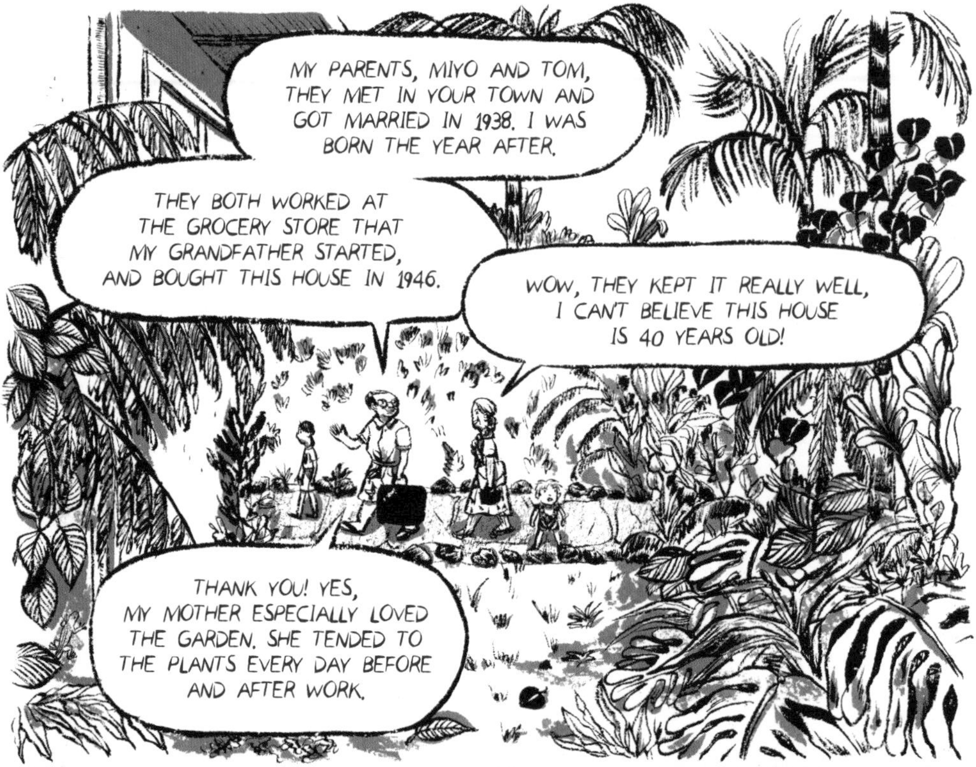
MY PARENTS, MIYO AND TOM, THEY MET IN YOUR TOWN AND GOT MARRIED IN 1938. I WAS BORN THE YEAR AFTER.
THEY BOTH WORKED AT THE GROCERY STORE THAT MY GRANDFATHER STARTED, AND BOUGHT THIS HOUSE IN 1946.
WOW, THEY KEPT IT REALLY WELL, I CAN'T BELIEVE THIS HOUSE IS 40 YEARS OLD!
THANK YOU! YES, MY MOTHER ESPECIALLY LOVED THE GARDEN. SHE TENDED TO THE PLANTS EVERY DAY BEFORE AND AFTER WORK.

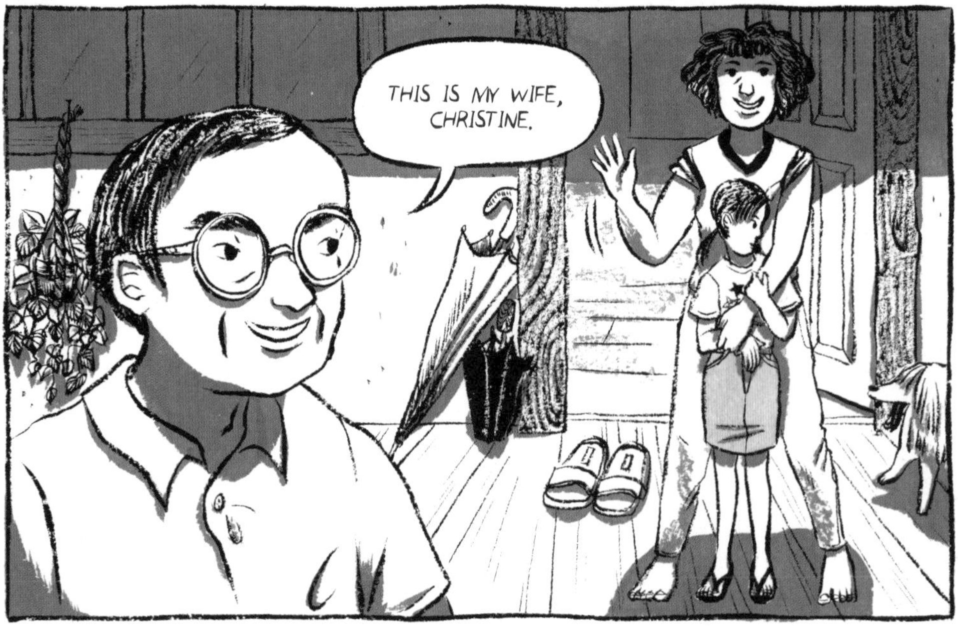
THIS IS MY WIFE, CHRISTINE.

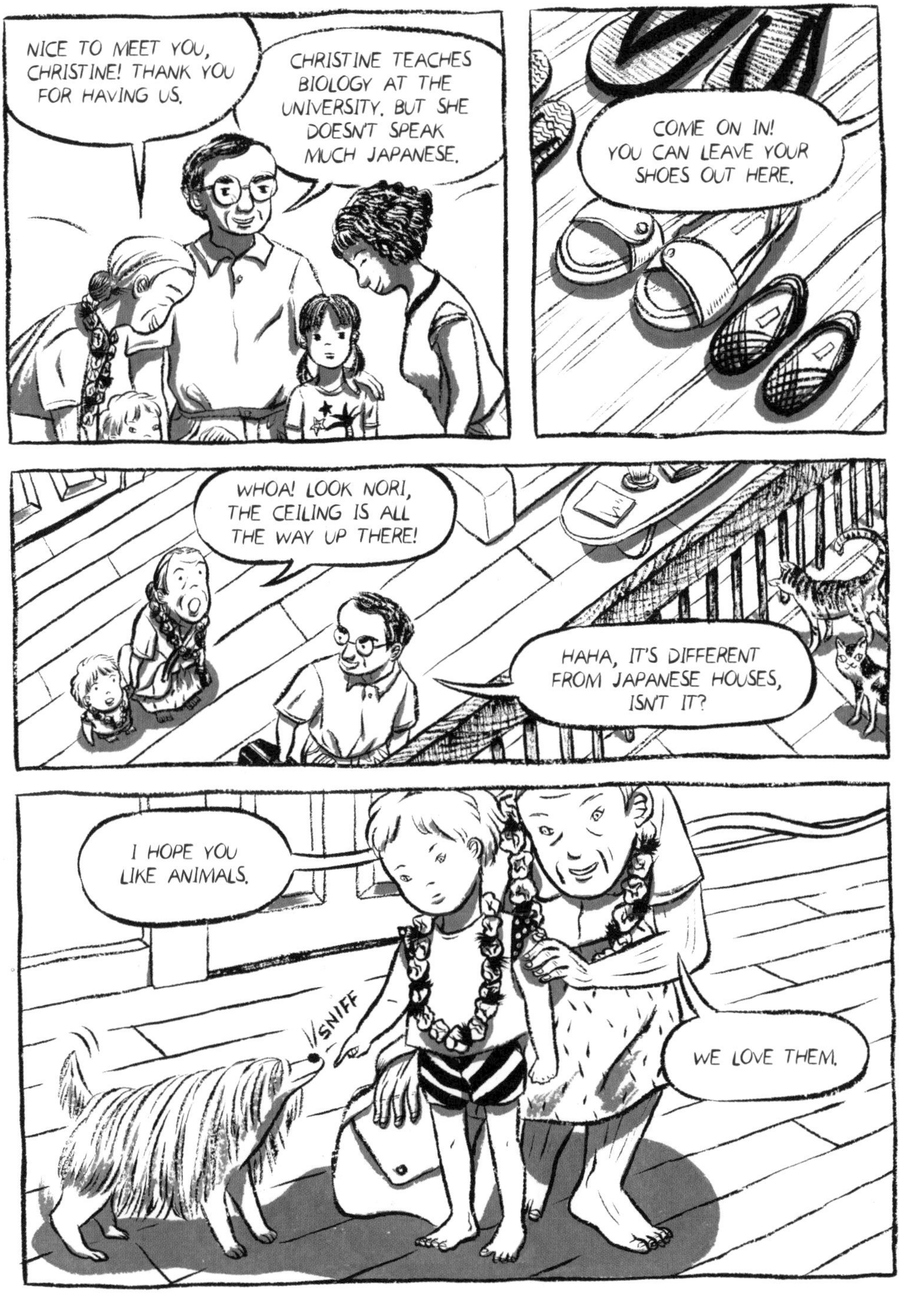
NICE TO MEET YOU, CHRISTINE! THANK YOU FOR HAVING US.
CHRISTINE TEACHES BIOLOGY AT THE UNIVERSITY. BUT SHE DOESN'T SPEAK MUCH JAPANESE.
COME ON IN! YOU CAN LEAVE YOUR SHOES OUT HERE.
WHOA! LOOK NORI, THE CEILING IS ALL THE WAY UP THERE!
HAHA, IT'S DIFFERENT FROM JAPANESE HOUSES, ISN'T IT?
I HOPE YOU LIKE ANIMALS.
SNIFF
WE LOVE THEM.

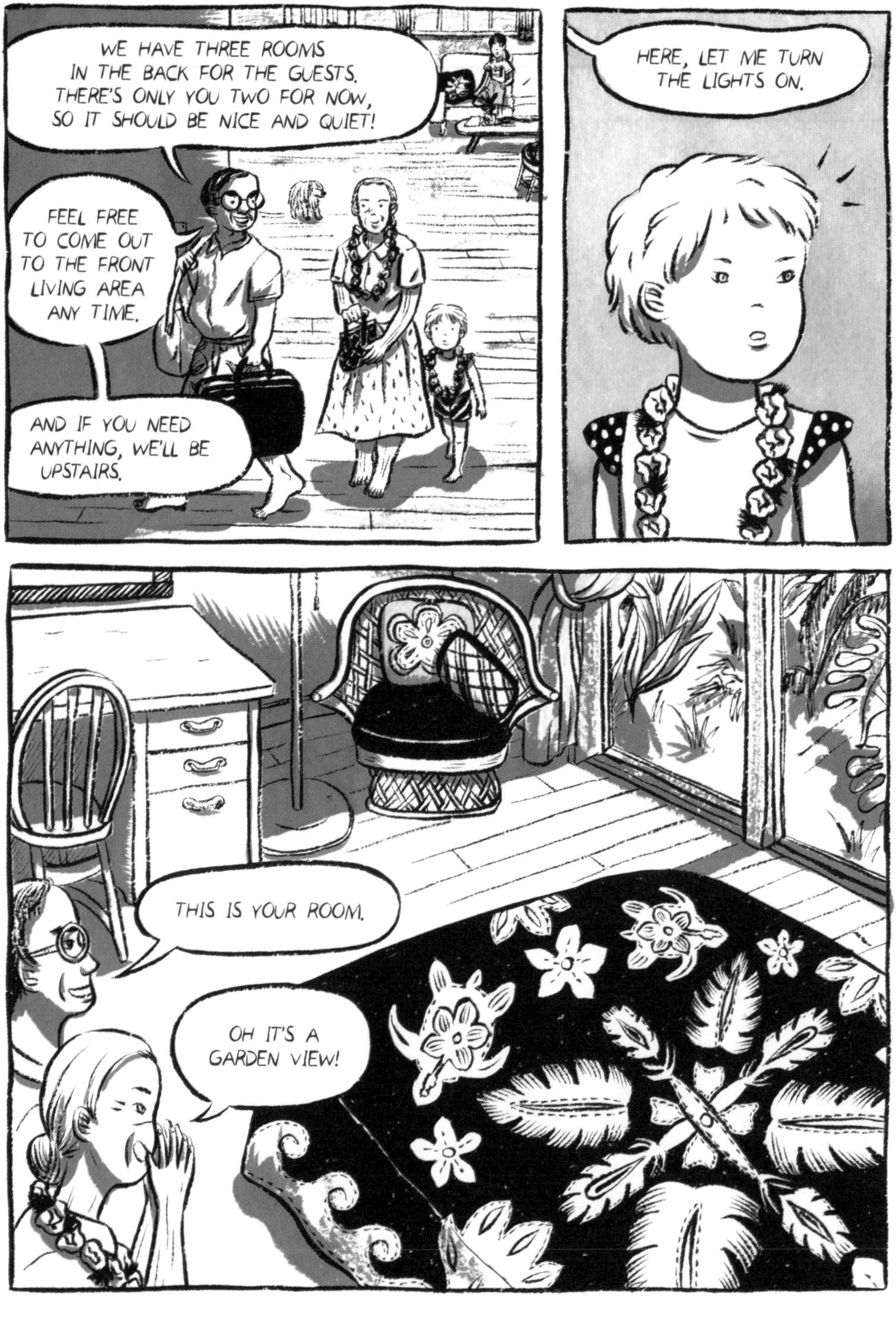
WE HAVE THREE ROOMS IN THE BACK FOR THE GUESTS. THERE'S ONLY YOU TWO FOR NOW, SO IT SHOULD BE NICE AND QUIET!
FEEL FREE TO COME OUT TO THE FRONT LIVING AREA ANY TIME.
AND IF YOU NEED ANYTHING, WE'LL BE UPSTAIRS.
HERE, LET ME TURN THE LIGHTS ON.
THIS IS YOUR ROOM.
OH IT'S A GARDEN VIEW!

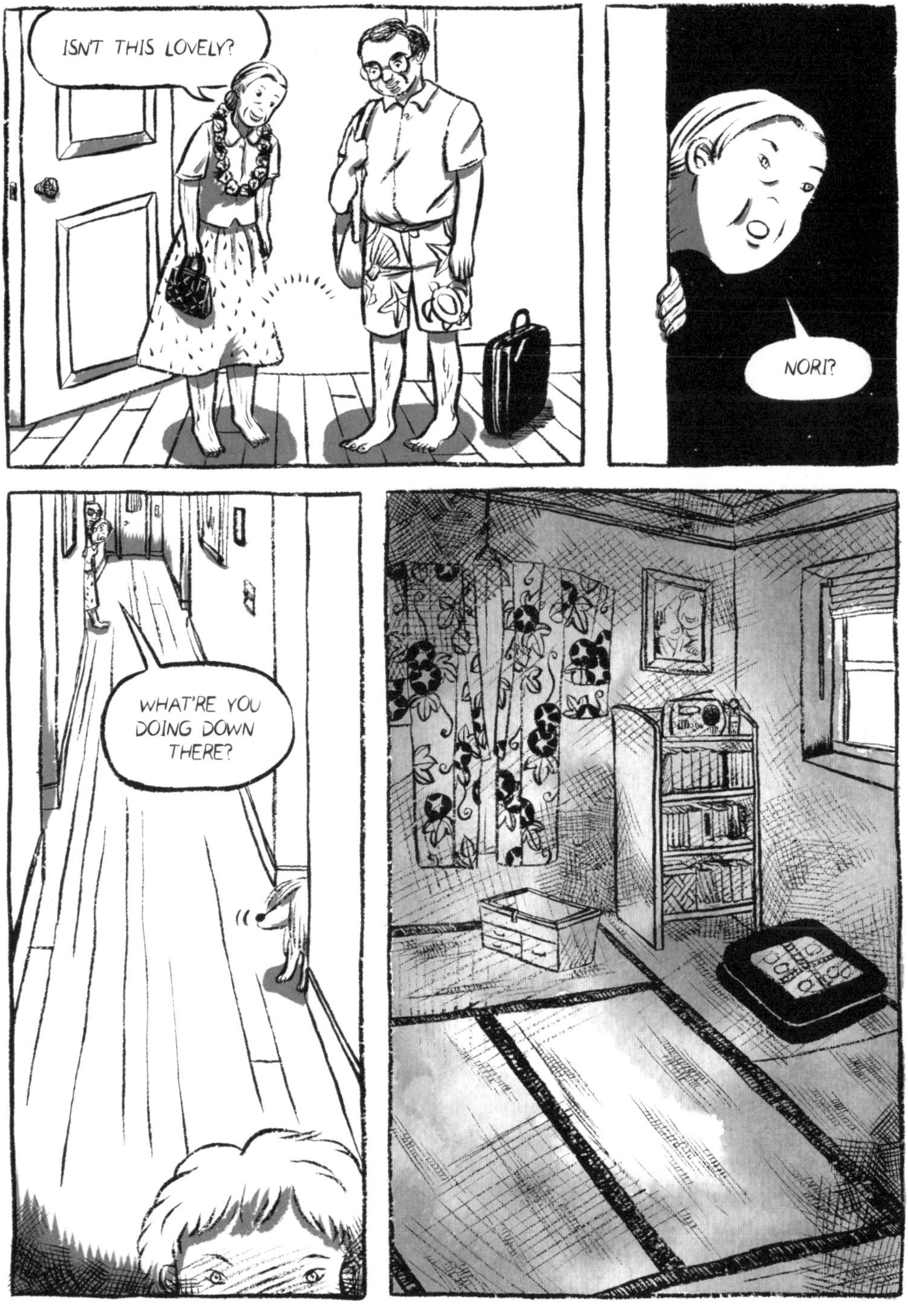
ISN'T THIS LOVELY?
NORI?
WHAT'RE YOU DOING DOWN THERE?

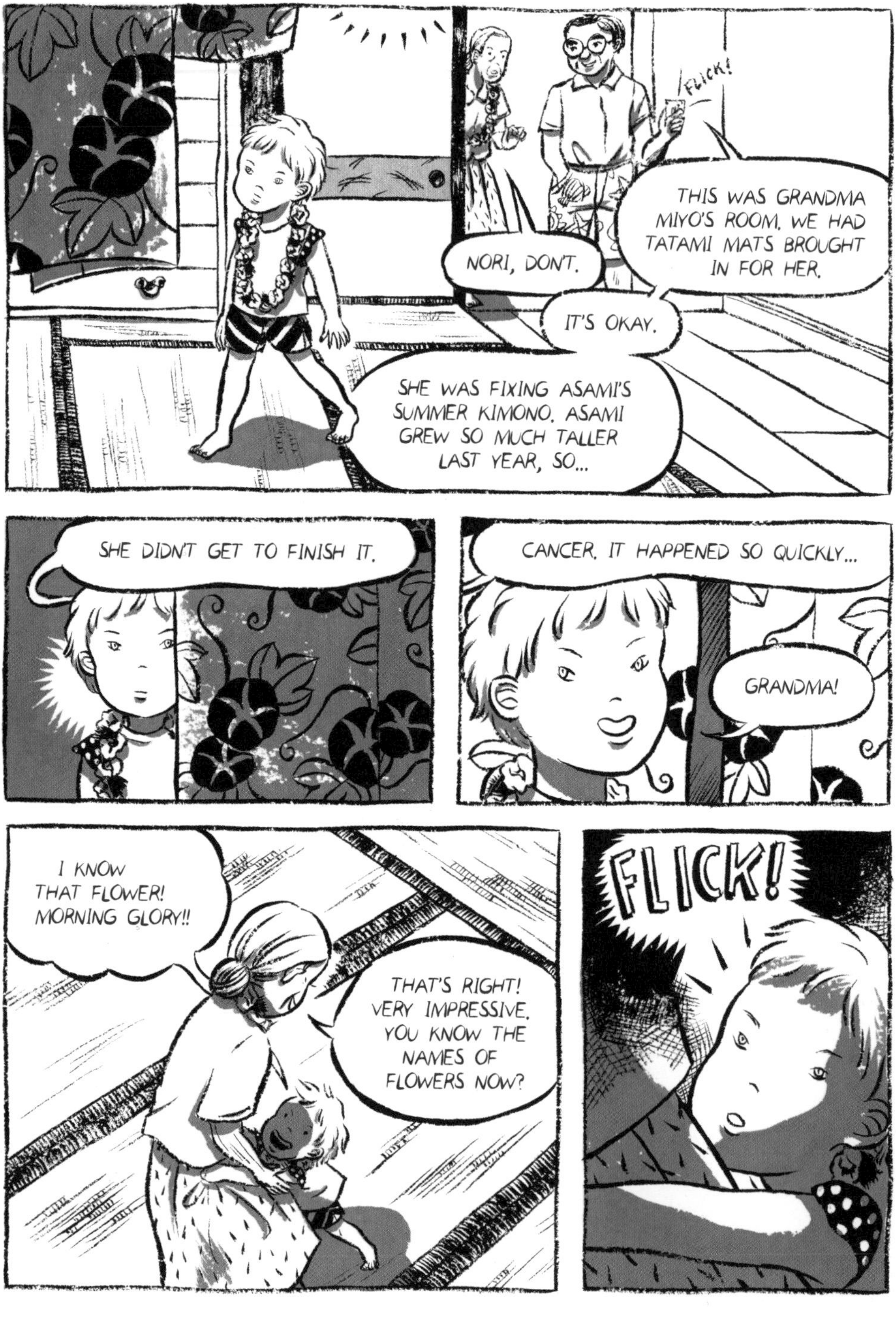
FLICK!
THIS WAS GRANDMA MIYO'S ROOM. WE HAD TATAMI MATS BROUGHT IN FOR HER.
NORI, DON'T.
IT'S OKAY.
SHE WAS FIXING ASAMI'S SUMMER KIMONO. ASAMI GREW SO MUCH TALLER LAST YEAR, SO...
SHE DIDN'T GET TO FINISH IT.
CANCER. IT HAPPENED SO QUICKLY...
GRANDMA!
I KNOW THAT FLOWER! MORNING GLORY!!
THAT'S RIGHT! VERY IMPRESSIVE. YOU KNOW THE NAMES OF FLOWERS NOW?
FLICK!

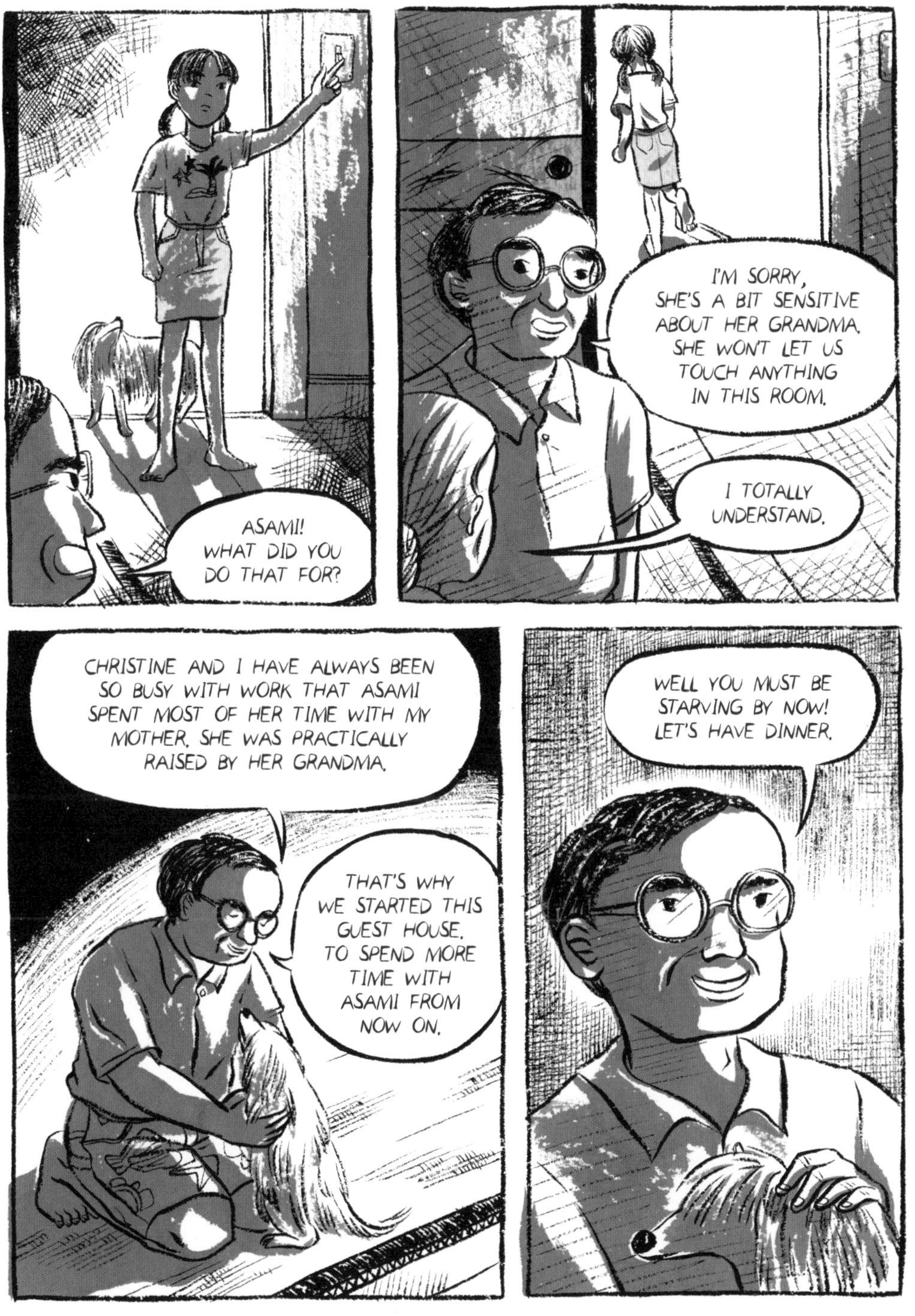
ASAMI! WHAT DID YOU DO THAT FOR?
I'M SORRY, SHE'S A BIT SENSITIVE ABOUT HER GRANDMA. SHE WON'T LET US TOUCH ANYTHING IN THIS ROOM.
I TOTALLY UNDERSTAND.
CHRISTINE AND I HAVE ALWAYS BEEN SO BUSY WITH WORK THAT ASAMI SPENT MOST OF HER TIME WITH MY MOTHER. SHE WAS PRACTICALLY RAISED BY HER GRANDMA.
THAT'S WHY WE STARTED THIS GUEST HOUSE. TO SPEND MORE TIME WITH ASAMI FROM NOW ON.
WELL YOU MUST BE STARVING BY NOW! LET'S HAVE DINNER.

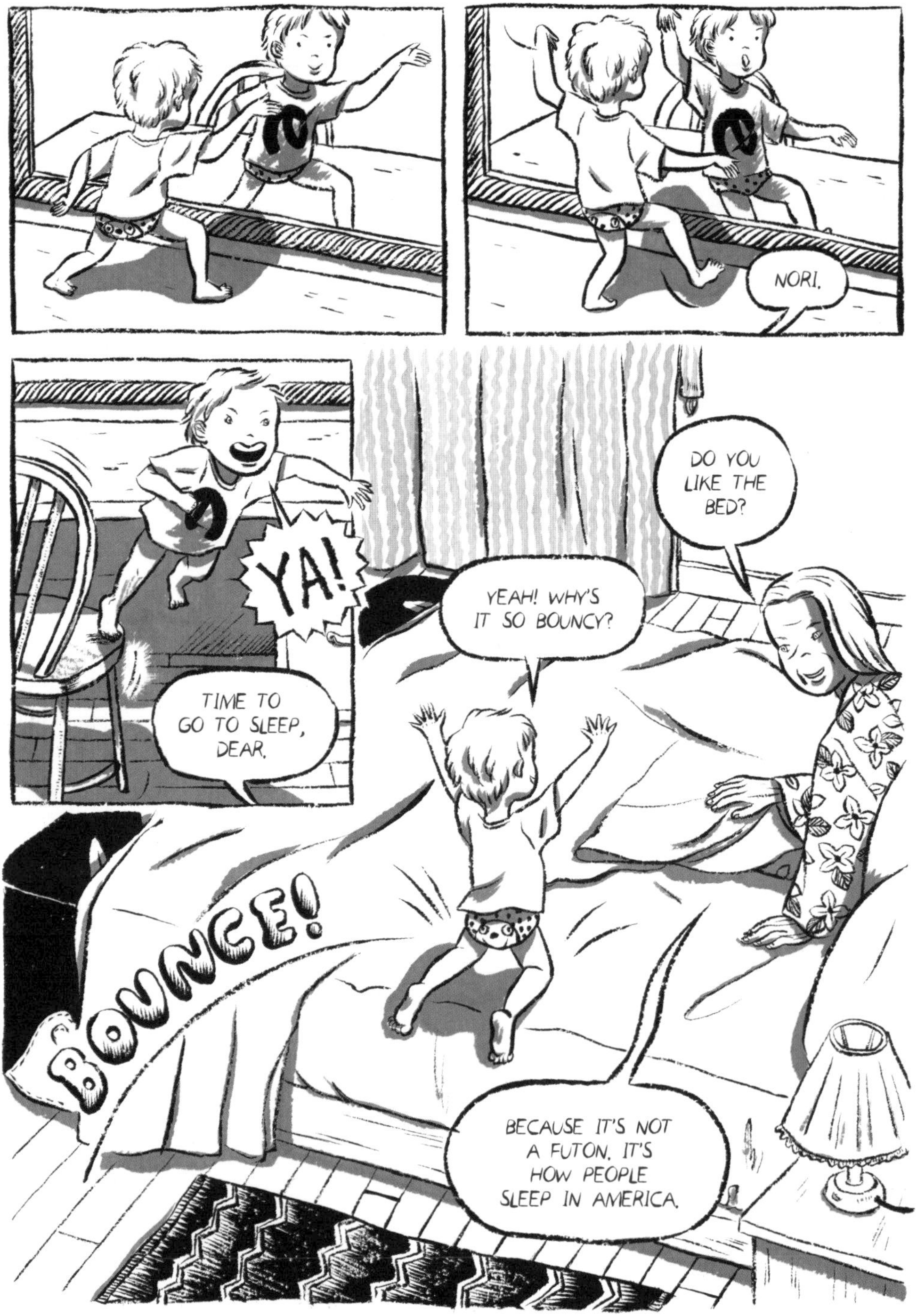
NORI.
YA!
TIME TO GO TO SLEEP, DEAR.
DO YOU LIKE THE BED?
YEAH! WHY'S IT SO BOUNCY?
BOUNCE!
BECAUSE IT'S NOT A FUTON. IT'S HOW PEOPLE SLEEP IN AMERICA.

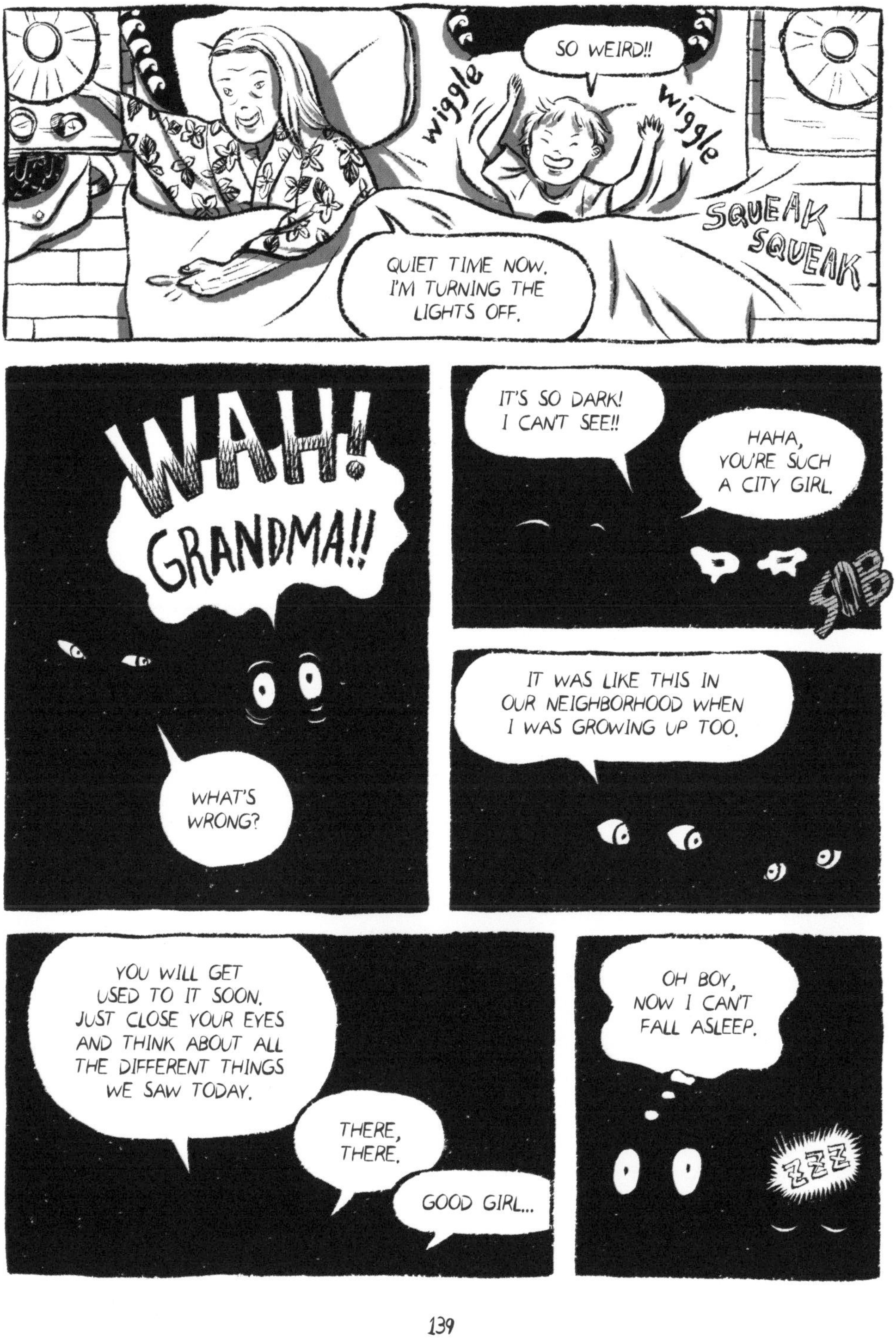
wiggle
SO WEIRD!!
wiggle
SQUEAK SQUEAK
QUIET TIME NOW. I'M TURNING THE LIGHTS OFF.
WAH! GRANDMA!!
WHAT'S WRONG?
IT'S SO DARK! I CAN'T SEE!!
HAHA, YOU'RE SUCH A CITY GIRL.
SOB
IT WAS LIKE THIS IN OUR NEIGHBORHOOD WHEN I WAS GROWING UP TOO.
YOU WILL GET USED TO IT SOON. JUST CLOSE YOUR EYES AND THINK ABOUT ALL THE DIFFERENT THINGS WE SAW TODAY.
THERE, THERE.
GOOD GIRL...
OH BOY, NOW I CAN'T FALL ASLEEP.
ZZZ

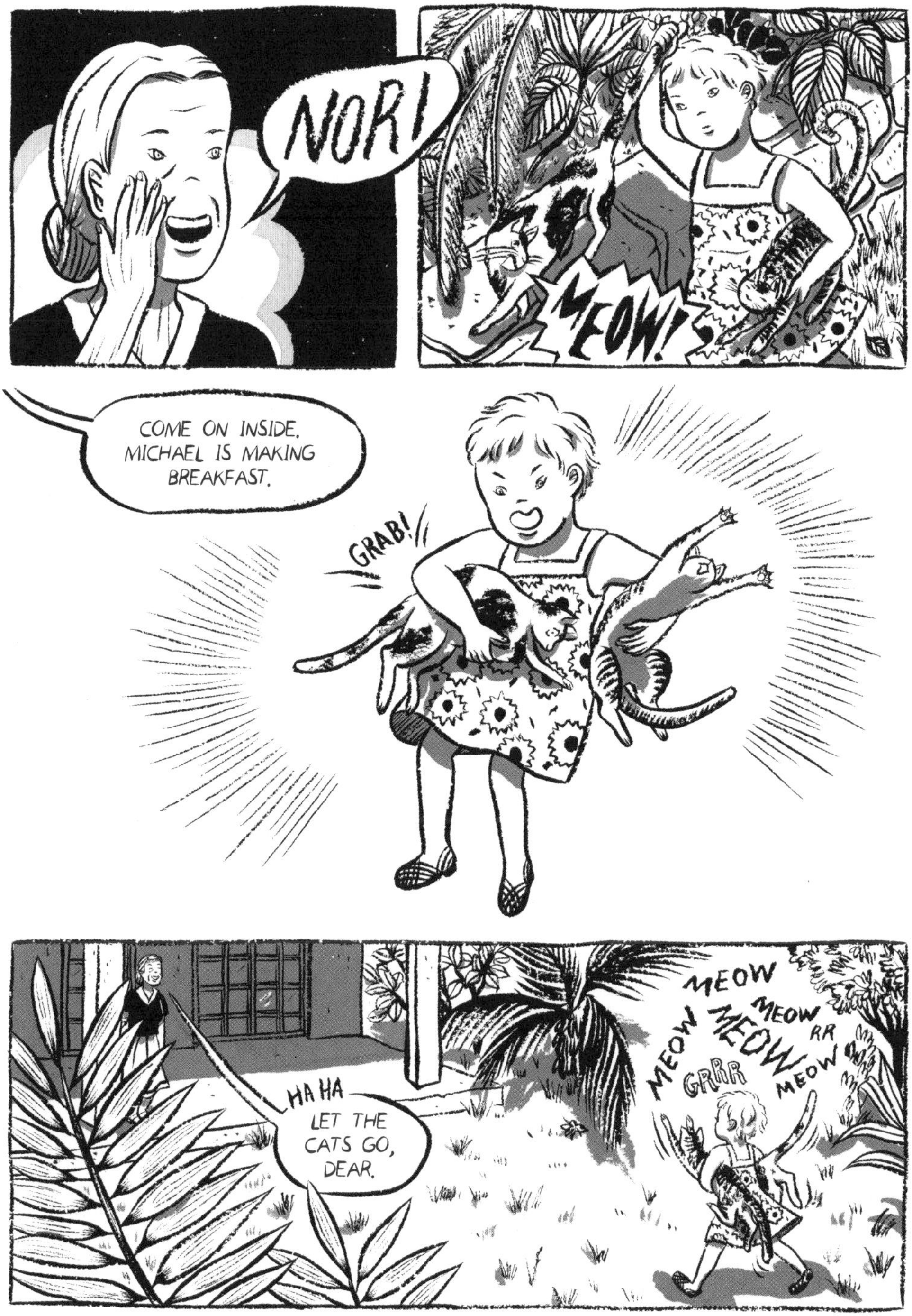
NORI
MEOW!
COME ON INSIDE. MICHAEL IS MAKING BREAKFAST.
GRAB!
MEOW
MEOW
MEOW
MEOW
RR
GRRR
MEOW
HA HA
LET THE CATS GO, DEAR.

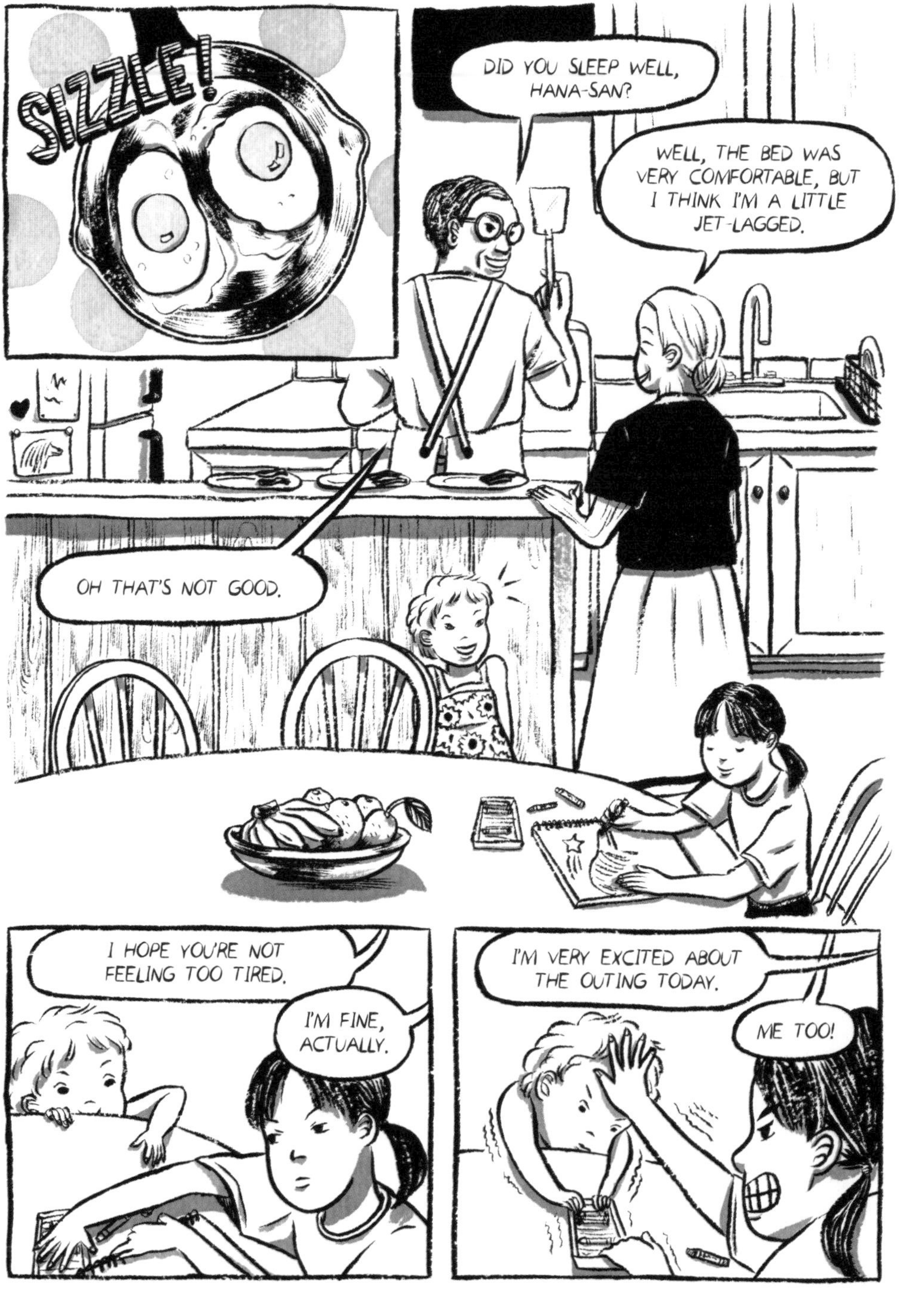
SIZZLE!
DID YOU SLEEP WELL, HANA-SAN?
WELL, THE BED WAS VERY COMFORTABLE, BUT I THINK I'M A LITTLE JET-LAGGED.
OH THAT'S NOT GOOD.
I HOPE YOU'RE NOT FEELING TOO TIRED.
I'M FINE, ACTUALLY.
I'M VERY EXCITED ABOUT THE OUTING TODAY.
ME TOO!

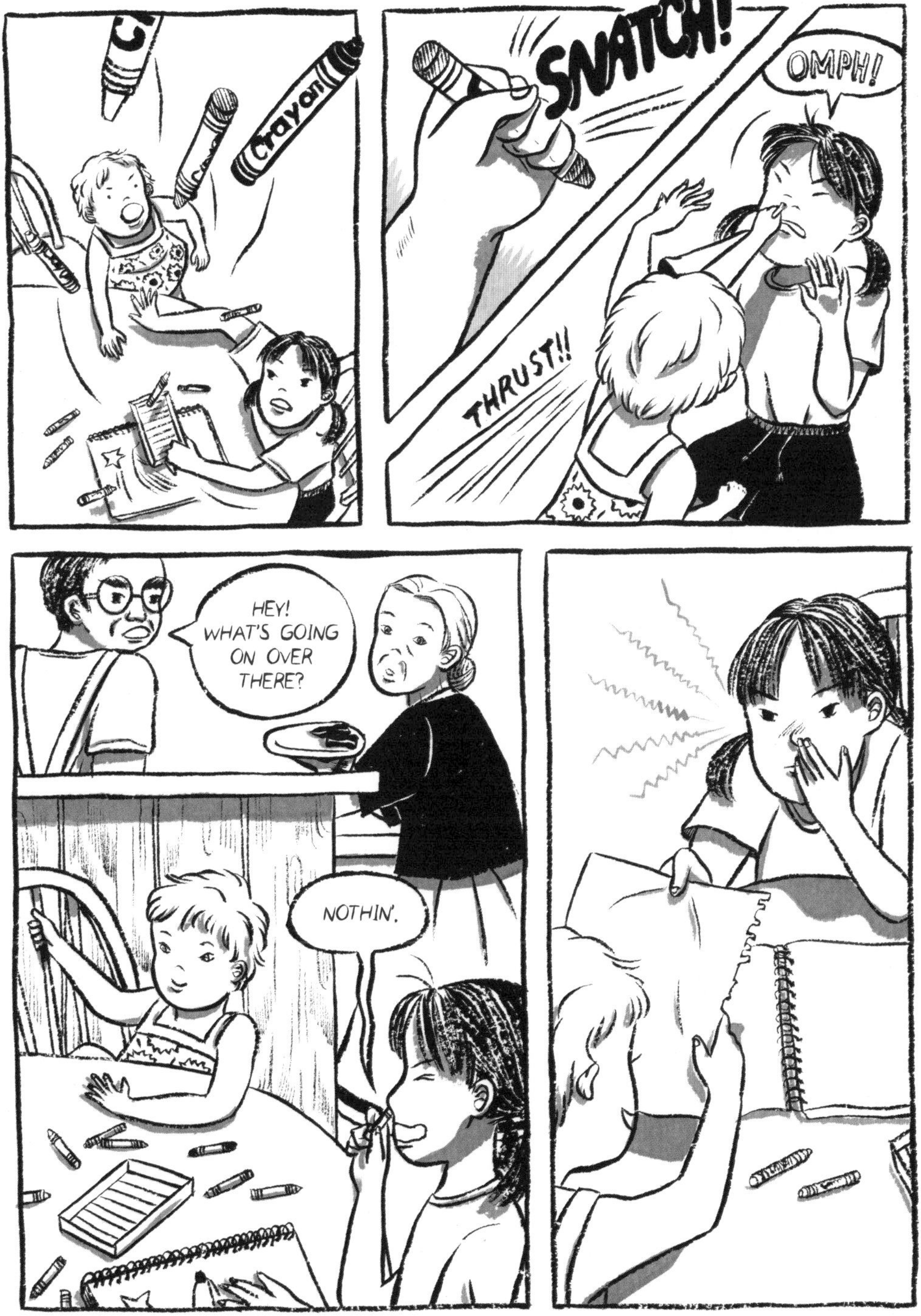
Crayon
SNATCH!
OMPH!
THRUST!!
HEY! WHAT'S GOING ON OVER THERE?
NOTHIN'.

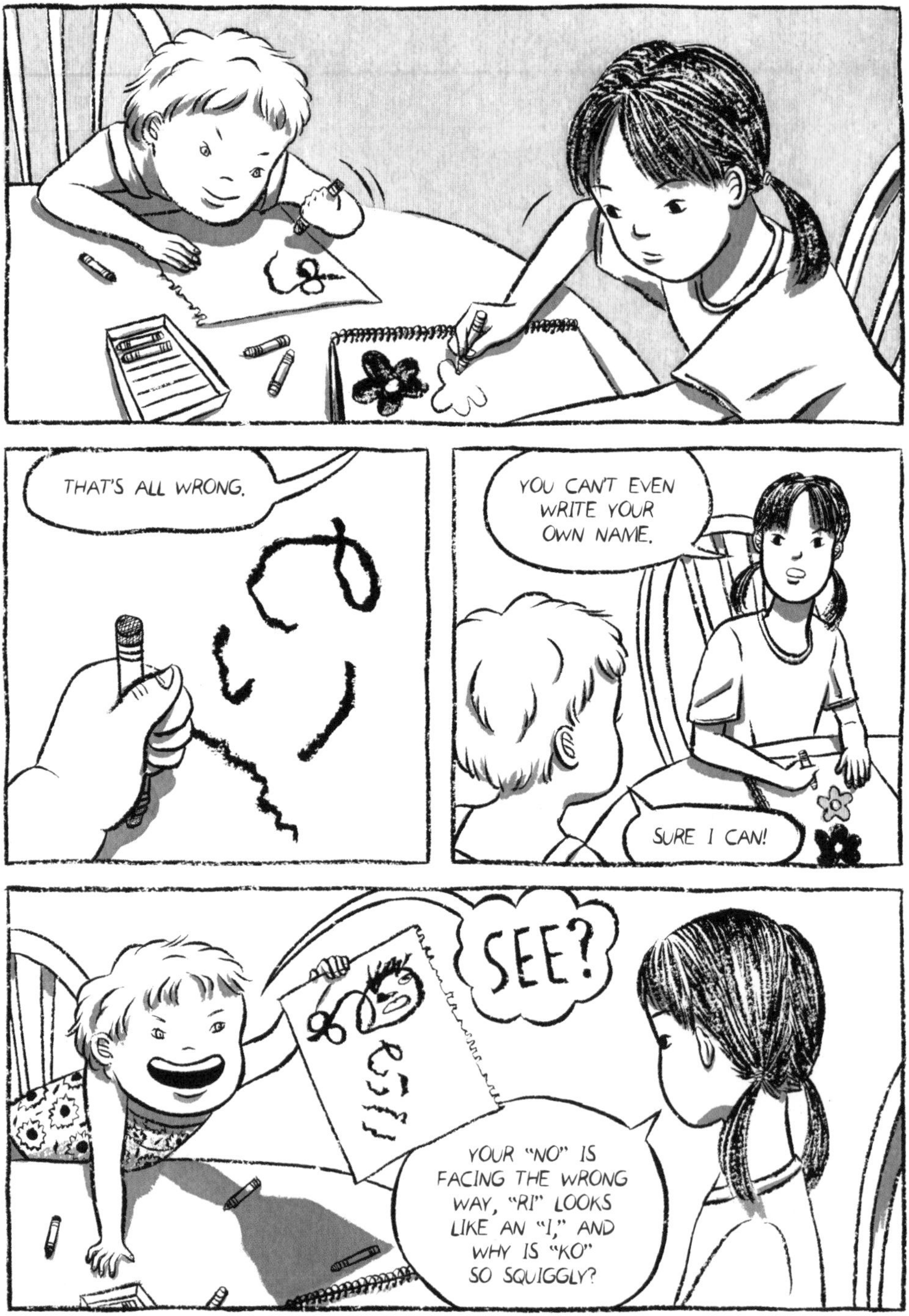
THAT'S ALL WRONG.
YOU CAN'T EVEN WRITE YOUR OWN NAME.
SURE I CAN!
SEE?
YOUR "NO" IS FACING THE WRONG WAY, "RI" LOOKS LIKE AN "I," AND WHY IS "KO" SO SQUIGGLY?

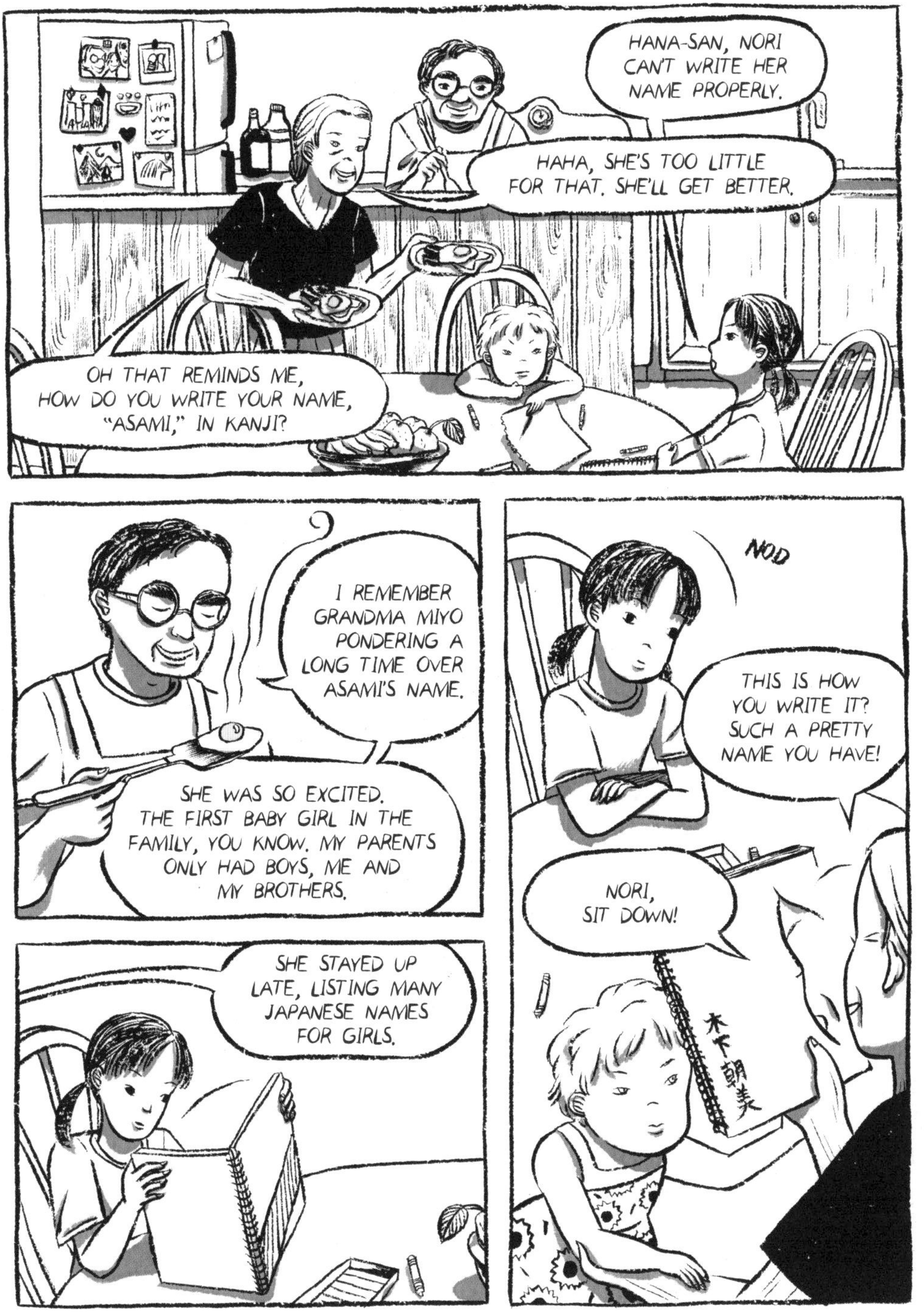
HANA-SAN, NORI CAN'T WRITE HER NAME PROPERLY.
HAHA, SHE'S TOO LITTLE FOR THAT. SHE'LL GET BETTER.
OH THAT REMINDS ME, HOW DO YOU WRITE YOUR NAME, "ASAMI," IN KANJI?
I REMEMBER GRANDMA MIYO PONDERING A LONG TIME OVER ASAMI'S NAME.
SHE WAS SO EXCITED. THE FIRST BABY GIRL IN THE FAMILY, YOU KNOW. MY PARENTS ONLY HAD BOYS, ME AND MY BROTHERS.
SHE STAYED UP LATE, LISTING MANY JAPANESE NAMES FOR GIRLS.
NOD
THIS IS HOW YOU WRITE IT? SUCH A PRETTY NAME YOU HAVE!
NORI, SIT DOWN!
木下朝美

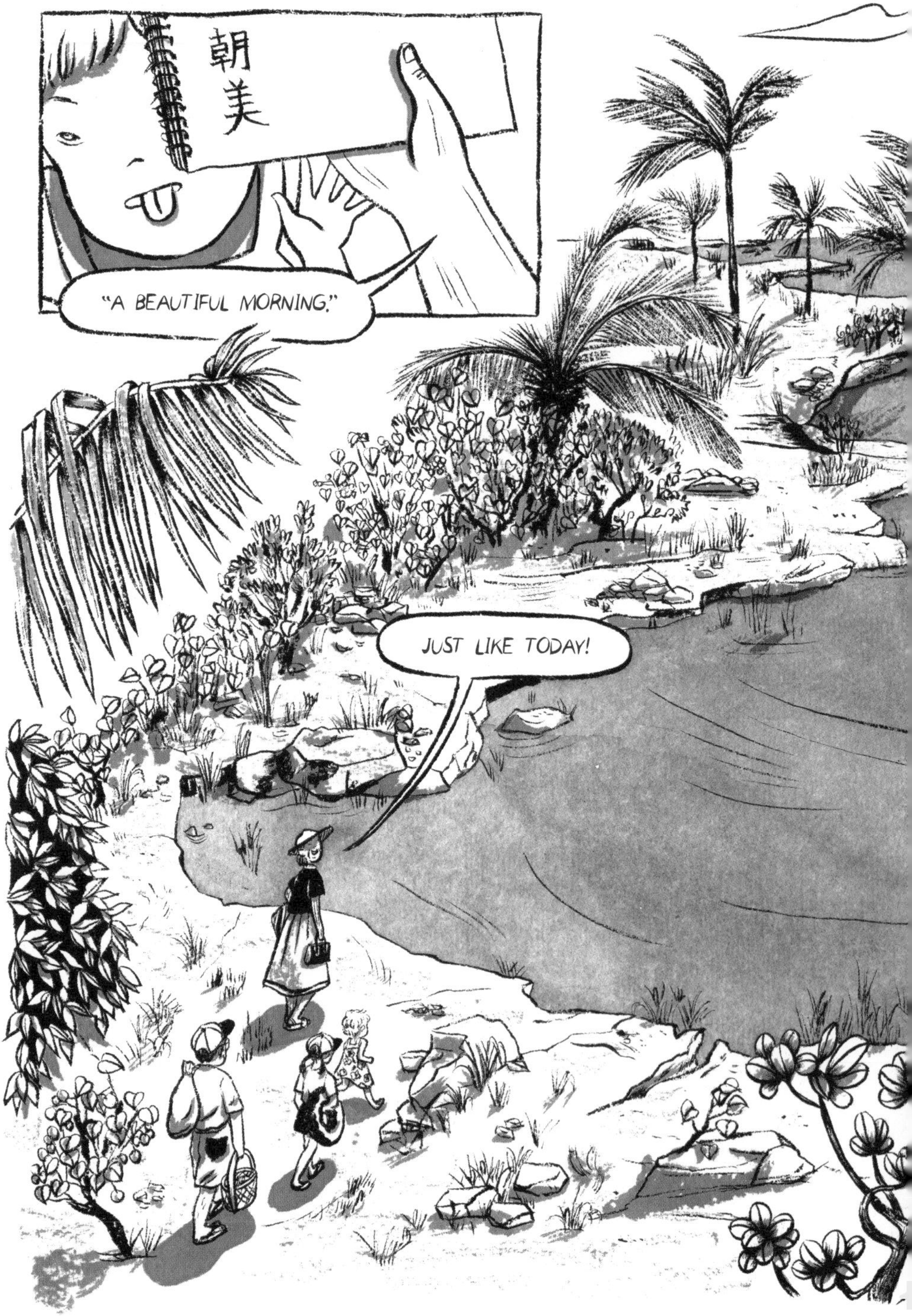
朝美
"A BEAUTIFUL MORNING."
JUST LIKE TODAY!

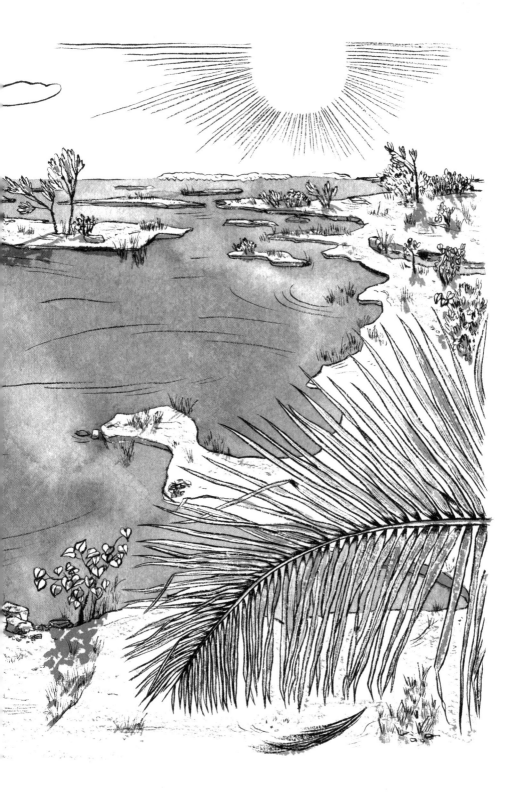

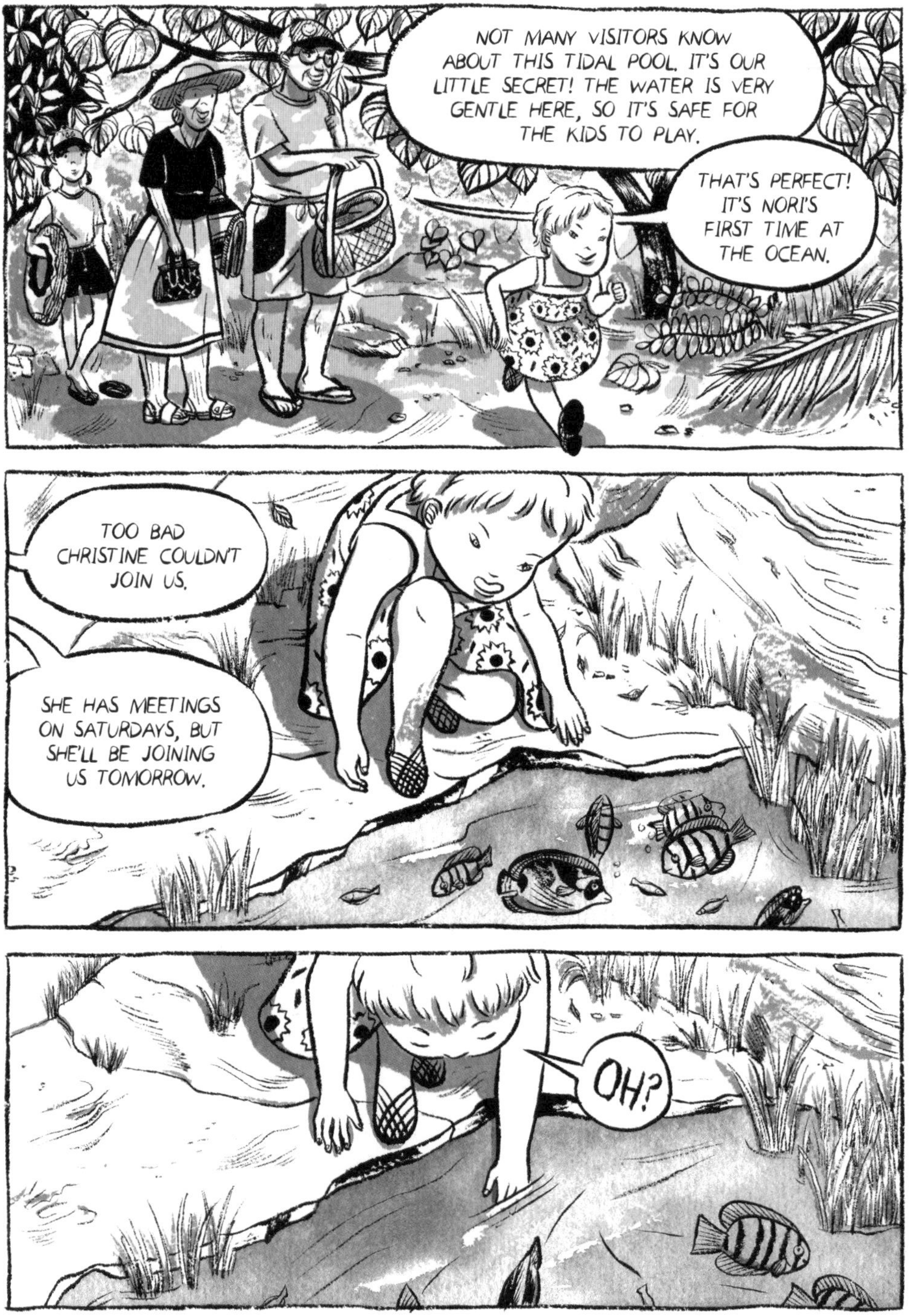
NOT MANY VISITORS KNOW ABOUT THIS TIDAL POOL. IT'S OUR LITTLE SECRET! THE WATER IS VERY GENTLE HERE, SO IT'S SAFE FOR THE KIDS TO PLAY.
THAT'S PERFECT! IT'S NORI'S FIRST TIME AT THE OCEAN.
TOO BAD CHRISTINE COULDN'T JOIN US.
SHE HAS MEETINGS ON SATURDAYS, BUT SHE'LL BE JOINING US TOMORROW.
OH?

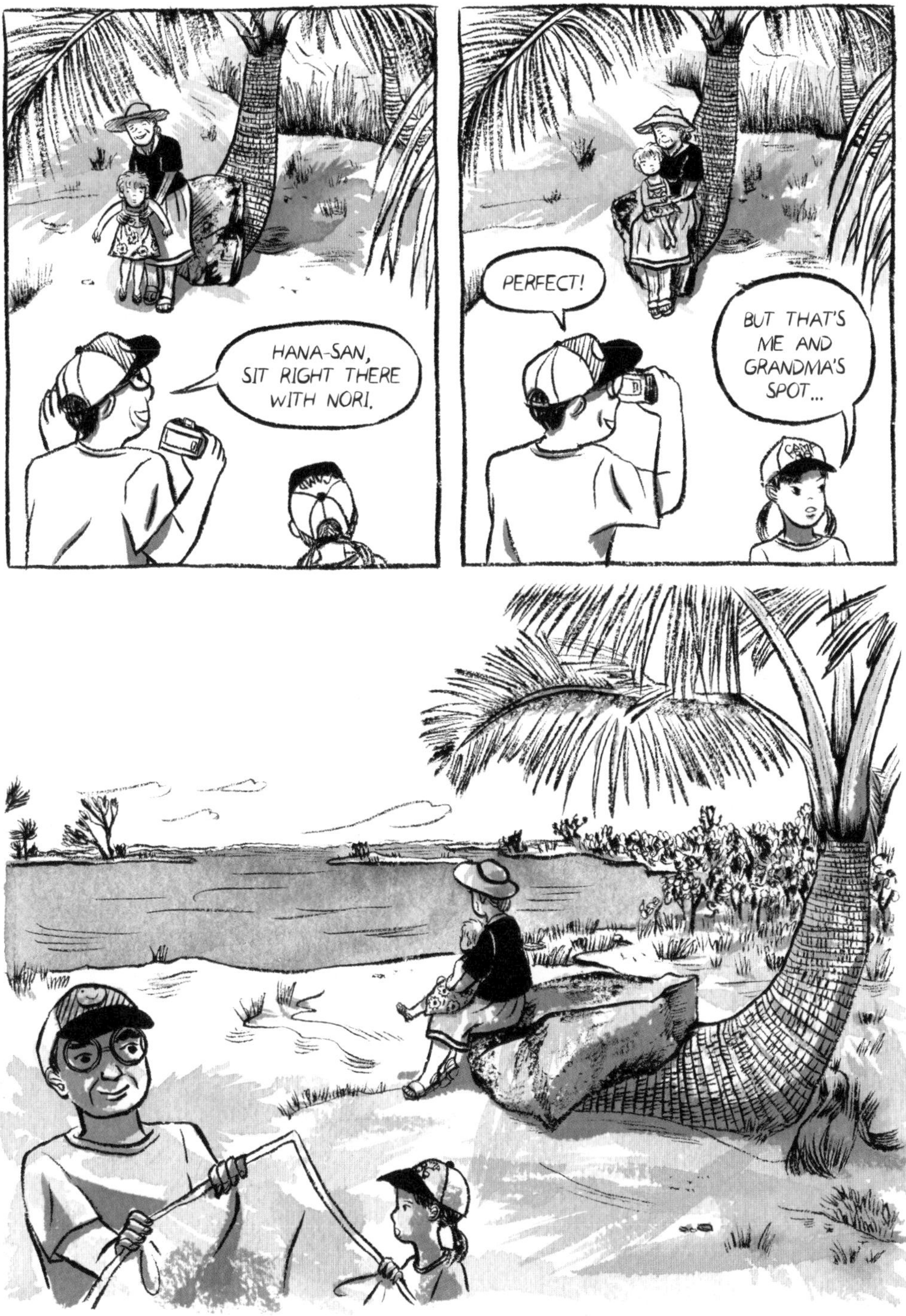
HANA-SAN, SIT RIGHT THERE WITH NORI.
PERFECT!
BUT THAT'S ME AND GRANDMA'S SPOT...

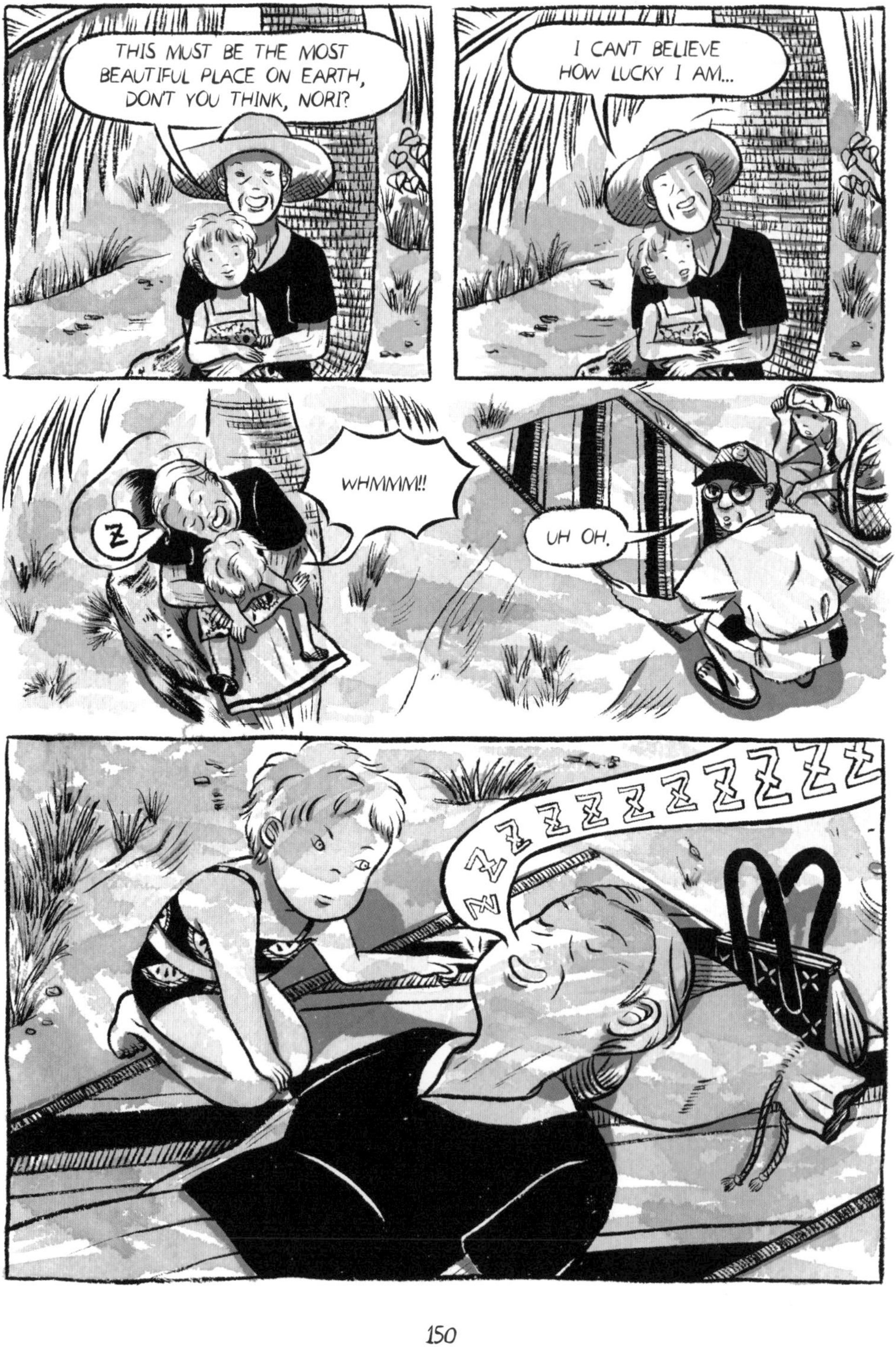
THIS MUST BE THE MOST BEAUTIFUL PLACE ON EARTH, DON'T YOU THINK, NORI?
I CAN'T BELIEVE HOW LUCKY I AM...
Z
WHMMM!!
UH OH.
ZZZZZZZZZZZZZZ

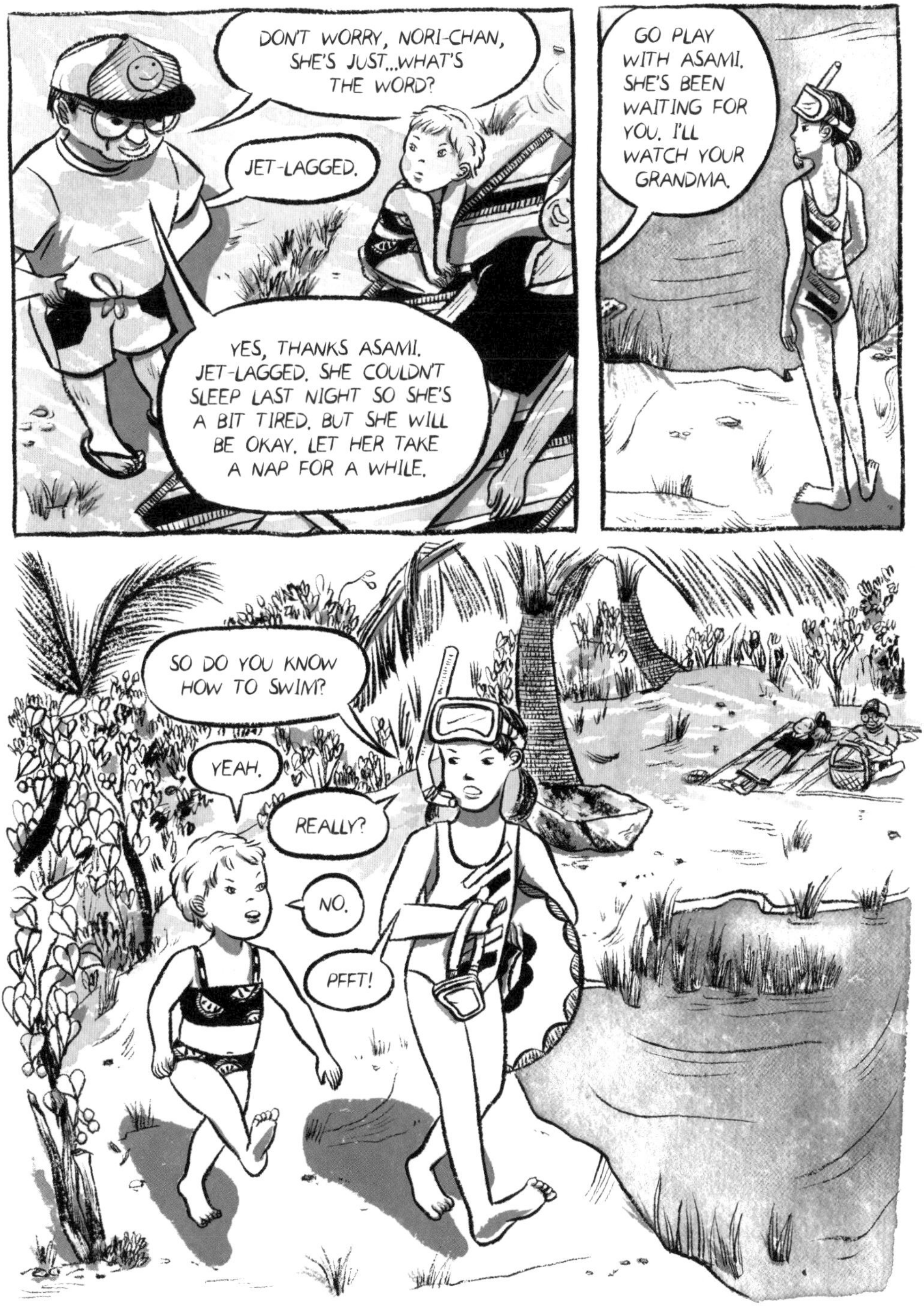
DON'T WORRY, NORI-CHAN, SHE'S JUST...WHAT'S THE WORD?
JET-LAGGED.
YES, THANKS ASAMI. JET-LAGGED. SHE COULDN'T SLEEP LAST NIGHT SO SHE'S A BIT TIRED. BUT SHE WILL BE OKAY. LET HER TAKE A NAP FOR A WHILE.
GO PLAY WITH ASAMI. SHE'S BEEN WAITING FOR YOU. I'LL WATCH YOUR GRANDMA.
SO DO YOU KNOW HOW TO SWIM?
YEAH.
REALLY?
NO.
PFFT!

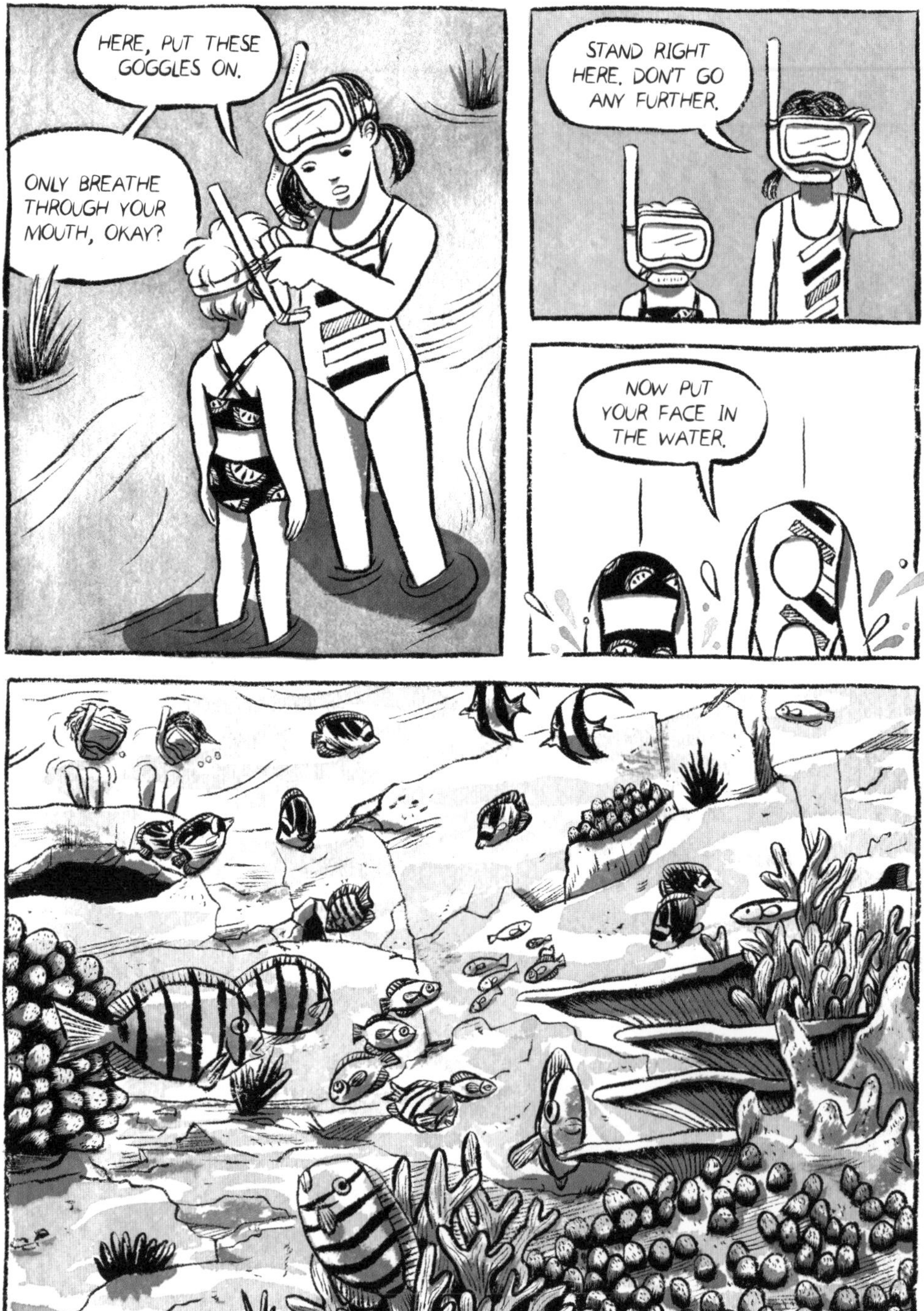
HERE, PUT THESE GOGGLES ON.
ONLY BREATHE THROUGH YOUR MOUTH, OKAY?
STAND RIGHT HERE. DON'T GO ANY FURTHER.
NOW PUT YOUR FACE IN THE WATER.

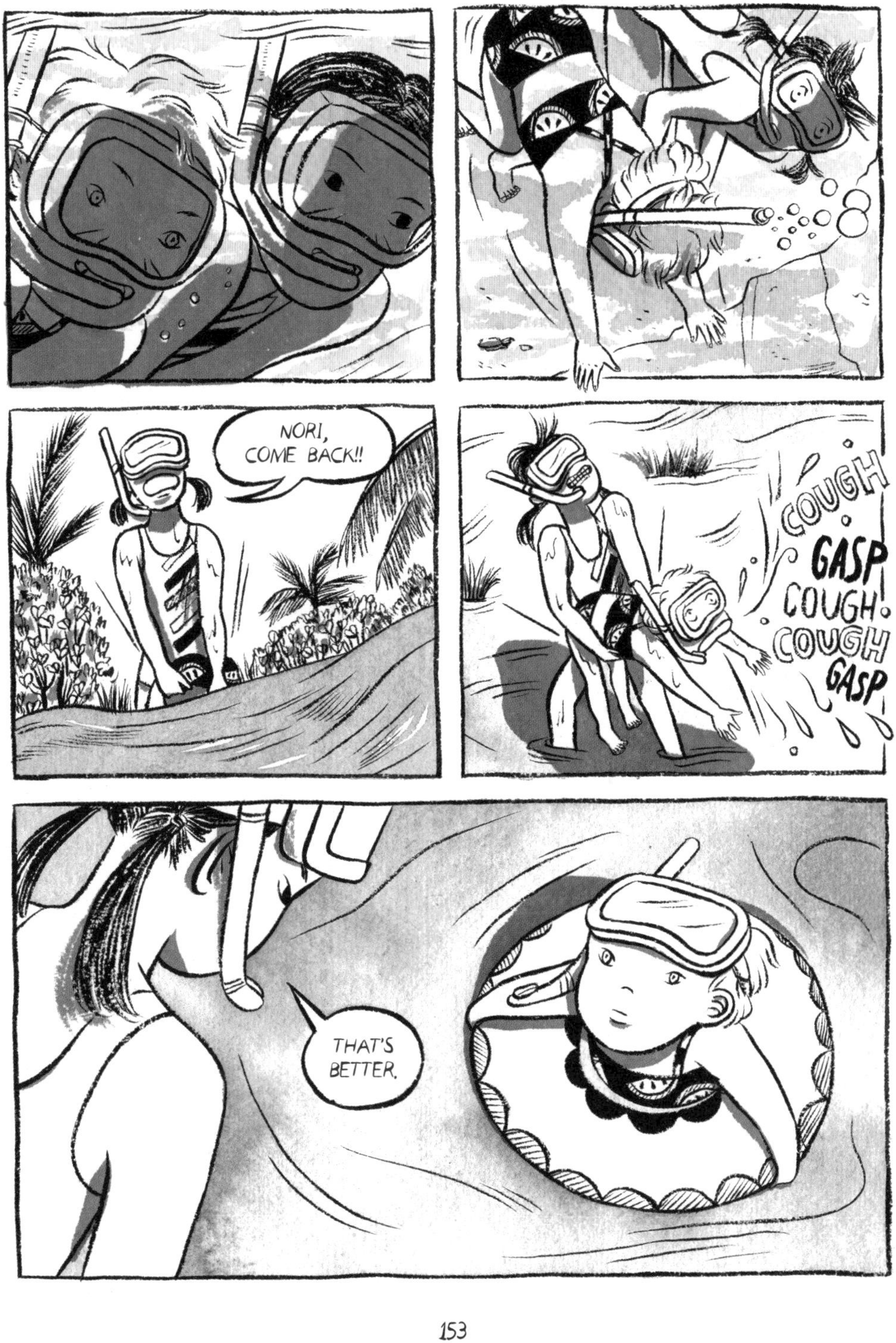
NORI, COME BACK!!
COUGH
GASP
COUGH
COUGH
GASP
THAT'S BETTER.

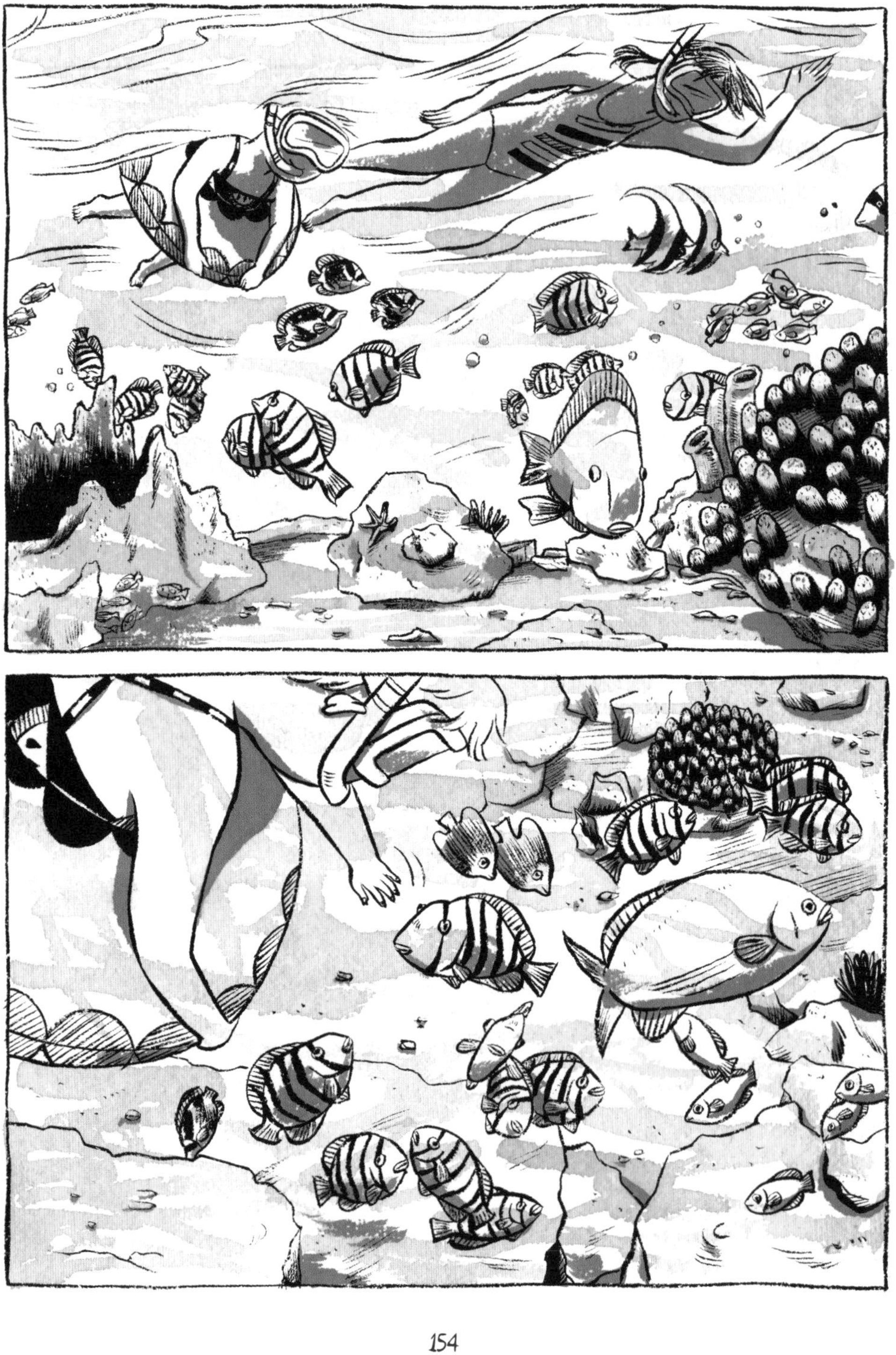

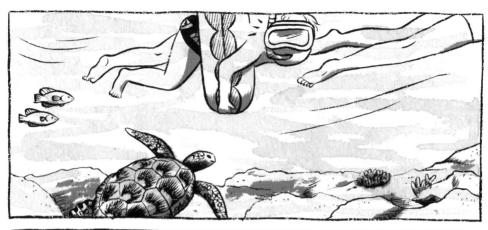

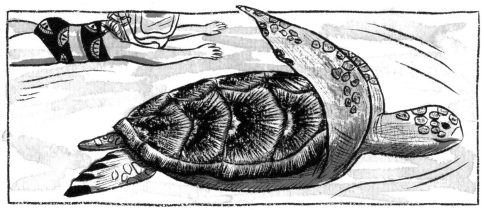

GRAB!

¡INHALE!

ARE YOU CRAZY?!
YOU COULD'VE DROWNED!

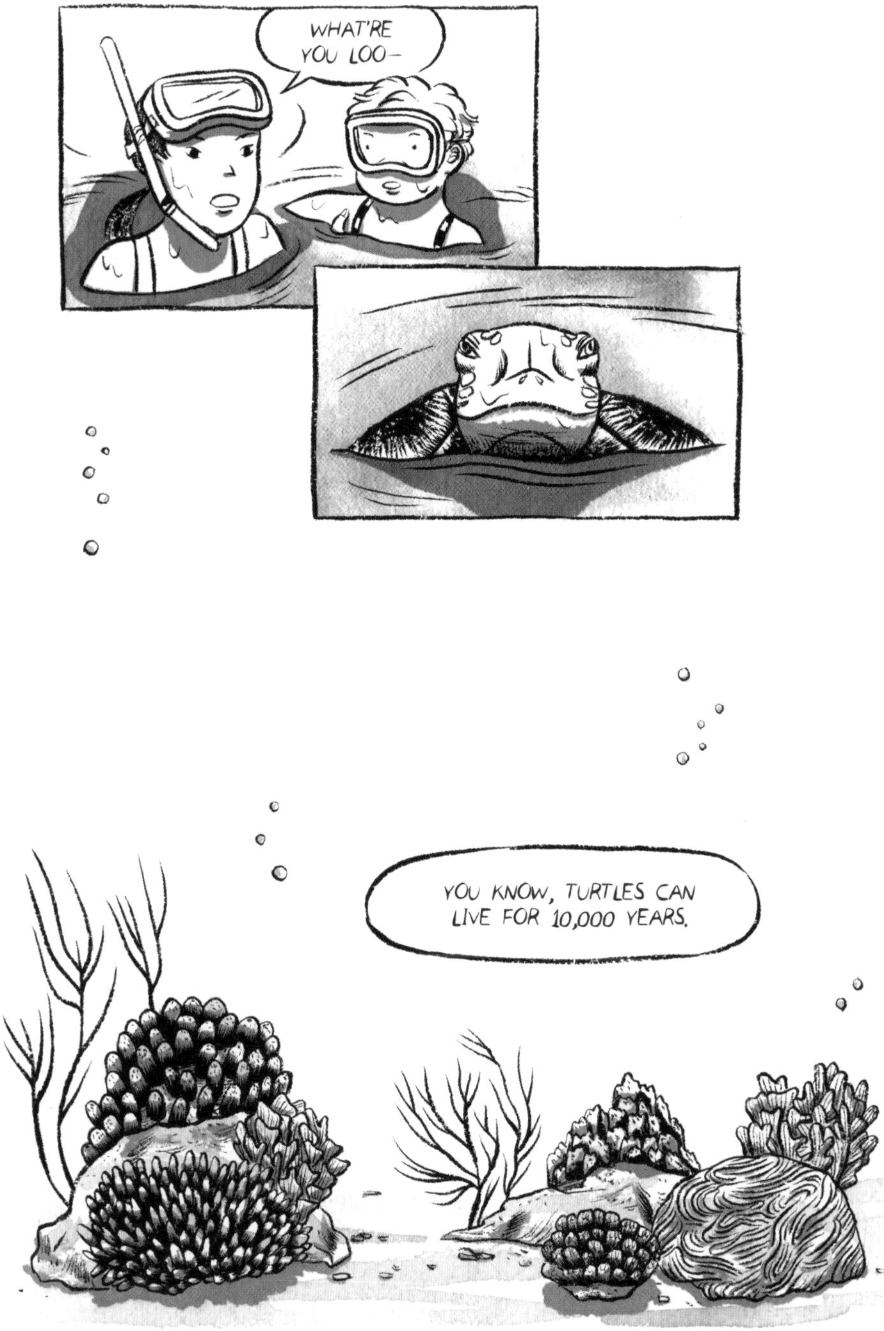
WHAT'RE YOU LOO—
YOU KNOW, TURTLES CAN LIVE FOR 10,000 YEARS.

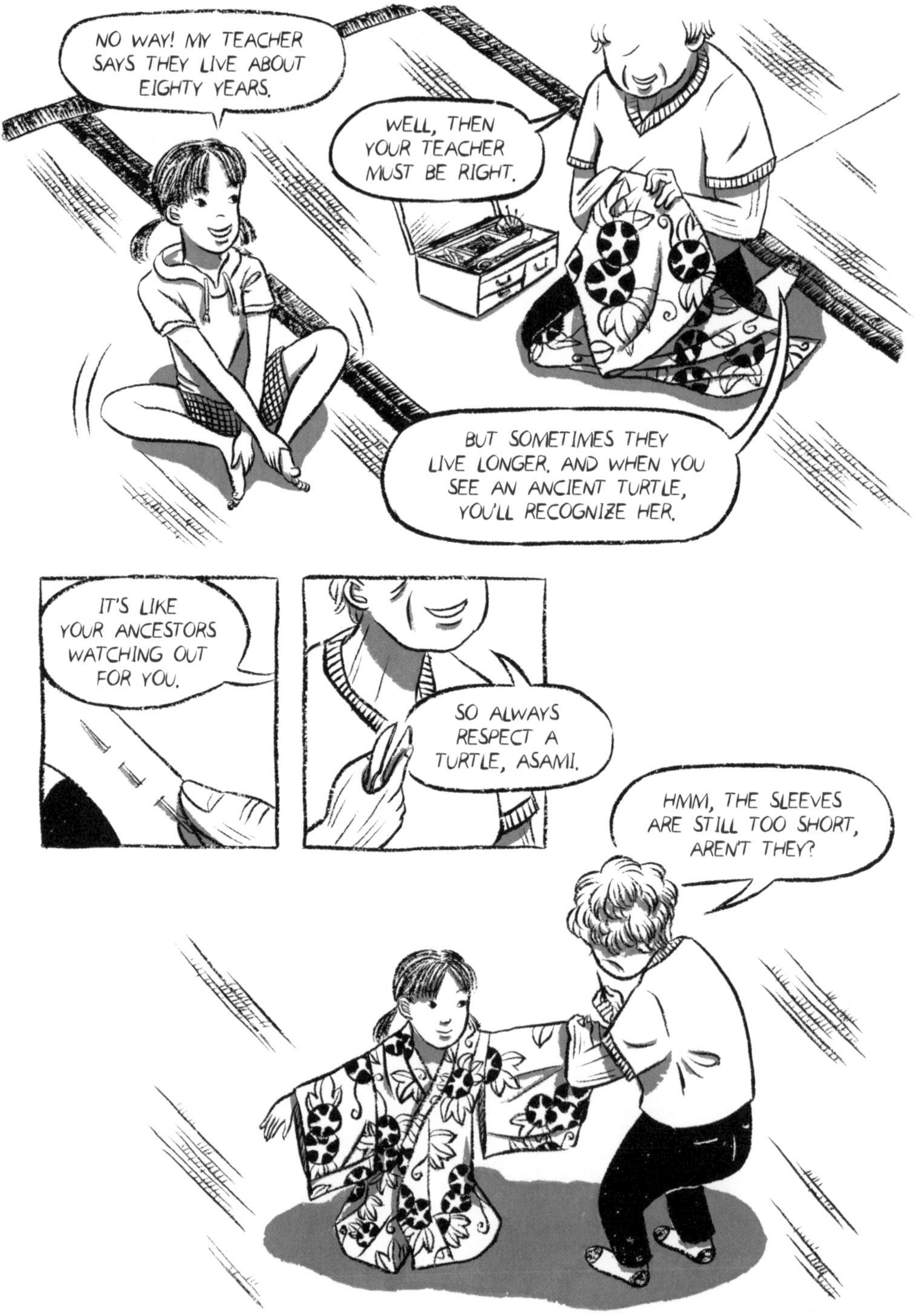
NO WAY! MY TEACHER SAYS THEY LIVE ABOUT EIGHTY YEARS.
WELL, THEN YOUR TEACHER MUST BE RIGHT.
BUT SOMETIMES THEY LIVE LONGER. AND WHEN YOU SEE AN ANCIENT TURTLE, YOU'LL RECOGNIZE HER.
IT'S LIKE YOUR ANCESTORS WATCHING OUT FOR YOU.
SO ALWAYS RESPECT A TURTLE, ASAMI.
HMM, THE SLEEVES ARE STILL TOO SHORT, AREN'T THEY?

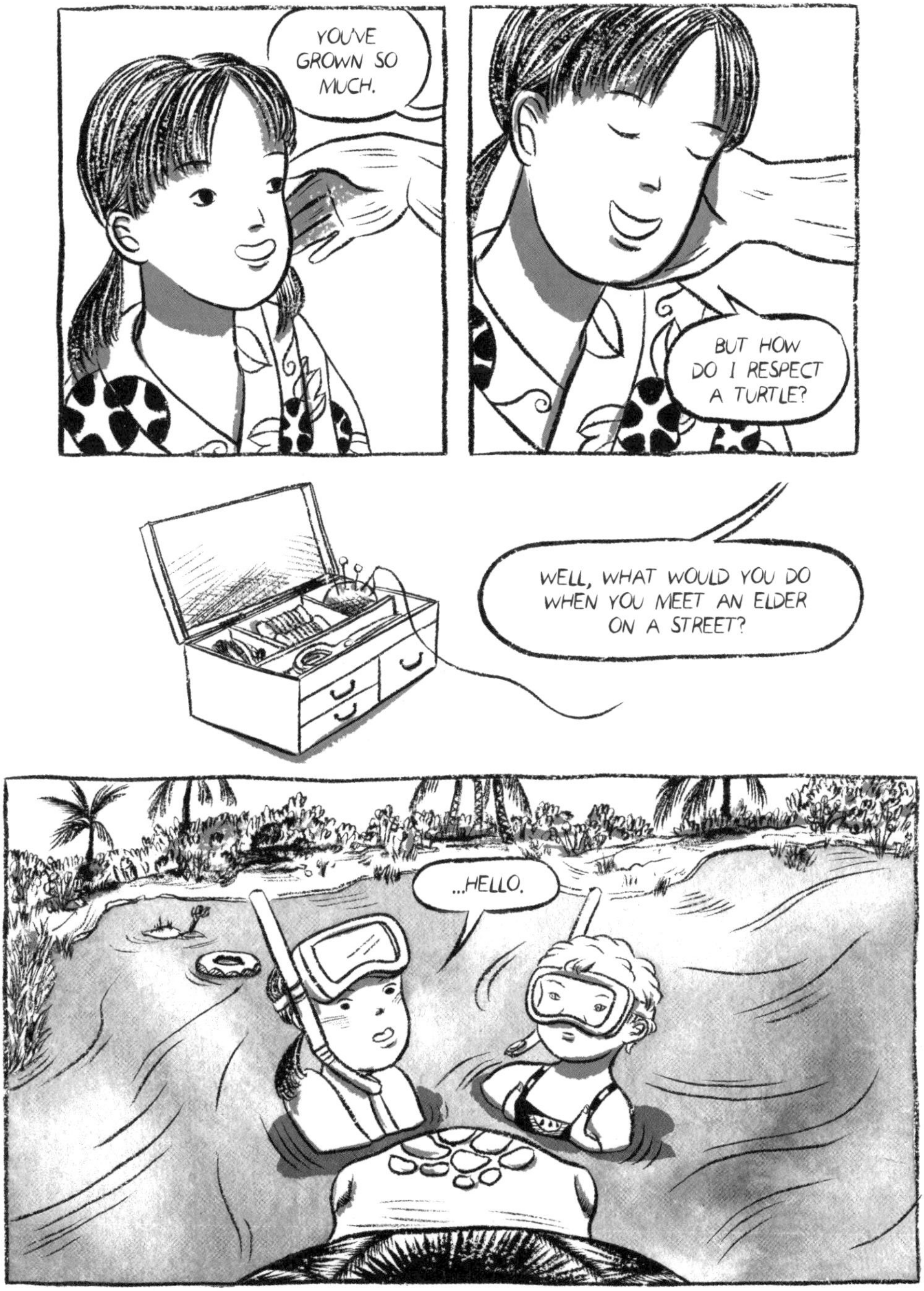
YOU'VE GROWN SO MUCH.
BUT HOW DO I RESPECT A TURTLE?
WELL, WHAT WOULD YOU DO WHEN YOU MEET AN ELDER ON A STREET?
...HELLO.

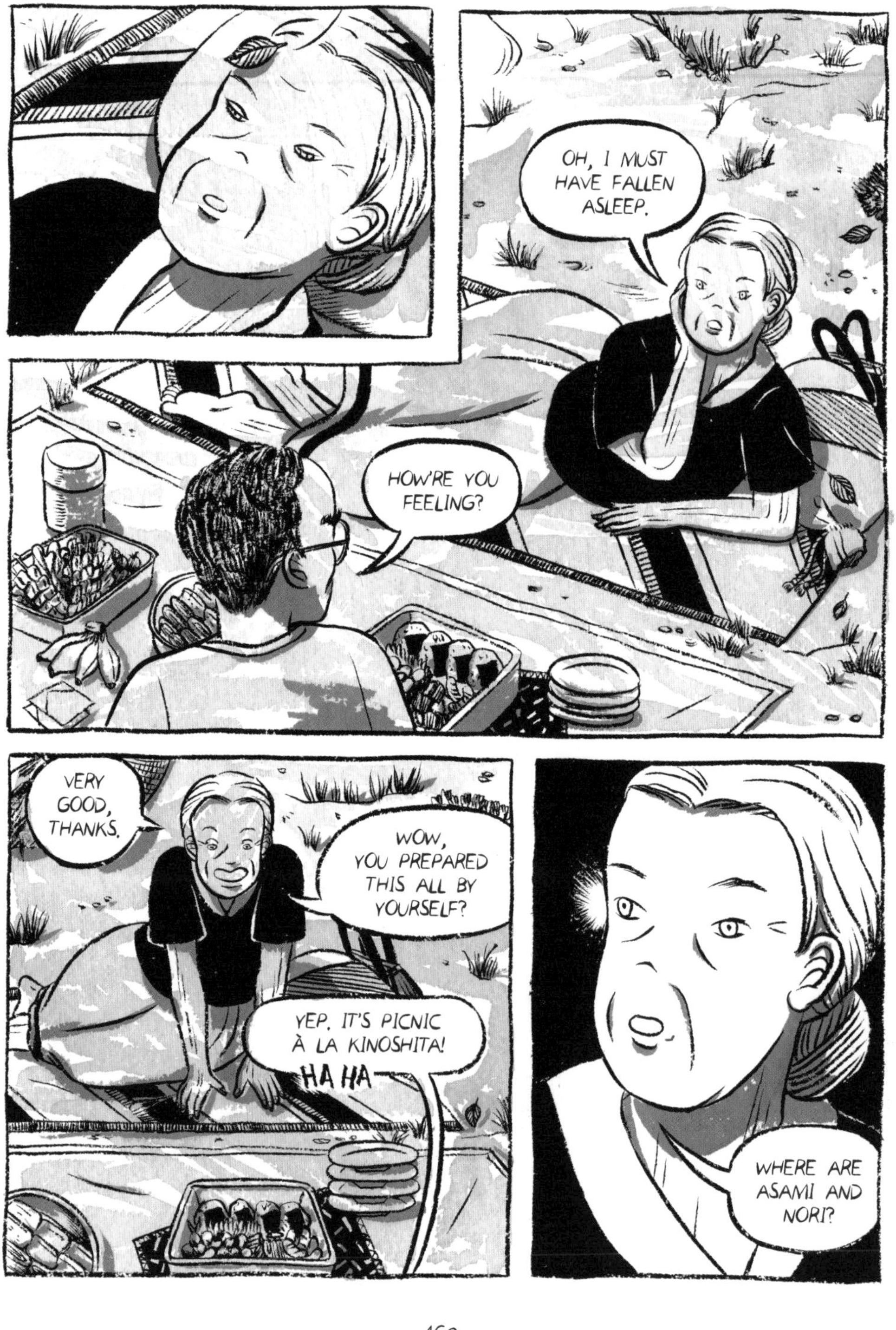
OH, I MUST HAVE FALLEN ASLEEP.
HOW'RE YOU FEELING?
VERY GOOD, THANKS.
WOW, YOU PREPARED THIS ALL BY YOURSELF?
YEP. IT'S PICNIC À LA KINOSHITA!
HA HA
WHERE ARE ASAMI AND NORI?

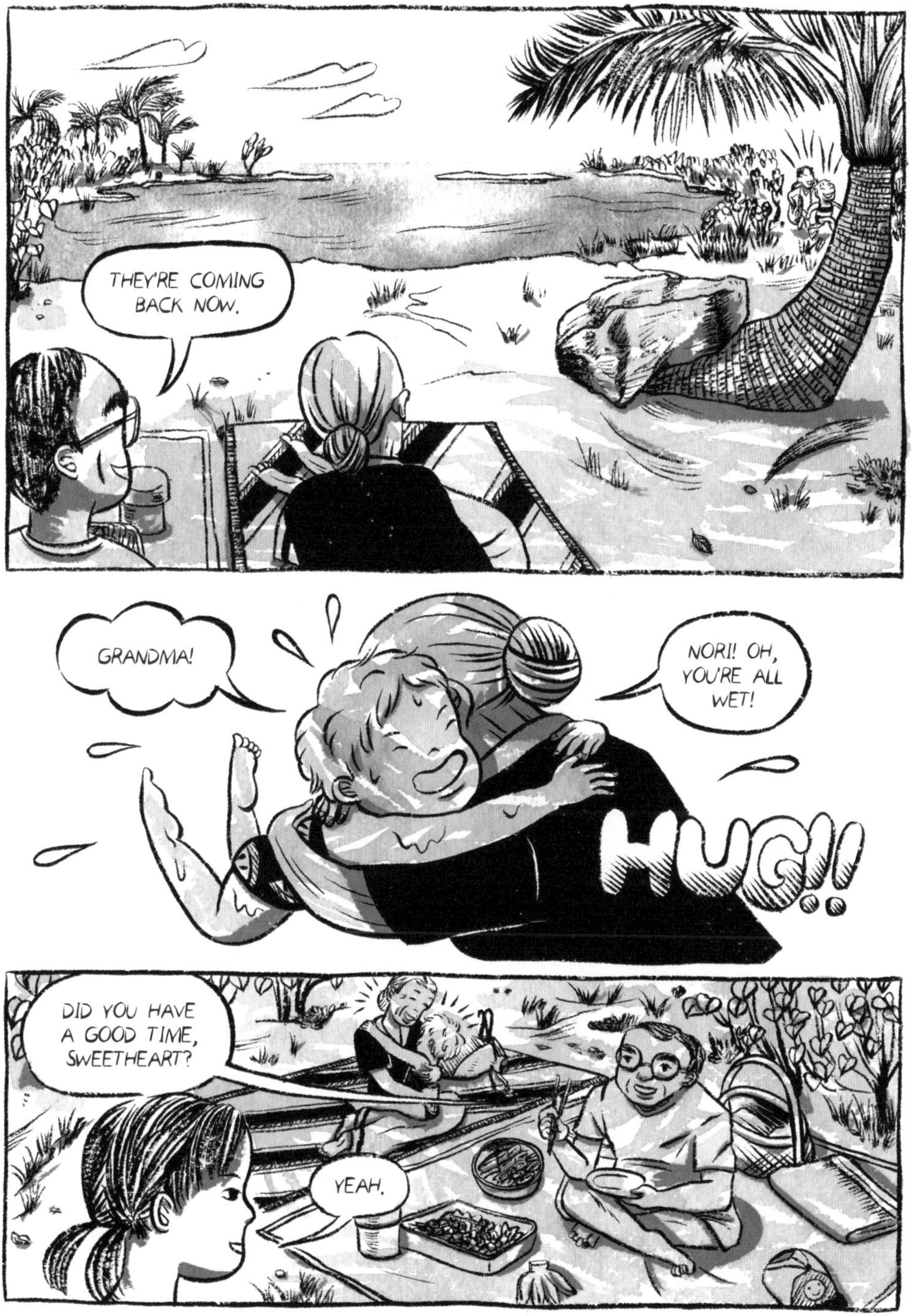
THEY'RE COMING BACK NOW.
GRANDMA!
NORI! OH, YOU'RE ALL WET!
HUG!!
DID YOU HAVE A GOOD TIME, SWEETHEART?
YEAH.

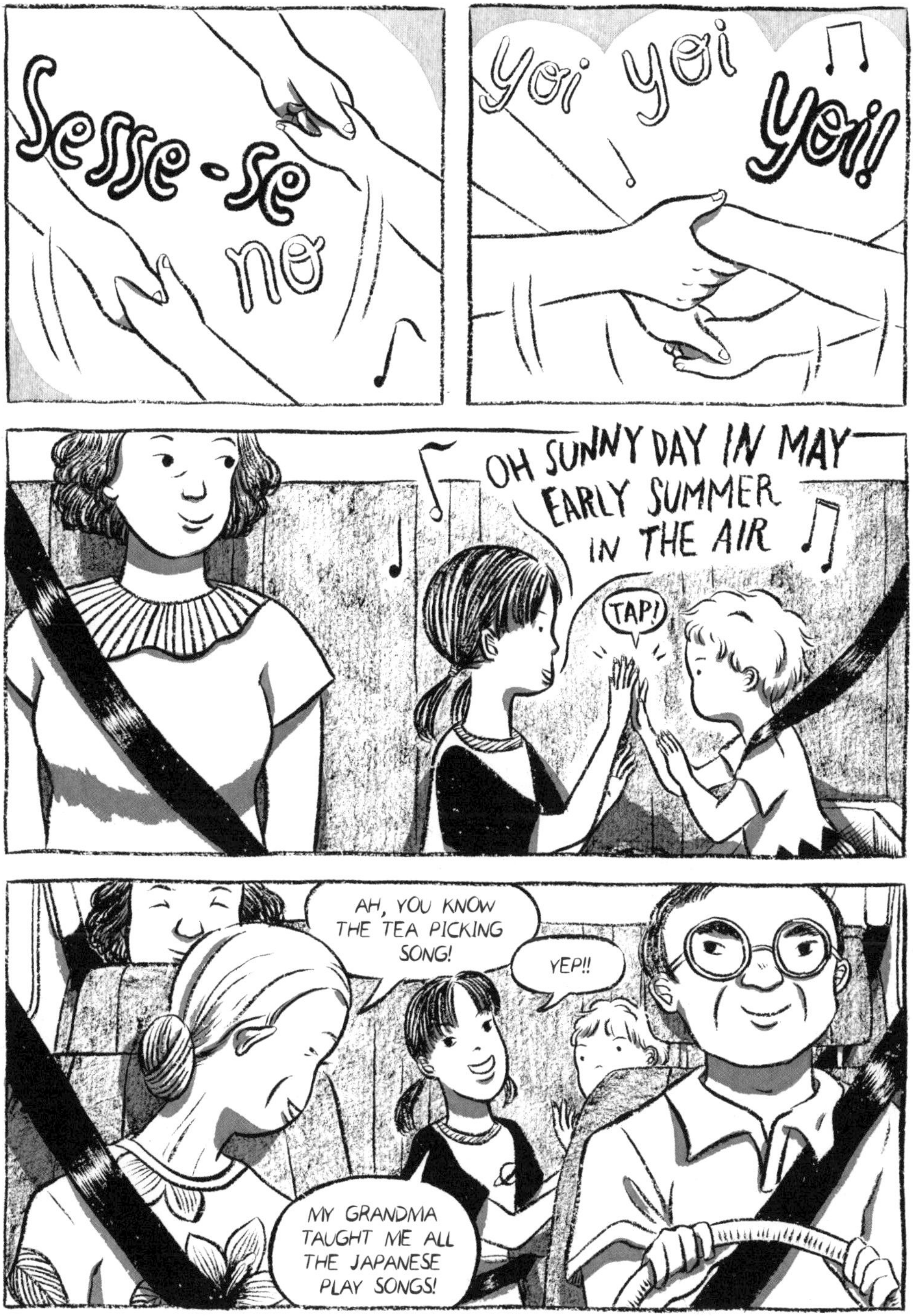

Sesse-se no
yoi yoi yoi!
OH SUNNY DAY IN MAY EARLY SUMMER IN THE AIR
TAP!
AH, YOU KNOW THE TEA PICKING SONG!
YEP!!
MY GRANDMA TAUGHT ME ALL THE JAPANESE PLAY SONGS!

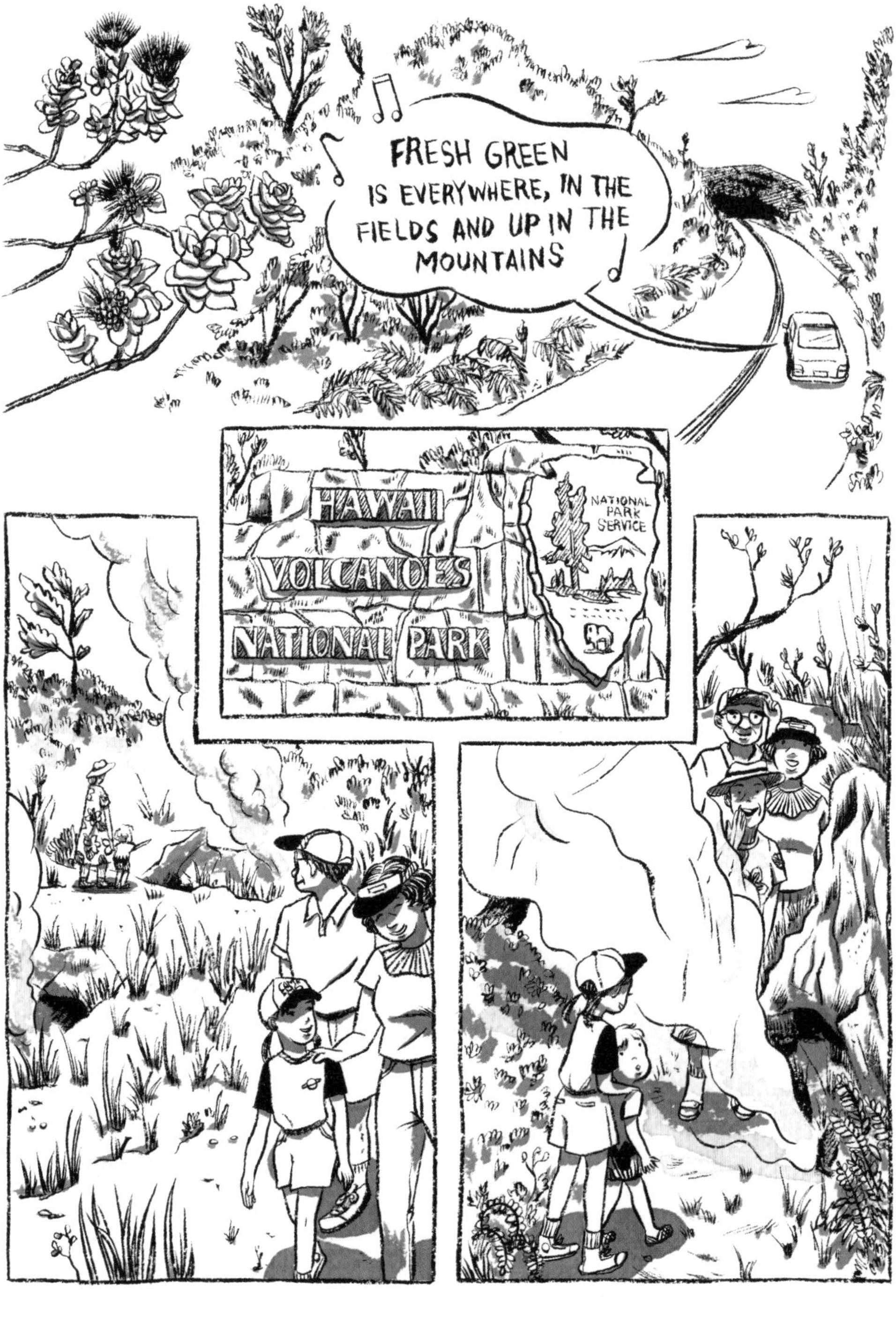
FRESH GREEN IS EVERYWHERE, IN THE FIELDS AND UP IN THE MOUNTAINS
HAWAII VOLCANOES NATIONAL PARK
NATIONAL PARK SERVICE

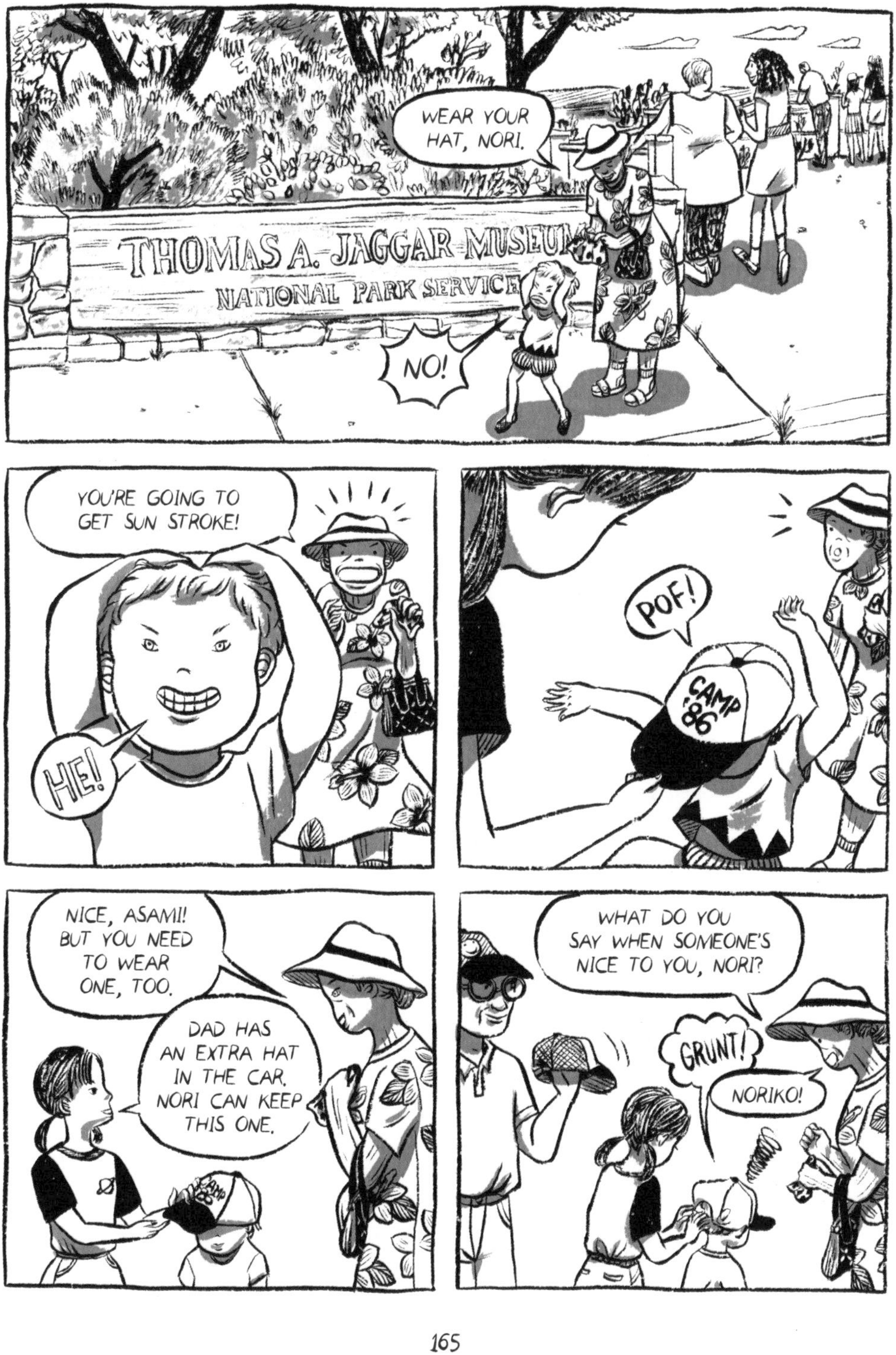

WEAR YOUR HAT, NORI.
THOMAS A. JAGGAR MUSEUM
NATIONAL PARK SERVICE
NO!
YOU'RE GOING TO GET SUN STROKE!
HE!
POF!
CAMP '86
NICE, ASAMI! BUT YOU NEED TO WEAR ONE, TOO.
DAD HAS AN EXTRA HAT IN THE CAR. NORI CAN KEEP THIS ONE.
WHAT DO YOU SAY WHEN SOMEONE'S NICE TO YOU, NORI?
GRUNT!
NORIKO!

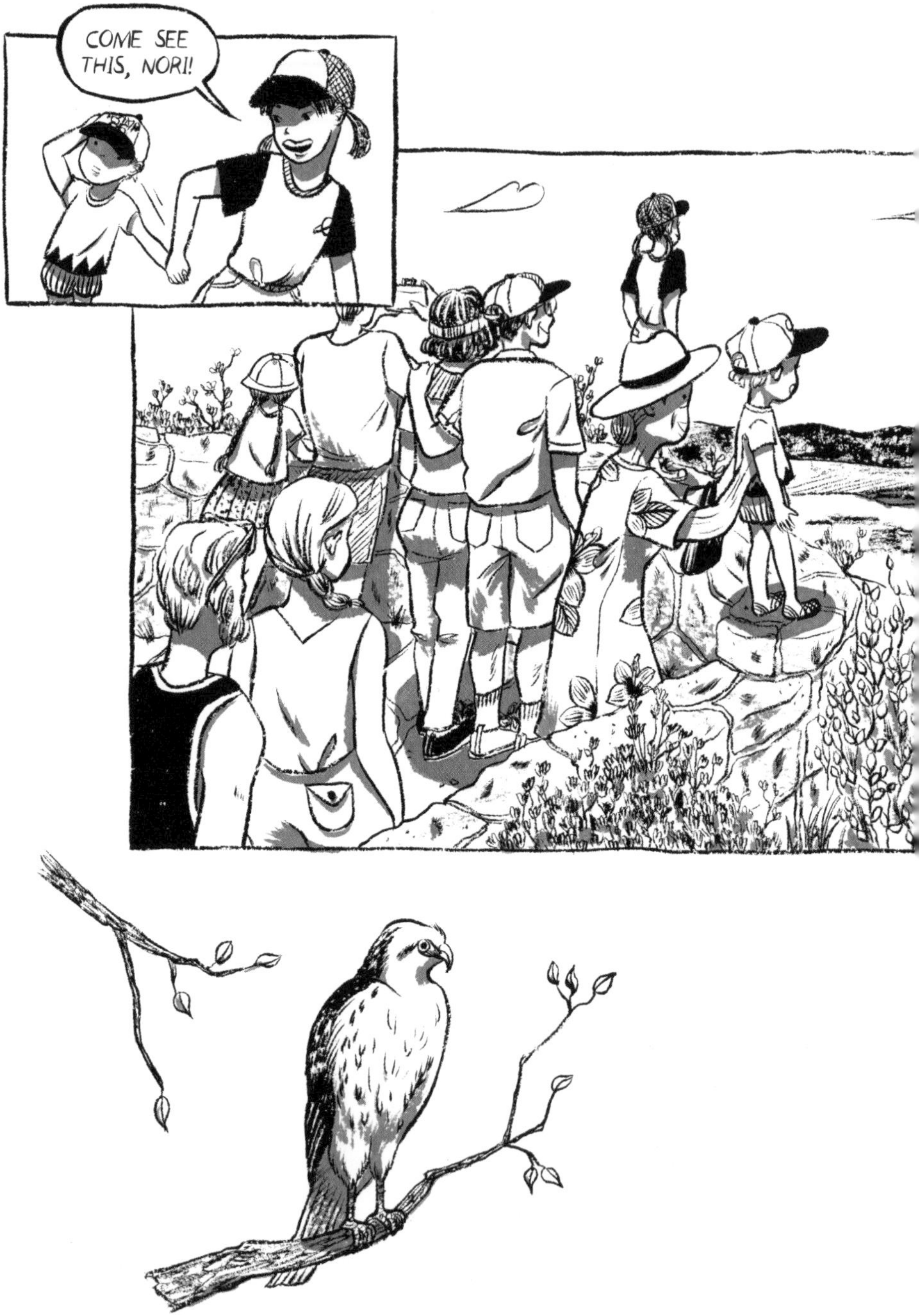
COME SEE THIS, NORI!

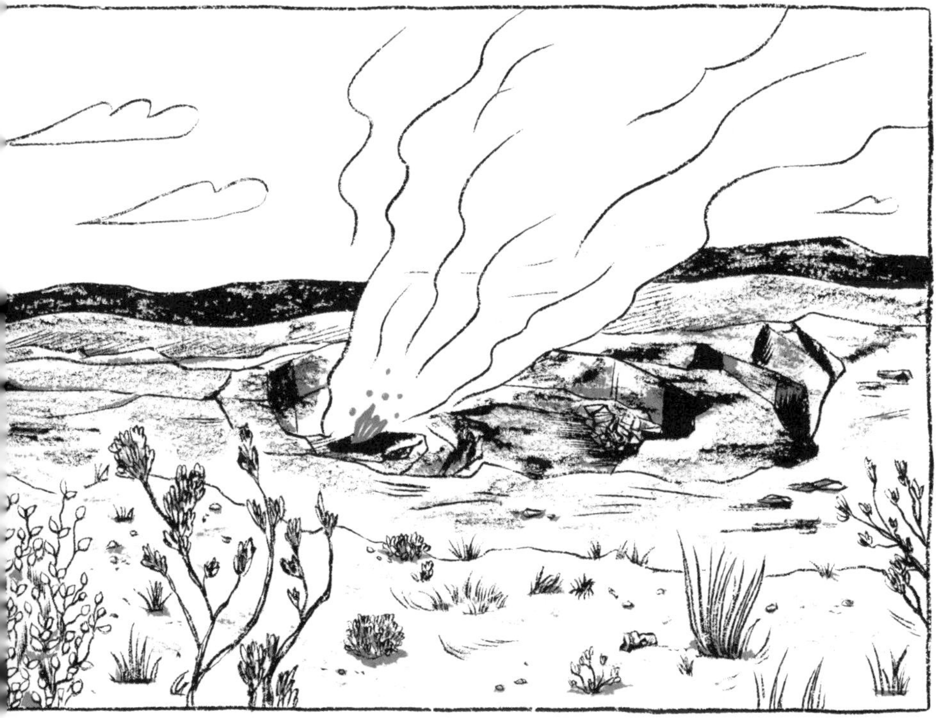

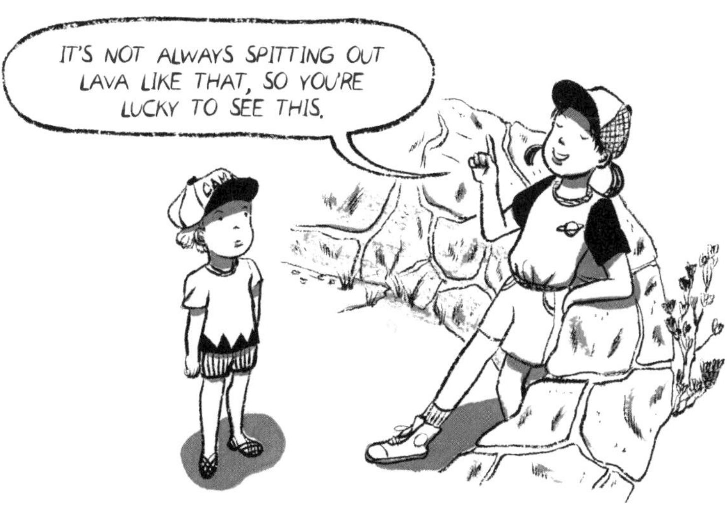
IT'S NOT ALWAYS SPITTING OUT LAVA LIKE THAT, SO YOU'RE LUCKY TO SEE THIS.

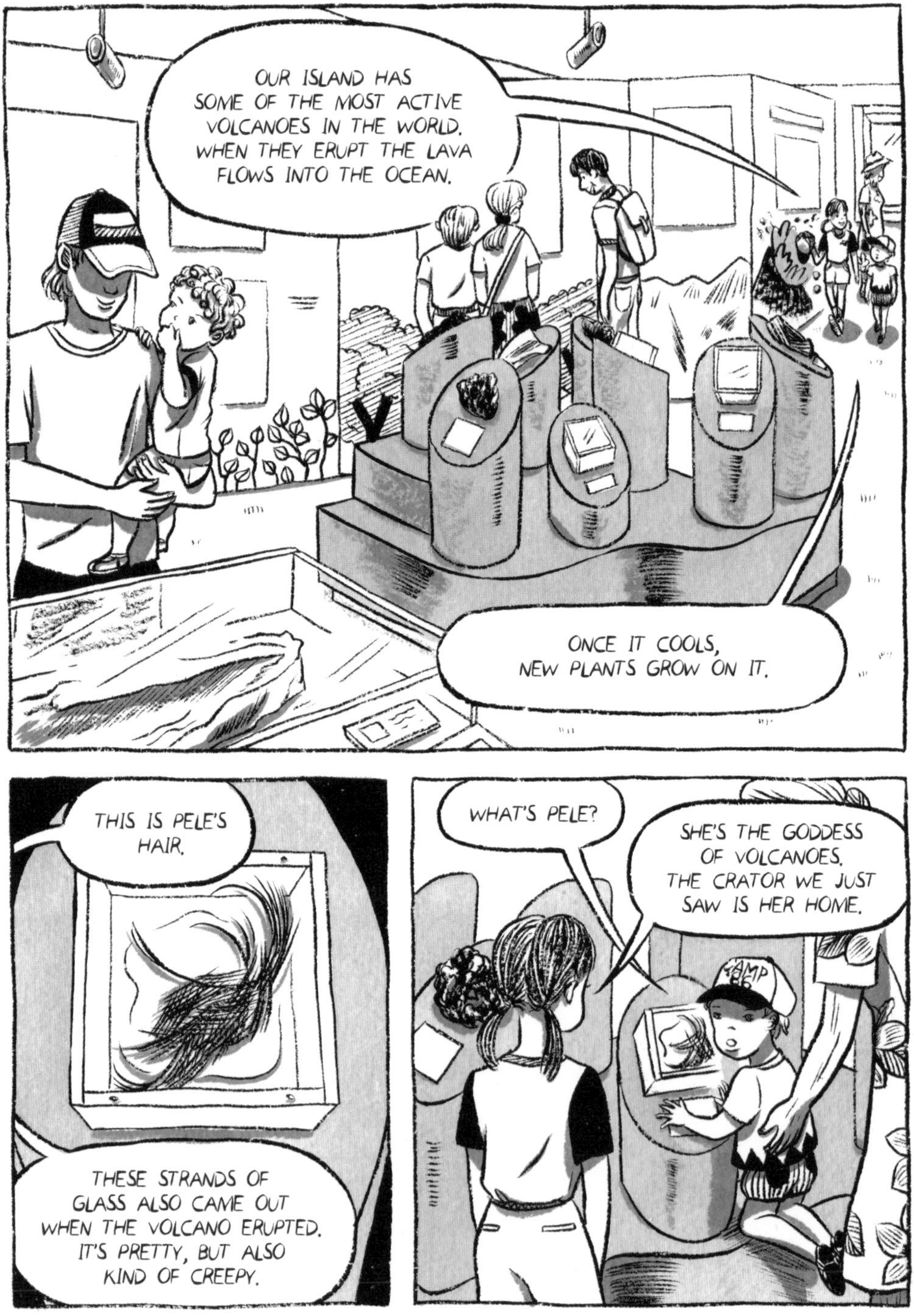
OUR ISLAND HAS SOME OF THE MOST ACTIVE VOLCANOES IN THE WORLD. WHEN THEY ERUPT THE LAVA FLOWS INTO THE OCEAN.
ONCE IT COOLS, NEW PLANTS GROW ON IT.
THIS IS PELE'S HAIR.
THESE STRANDS OF GLASS ALSO CAME OUT WHEN THE VOLCANO ERUPTED. IT'S PRETTY, BUT ALSO KIND OF CREEPY.
WHAT'S PELE?
SHE'S THE GODDESS OF VOLCANOES. THE CRATOR WE JUST SAW IS HER HOME.

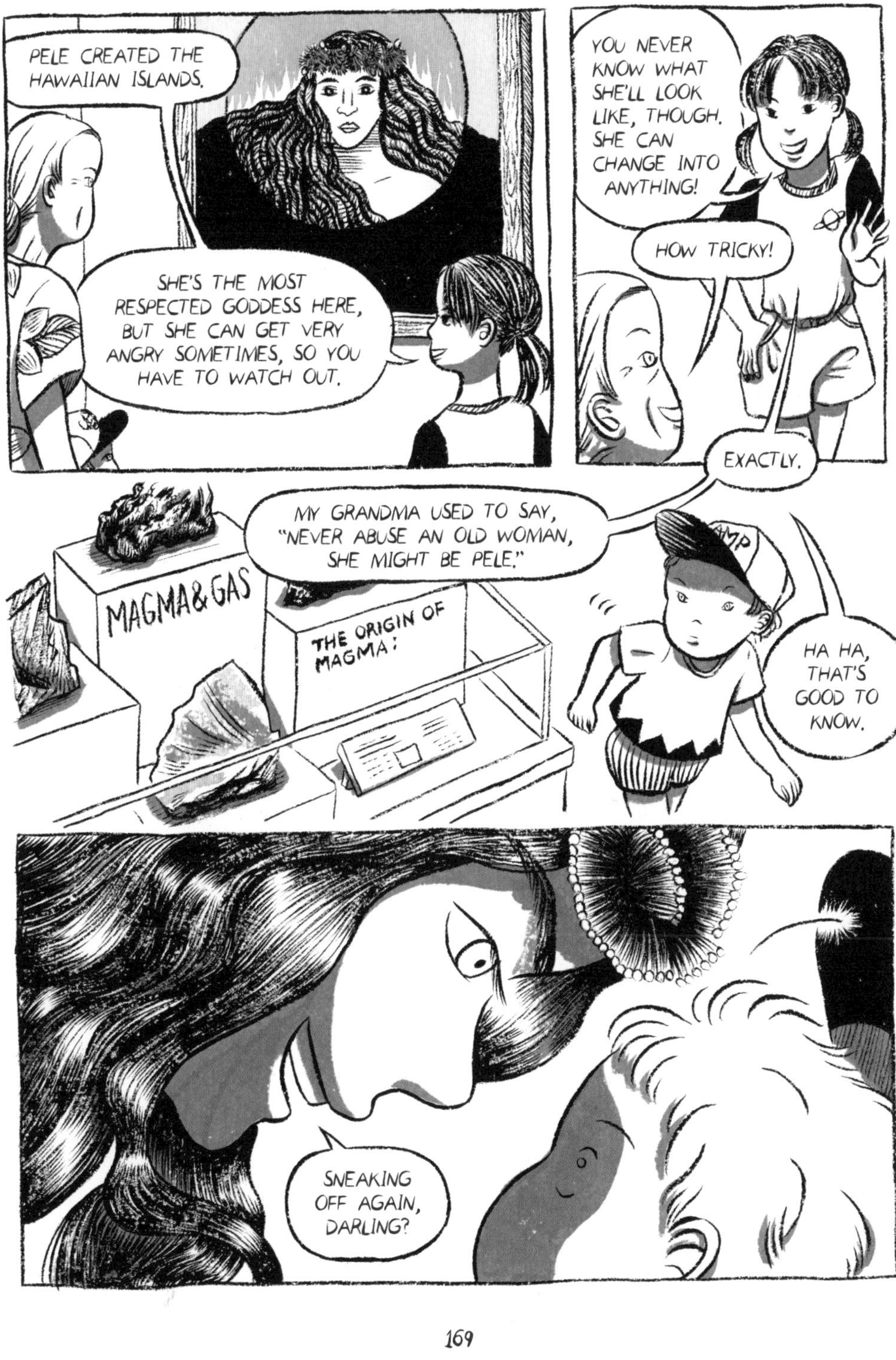
PELE CREATED THE HAWAIIAN ISLANDS.
SHE'S THE MOST RESPECTED GODDESS HERE, BUT SHE CAN GET VERY ANGRY SOMETIMES, SO YOU HAVE TO WATCH OUT.
YOU NEVER KNOW WHAT SHE'LL LOOK LIKE, THOUGH. SHE CAN CHANGE INTO ANYTHING!
HOW TRICKY!
EXACTLY.
MY GRANDMA USED TO SAY, "NEVER ABUSE AN OLD WOMAN, SHE MIGHT BE PELE."
MAGMA & GAS
THE ORIGIN OF MAGMA:
HA HA, THAT'S GOOD TO KNOW.
SNEAKING OFF AGAIN, DARLING?

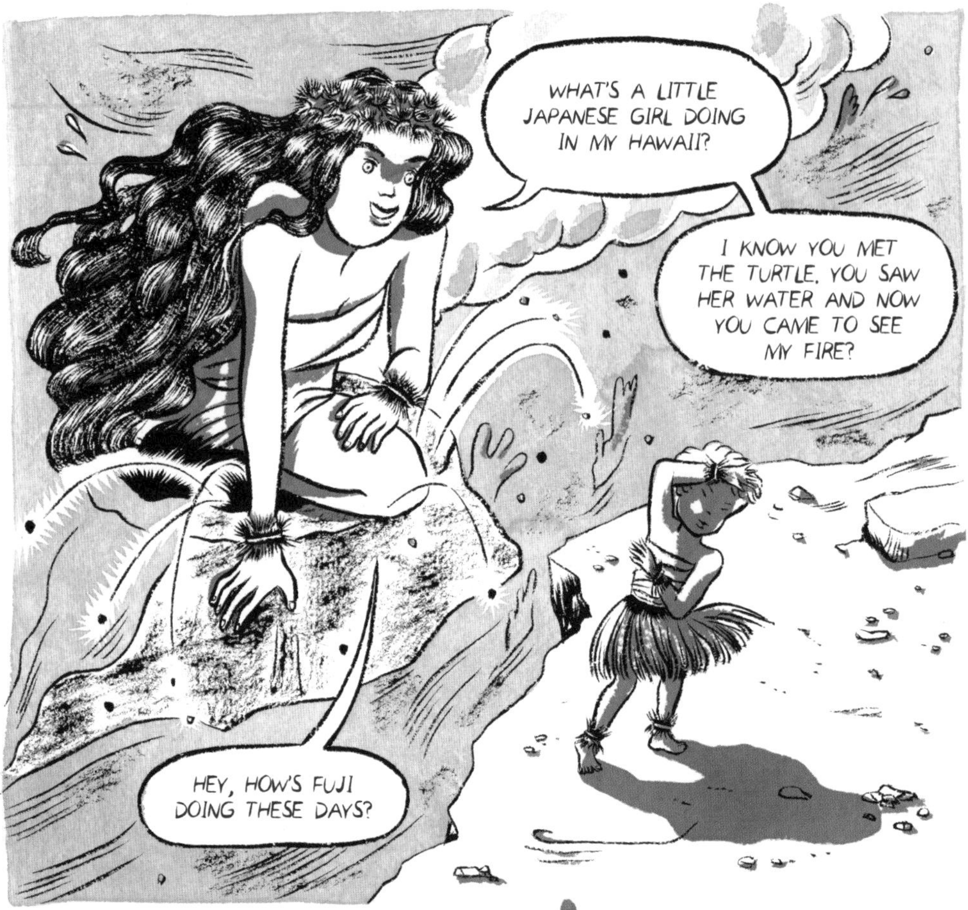
WHAT'S A LITTLE JAPANESE GIRL DOING IN MY HAWAII?
I KNOW YOU MET THE TURTLE. YOU SAW HER WATER AND NOW YOU CAME TO SEE MY FIRE?
HEY, HOW'S FUJI DOING THESE DAYS?

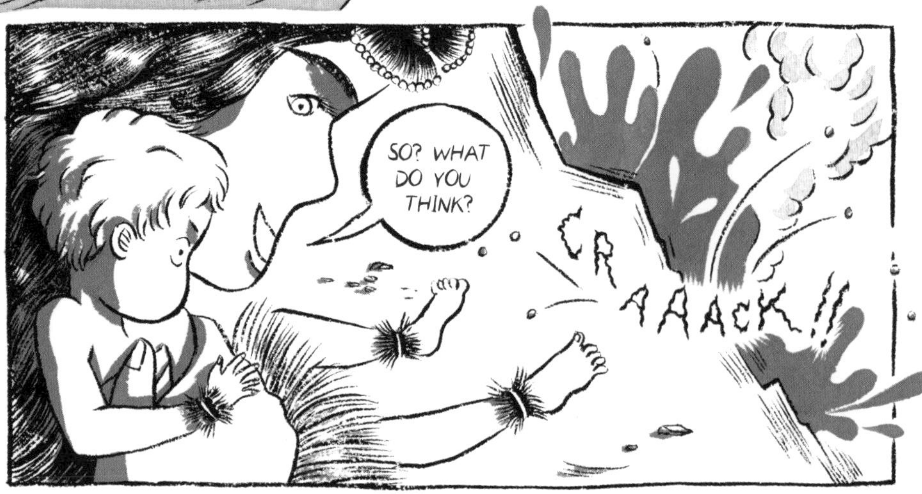
SO? WHAT DO YOU THINK?
CRAAACK!!

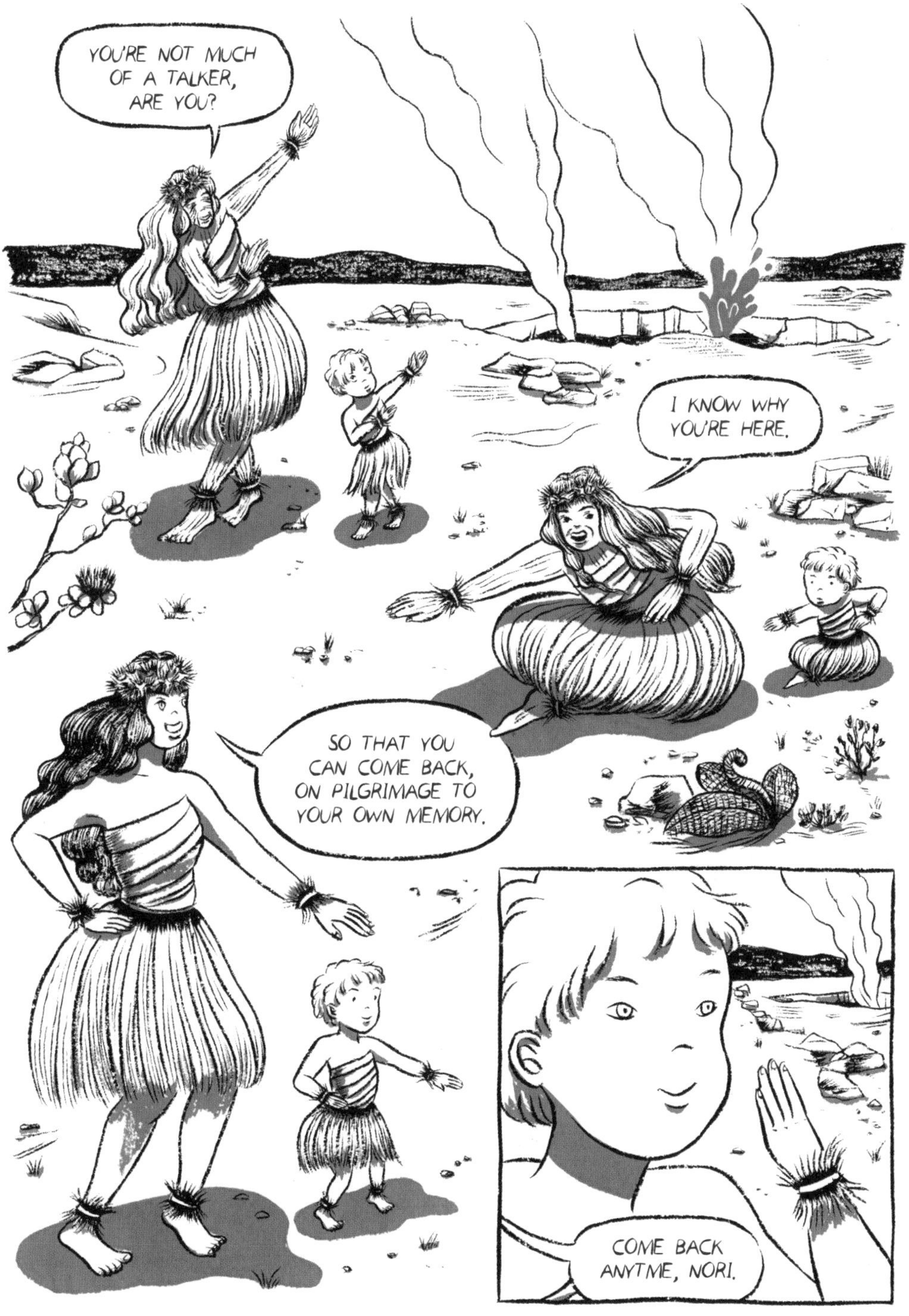
YOU'RE NOT MUCH OF A TALKER, ARE YOU?
I KNOW WHY YOU'RE HERE.
SO THAT YOU CAN COME BACK, ON PILGRIMAGE TO YOUR OWN MEMORY.
COME BACK ANYTME, NORI.

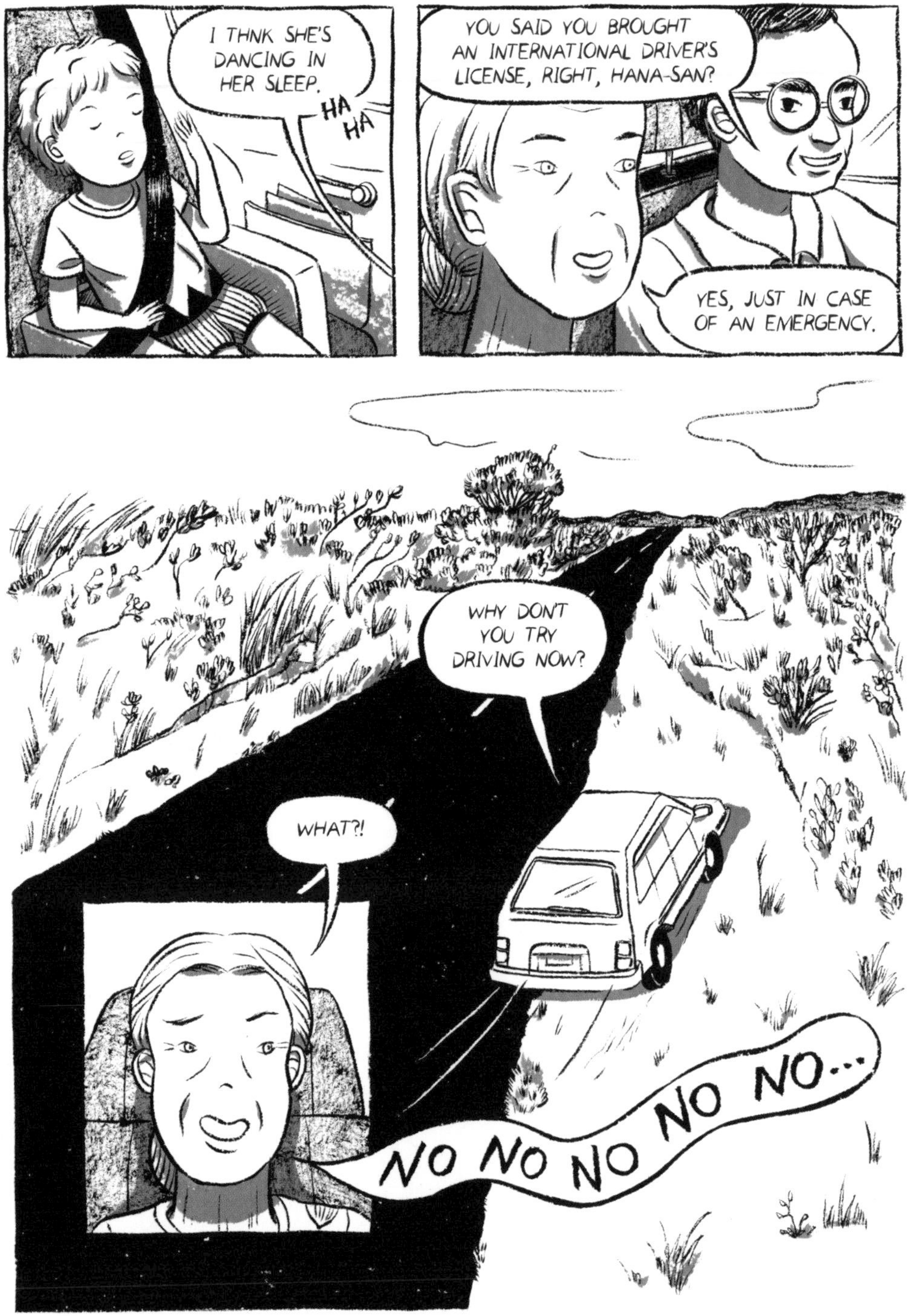
I THNK SHE'S DANCING IN HER SLEEP.
HA HA
YOU SAID YOU BROUGHT AN INTERNATIONAL DRIVER'S LICENSE, RIGHT, HANA-SAN?
YES, JUST IN CASE OF AN EMERGENCY.
WHY DON'T YOU TRY DRIVING NOW?
WHAT?!
NO NO NO NO NO...

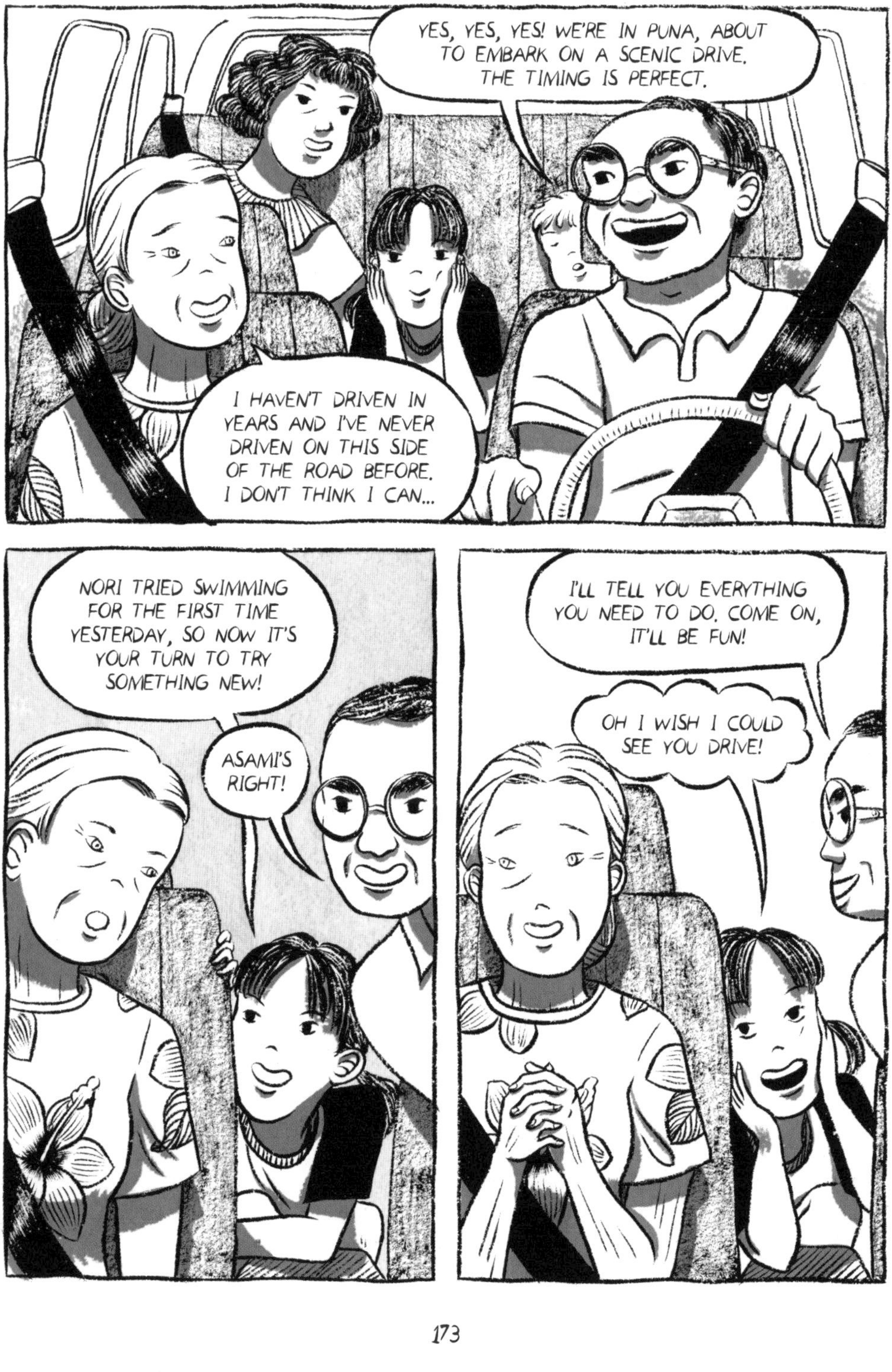
YES, YES, YES! WE'RE IN PUNA, ABOUT TO EMBARK ON A SCENIC DRIVE. THE TIMING IS PERFECT.
I HAVEN'T DRIVEN IN YEARS AND I'VE NEVER DRIVEN ON THIS SIDE OF THE ROAD BEFORE. I DON'T THINK I CAN...
NORI TRIED SWIMMING FOR THE FIRST TIME YESTERDAY, SO NOW IT'S YOUR TURN TO TRY SOMETHING NEW!
ASAMI'S RIGHT!
I'LL TELL YOU EVERYTHING YOU NEED TO DO. COME ON, IT'LL BE FUN!
OH I WISH I COULD SEE YOU DRIVE!

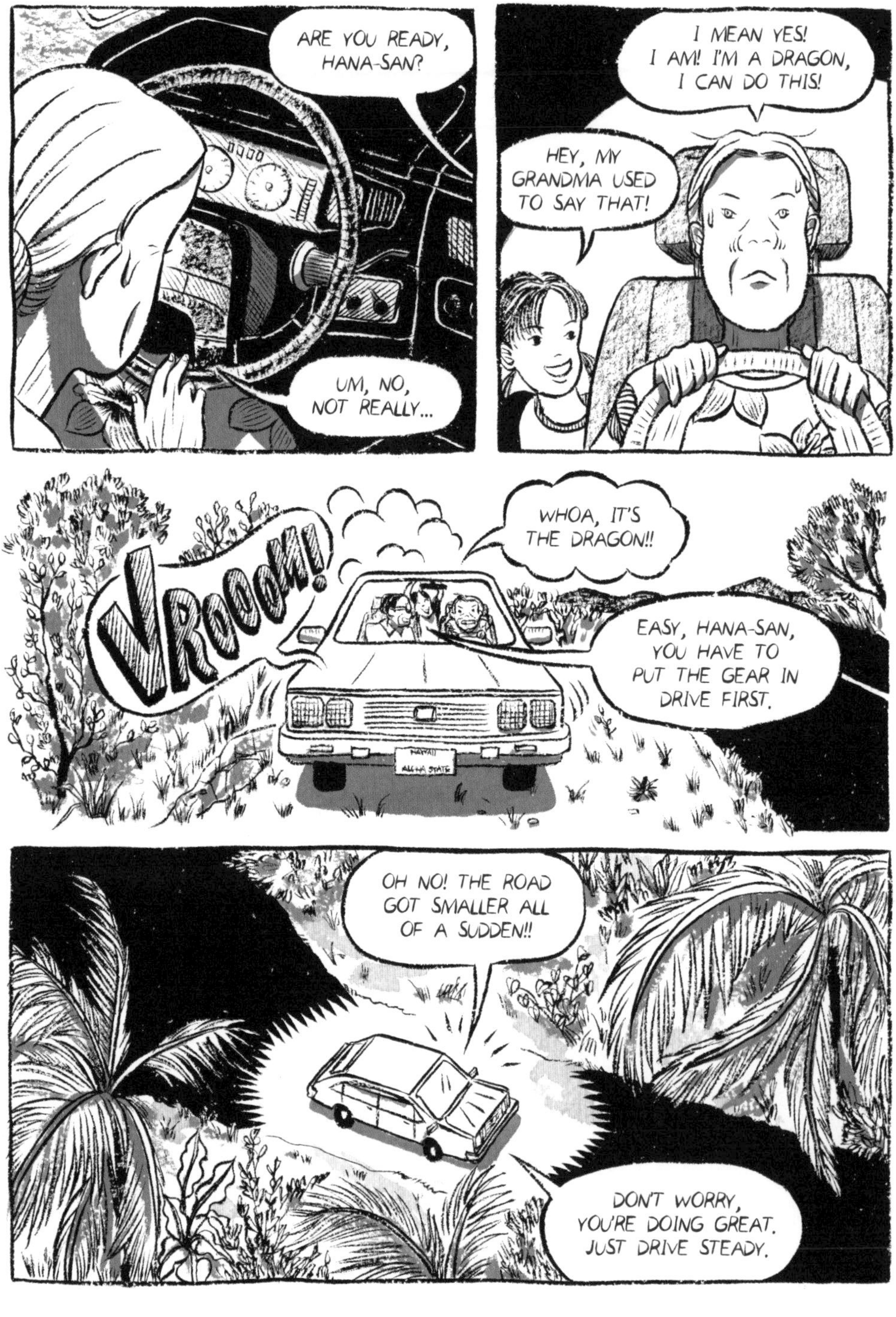
ARE YOU READY, HANA-SAN?
UM, NO, NOT REALLY...
I MEAN YES! I AM! I'M A DRAGON, I CAN DO THIS!
HEY, MY GRANDMA USED TO SAY THAT!
VROOOM!
WHOA, IT'S THE DRAGON!!
EASY, HANA-SAN, YOU HAVE TO PUT THE GEAR IN DRIVE FIRST.
OH NO! THE ROAD GOT SMALLER ALL OF A SUDDEN!!
DON'T WORRY, YOU'RE DOING GREAT. JUST DRIVE STEADY.

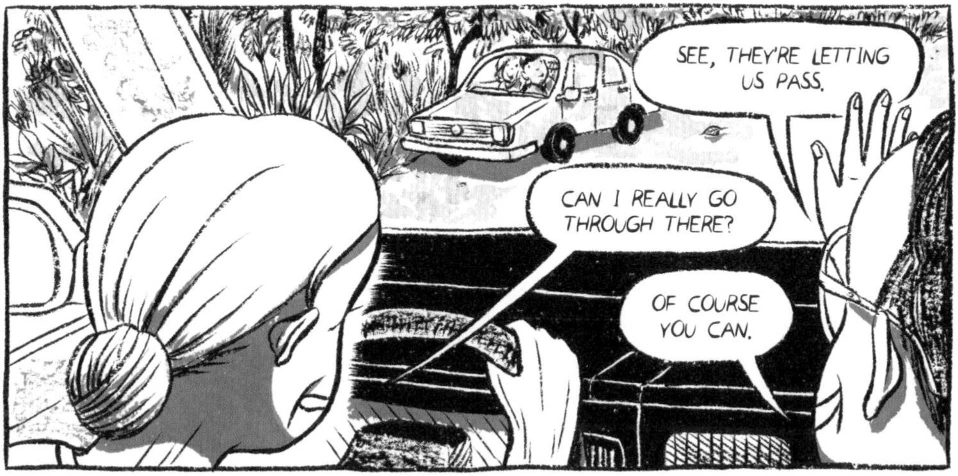
SEE, THEY'RE LETTING US PASS.
CAN I REALLY GO THROUGH THERE?
OF COURSE YOU CAN.

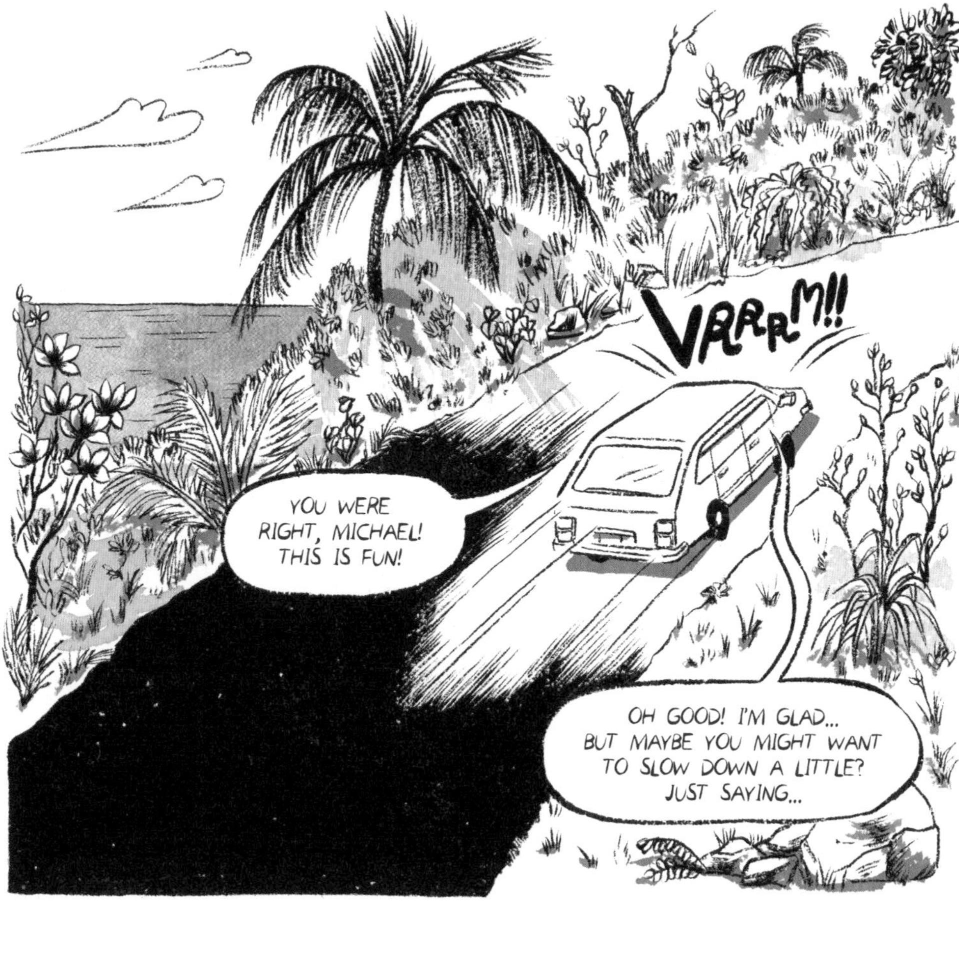
VRRRM!!
YOU WERE RIGHT, MICHAEL! THIS IS FUN!
OH GOOD! I'M GLAD... BUT MAYBE YOU MIGHT WANT TO SLOW DOWN A LITTLE? JUST SAYING...

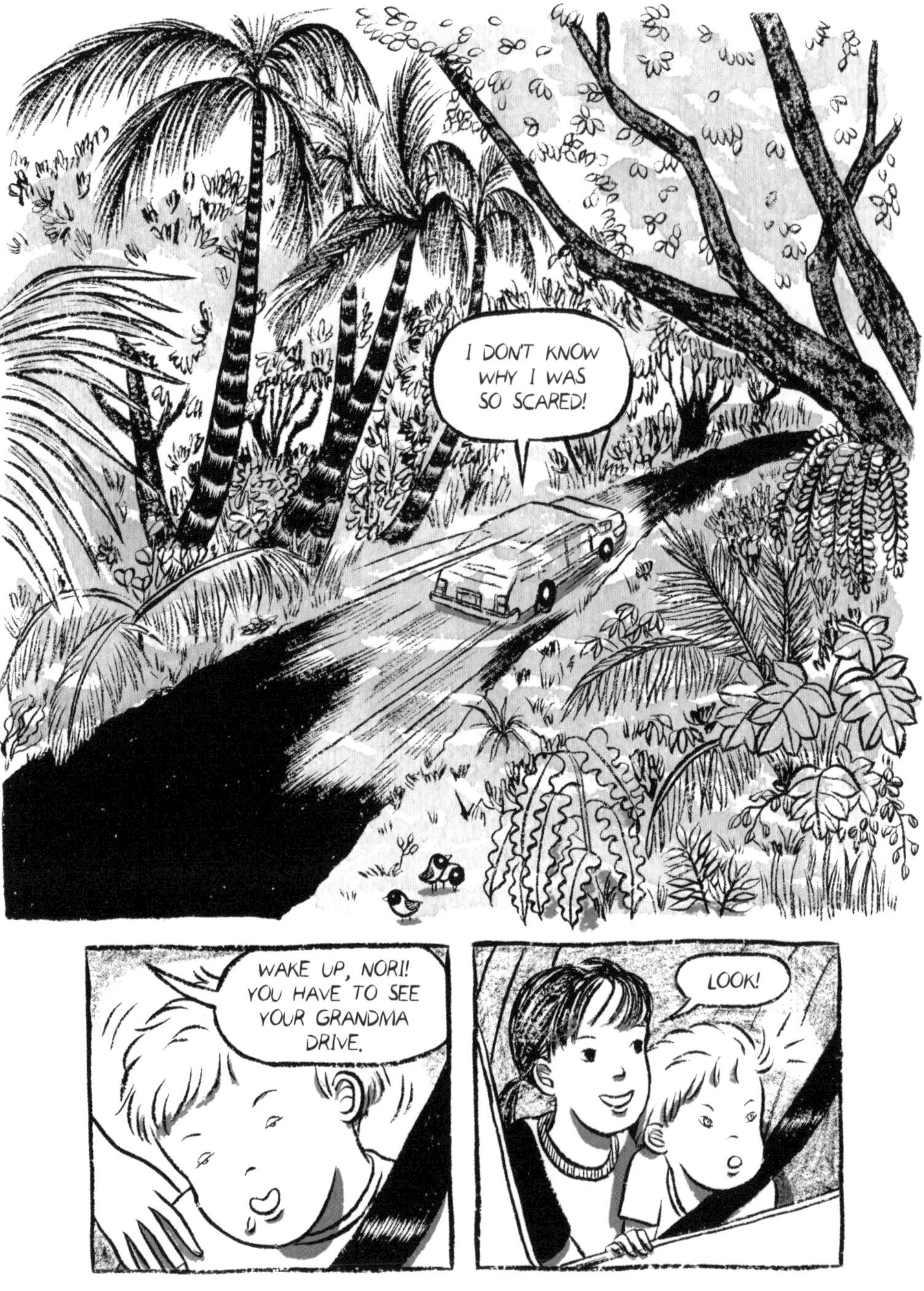
I DON'T KNOW WHY I WAS SO SCARED!
WAKE UP, NORI! YOU HAVE TO SEE YOUR GRANDMA DRIVE.
LOOK!

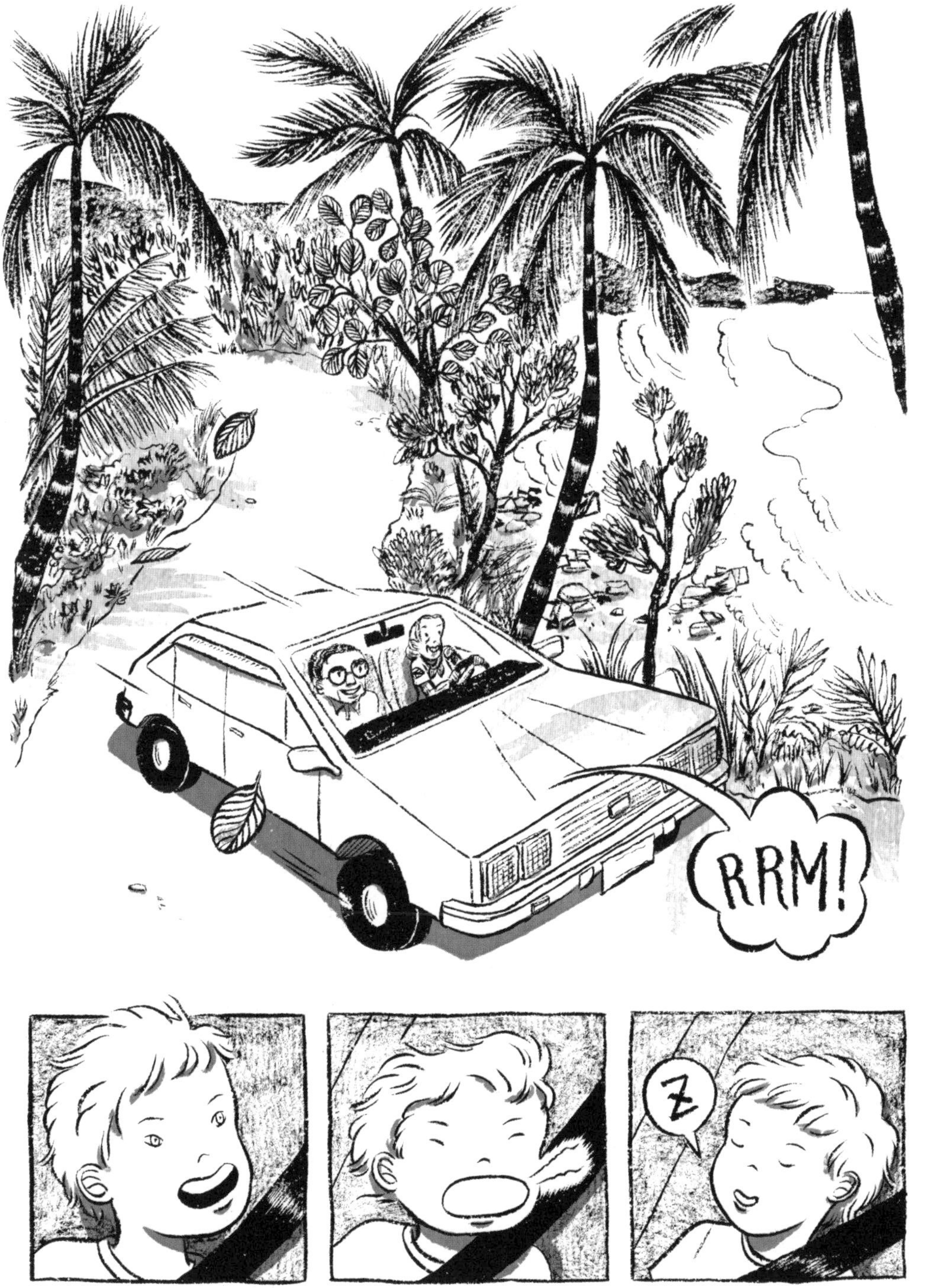
RRM!
Z

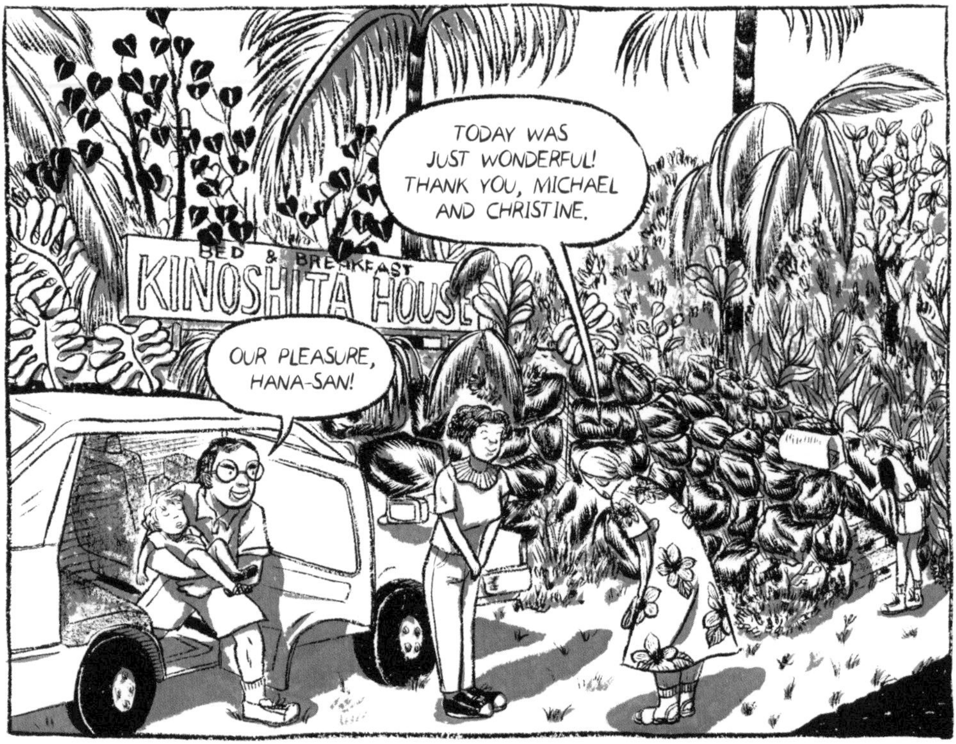
BED & BREAKFAST
KINOSHITA HOUSE
TODAY WAS JUST WONDERFUL! THANK YOU, MICHAEL AND CHRISTINE.
OUR PLEASURE, HANA-SAN!

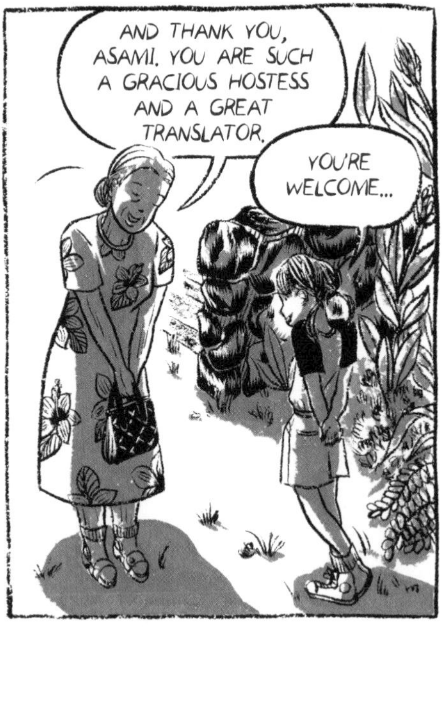
AND THANK YOU, ASAMI. YOU ARE SUCH A GRACIOUS HOSTESS AND A GREAT TRANSLATOR.
YOU'RE WELCOME...

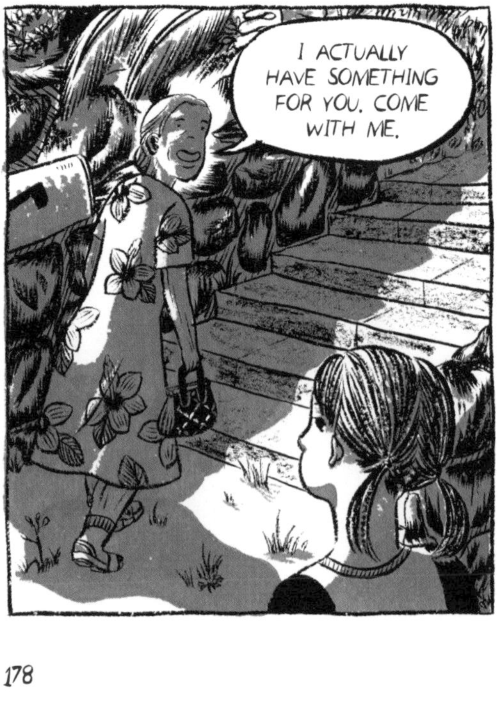
I ACTUALLY HAVE SOMETHING FOR YOU. COME WITH ME.

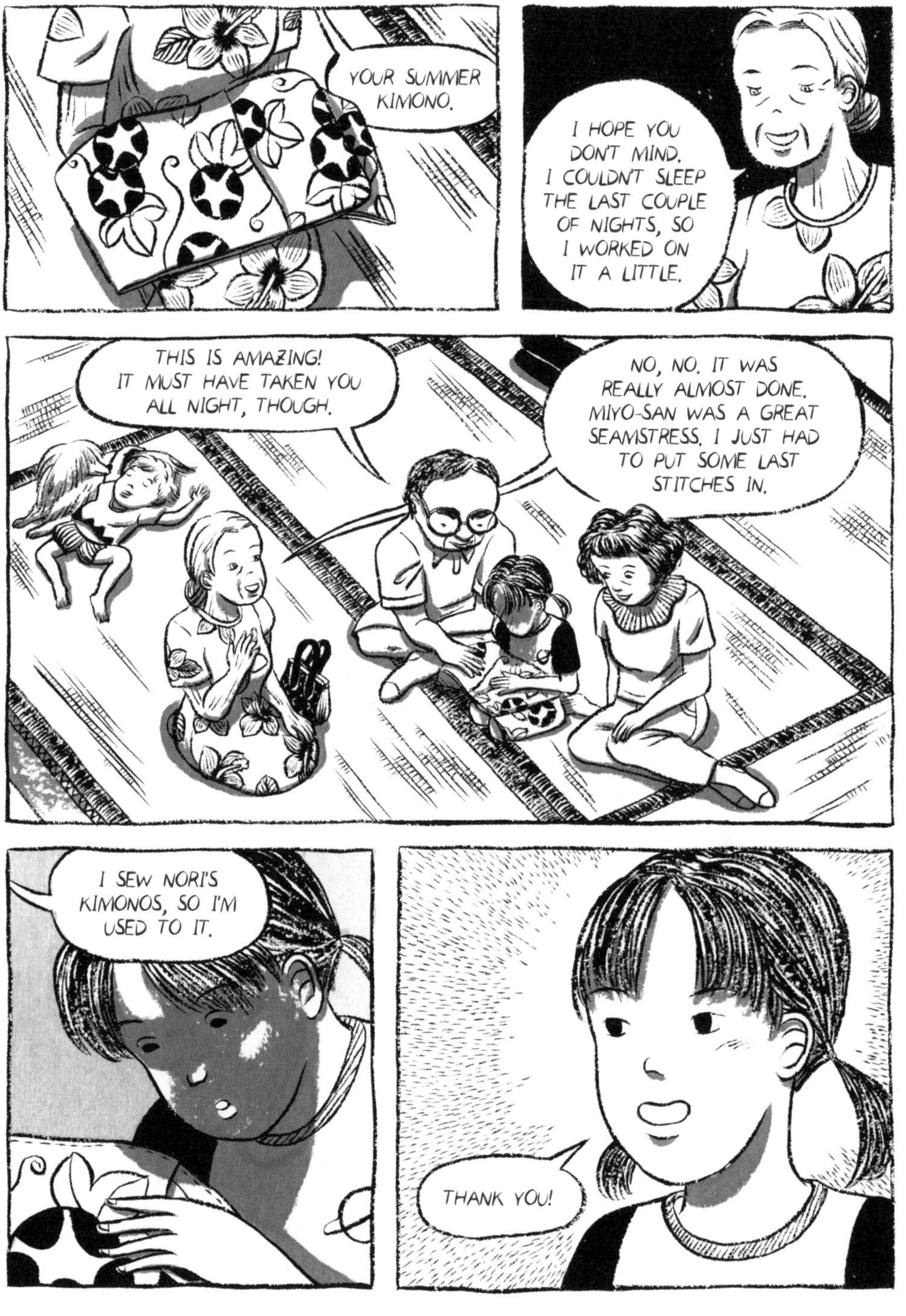
YOUR SUMMER KIMONO.
I HOPE YOU DON'T MIND. I COULDN'T SLEEP THE LAST COUPLE OF NIGHTS, SO I WORKED ON IT A LITTLE.
THIS IS AMAZING! IT MUST HAVE TAKEN YOU ALL NIGHT, THOUGH.
NO, NO. IT WAS REALLY ALMOST DONE. MIYO-SAN WAS A GREAT SEAMSTRESS. I JUST HAD TO PUT SOME LAST STITCHES IN.
I SEW NORI'S KIMONOS, SO I'M USED TO IT.
THANK YOU!

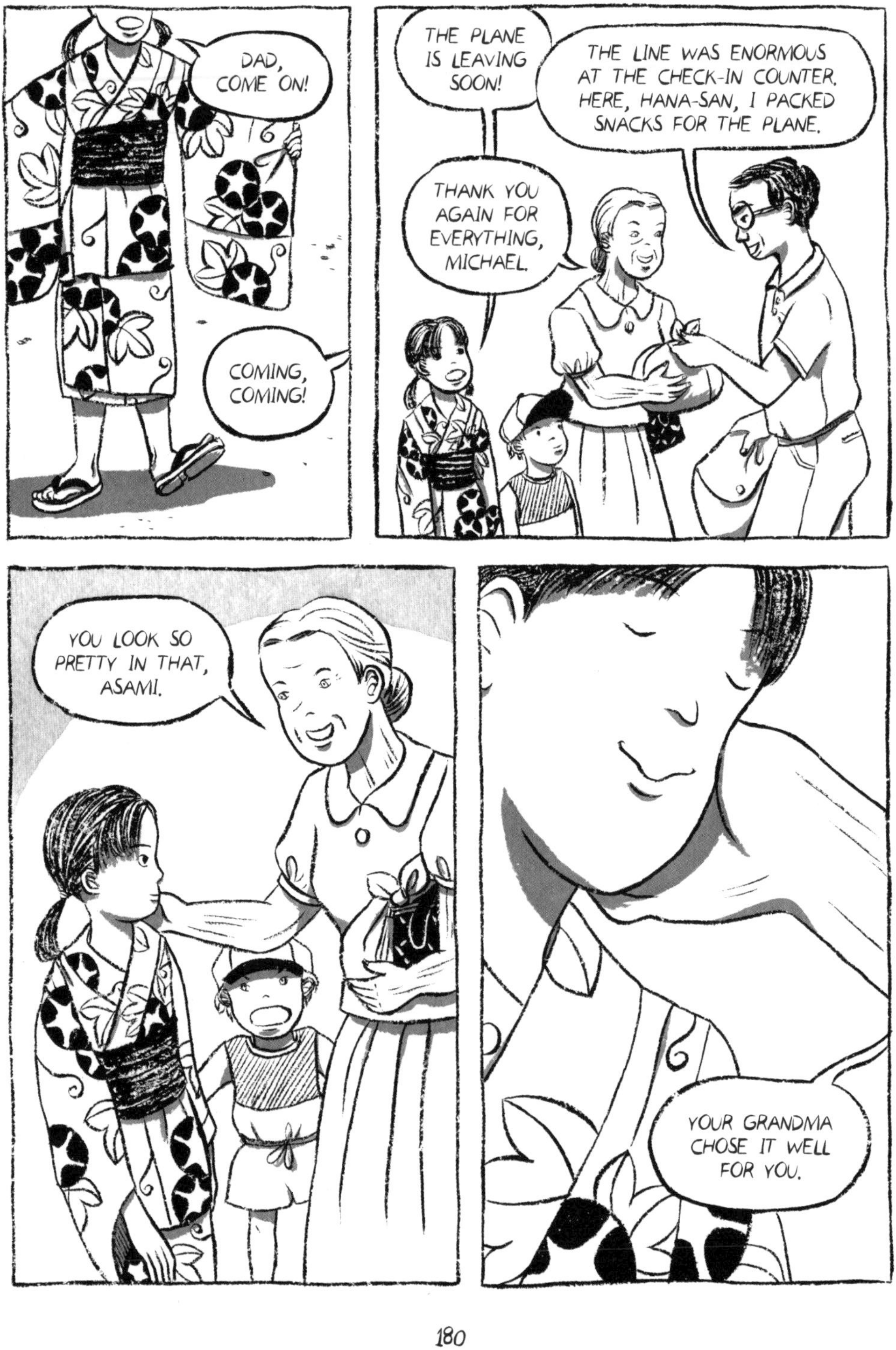
DAD, COME ON!
COMING, COMING!
THE PLANE IS LEAVING SOON!
THE LINE WAS ENORMOUS AT THE CHECK-IN COUNTER. HERE, HANA-SAN, I PACKED SNACKS FOR THE PLANE.
THANK YOU AGAIN FOR EVERYTHING, MICHAEL.
YOU LOOK SO PRETTY IN THAT, ASAMI.
YOUR GRANDMA CHOSE IT WELL FOR YOU.

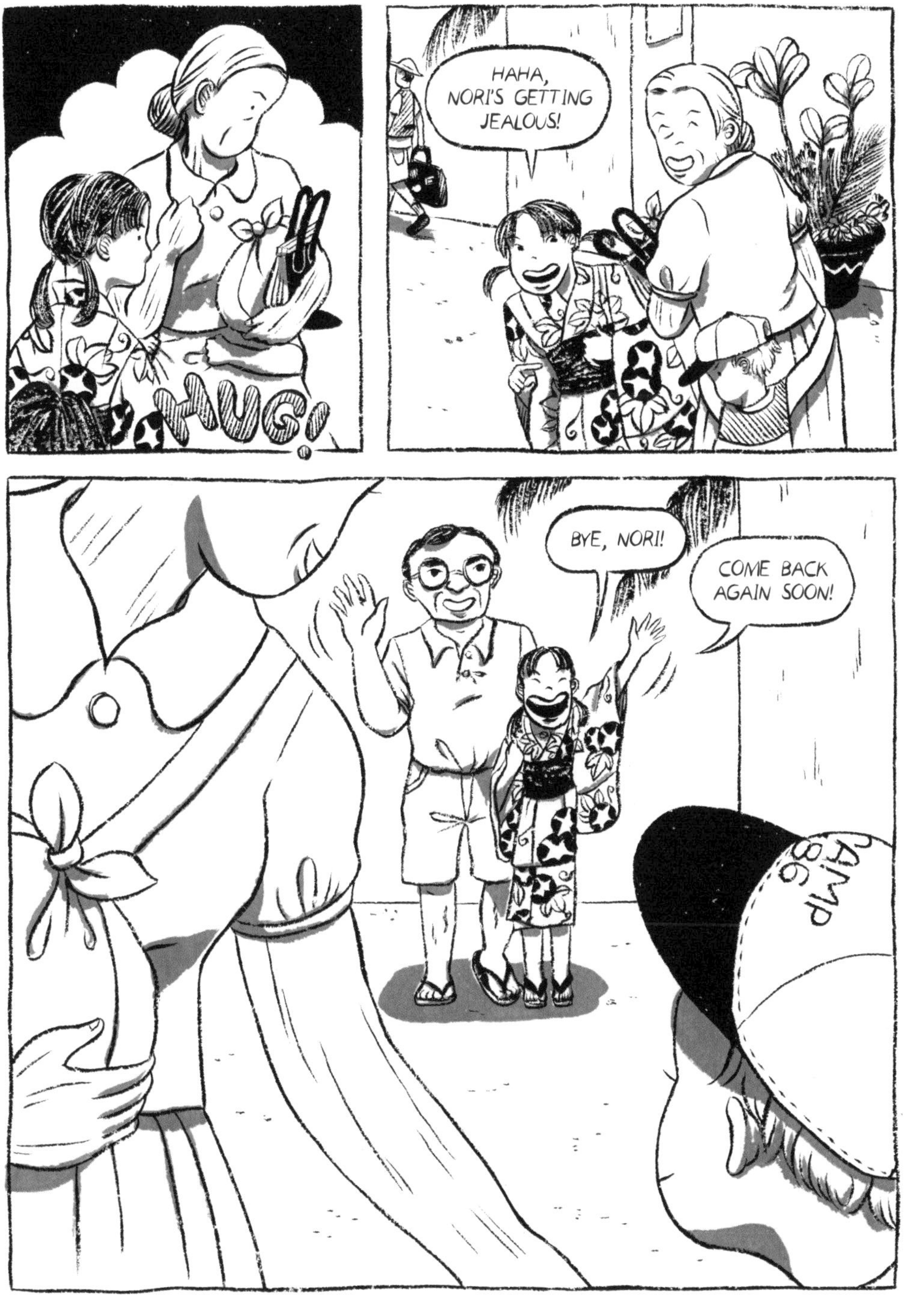
HUG!
HAHA, NORI'S GETTING JEALOUS!
BYE, NORI!
COME BACK AGAIN SOON!

JAGGAR MUSEUM AND THE OVERLOOK IN HAWAI'I VOLCANOES NATIONAL PARK THAT NORI
AND GRANDMA VISITED WERE INDEFINITELY CLOSED IN 2018 DUE TO VOLCANIC ACTIVITIES.

5

五

NORI
AND THE
DOGS
OF
WINTERLAND

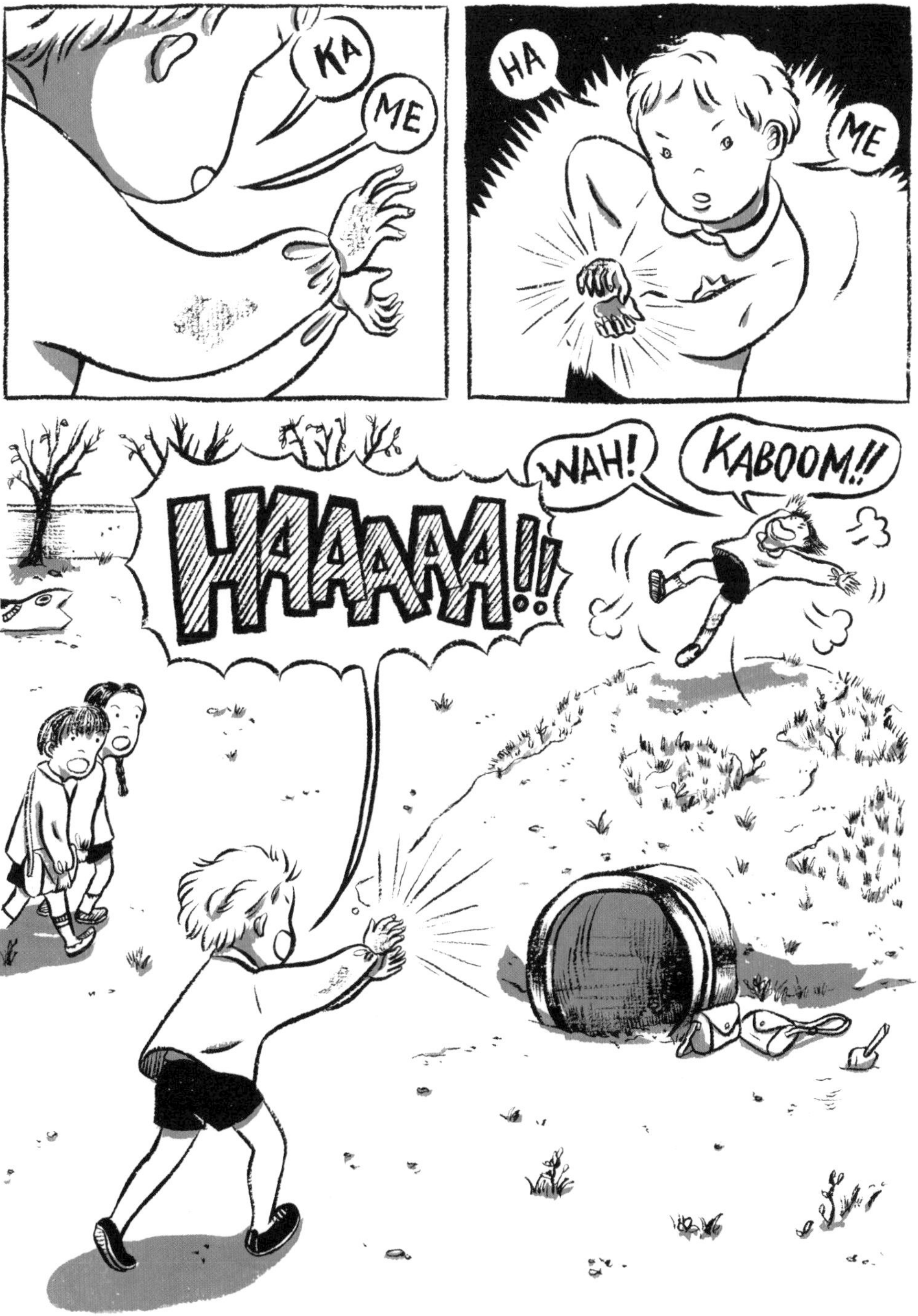
KA
ME
HA
ME
HAAAAA!!
WAH!
KABOOM!!

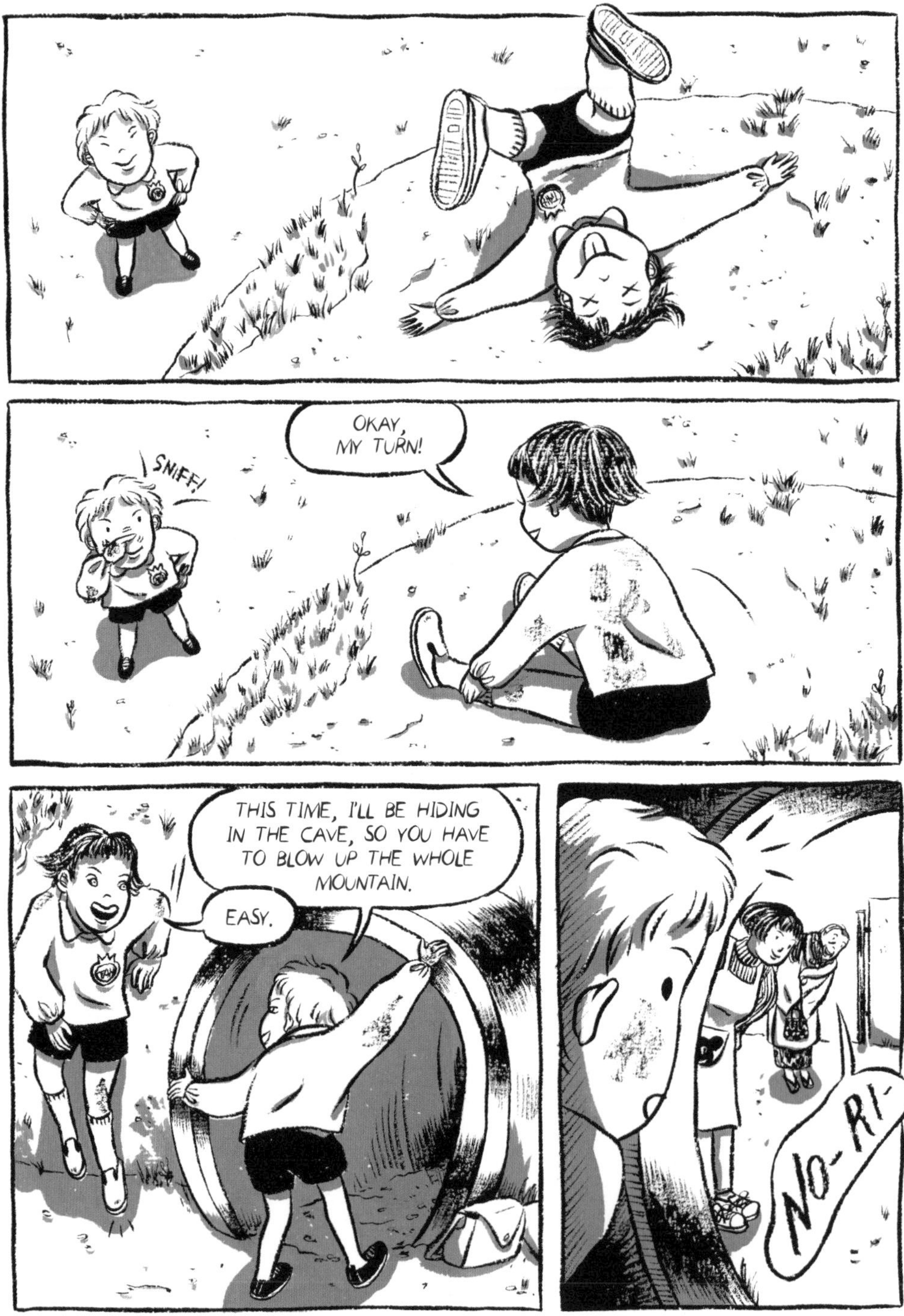
OKAY, MY TURN!
SNIFF!
THIS TIME, I'LL BE HIDING IN THE CAVE, SO YOU HAVE TO BLOW UP THE WHOLE MOUNTAIN.
EASY.
NO-RI-

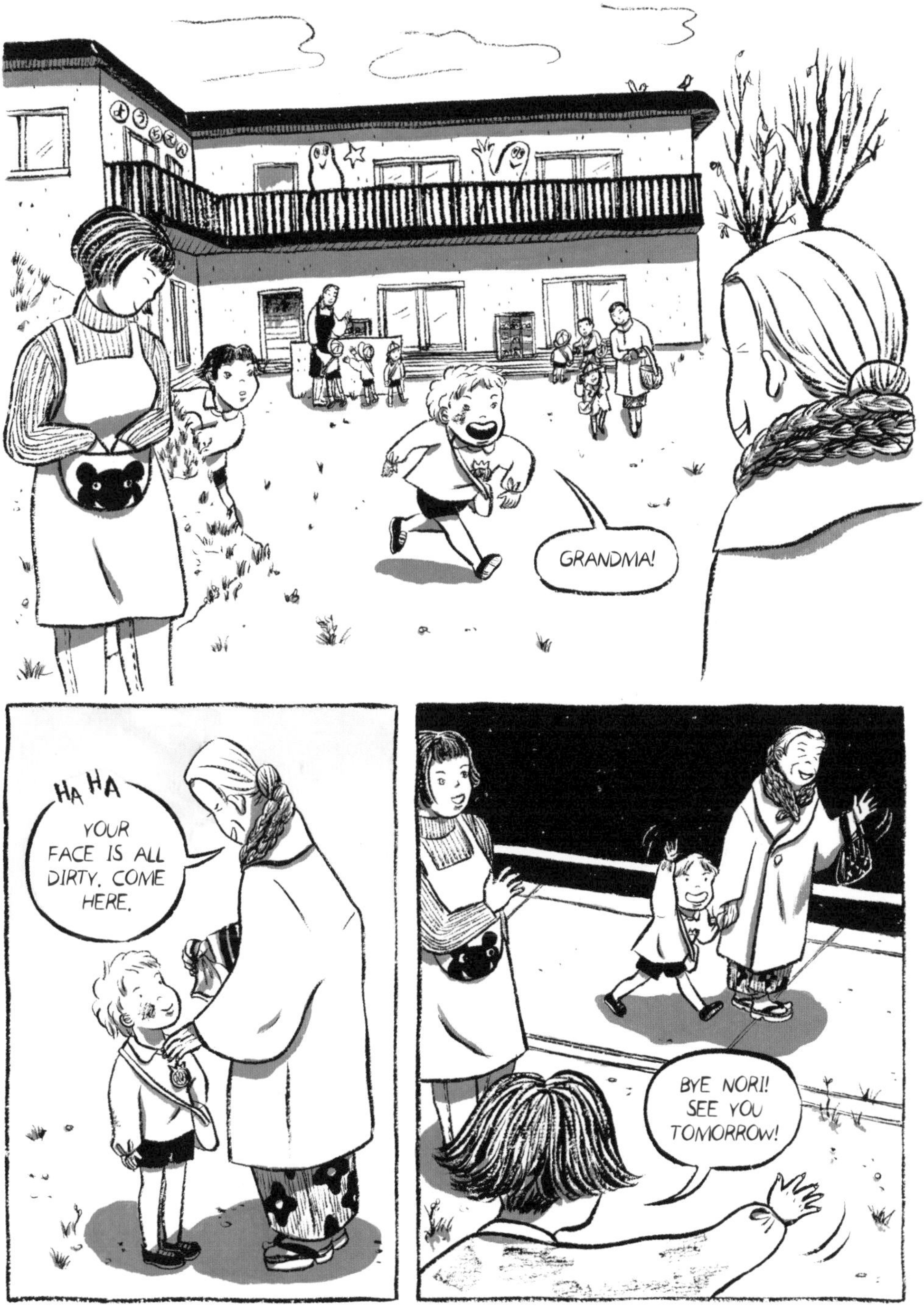
GRANDMA!
HA HA
YOUR FACE IS ALL DIRTY. COME HERE.
BYE NORI! SEE YOU TOMORROW!

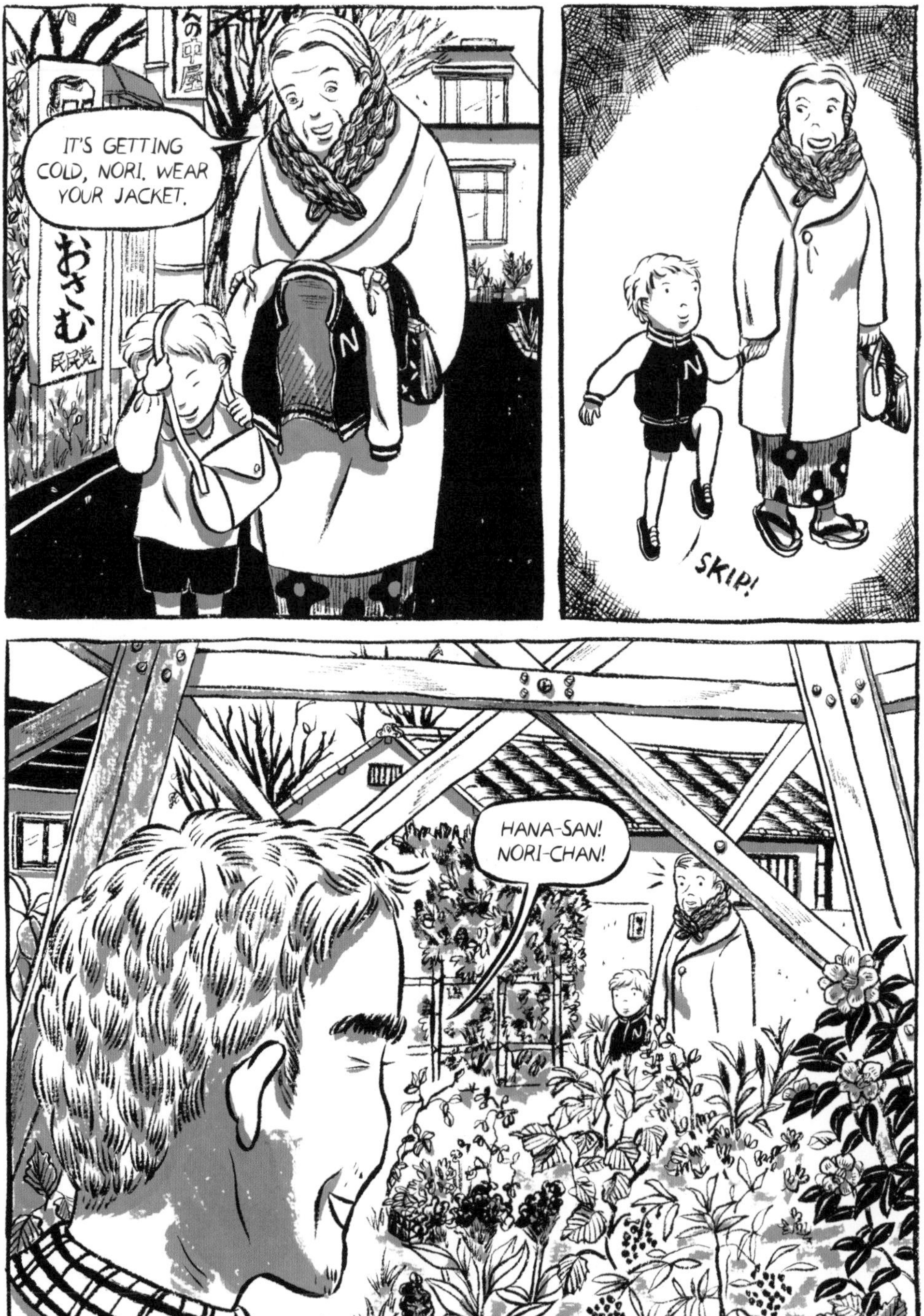
IT'S GETTING COLD, NORI. WEAR YOUR JACKET.
おさむ
民民党
SKIP!
HANA-SAN! NORI-CHAN!

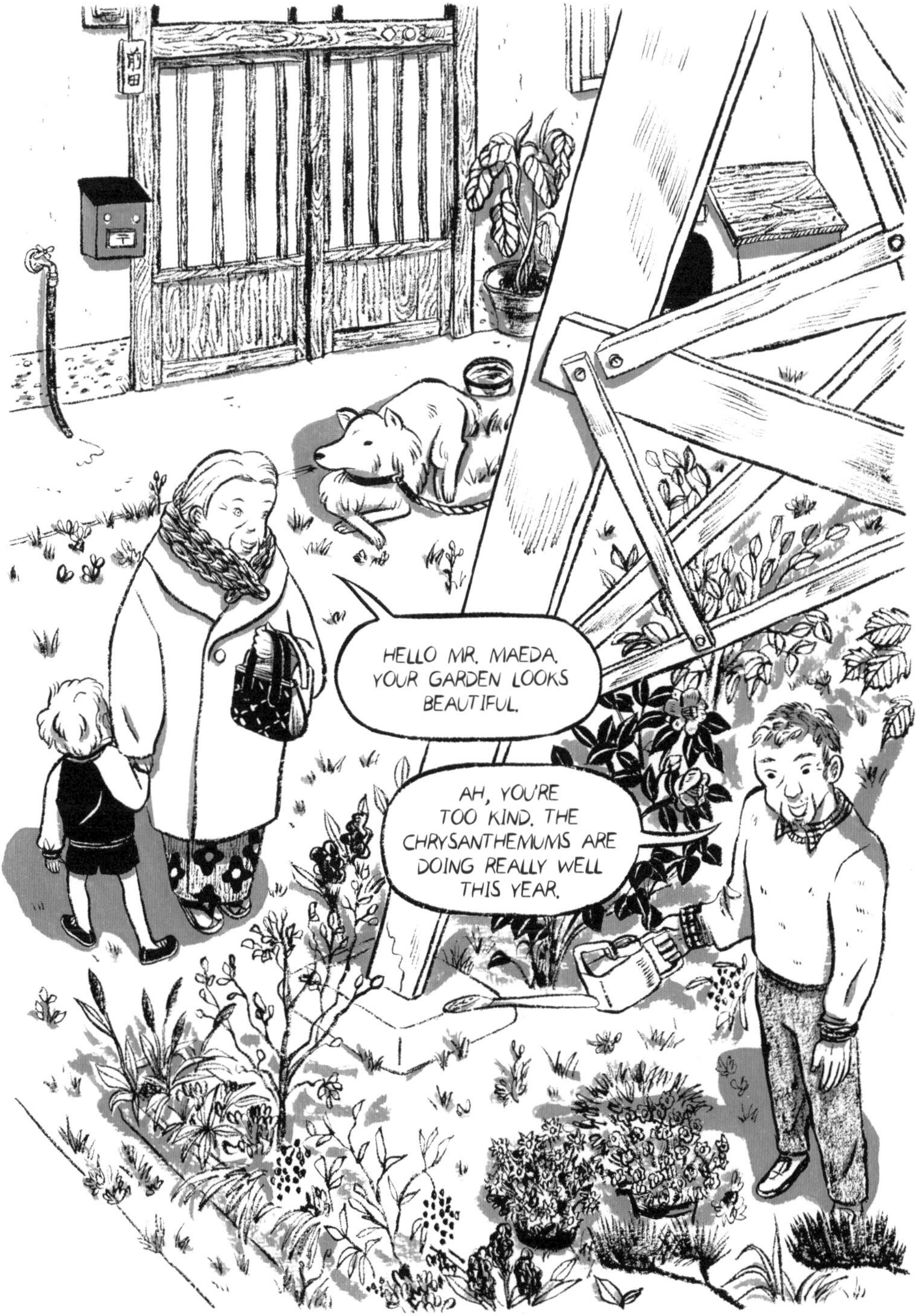
前田
HELLO MR. MAEDA. YOUR GARDEN LOOKS BEAUTIFUL.
AH, YOU'RE TOO KIND. THE CHRYSANTHEMUMS ARE DOING REALLY WELL THIS YEAR.

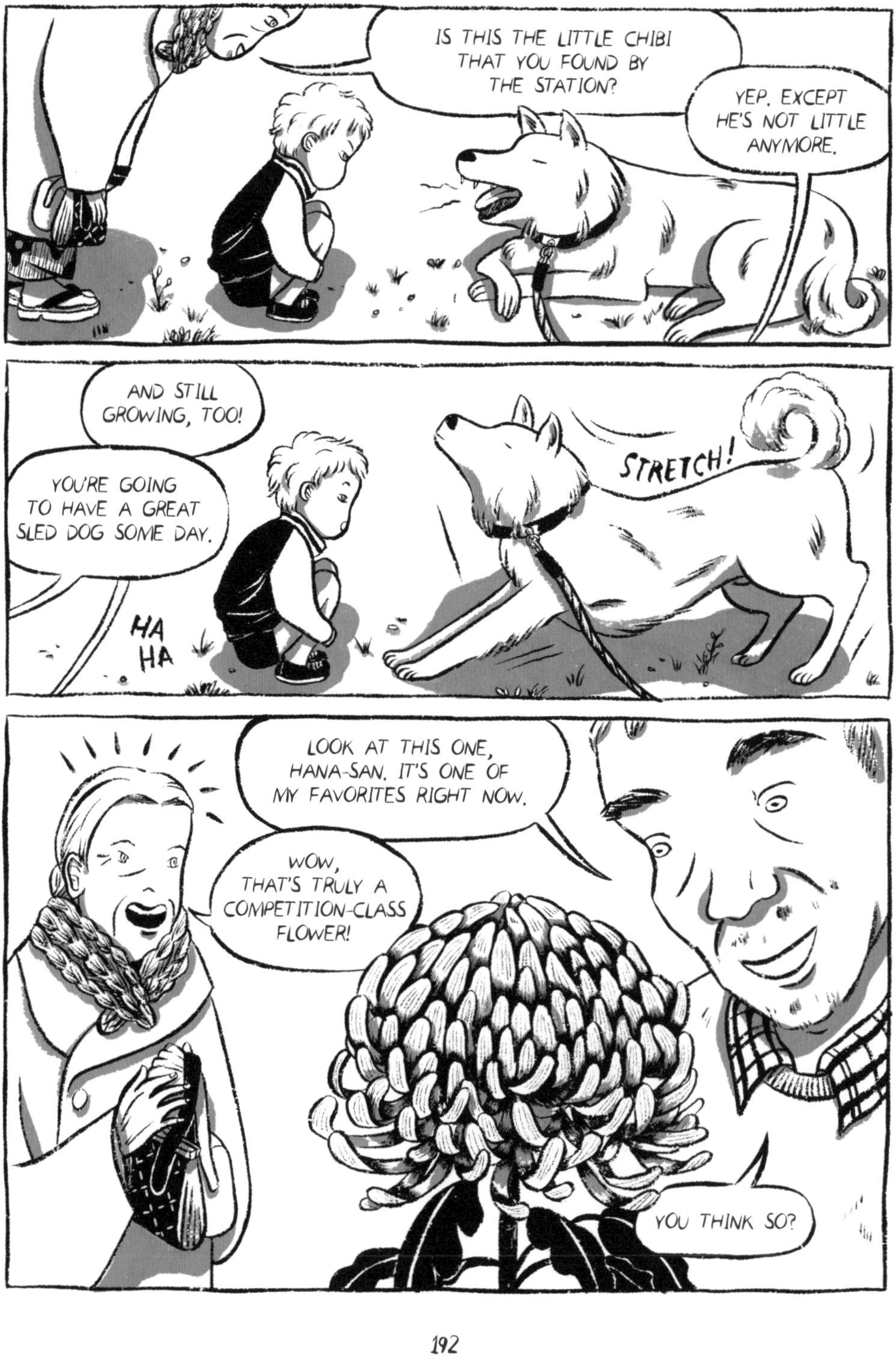

IS THIS THE LITTLE CHIBI THAT YOU FOUND BY THE STATION?
YEP. EXCEPT HE'S NOT LITTLE ANYMORE.
AND STILL GROWING, TOO!
STRETCH!
YOU'RE GOING TO HAVE A GREAT SLED DOG SOME DAY.
HA HA
LOOK AT THIS ONE, HANA-SAN. IT'S ONE OF MY FAVORITES RIGHT NOW.
WOW, THAT'S TRULY A COMPETITION-CLASS FLOWER!
YOU THINK SO?

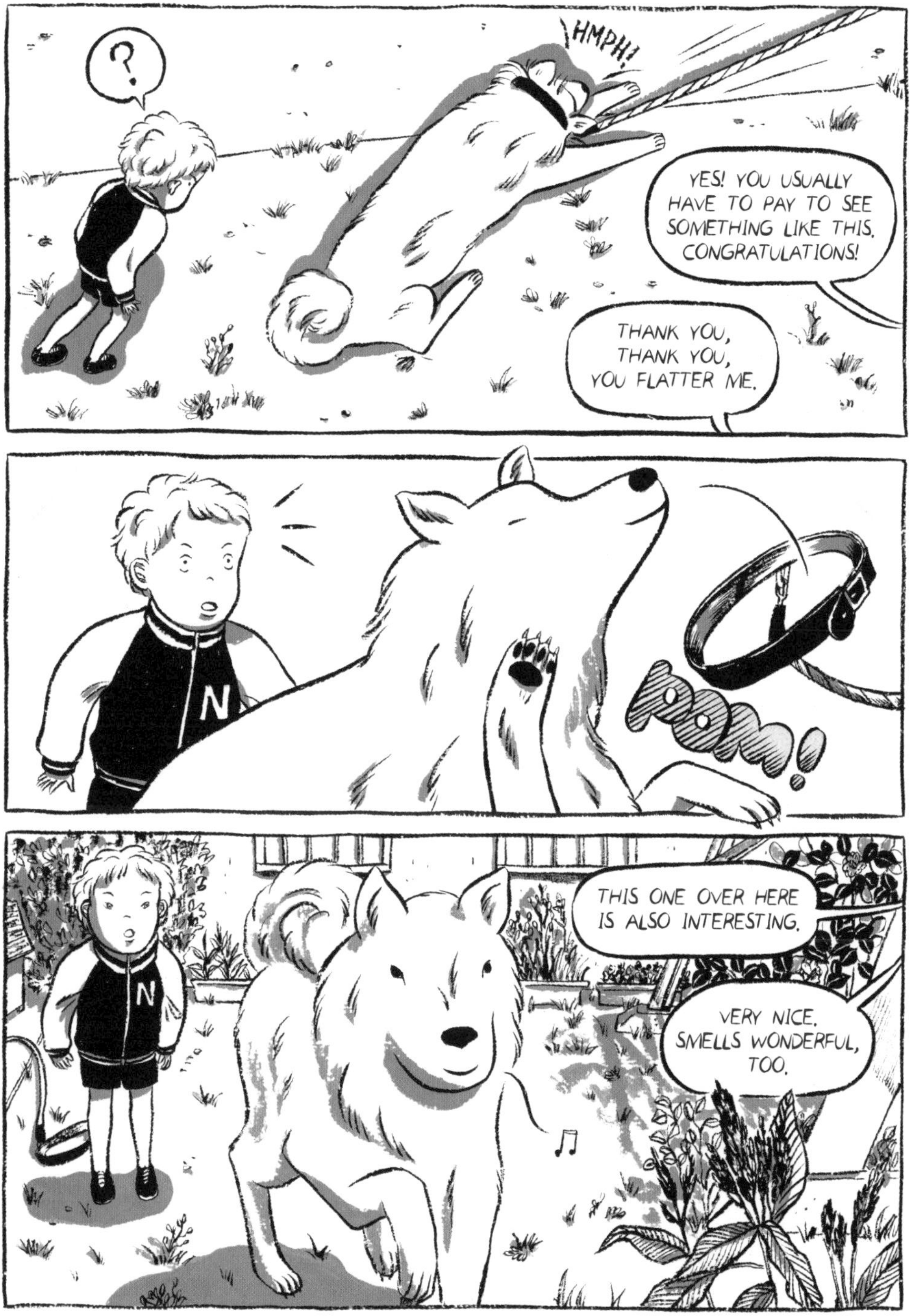
?
HMPH!
YES! YOU USUALLY HAVE TO PAY TO SEE SOMETHING LIKE THIS. CONGRATULATIONS!
THANK YOU, THANK YOU, YOU FLATTER ME.
N
POOM!
N
THIS ONE OVER HERE IS ALSO INTERESTING.
VERY NICE. SMELLS WONDERFUL, TOO.

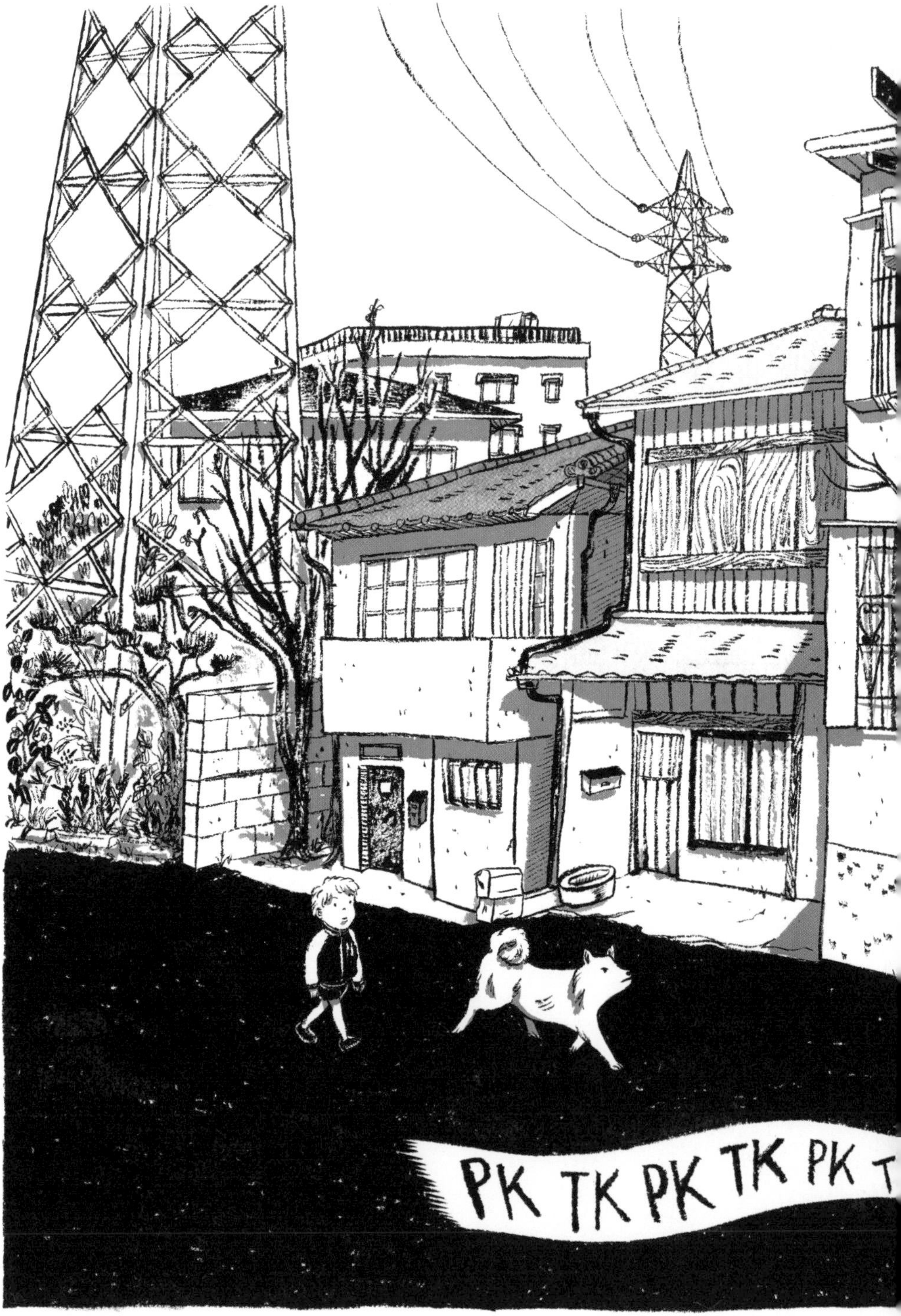
PK TK PK TK PK T

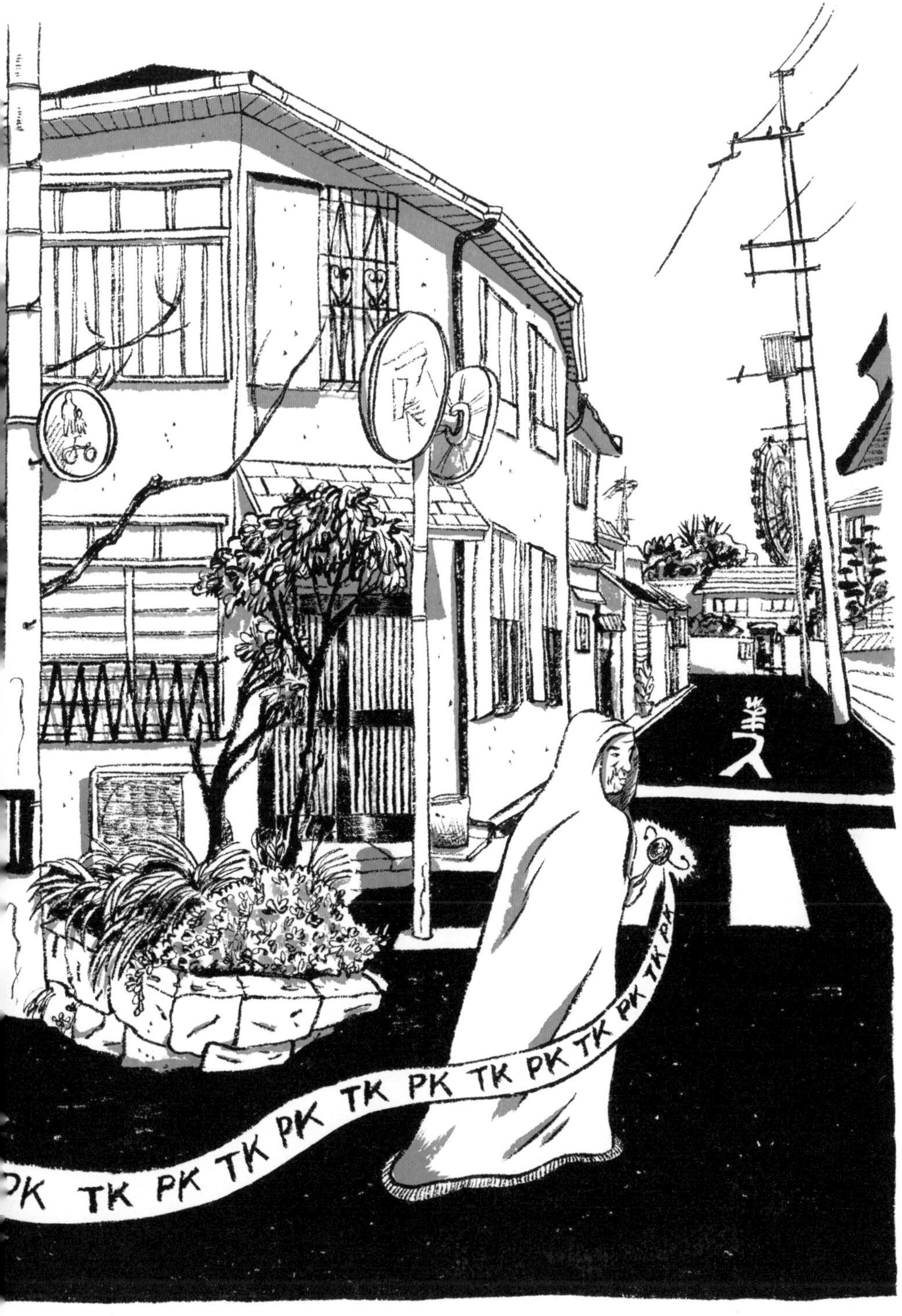
PK TK PK TK PK TK PK TK PK TK PK TK PK

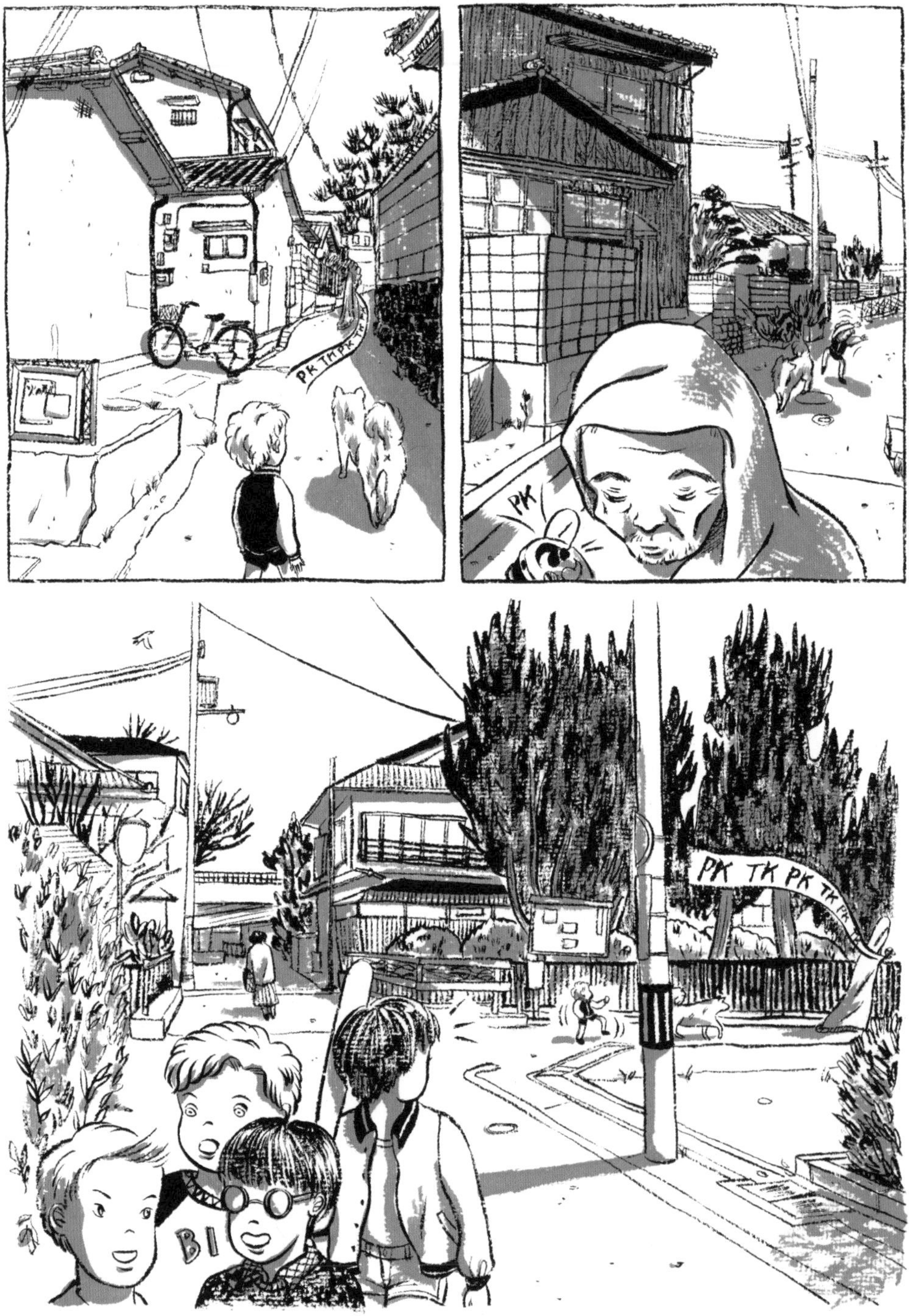
PK TK PK
PK
PK TK PK TK
BI

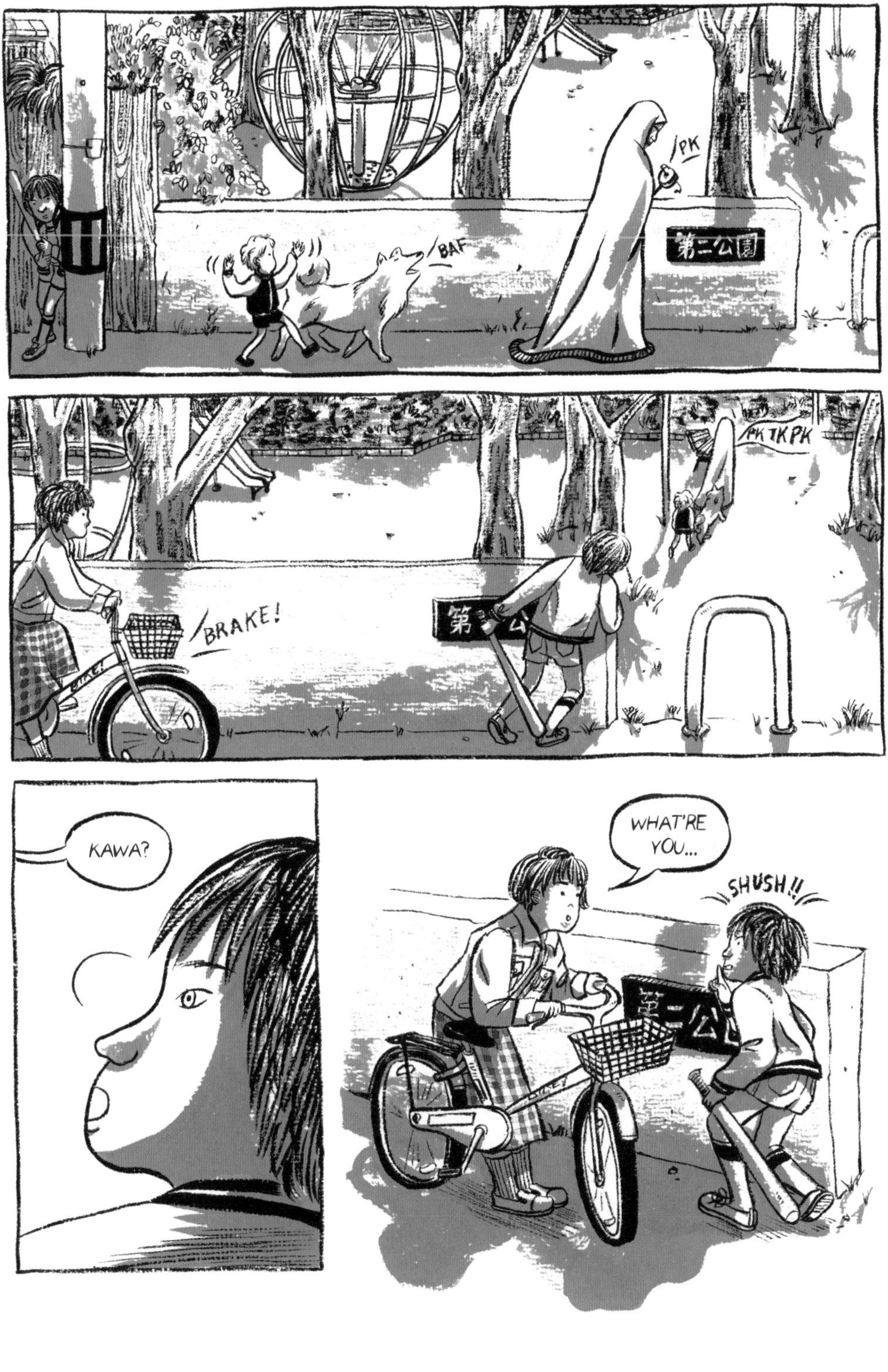
PK
BAF
第二公園
BRAKE!
PKTKPK
KAWA?
WHAT'RE YOU...
SHUSH!!

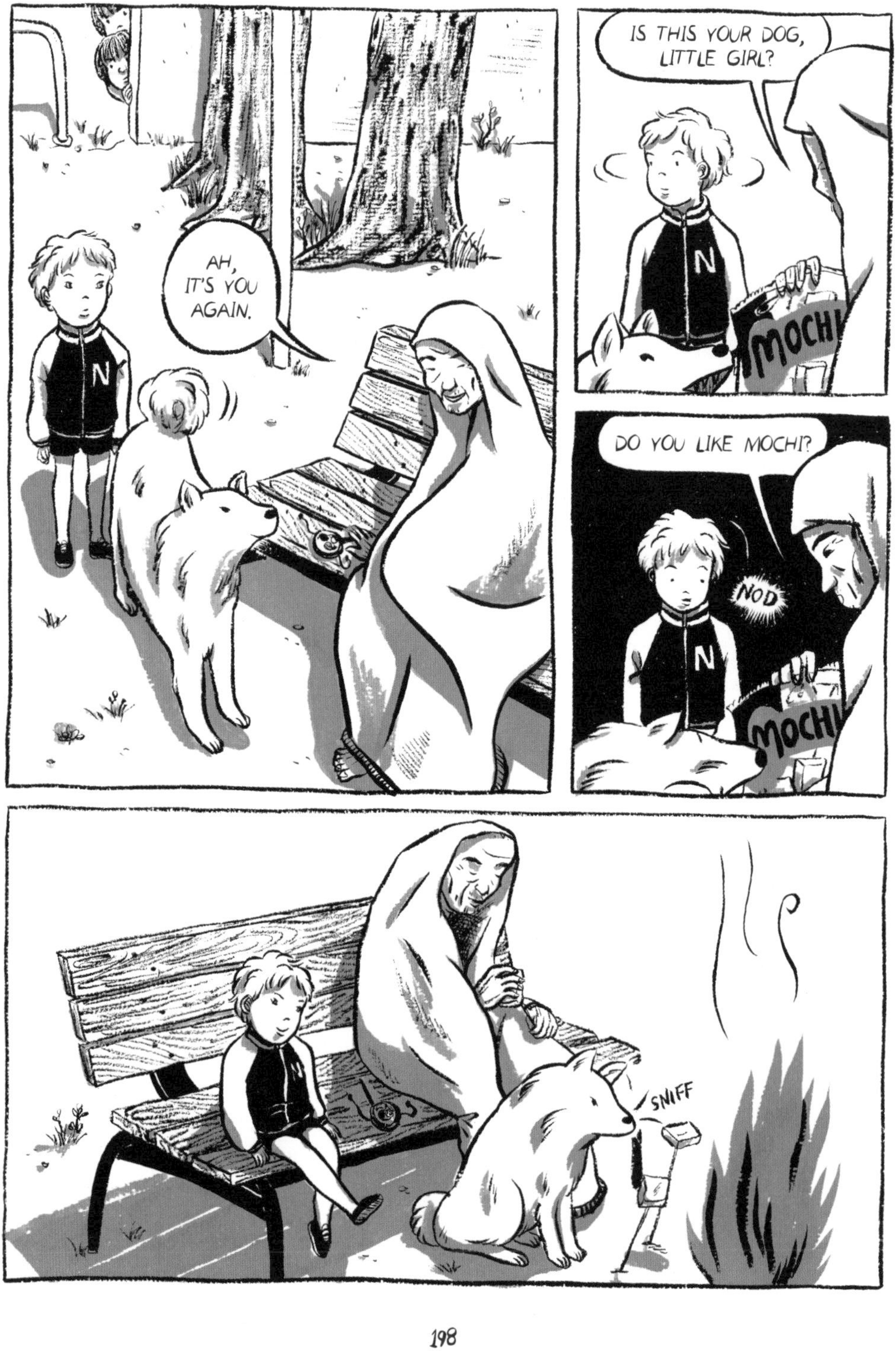
AH, IT'S YOU AGAIN.
IS THIS YOUR DOG, LITTLE GIRL?
MOCHI
DO YOU LIKE MOCHI?
NOD
MOCHI
SNIFF

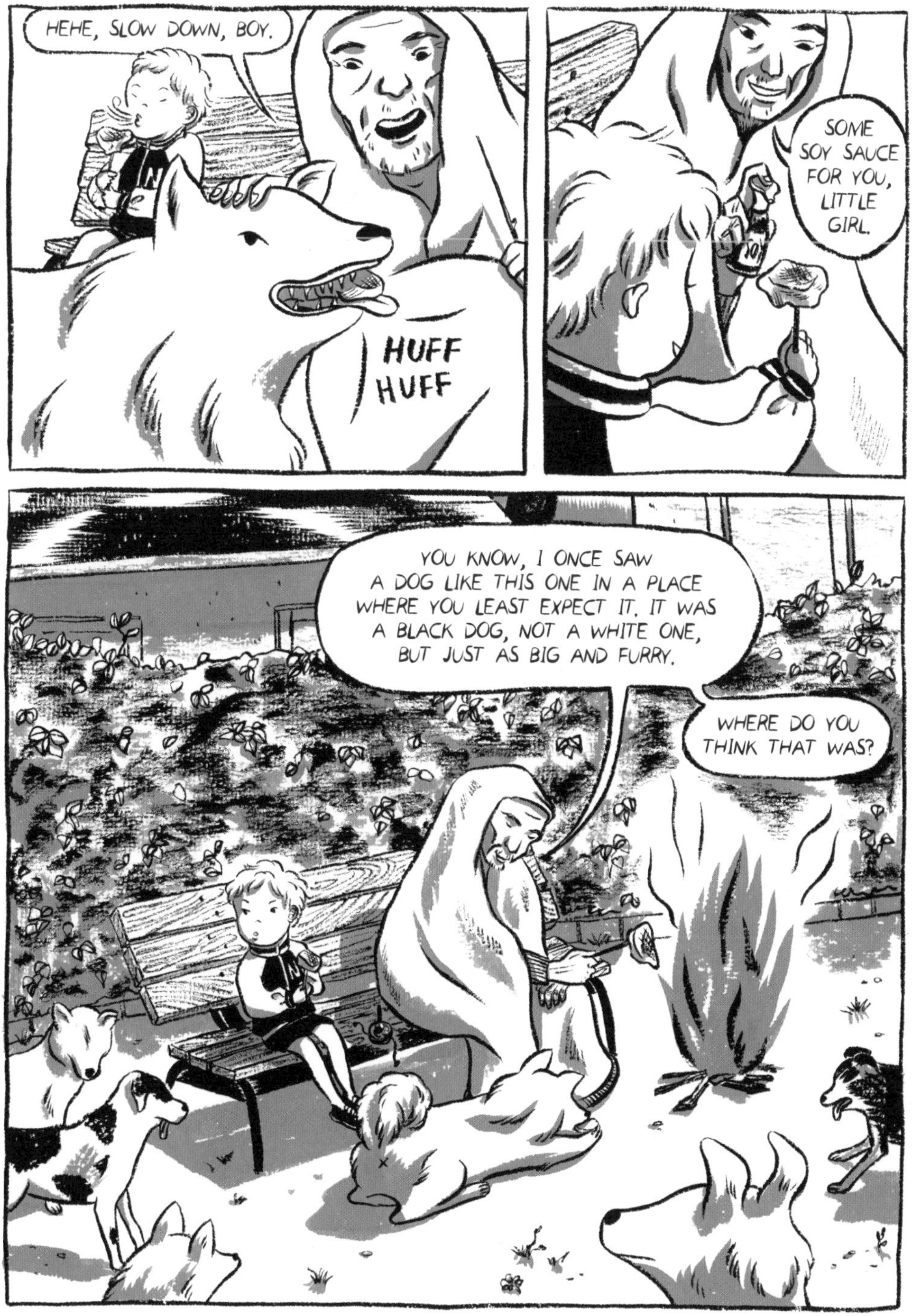
HEHE, SLOW DOWN, BOY.
HUFF HUFF
SOME SOY SAUCE FOR YOU, LITTLE GIRL.
YOU KNOW, I ONCE SAW A DOG LIKE THIS ONE IN A PLACE WHERE YOU LEAST EXPECT IT. IT WAS A BLACK DOG, NOT A WHITE ONE, BUT JUST AS BIG AND FURRY.
WHERE DO YOU THINK THAT WAS?

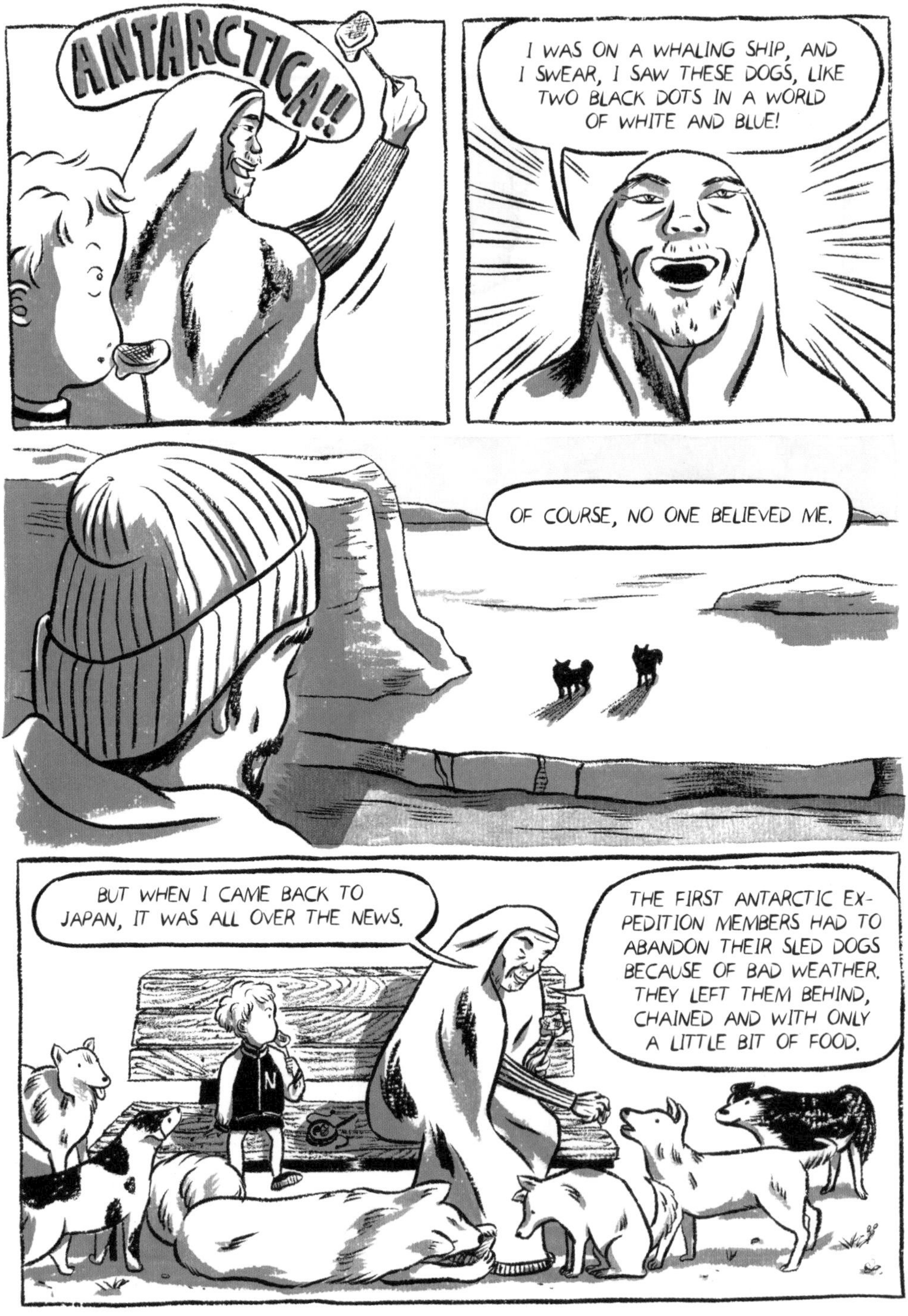
ANTARCTICA!!
I WAS ON A WHALING SHIP, AND I SWEAR, I SAW THESE DOGS, LIKE TWO BLACK DOTS IN A WORLD OF WHITE AND BLUE!
OF COURSE, NO ONE BELIEVED ME.
BUT WHEN I CAME BACK TO JAPAN, IT WAS ALL OVER THE NEWS.
THE FIRST ANTARCTIC EXPEDITION MEMBERS HAD TO ABANDON THEIR SLED DOGS BECAUSE OF BAD WEATHER. THEY LEFT THEM BEHIND, CHAINED AND WITH ONLY A LITTLE BIT OF FOOD.
N

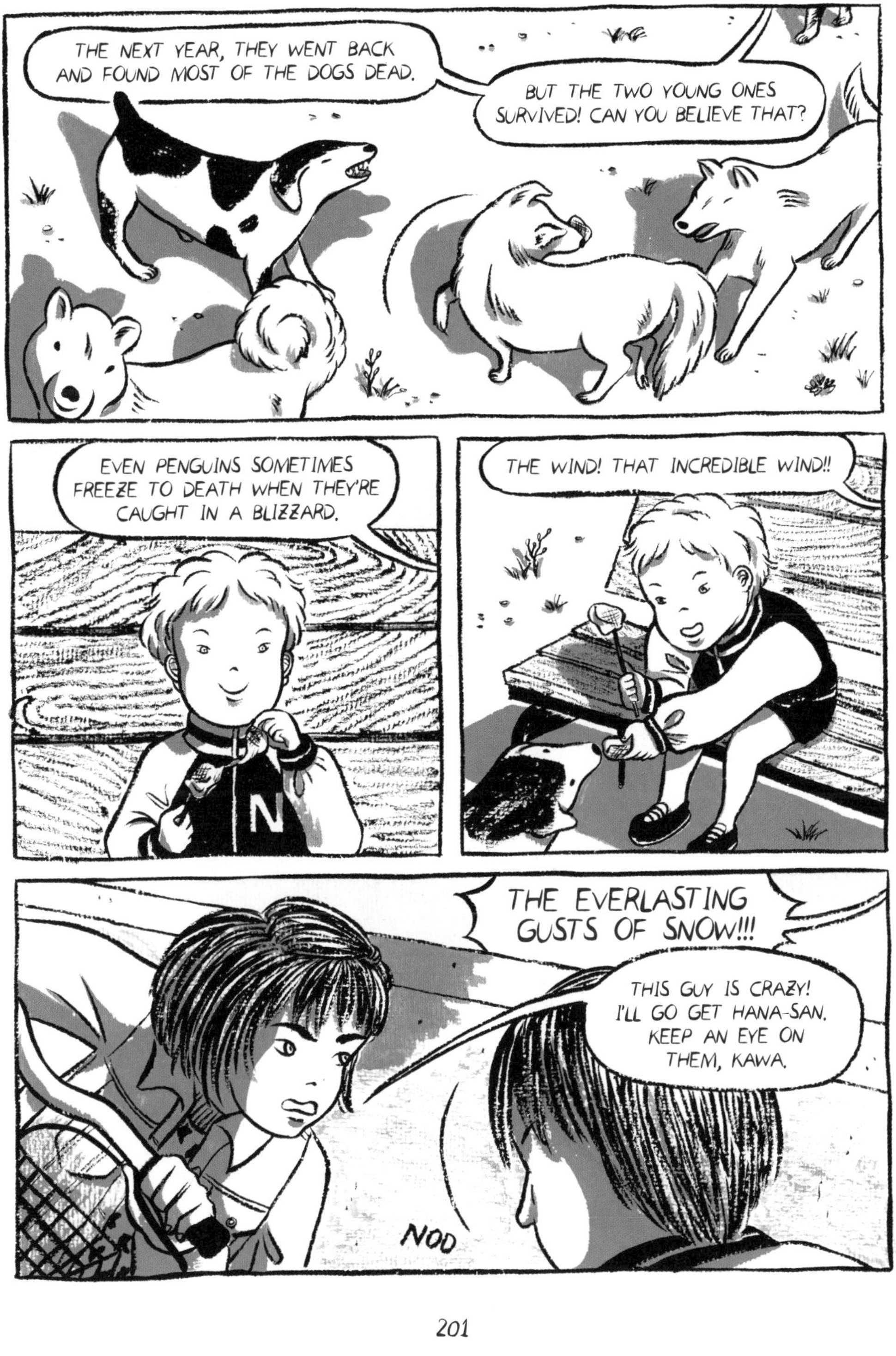
THE NEXT YEAR, THEY WENT BACK AND FOUND MOST OF THE DOGS DEAD.
BUT THE TWO YOUNG ONES SURVIVED! CAN YOU BELIEVE THAT?
EVEN PENGUINS SOMETIMES FREEZE TO DEATH WHEN THEY'RE CAUGHT IN A BLIZZARD.
N
THE WIND! THAT INCREDIBLE WIND!!
THE EVERLASTING GUSTS OF SNOW!!!
THIS GUY IS CRAZY! I'LL GO GET HANA-SAN. KEEP AN EYE ON THEM, KAWA.
NOD

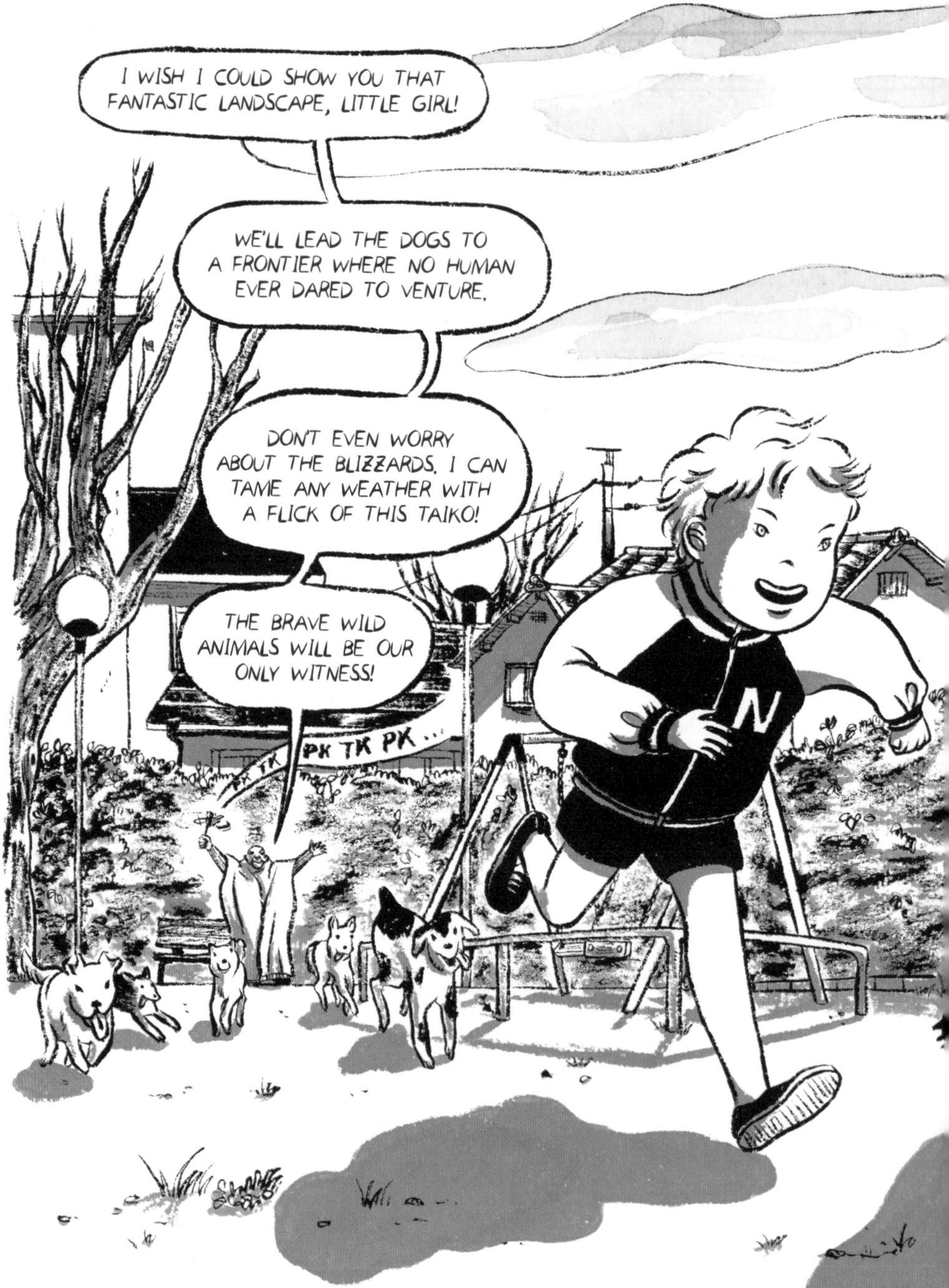
I WISH I COULD SHOW YOU THAT FANTASTIC LANDSCAPE, LITTLE GIRL!
WE'LL LEAD THE DOGS TO A FRONTIER WHERE NO HUMAN EVER DARED TO VENTURE.
DON'T EVEN WORRY ABOUT THE BLIZZARDS. I CAN TAME ANY WEATHER WITH A FLICK OF THIS TAIKO!
THE BRAVE WILD ANIMALS WILL BE OUR ONLY WITNESS!
PK TK PK TK PK...

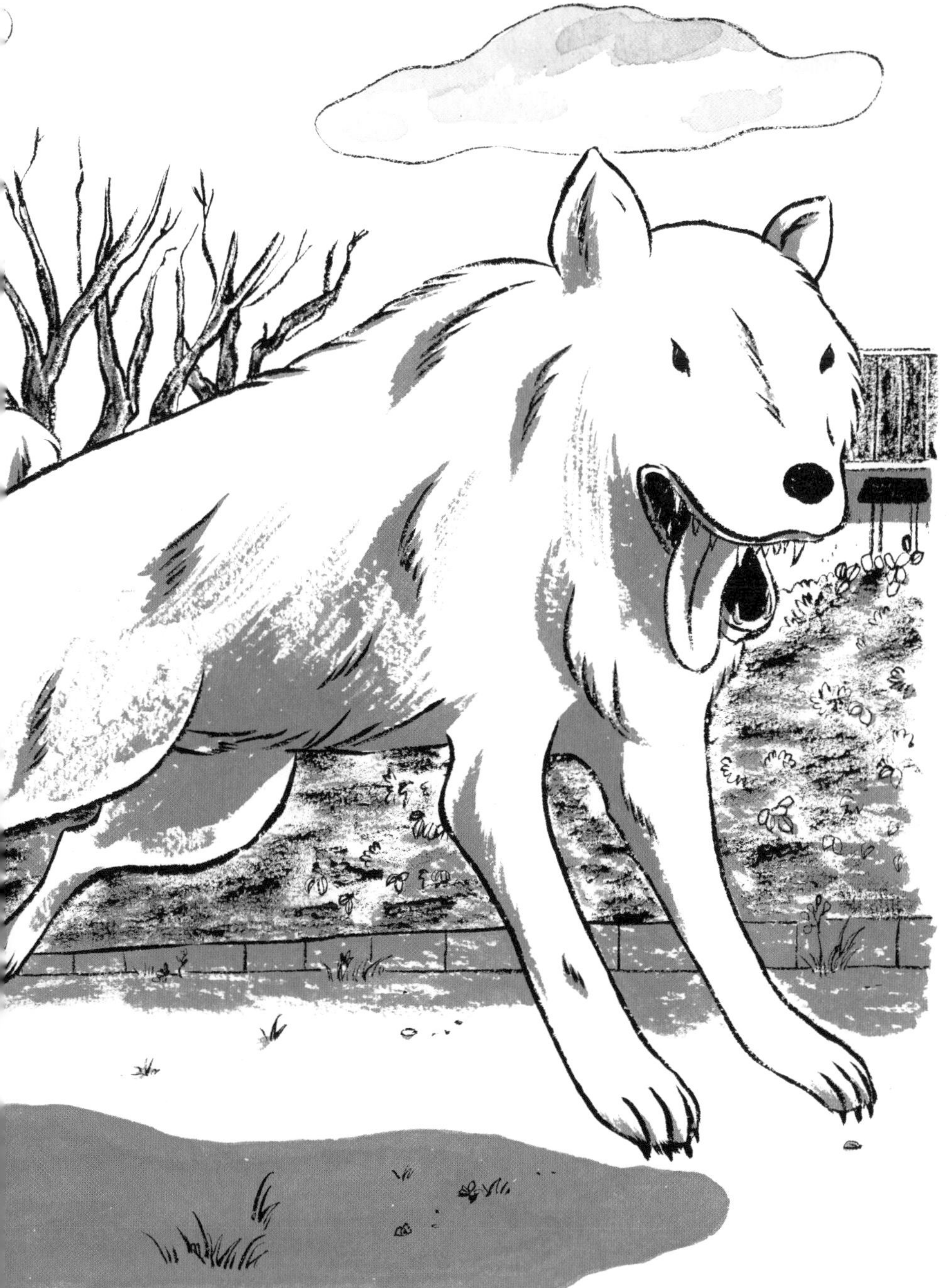

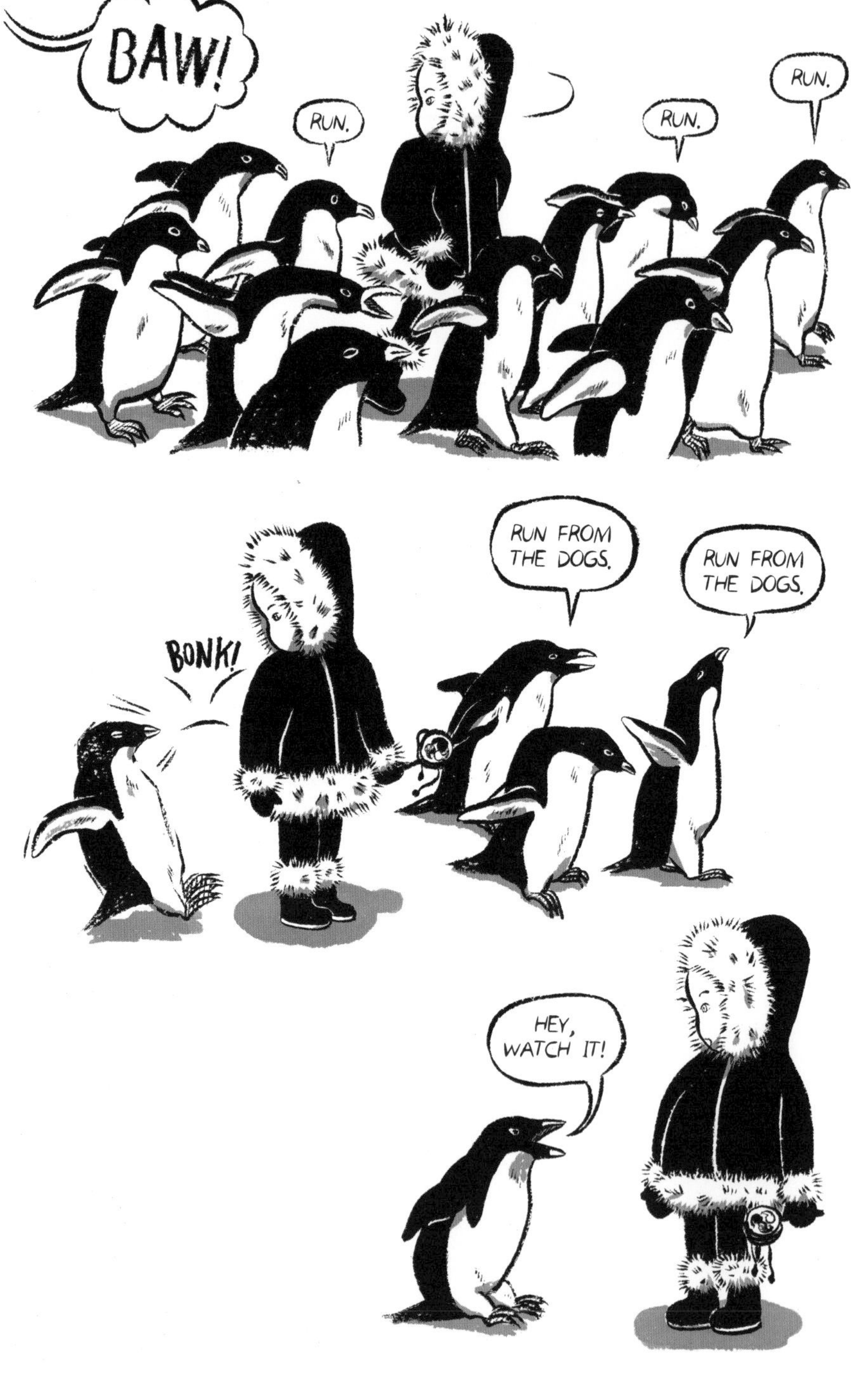
BAW!
RUN.
RUN.
RUN.
RUN FROM THE DOGS.
RUN FROM THE DOGS.
BONK!
HEY, WATCH IT!

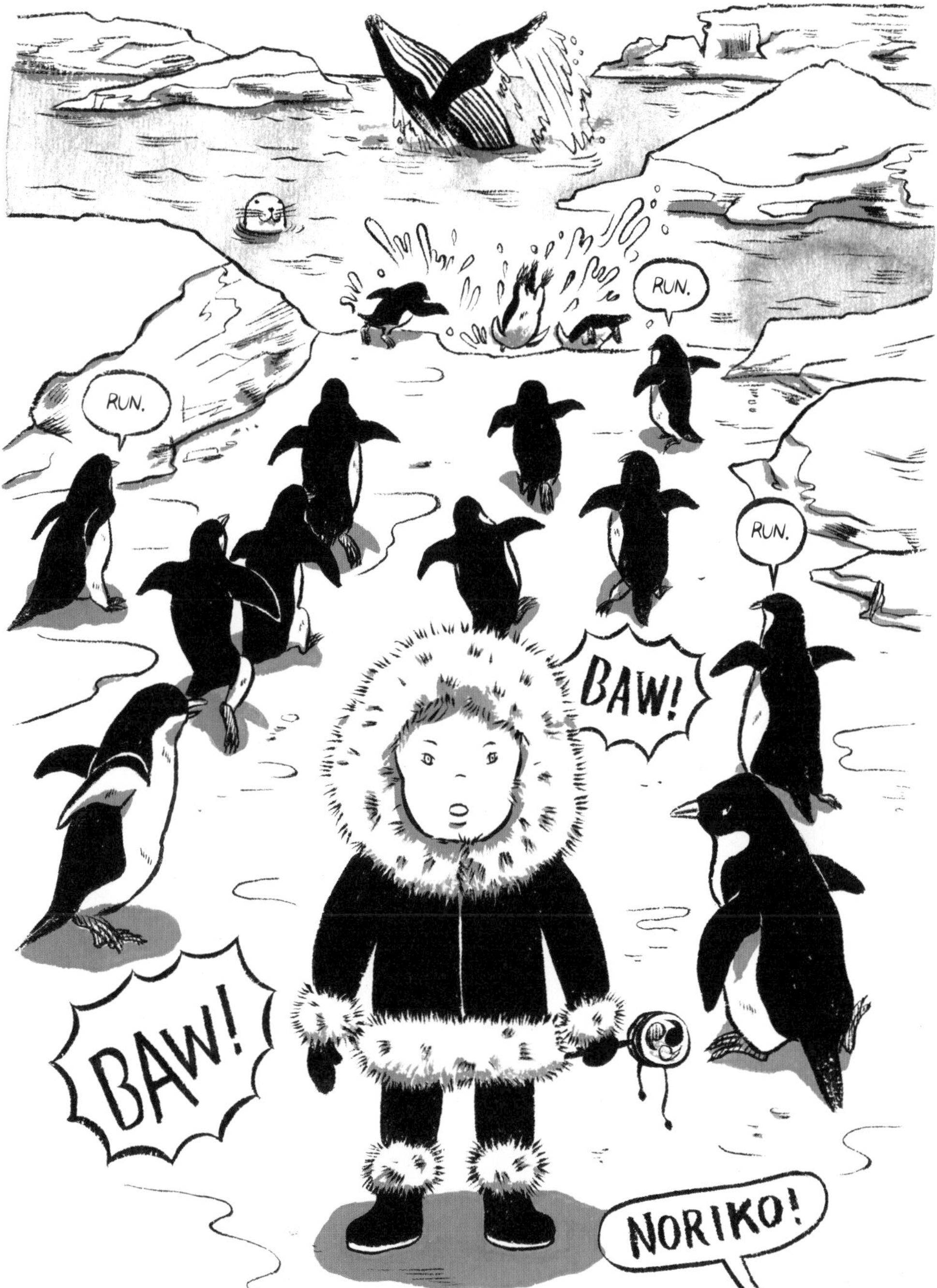
RUN.
RUN.
RUN.
BAW!
BAW!
NORIKO!

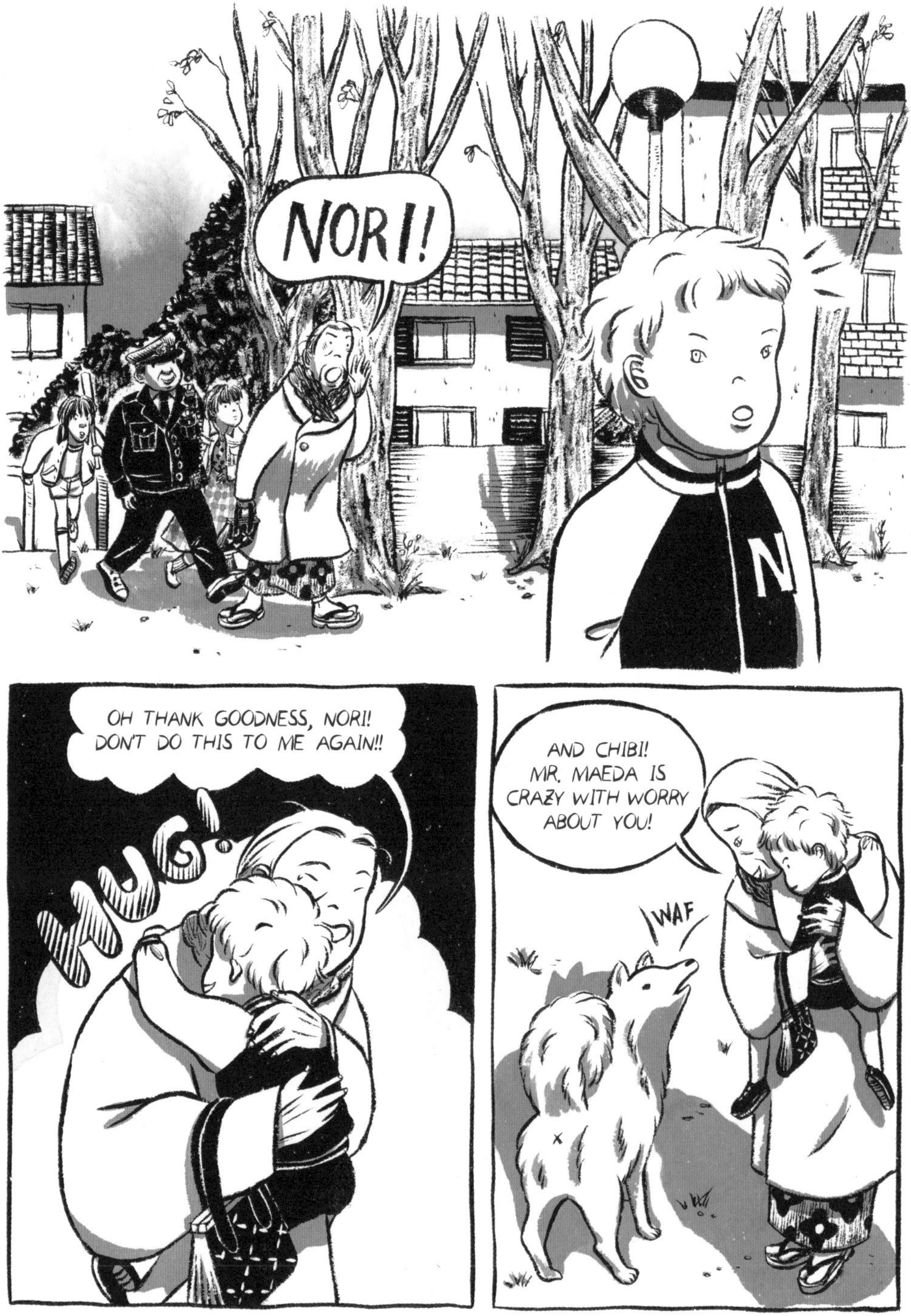
NORI!
OH THANK GOODNESS, NORI! DON'T DO THIS TO ME AGAIN!!
HUG!
AND CHIBI! MR. MAEDA IS CRAZY WITH WORRY ABOUT YOU!
WAF

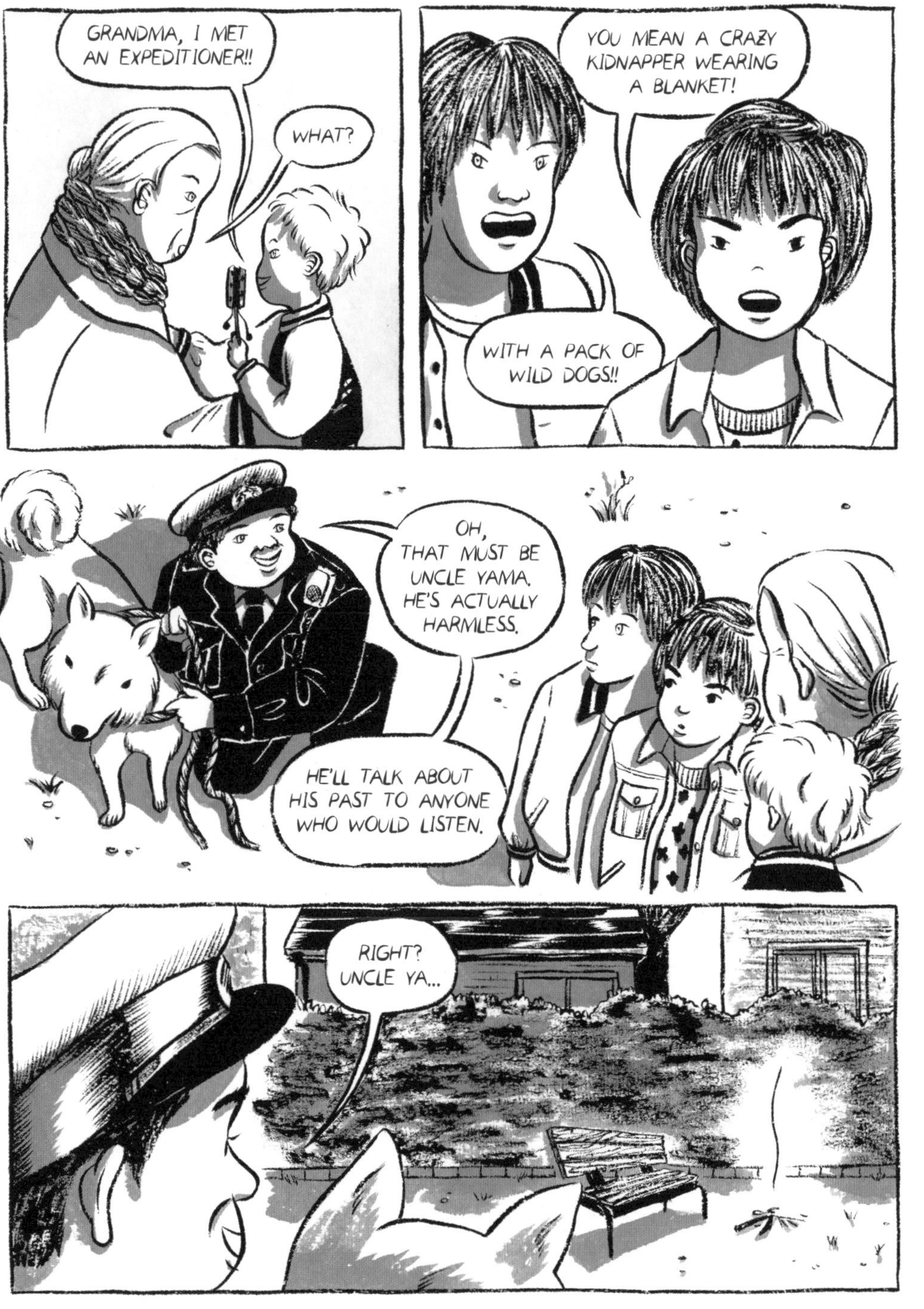
GRANDMA, I MET AN EXPEDITIONER!!
WHAT?
YOU MEAN A CRAZY KIDNAPPER WEARING A BLANKET!
WITH A PACK OF WILD DOGS!!
OH, THAT MUST BE UNCLE YAMA. HE'S ACTUALLY HARMLESS.
HE'LL TALK ABOUT HIS PAST TO ANYONE WHO WOULD LISTEN.
RIGHT? UNCLE YA...

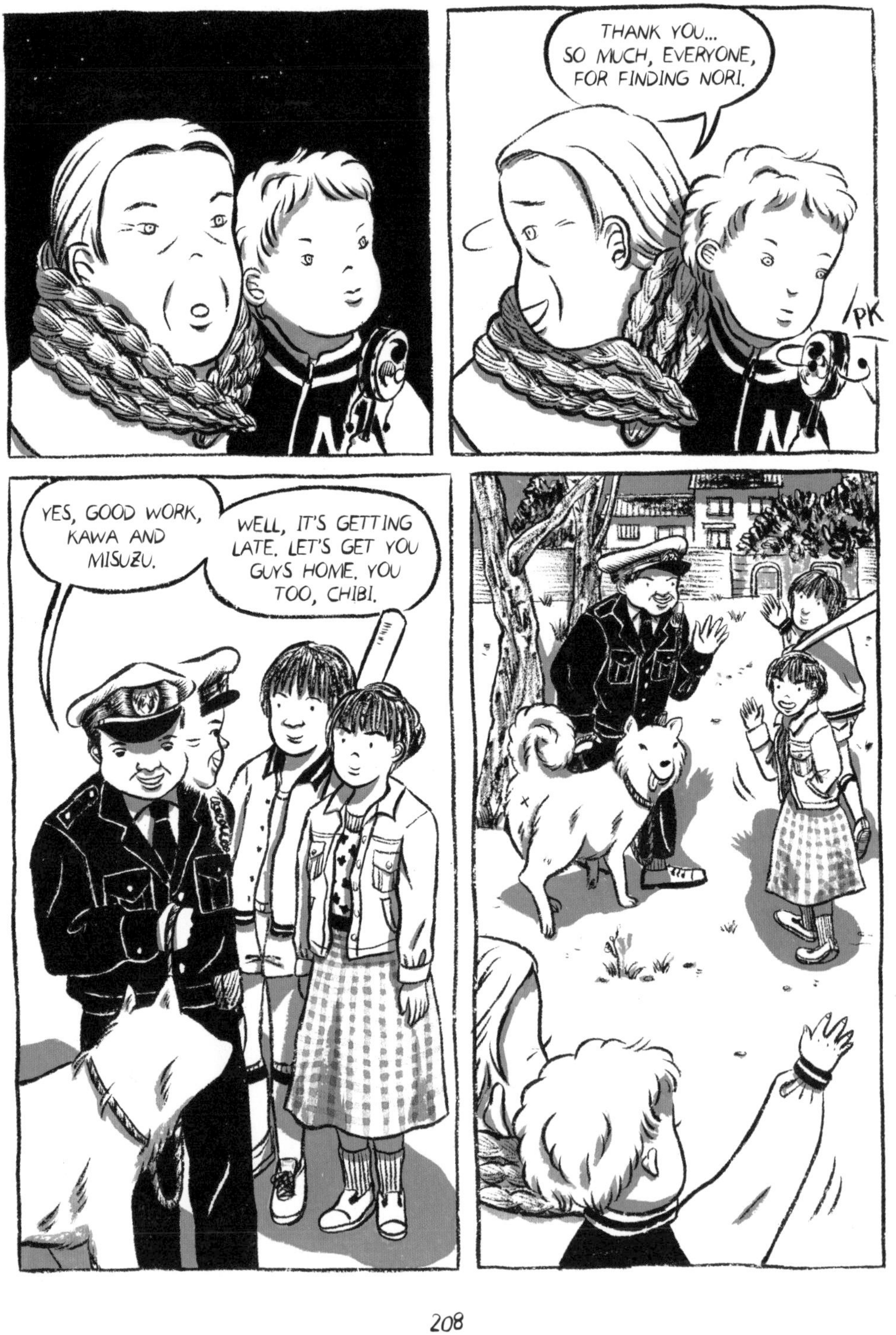
THANK YOU... SO MUCH, EVERYONE, FOR FINDING NORI.
PK
YES, GOOD WORK, KAWA AND MISUZU.
WELL, IT'S GETTING LATE. LET'S GET YOU GUYS HOME. YOU TOO, CHIBI.

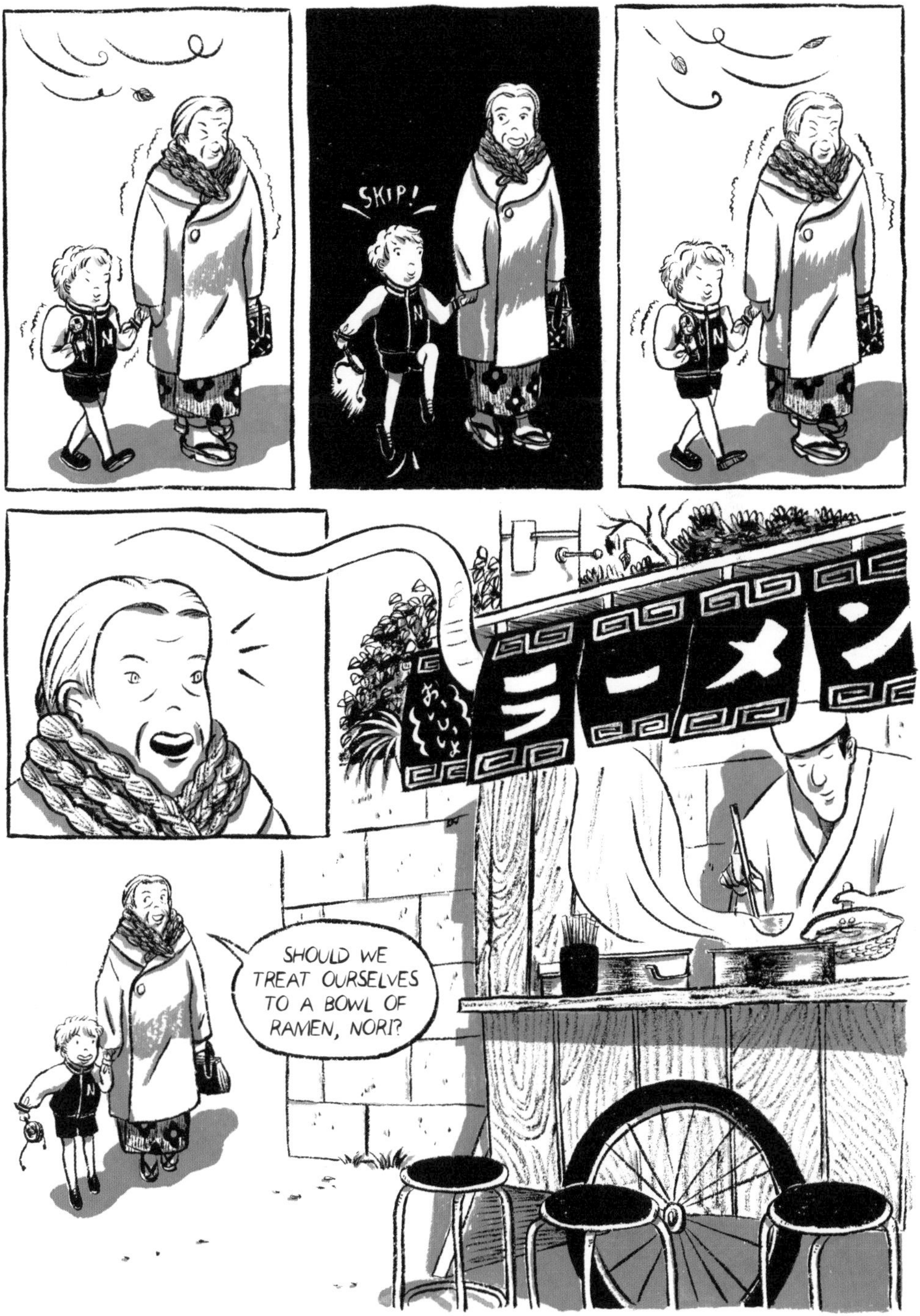
SKIP!
おいしいよ
ラーメン
SHOULD WE TREAT OURSELVES TO A BOWL OF RAMEN, NORI?

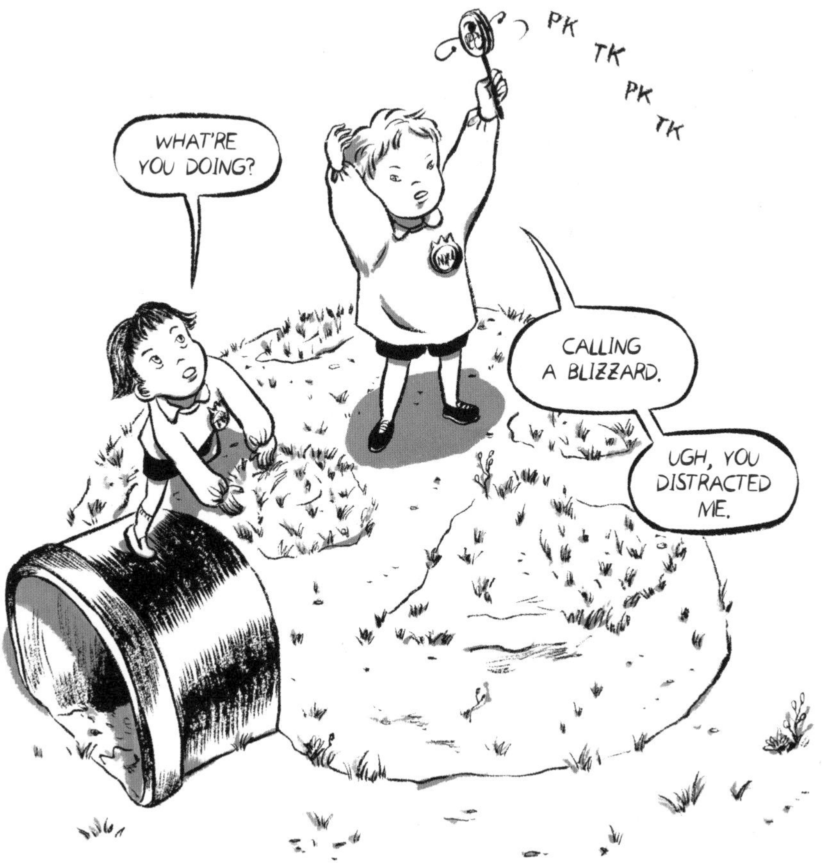
WHAT'RE YOU DOING?
PK TK PK TK
CALLING A BLIZZARD.
UGH, YOU DISTRACTED ME.

6

六

NORI
AND THE BATS IN THE HOUSE
AGAIN

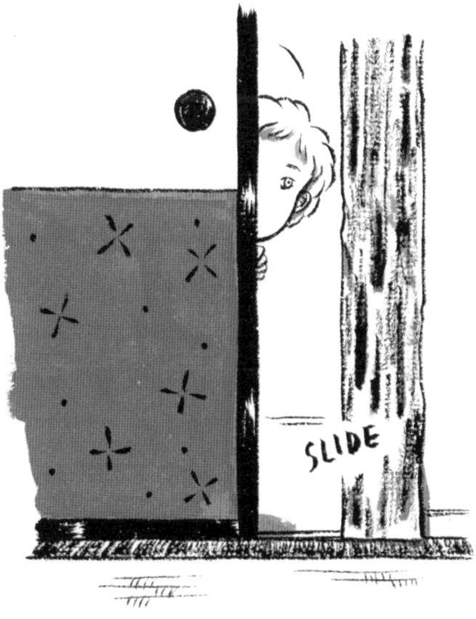
SLIDE

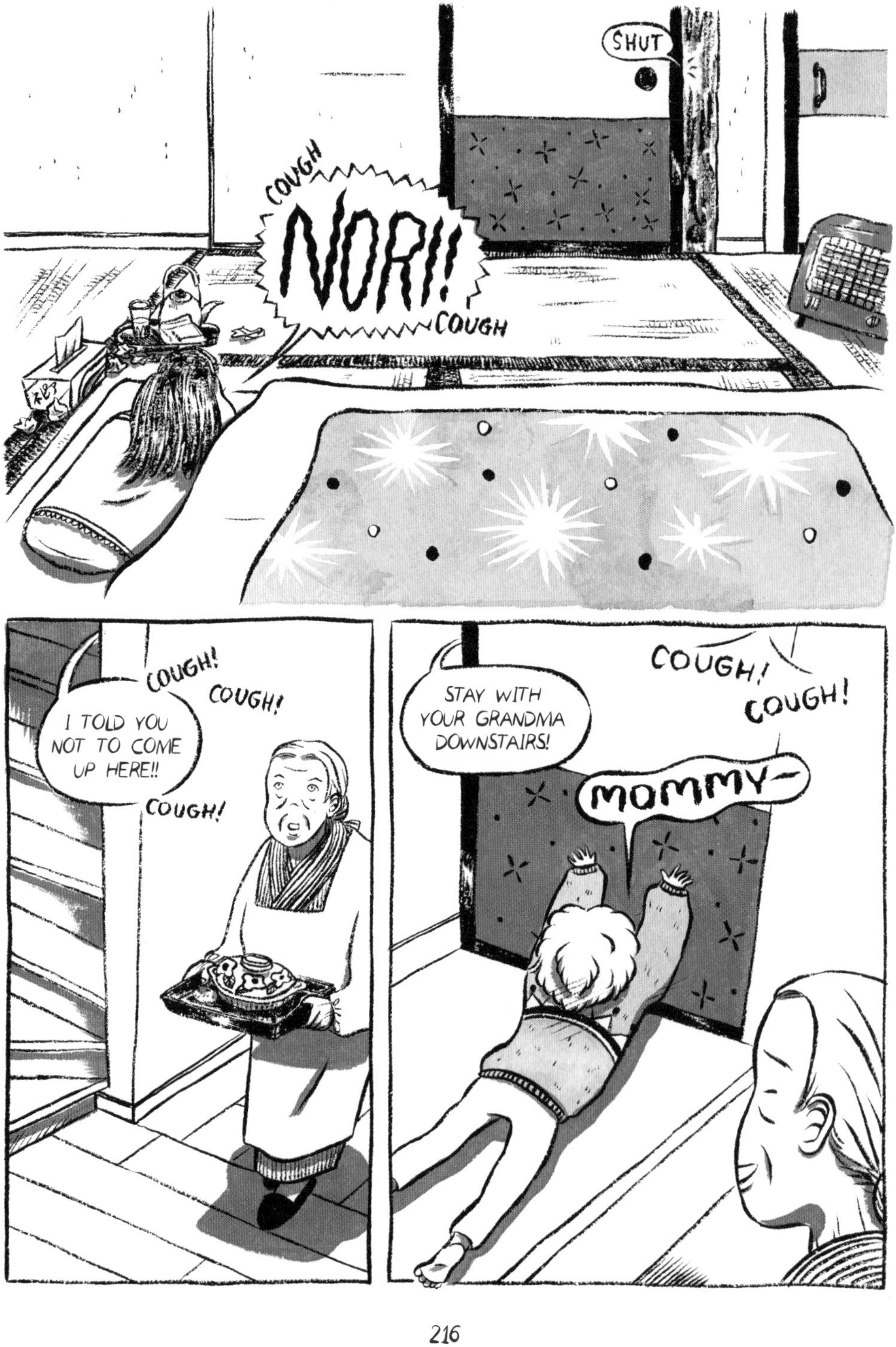
SHUT
COUGH
NORI!
COUGH
COUGH!
COUGH!
I TOLD YOU NOT TO COME UP HERE!!
COUGH!
STAY WITH YOUR GRANDMA DOWNSTAIRS!
COUGH!
COUGH!
MOMMY-

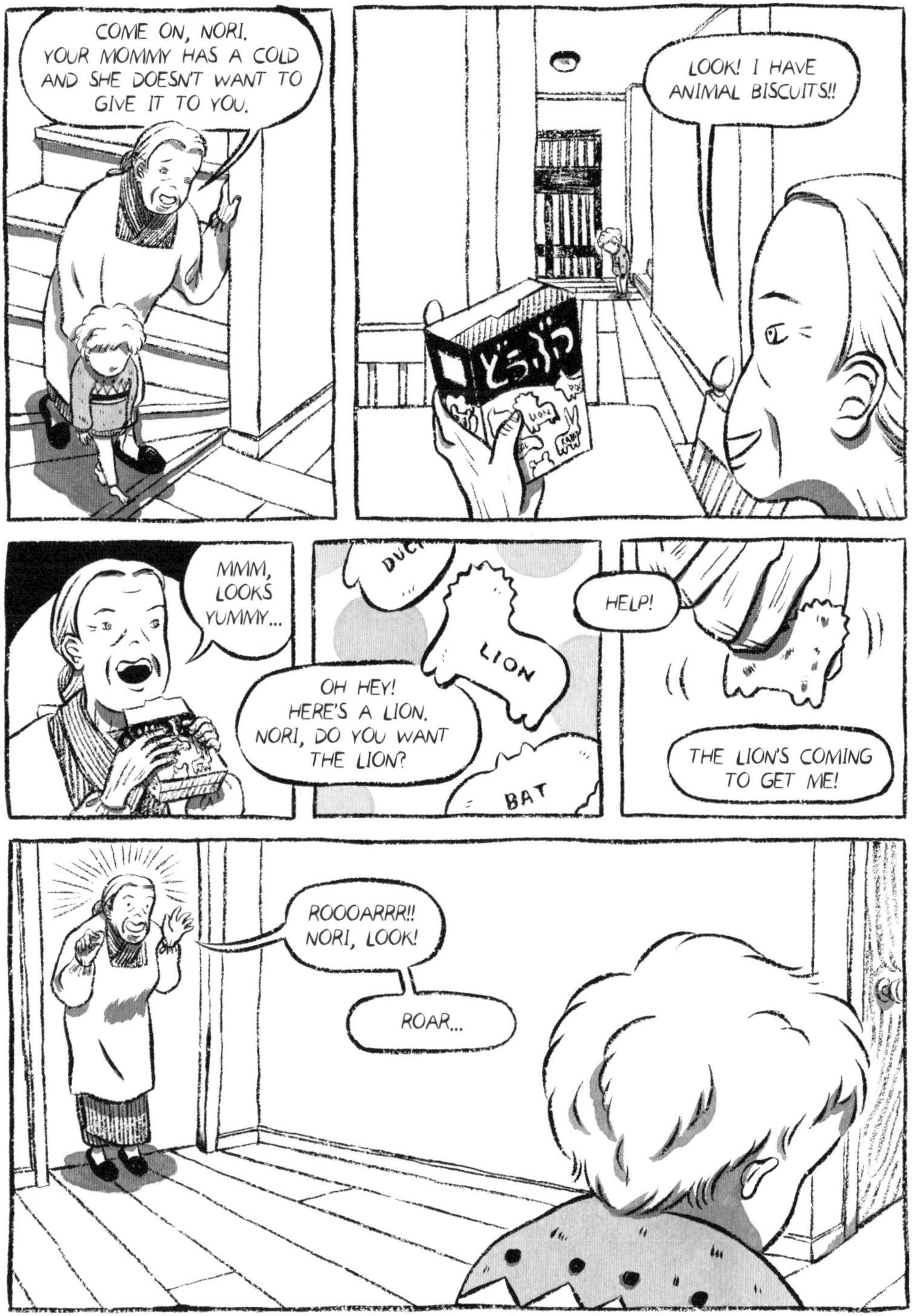
COME ON, NORI. YOUR MOMMY HAS A COLD AND SHE DOESN'T WANT TO GIVE IT TO YOU.
LOOK! I HAVE ANIMAL BISCUITS!!
MMM, LOOKS YUMMY...
DUC
LION
OH HEY! HERE'S A LION. NORI, DO YOU WANT THE LION?
BAT
HELP!
THE LION'S COMING TO GET ME!
ROOOARRR!! NORI, LOOK!
ROAR...

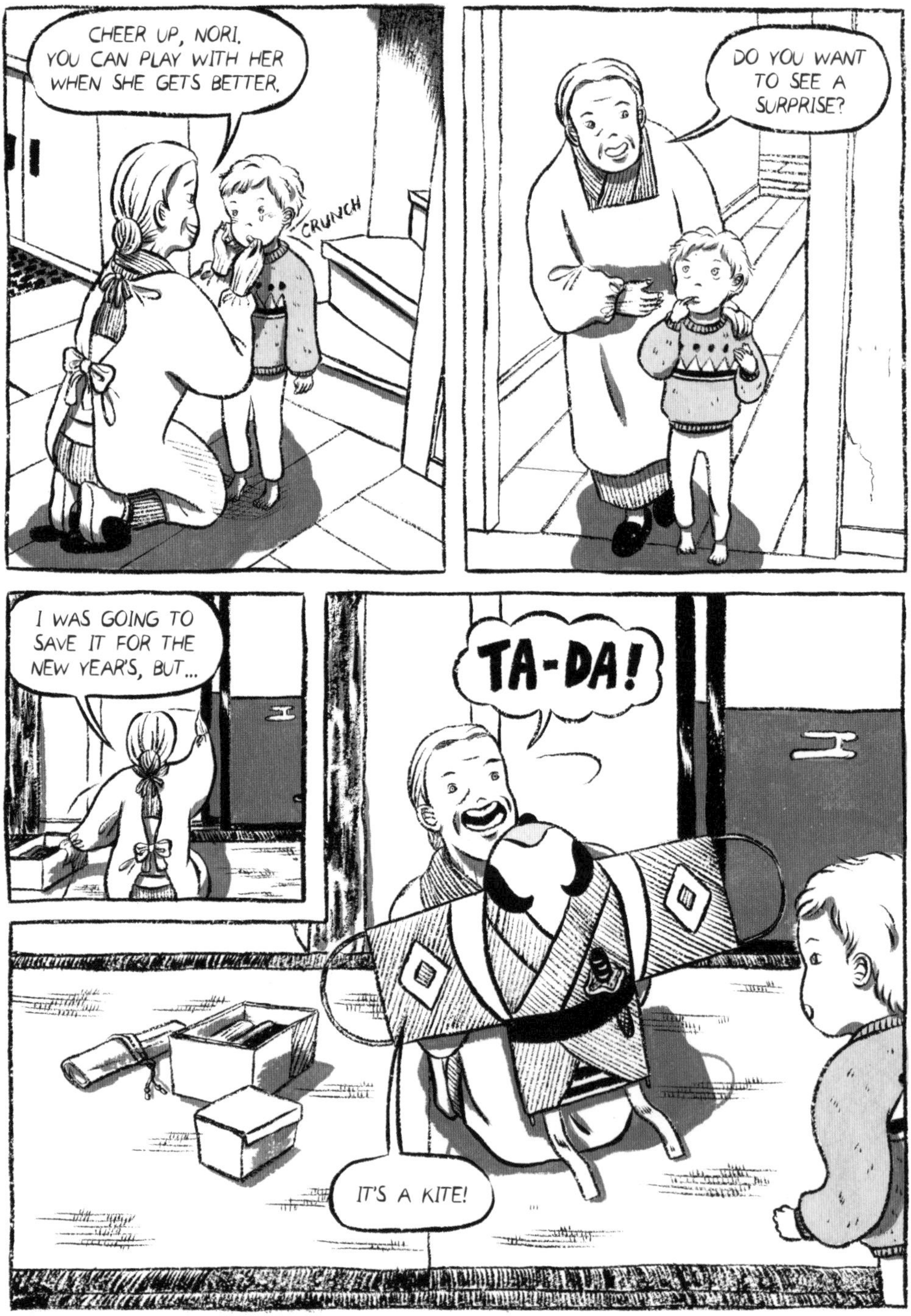
CHEER UP, NORI. YOU CAN PLAY WITH HER WHEN SHE GETS BETTER.
CRUNCH
DO YOU WANT TO SEE A SURPRISE?
I WAS GOING TO SAVE IT FOR THE NEW YEAR'S, BUT...
TA-DA!
IT'S A KITE!

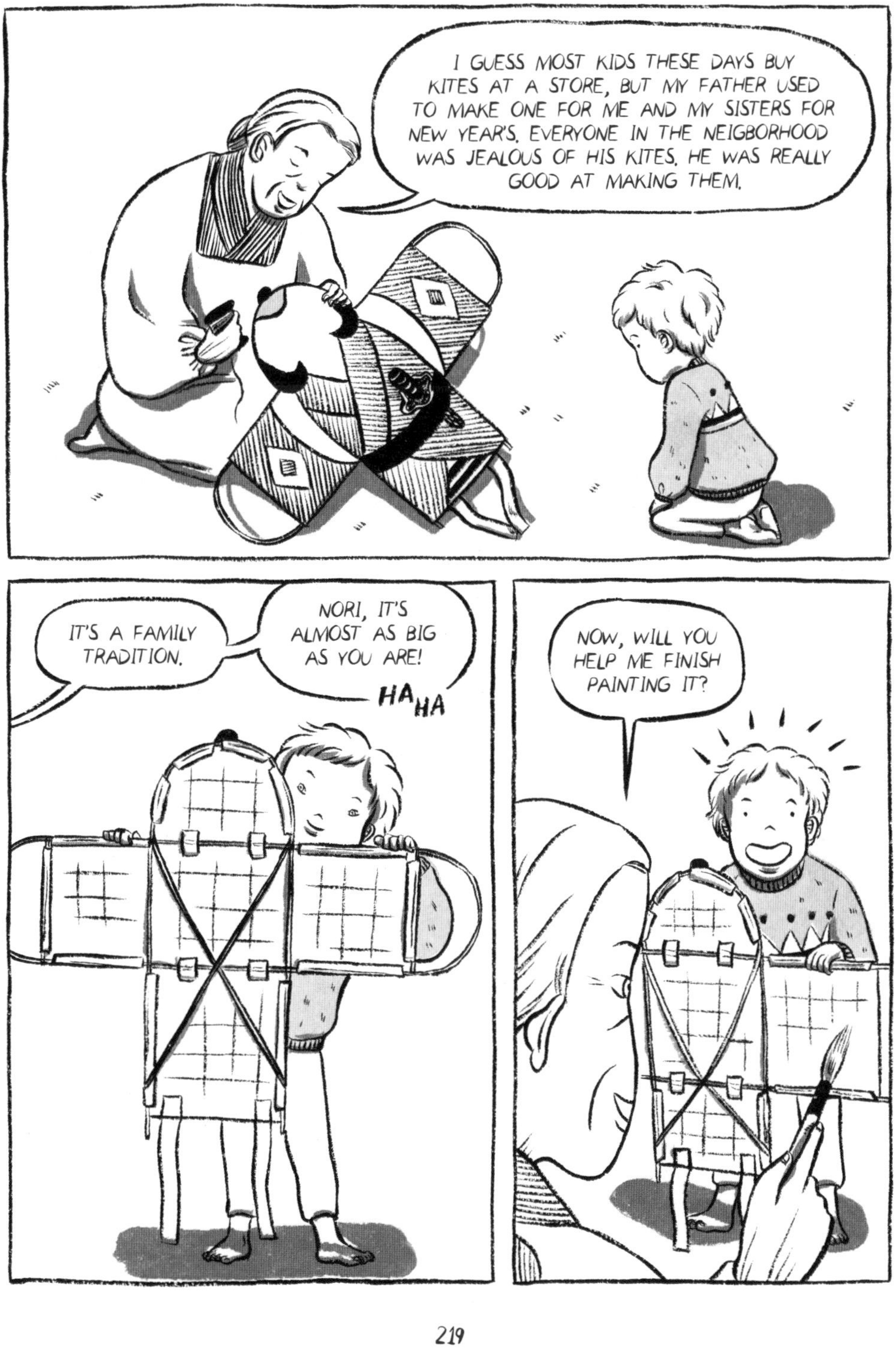

I GUESS MOST KIDS THESE DAYS BUY KITES AT A STORE, BUT MY FATHER USED TO MAKE ONE FOR ME AND MY SISTERS FOR NEW YEAR'S. EVERYONE IN THE NEIGBORHOOD WAS JEALOUS OF HIS KITES. HE WAS REALLY GOOD AT MAKING THEM.
IT'S A FAMILY TRADITION.
NORI, IT'S ALMOST AS BIG AS YOU ARE!
HA HA
NOW, WILL YOU HELP ME FINISH PAINTING IT?

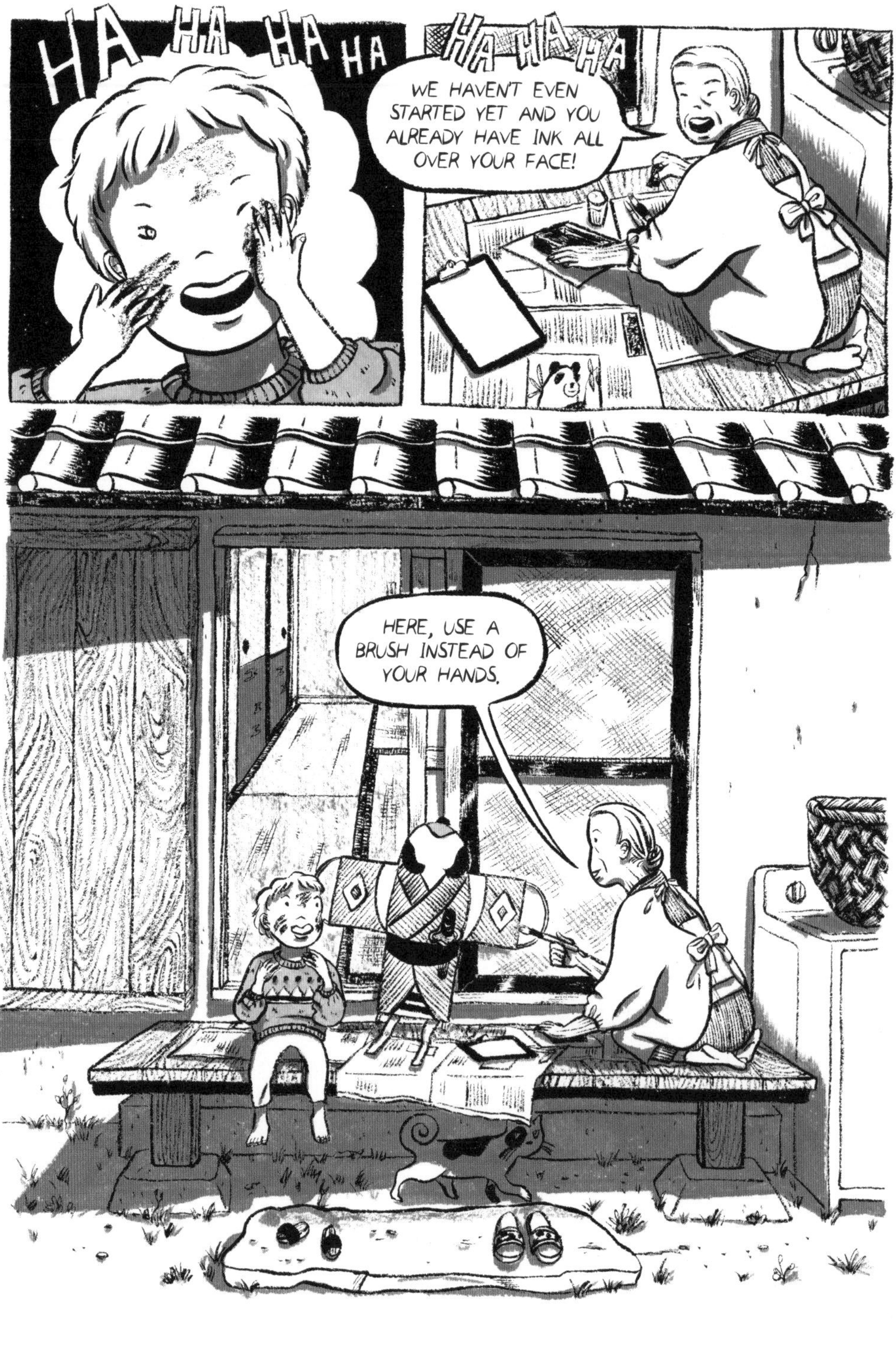
HA HA HA HA
HA HA HA
WE HAVEN'T EVEN STARTED YET AND YOU ALREADY HAVE INK ALL OVER YOUR FACE!
HERE, USE A BRUSH INSTEAD OF YOUR HANDS.

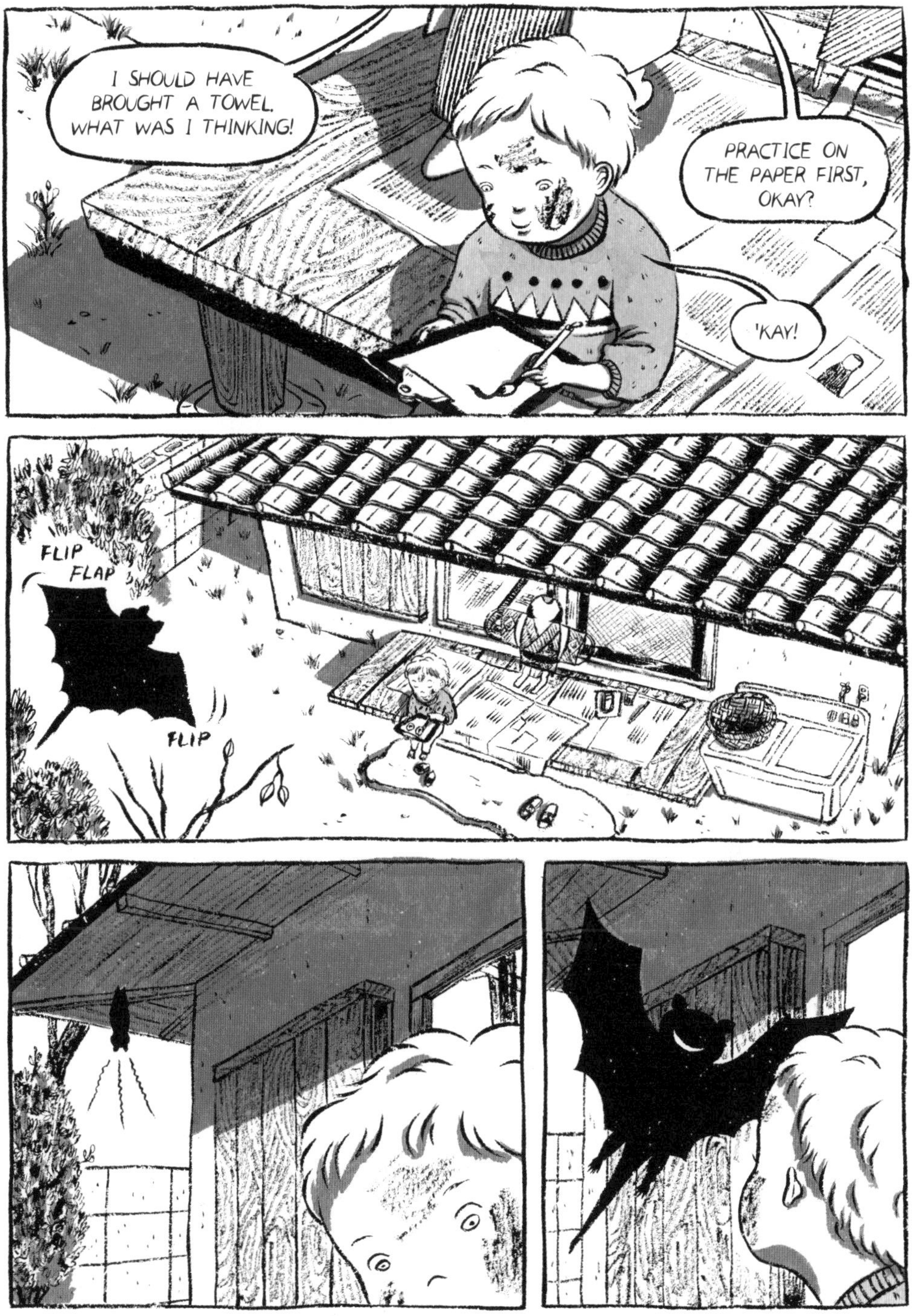
I SHOULD HAVE BROUGHT A TOWEL. WHAT WAS I THINKING!
PRACTICE ON THE PAPER FIRST, OKAY?
'KAY!
FLIP
FLAP
FLIP

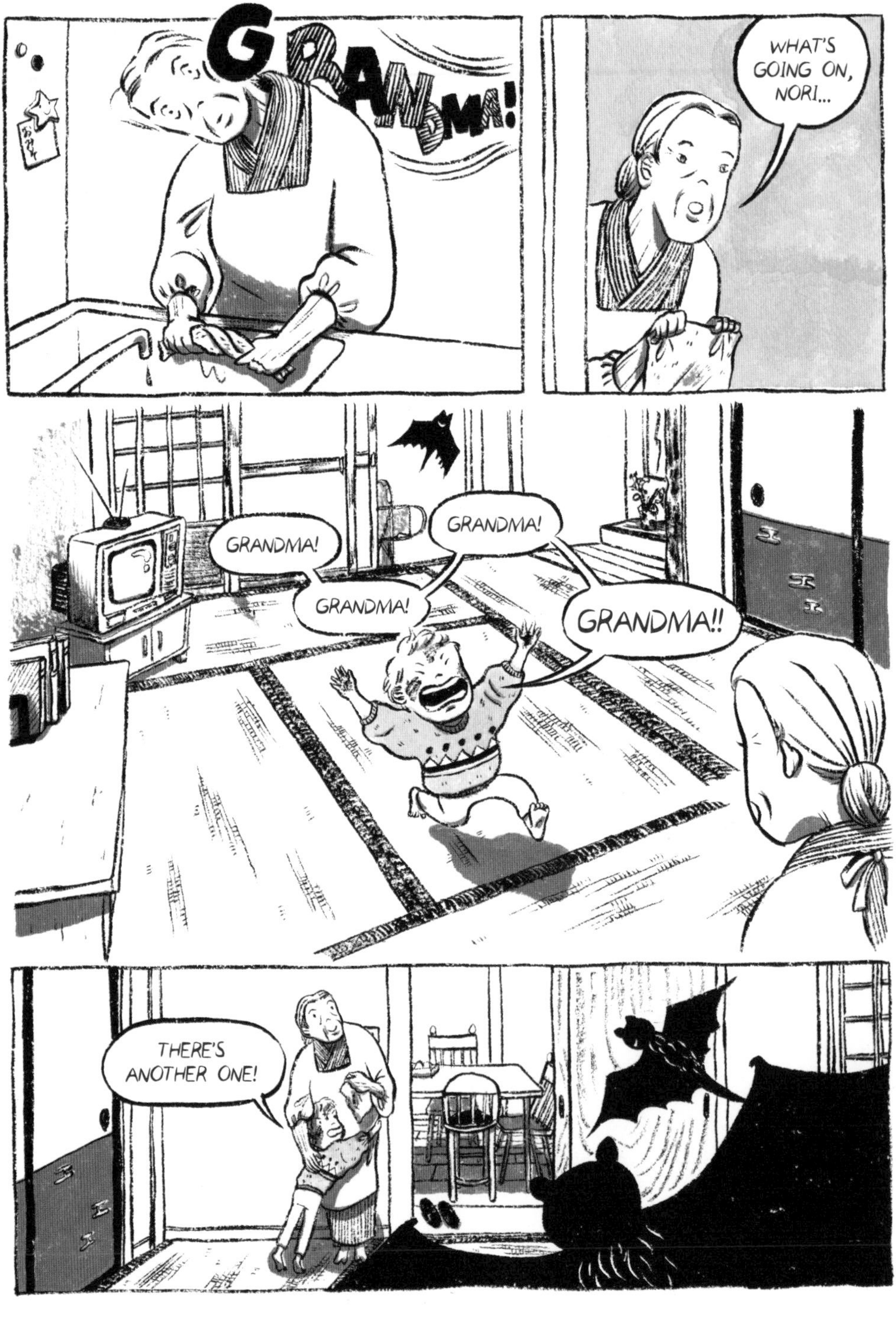
GRANDMA!
WHAT'S GOING ON, NORI...
GRANDMA!
GRANDMA!
GRANDMA!
GRANDMA!!
THERE'S ANOTHER ONE!

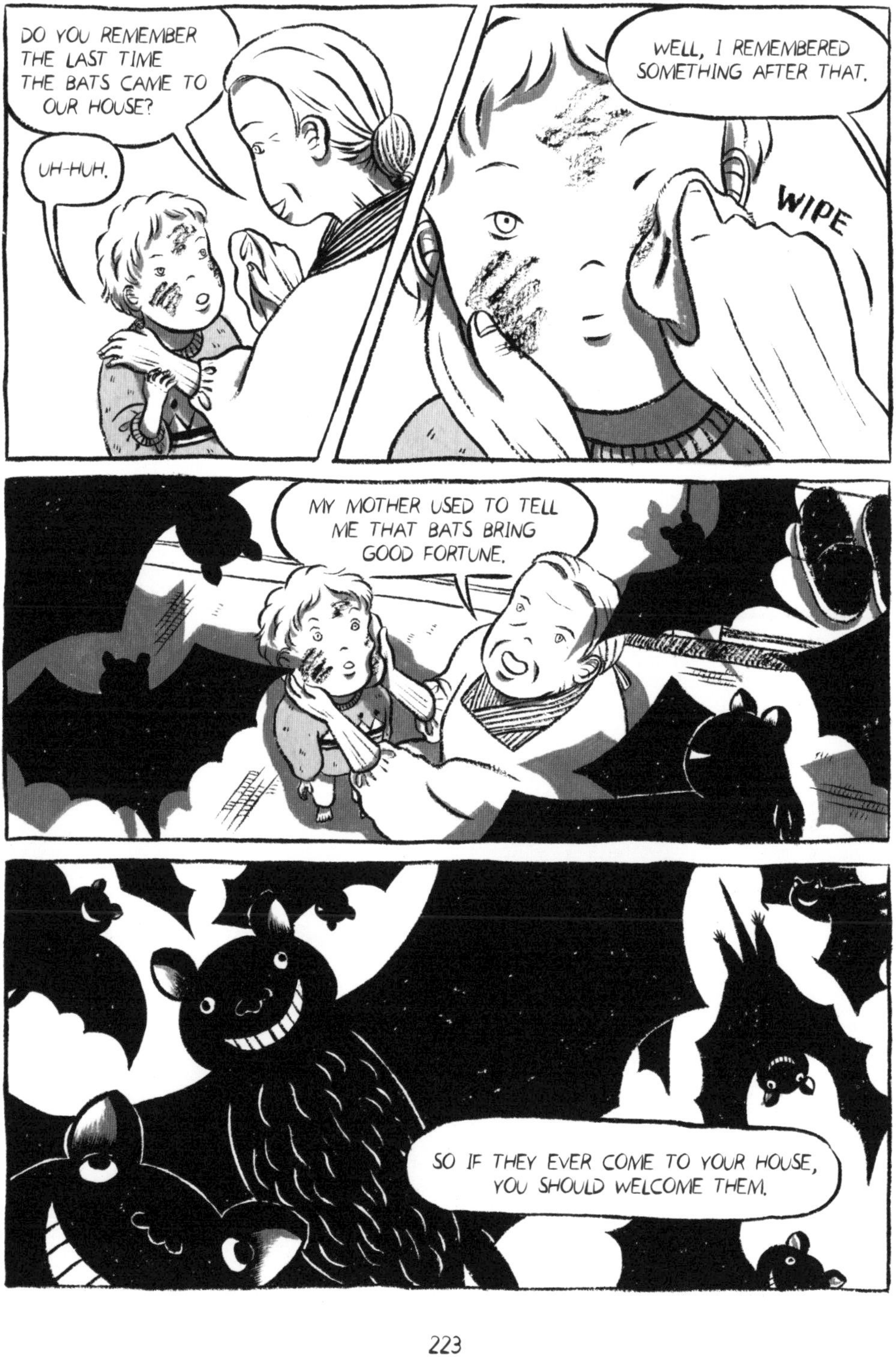
DO YOU REMEMBER THE LAST TIME THE BATS CAME TO OUR HOUSE?
UH-HUH.
WELL, I REMEMBERED SOMETHING AFTER THAT.
WIPE
MY MOTHER USED TO TELL ME THAT BATS BRING GOOD FORTUNE.
SO IF THEY EVER COME TO YOUR HOUSE, YOU SHOULD WELCOME THEM.

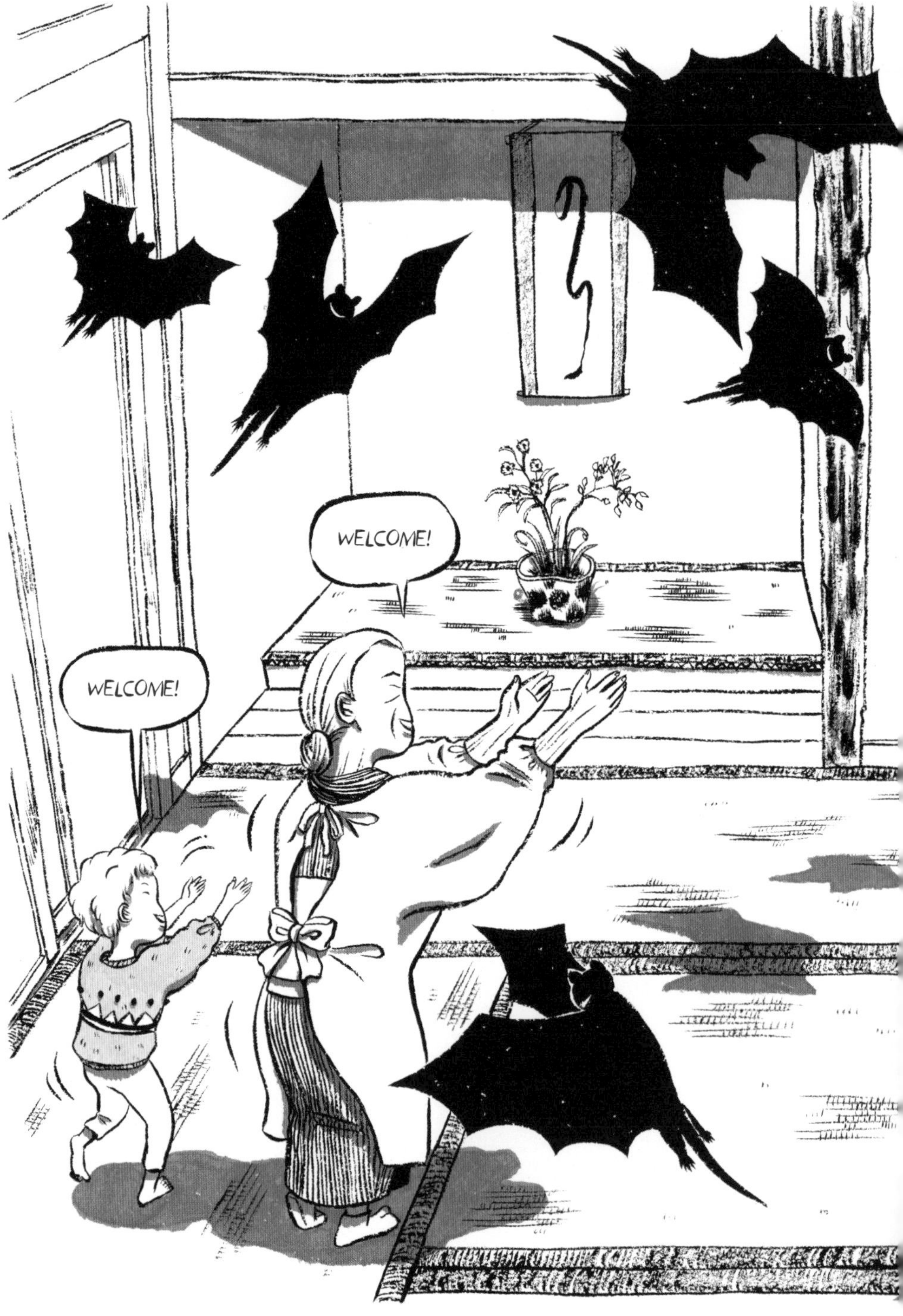
WELCOME!
WELCOME!

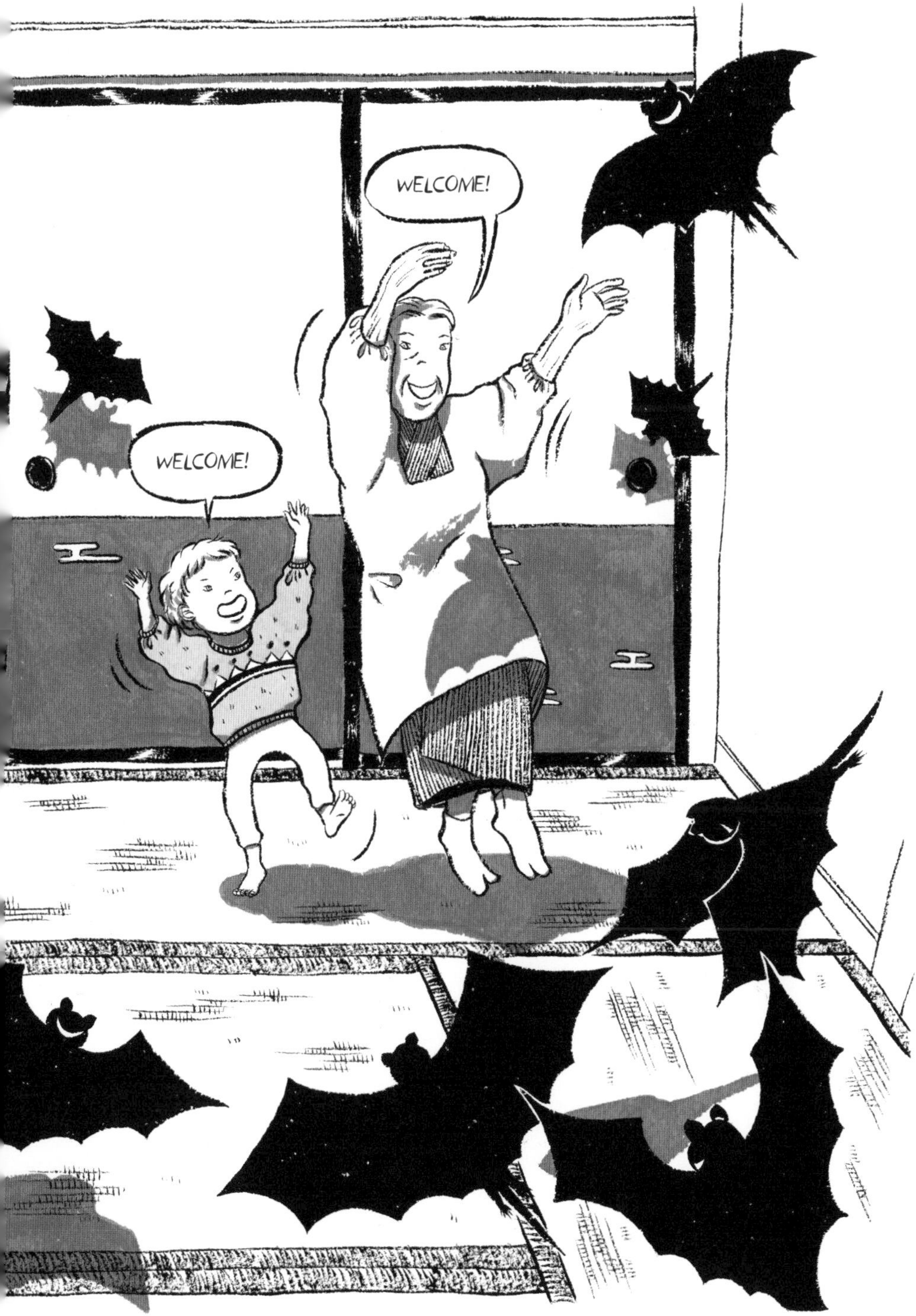
WELCOME!
WELCOME!

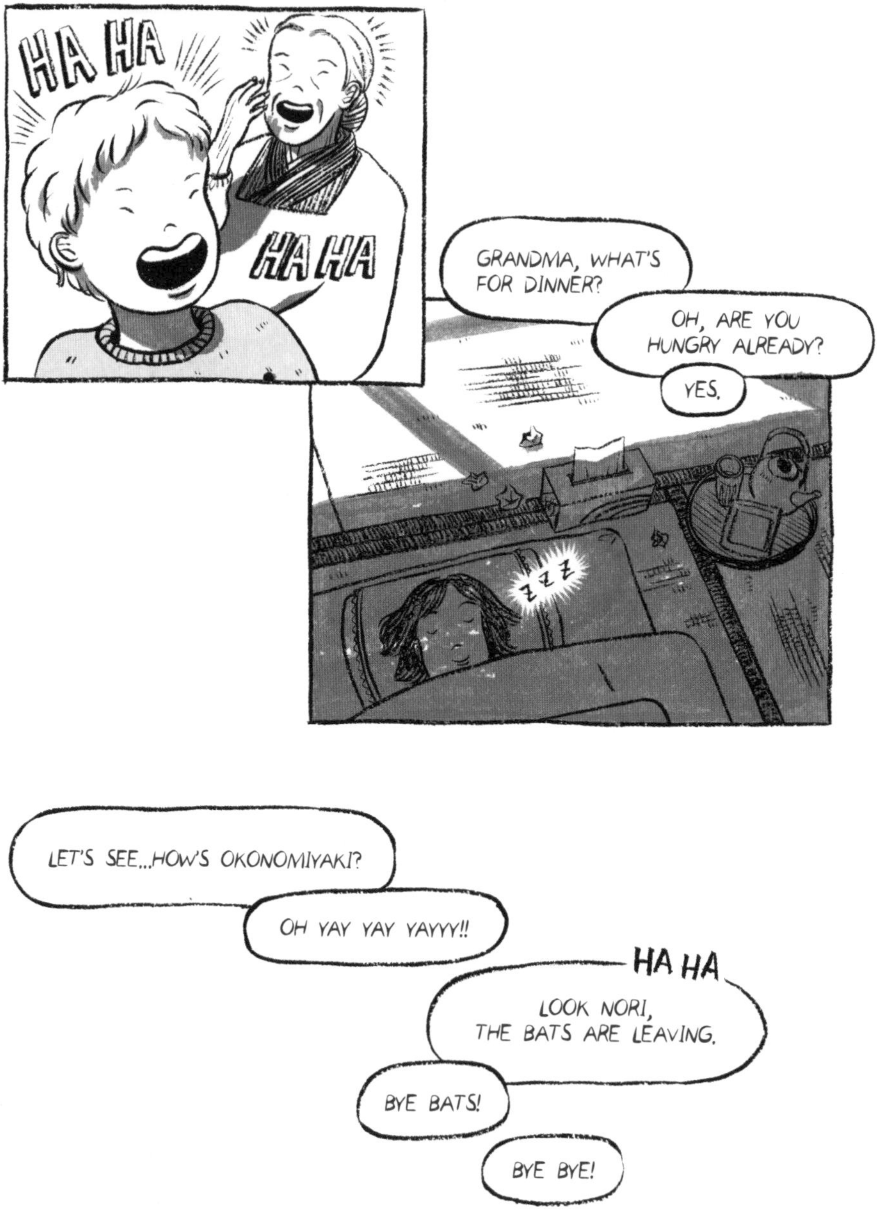
HA HA
HA HA
GRANDMA, WHAT'S FOR DINNER?
OH, ARE YOU HUNGRY ALREADY?
YES.
Z Z Z
LET'S SEE...HOW'S OKONOMIYAKI?
OH YAY YAY YAYYY!!
HA HA
LOOK NORI, THE BATS ARE LEAVING.
BYE BATS!
BYE BYE!

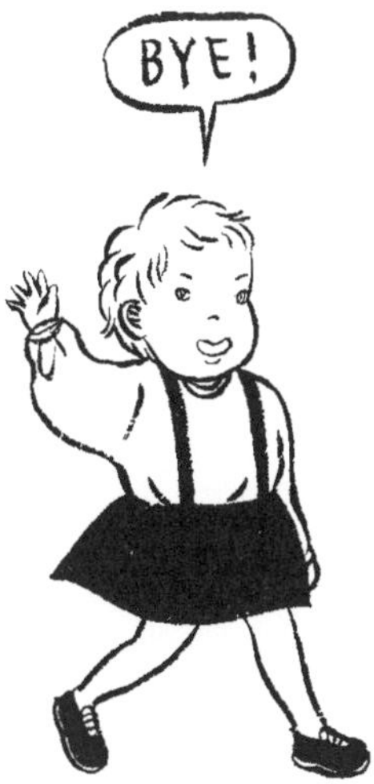
BYE!

Rumi Hara was born in Kyoto, Japan, in 1982 and grew up with her two loving grandmothers helping to take care of her and her little brother. While working as a translator in Tokyo, she started printing her comics on a tiny home printer in 2010. After attending Savannah College of Art and Design, Hara moved to New York City in 2014, where she now lives and works as an illustrator and comics artist. *Nori* was first self-published as a series of minicomics that was nominated for an Ignatz Award in 2018.